OBLIVIOUS

Reviews for Oblivious

4½ Stars! "The well-plotted, delicious mystery keeps readers guessing from the start with laugh-out-loud moments mixed with poignant scenes. The characters are well-developed and multifacted."
—Donna M. Brown, Romantic Times Book Reviews

4 Cups! *"Oblivious* is a page-turner. Depre sketches a story that allows the reader to become absorbed with the events and holds them captive until the end."
—Cherokee, Coffee Time Romance

4½ Stars! "This is a laugh out loud masterpiece. Wholly clean, it intrigues you and keeps you smiling from beginning to end. I love this book and it goes on my virtual keeper shelf."
—Amanda Killgore, Huntress Reviews

"My Evanovich customers will love this book!"
—Ani Sorenson, Proprietor J. O'Donoghue Books

"A charming story with a likeable heroine and a small-town mystery, this book was a complete delight to read."
—Wendy Hines, Armchair Reviews

Books by Cyndia Depre

Amanda's Rib

Oblivious

8/16/10
For Cathy —
Thanks so much for
reading Oblivious!
Cyndia Depre

CYNDIA DEPRE

OBLIVIOUS

Mundania Press

Oblivious Copyright © 2008 by Cyndia Depre

All rights reserved under the International and Pan-American Copyright Conventions. No part of this book may be reproduced or transmitted in any form or by any means, electronic or mechanical including photocopying, recording, or by any information storage and retrieval system, without permission in writing from the publisher.

The scanning, uploading and distribution of this book via the Internet or via any other means without the permission of the publisher is illegal, and punishable by law. Please purchase only authorized electronic editions, and do not participate in or encourage the electronic piracy of copyrighted materials. Your support of the author's rights is appreciated.

This is a work of fiction. Names, characters, places and incidents either are the product of the author's imagination or are used fictitiously, and any resemblance to any actual persons, living or dead, events, or locales is entirely coincidental.

A Mundania Press Production
Mundania Press LLC
6470A Glenway Avenue, #109
Cincinnati, Ohio 45211-5222

To order additional copies of this book, contact:
books@mundania.com
www.mundania.com

Cover Art © 2008 by SkyeWolf
SkyeWolf Images (http://www.skyewolfimages.com)
Book Design, Production, and Layout by Daniel J. Reitz, Sr.
Marketing and Promotion by Bob Sanders

Trade Paperback ISBN: 978-1-59426-723-9
eBook ISBN: 978-1-59426-722-2

First Edition • February 2008

Production by Mundania Press LLC
Printed in the United States of America
10 9 8 7 6 5 4 3 2 1

Warning: The unauthorized reproduction or distribution of this copyrighted work is illegal. Criminal copyright infringement, including infringement without monetary gain, is investigated by the FBI and is punishable by up to 5 years in federal prison and a fine of $250,000.

DEDICATION

This is for my husband, John, and my parents, Betty and Darrell Newell. I love you.

Jana Thomson at Artistic Treasures, Cathy Plys, Bill C. and Di have gone above and beyond in their support, and I thank them for all they've done. Jackie gave me a wonderful 'Livvy-ism' that still makes me laugh! Janice remains the best critique partner ever. Nothing slips by her eagle eye.

Jo Taylor deserves special mention. Compassion, talent and creativity make her truly unique. I couldn't ask for a better friend.

CHAPTER ONE

She was born in April, but her parents named her January. By the following morning they had second thoughts and changed the forms. Now, nearly thirty years later, Olivia, nee January, Chatham slipped an emerald green dress over her head and wiggled her hips to adjust it. The top half of the silk and satin sheath fit like a second skin. The skirt flared just below her waist and ended primly at the middle of her knees. Olivia studied her reflection in the mirror, twisting right and left as she tried to see if it made her behind look big. The phone interrupted her inspection.

"Merry Christmas!" she said into the receiver.

"You're still in your room? Why aren't you on the way over?" Josephine Bookman, Olivia's best friend, sounded stressed. She always fretted over her parties, worrying each detail to pieces. Olivia often told her to throw some old records on the stereo, pour potato chips into a few bowls, and get the Twister® game out, but Josie never listened. Poor thing. Twister® was a marvelous ice-breaker. Even when there wasn't any ice to break.

"Calm down, Josie. I'm on my way downstairs to do some mingling. Then I'll head over to your house."

"Mingle fast, okay? Whatever you do, don't let Alice Parker corner you. She'll start talking about her cats, and that could take hours."

"They're her family. She's just lonely, Josie. It wouldn't hurt you to listen to her sometime, too. You'd make her so happy."

"It'll be my New Year's resolution. I promise to listen to Alice babble about Tinker Bell and Snowflake if you promise to get over here in half an hour."

"Don't worry. I won't lollygag." She hung up before Josie could answer. Josie may stew before her parties, but Olivia had a quirk of her own. She got so excited at the notion of seeing so many friends at once, she turned into a clumsy fool. What was the saying? Two thumbs on left feet? Something like that.

Fluffing her hair, she took a deep, calming breath and crossed to the bathroom to check her makeup a fifth and final time. She hummed Jingle Bells while dabbing Mariella Burani behind her ears. Olivia knew she sang off-key at church and during festive sing-alongs, but for some reason, in this large marble and tile room, she thought she sounded exactly like Barbra Streisand. Marveling at the vagaries of acoustics, she shut the light off and left the room.

Olivia picked her satin purse off the bed and climbed into matching high heel shoes. She turned off the stereo and all but one lamp in the sitting room, then left her suite, closing the door firmly behind her.

As she walked down the hallway toward the second story landing she looked over the mahogany railing, admiring the decorations in the vast entry one floor below. The chandelier had been dimmed, and soft light reflected off gold and silver ribbons and bows, making them appear fuzzy, as if she were looking at an unfocused photograph. Slowly descending the wide staircase, she trailed her hand along the banister. Wreaths, flocking, lights, candles, and miniature towns sitting on tables made the place feel like a fairyland. Her mother had outdone herself with decorations for this year's Christmas gala.

Moving home had seemed natural after the breakup of her marriage to Sam Wallace. She'd shut herself in her rooms, planning to lick her wounds and heal her heart. Two days later Josie barged in and told her she'd wasted enough time mewling over a two-timing warthog like Sammy. Olivia readily agreed, and considered Josie's suggestion that they go on a shopping spree absolutely brilliant. The two women spent a frenzied week in Chicago, giving the term 'Windy City' a whole new meaning. That was six months ago, and Olivia was still living with her parents, still trying to figure out what to do with her life. Leaving Chatham, Wisconsin, was out of the question. This was home. She knew everyone in town, and could only think of a handful of people she didn't like. Reaching the bottom of the stairs, she slapped a palm on the newel post. Nope, she wasn't leaving Chatham. She'd have to find her future here. Something would come along to spark her interest.

People wandered between rooms on the lower level of the large house. Olivia stopped and exchanged words with most of them. She plucked a glass of wine off the tray a passing waiter held out to her. Another uniformed arm offered a platter of hors d'oeuvres. She picked up a cracker topped with something, stared at it for a moment, and popped it into her mouth as she moved from the library to the living room. Not bad, she thought, and looked for more appetizers. She found several trays of food sitting on a table and sipped her wine as she picked up another mystery tidbit.

Olivia swiveled to survey the room, and as she did her clutch purse slipped from under her arm. She caught it but dropped the cracker. *Oh Lordy, why do they always land upside down?* Olivia glanced around in embarrassment as she picked up a napkin and bent to clean up her mess. Finished with her task, and certain that no one had seen, she turned and looked into a pair of amused gray eyes.

Good grief, what was *he* doing here? And why was he standing by her parents? Another lady, one she recognized, completed the grouping. She'd seen the man around town a few times the past couple of weeks, but had never spoken to him and didn't even know his name. He usually wore jeans and sweatshirts, and was handsome in a rugged, outdoorsy way. He wore his dark hair a shade too long, and Olivia sometimes wondered if he'd bothered to comb it that day. Tonight, in his suit and tie and with his hair smoothed back, he looked like the "Marlboro Man" gone Wall Street. No, she corrected herself. He looked like a predator. A shiver raced up her spine.

"Livvy," her father called out and waved his hand in the air, motioning her over. "There's someone I want you to meet."

Olivia bumped a table topped with full champagne flutes as she moved toward her parents. She glanced down and saw liquid sloshing over the sides of the Waterford crystal, but none of the glasses fell and broke. The tablecloth was probably a goner, though.

"Hi Mom, Dad." Olivia brushed the air beside their cheeks, not wanting to get lipstick on them.

"Livvy," her father said, "this is Professor Mecklenberg. Teaches at the college over in Deerwood. Professor, our daughter, Olivia."

"Call me Cheryl," the woman said as she shook Olivia's hand. Chin-length chestnut curls danced around Cheryl's head. She smiled, but Olivia thought it appeared forced. Her eyes held no warmth. Olivia had taken one of Professor Mecklenberg's classes. She hadn't liked her then and didn't feel comfortable with her now. Taking a small step back, Olivia wondered why Cheryl would have such an immediate and unusual affect on her.

"And this is Tucker Monroe," her father continued, indicating the tall, broad-shouldered man with smoky gray eyes standing next to Cheryl.

"Nice to meet you." Tucker shook Olivia's hand. "I was just telling your parents how much I'm enjoying their party. I think the canapés are the best I've ever had." His eyes sparkled, and Olivia knew he was making fun of her for dropping one.

Olivia raised her chin and looked up at him. "Mom always throws the best parties in town. And she does all the menu planning herself, don't you, Mom?"

Eleanor Chatham blushed as she fingered the pearls at her throat. "Don't carry on, Livvy. It's not as if I make them."

"Tucker here's in the market," Olivia's father told her.

She stifled a sigh. There were few things Richard Chatham

enjoyed more than talking about the stock market. That and beating the IRS at their own game were his passions. If this Tucker guy had any tax tricks up his sleeve, he was in for a very long night.

"I dabble in it," Tucker said. "It's a hobby."

"Damn lucrative one by the looks of things." Richard glanced at his Olivia. "Drove up in one of those new sports cars. What's the name of it again?"

"Porsche," Tucker answered with a shrug. "I've always liked cars."

"Another thing we have in common," Richard told him.

Olivia's mouth almost fell open. She'd never seen her father look twice at a car. She doubted he'd know how to lift the hood of one. Why was he kissing up to this guy? And why did the name Tucker Monroe sound familiar? She quickly drank from her wineglass as the answer registered. He was the mysterious man Josie had been raving about lately. Olivia looked at his lopsided grin, dimpled cheeks, and masculine frame. For once Josie hadn't exaggerated. She'd be green with envy when she found out Olivia had actually met him.

"If you plan on sticking around town, you might want to invest in a four-wheel drive car for the winter. We've been lucky, it hasn't snowed yet, but it will. I doubt Porsches do well on icy roads." Olivia set her glass near the edge of a table.

"Good advice. I'll put that on my to-do list." Tucker grabbed the teetering goblet, then moved it to the center of the table.

"Thank you. I seem to be clumsy tonight."

"Livvy's always over-excited before going to a party." Eleanor smiled as if proud of the fact.

"Then you can relax," Tucker said. "You're at the party."

Olivia shook her head. "Not this one. Josie's."

"Josie?"

"One of Livvy's little friends," Eleanor explained.

Olivia put an arm around her mother's shoulder and gave her a gentle squeeze. She was almost thirty years old, yet her mother still referred to her buddies as her 'little friends'.

"Cheryl recently moved here from Deerwood, Livvy. Tucker's new in town, too. Where are you from, Tucker?" Eleanor asked.

"Chicago, Buffalo, Minneapolis, LA, all over really."

"What an exciting life! How long do you plan to stay in Chatham?"

"I don't know, Eleanor. I guess until I decide to leave. That's usually how it works."

Olivia looked at him suspiciously. Why would anyone move all around the country? Maybe he was running from the law, a fugitive on the lam. The thought made her shiver again. Then he smiled at her and she knew he couldn't possibly be a criminal. He probably just got bored easily.

"I thought I recognized you from the college, but I must have been wrong. The name of the person I'm thinking of wasn't Chatham," Cheryl interjected.

"I took one of your English classes, but my name was Armstrong then."

"Oh," her father said with a nod. "That was when you were married to Eric." He turned to Cheryl and Tucker. "Livvy always takes her maiden name back and moves in with us when she's between husbands."

"You make it sound like I run through husbands the way Elizabeth Taylor does." Olivia felt her face grow warm. "And living here is only temporary, you know that."

"Temporary since June."

Eleanor patted her arm. "There, there, dear. Your father and I love having you here."

"What line of work are you in, Ms. Chatham?" Tucker asked.

"Call me Olivia. I'm sort of between things right now."

"Livvy is very civic minded," Eleanor said. "She does a lot of volunteer work."

"Where do you volunteer?" Tucker stuck a hand in his pocket. He seemed relaxed and at ease. Cheryl put an arm through his and stared at Olivia with the expression of someone who'd found a fly in their soup.

Olivia shrugged. "Nowhere right now. I did work at the library, but the head librarian, Glory Bea Carter, wouldn't let me do anything but check books in and out. Stamp, stamp, stamp all day long. I was almost happy when she fired me."

"Why would anyone fire a volunteer?" Tucker inquired.

"She wanted me to fine people if they brought their books back late. For Pete's sake, how can you fine someone for being a slow reader? The very idea is ridiculous and could break their spirits, make them feel inadequate."

"Why didn't you pay their fines? You could probably afford a quarter here and a quarter there."

"She did, Tucker," Eleanor said. "Glory Bea said that was wrong and encouraged people not to be responsible for themselves. She called Livvy a neighbor. Mercy me, we're all neighbors."

"She said enabler, Mom."

"I don't care what she called it, dear. It was just an excuse to let you go. I think she's one of those people who holds a grudge all their lives." Eleanor turned her attention to Tucker and Cheryl. "When Livvy was a little girl she adored Glory Bea Carter. Every time she saw her she'd shout, 'Golly gee, it's Glory Bea!' and run to her and throw her little arms around the poor woman's legs. Glory Bea never married, never had children. I imagine a youngster with Livvy's enthusiasm was a tad overwhelming to her." Eleanor reached for Olivia's hand and squeezed it. "But we don't let little things upset us. Livvy went on to volunteer at the local clinic. They made her hostess."

"A clinic with a hostess?" Tucker raised his eyebrows.

"Nurse Weathers was mighty territorial. She wouldn't let me behind the counter, not even to answer phones. I suppose a person has to be a bit aggressive to reach her level of success. She and Doctor Plys ended up making a new position just for me. Chatham Clinic Hostess."

Tucker cleared his throat. "Sounds like an interesting job."

"I loved it. I mingled in the waiting room and tried to ease the fears of patients and their families. Sometimes I bought small gifts for them. It's amazing how much a tiny little thing can cheer a person up."

Olivia's father looked at Tucker. "I'm afraid Livvy took her hostess duties a bit too far. So many people stopped in to visit every day, Doc Plys said his waiting room was becoming a social club."

"I got the boot. Personally, I think Doctor Plys overreacted. Firing a person who brings potential customers to your business doesn't make sense to me. Everyone needs a doctor now and then. Why not make a nice impression so they remember him?" Olivia smiled, trying not to let the hurt show. Being fired from two volunteer jobs could certainly lower a gal's self-esteem. Olivia didn't know what she was going to do with her time. Apparently she couldn't even give it away. Pulling her thoughts to the present, she remembered Josie's party and glanced at her watch.

"Good grief, I'm late." Olivia pecked the air by her parents' faces again, and then turned to the others. "Nice to have met you. Enjoy yourselves."

"I hope to see you again, Olivia. It's nice to meet someone so public-spirited." Tucker gave her a wide grin, displaying a bright set of pearly white teeth. Cheryl looked as if she'd just stepped on a bee.

As Olivia moved away from the group, she heard her mother say, "Livvy's always in a hurry."

"Came into the world two weeks early, and hasn't stopped moving long enough to take a deep breath since," her father added.

Her dad, what a kidder. Olivia turned to look at him and saw Tucker staring at her. Ducking her head, she went to the entry, fanning her warm cheeks with one hand. That Tucker, talk about magnetism. The air around him practically crackled. He was even better than Josie had claimed. He had an aura. That was it. She'd explain him to Josie as a man with a huge aura.

Olivia bumped into a woman in a white dress as she backed out of the coat closet. Unfortunately the woman had been drinking a glass of red wine. Zinfandel now decorated her ample bosom.

Olivia grabbed the lady by an arm and steered her toward the kitchen. "I'm so sorry. I'm sure we can get that out. Isn't there some kind of fizzy water that works wonders on red wine?"

The woman patted her hand. "Don't fret, Livvy."

Olivia blinked at her. "Aunt Lucille. I didn't even recognize you. You've lost so much weight."

Aunt Lucille pulled her shoulders straight, clearly pleased by the compliment. "You're the only one who's mentioned it."

"I'm sure everyone else meant to. The party, you know. People forget what they're about to say most of the time."

"You go on to wherever you were headed, honey. I know where the kitchen is."

Olivia blew another air kiss and wiggled her fingers at her aunt as she turned to leave. Poor Aunt Lucille hadn't lost an ounce. She threw her coat over her shoulders and opened the door to find Sammy standing on the veranda, his finger an inch from the doorbell.

"Were you invited or are you crashing?" Olivia asked.

Sammy nodded in the direction of the guests' parked cars. "Does that Porsche belong to Tucker Monroe?"

"Uh huh." Olivia hurried out the door and pulled it shut behind her.

"If he's invited, I ought to be welcome, too."

"What's wrong with him?"

"He gambles."

"So what? Why are you really here?" Olivia didn't see her car under the portico and remembered she'd had to move it to make room for other vehicles. She turned toward the garage.

Sammy fell into step beside her. "I think we should try again."

"Try with someone else." She stopped and snapped her fingers. "I know, try with your exercise guru. I could hardly believe my eyes when I walked in on you two. She must be double jointed everywhere."

"I made one little mistake. Haven't you ever done something you shouldn't have?"

Olivia put her hands on her hips and looked at Sam Wallace's petulant face. Shaking her head, she bit back an answer. "No, that one's too easy." She began walking again. "Sammy, it's over. It was over the last time you wanted to try again and it'll still be over the next time you think of asking so don't ask because I'm telling you now, it's over." Olivia ground her teeth, hating the way Sammy brought out the ugly side of her. She pulled her keys from her purse when she reached her new Lexus SUV.

"When did you get this?"

"Two weeks ago. It's an early Christmas present from Mom and Dad." Olivia opened the door and climbed into her gift. "You kept our SUV, remember?"

"You got our 'Vette. Did you sell it?"

"It's in storage until summer, and it was mine before we got married, so it wasn't *ours*. Go away, Sammy. Have a nice life." She pulled the door shut, ignoring his protests.

Olivia started the car and, checking her makeup in the mirror, rubbed a smudge of mascara off her cheek. No wonder that Monroe guy had stared at her. She couldn't even get her makeup on right.

Olivia made her way slowly down the winding drive, awestruck as always at the beauty of the landscape in front of her house. She wondered if her mother had bought every Christmas light in town.

≈≈

The next day Tucker Monroe got what he'd been hoping for, something to get his mind off Olivia Chatham. Her father's comment about her moving home between husbands had given him pause, but since he never planned to marry, he shrugged it off. His mind kept straying to long, taffy-colored hair and wide, guileless green eyes. It took the police to snap him out of his musings. When they came to his door, and asked him to go to the station with them for questioning, all thoughts of her flew out of his head.

"Questioning about what?"

"The murder of Cheryl Mecklenberg. Is that your coat, sir?" one of the officers asked, nodding at a jacket hanging over the back of a chair.

"Yeah," Tucker replied absently. Cheryl had been murdered? She hadn't made much of an impression on him, but it shook him to hear she was dead. "When was she killed? How?"

The officer picked up the jacket, ignoring Tucker's questions, and felt in the pockets before handing it to Tucker. "We'll talk at the station."

"I'll follow you." Tucker pulled his coat on.

"We'd prefer you ride with us. We'll see that you get home when we're finished." The officer's tone left no room for argument.

Tucker wondered if he should get an attorney, but decided to hold off. It might be something he could handle alone. Asking for a lawyer right away would look suspicious, and the last thing Tucker wanted was public attention and another discussion with an attorney. He'd had enough of both to last three lifetimes.

Olivia Chatham wasn't out of Tucker's thoughts for long. Less than an hour later he realized she was half his alibi.

CHAPTER TWO

"How did you meet Tucker Monroe?" Olivia asked the next morning. She twirled a forkful of pancakes in a thick puddle of syrup.

Her father sat in his usual seat at the head of the table. The morning paper lay open beside his plate. "I hadn't until last night. Your mother met Cheryl at a fund-raiser and invited her to the party. She brought him. Damn good thing, too. Been wanting to meet him."

"Why?"

"He's got the Midas touch with the market."

"How do you know?"

"Sammy told me last week. Says Monroe's a gambler, too. Guess it's pretty much the same thing," Richard added with a shrug.

Olivia's fork clattered onto her plate. "You talked to Sammy last week?"

"He called. Didn't I tell you?"

"Honestly, Richard," Eleanor said from the opposite end of the table. "How many times do I have to ask you to write things down?"

Olivia watched her father shove more pancakes into his mouth, and knew he was avoiding the topic. "Must have slipped your mind, Dad. Are you planning on asking Tucker for stock tips?"

"You bet I am. The kid reminds me of myself at that age. A real go-getter. Man of action. I like him."

"If by 'kid' you mean Tucker, he's got to be at least thirty-five." Olivia wondered if she should tell them she'd seen Tucker after the party last night. Her mother would probably worry about her driving alone that late, she decided, and didn't bring it up.

"That's a kid to me." Richard lifted the paper and turned from the business section to sports. "What do you have going on today, Livvy?"

"I have to run an errand, then help Josie clean the party mess."

"Sounds like fun," he said absently.

Olivia scowled, knowing he hadn't paid attention to her answer. She wished she could ask him how a person went about buying a new tire without her mother overhearing. He might not know much about cars, but he'd surely had a flat tire once or twice in his life. Before she could think of a way to get him alone, he folded the paper and stood.

Richard went to the kitchen door and pushed it open. "Mighty fine stack, Dorothy."

"Thanks, Mr. C. Glad you liked them."

The door swung shut as he turned and crossed to the table. Leaning over, he pecked Eleanor on the cheek, and then did the same to Olivia before leaving the dining room.

Eleanor put her napkin beside her empty plate and rose. "I've got to run, too, dear. Will we see you at dinner?"

"I'll be here." Olivia squeezed the hand her mother placed on her shoulder.

Eleanor left as Dorothy Keller entered, wiping her hands on a towel. The Chathams owned the house, but Dorothy ran it. "He says that every time I make pancakes."

"He means it every time." Olivia stood and reached for her plate.

"I'll get that, Livvy," Dorothy said, rushing to her side. "You run along."

"I'm not going to drop it."

"I know, sweetie. Just doing my job."

Olivia saw the relief on the other woman's face when she

got her hands on the sticky, syrup-covered plate. "I'm not clumsy after a party."

"I thought you might have another one tonight."

"I don't," Olivia said, leaving the room. Her father had closed his study's door, meaning Do Not Disturb. She was on her own as far as tire buying went.

⁕⁕

Tucker sat at a table in a dingy interrogation room at the police station. He sipped coffee from a Styrofoam cup and eyed the three policemen. Sheriff Strickland settled on the chair across from him and deputies occupied seats on each side of the table. The county sheriff wore a crisply ironed uniform and his shoes were buffed to a shine. His thinning brown hair and full mustache were neatly trimmed. The deputies were equally tidy. Tucker waited for the questions to begin.

"How well did you know Ms. Mecklenberg?" Strickland asked.

"Not well at all. We were introduced by a mutual acquaintance. I was surprised she invited me to the party." Tucker saw the deputy to his left make a note on a pad he held on his lap.

"But you went? Even though you didn't know her well?" Strickland's eyes narrowed behind the lenses of his glasses.

Tucker had been around cops enough during the last year to recognize 'The Look'. It reminded him of an animal on the prowl. He assumed an air of indifference. "Sure. How else am I going to meet people?"

"What time did you take her home?"

"I think it was around a quarter to twelve. Somewhere in there."

"Define 'somewhere'."

"Five minutes either way," Tucker answered.

"How long did you stay?"

"Long enough to see her to the door."

"You didn't go in?" Strickland's eyebrows rose. The deputy continued making notes. The other officer studied Tucker as if he was a new breed of ape on exhibit at a zoo.

"No. How was she murdered? When did it happen?"

"Did you go straight home?"

Tucker finished his coffee, and put the cup on the table as he shook his head. "I felt restless, so I decided to go to the cafe. On the way there I came across Olivia Chatham. She was having car trouble, and I stopped to help her."

"What kind of car trouble? That Lexus can't be a month old."

"Flat tire. I helped her change it."

"This is a small town, Monroe. I don't know if you're familiar with life in a place this size, but we know each other. Olivia would never stop to change a tire. She'd just keep going on the flat one."

"It'd slow her down some," the deputy to Tucker's left said, looking up from his notes. Strickland glared at him.

Funny, Tucker thought. That's exactly what happened. "She was going so slow I knew something was wrong. I passed her and saw the flat and motioned her to the side of the road."

"What time was this?"

"A little after midnight. She might have a better idea."

"We'll ask her. How long did it take you to change the tire?"

"Changing the tire didn't take long. Convincing her it needed to be changed was an uphill climb. She seemed to think the tire was already ruined, so why worry about it? It took a while to explain the importance of a rim to the overall performance of a vehicle. When she understood, she let me change it."

"*Let* you?"

"That's how it felt." Tucker twirled his empty cup. "Like she was doing me a favor."

The cop to his left nodded. "Sounds like Livvy, all right."

"Mind if I handle this, Benjy?" Strickland said.

"Sorry."

"What time did you get done with the tire?"

"Had to have been close to one. I followed Ms. Chatham

home, then went to the 24 Hour Café. It was closed so I went to the truck stop on Route 12."

"What time did you get there?"

"One-twenty, one-thirty. I'm not sure, I wasn't watching the clock."

"We can check that out easily enough. They have cameras. Frank, see if you can round up someone in charge at the truck stop and get a look at last night's tape. Find out if anyone remembers seeing Mr. Monroe."

The cop on Tucker's right stood and left the room. He hadn't spoken a word in Tucker's presence.

"When did you leave the truck stop?" Strickland asked.

"Around four. I got caught up in a poker game."

Strickland made an undecipherable noise and rose. "Come on, Ben. We need to call Olivia and invite her to the station."

Tucker watched the door close behind them and wondered how long this would take. He wished he'd asked for more coffee.

❧❧

"Tanya," Olivia said in dismay when she saw the woman exit the sheriff's office. "Not Donny Jr. again?"

Tanya shook her head. "No, Livvy. This time *they* needed *me*." Her chest puffed out. "I'm an alibi."

"An alibi! How exciting!"

"What about you, Livvy? Why are you here?"

"I don't know. Ben tracked me down at Josie's and asked me to come in to talk to Eugene. Didn't seem polite to say 'no'. Whose alibi are you?"

"That's enough, ladies. No comparing notes." Sheriff Strickland touched Olivia's arm.

"Talk to you later, Tanya," Olivia said. "I'm glad it wasn't about Donny Jr."

"Just a matter of time before it is again." Tanya's shoulders lowered.

Olivia didn't know what to say. Tanya was probably right. Her son had a gift for finding mischief and getting caught.

She looked up at the Sheriff. "What's going on Eugene?"

Strickland motioned her into his office. She shrugged out of her coat, draped it over the back of a chair, then settled on the seat and waited. Eugene shut the door before sitting behind his desk.

He leaned on his forearms. "Olivia, I'd appreciate it if you'd call me Sheriff or Sheriff Strickland around here." He lifted a hand and waved it toward the room on the other side of the glass walls, then dropped his hand to the desk again. "It's a matter of keeping their respect."

"Of course, Eugene. I'm sorry." Olivia heard the door open and turned in her seat as Frank Rothstein and Ben Appleby entered. "Hiya, guys."

"Hi, Livvy," Frank said. Ben nodded at her, then shut the door and both men took seats behind Olivia.

She turned to the sheriff. "What can I do for you?"

"Tell me about last night."

"What about it? I went to a party at Josie's. Jimmy Zeigler got drunk, but Jimmy always gets drunk. I took his keys and he was real polite about it, just like he always is. Such a happy lush. Let's see…what else?" Olivia drummed her fingertips on an arm of her chair.

"No, Olivia. I mean did you run into any trouble?"

Olivia drew her eyebrows together as she thought. "No," she said after a few moments. "Unless a flat tire could be called trouble."

"Tell me about it." Strickland sat back in his chair.

"I had a flat tire. I didn't want to bother with it, and thought if I went real slow, it wouldn't matter. Then someone drove next to me and motioned for me to pull over. Nearly gave me a heart attack until I saw who it was."

"Who was it?"

"Tucker Monroe. He's new in town and I'd met him earlier at Mom and Dad's party. I'm so sorry you and Betty couldn't make it, Eu…Sheriff."

"Where were you when he motioned you over?"

"Between my house and Josie's." Olivia noticed Eugene

press his lips together, and wondered if the holiday season was causing him too much stress.

"Could you be more specific? Do you remember what road?"

"Oh, sure. Old Mill Road."

"Did you happen to notice the time?"

"Twelve-oh-six." She straightened. "I looked at the clock when I saw someone pull alongside me. I thought I was about to be robbed by a highway bandit and wanted to have all kinds of details and clues for you."

Eugene looked over her shoulder, and Olivia had the feeling she'd said something important. "Frank, run out to Livvy's car and see if her clock is correct."

Olivia reached in her pocket. "It's in the front row. A white Lexus. Or maybe it's called eggshell." She pulled out her keys and handed them to Frank. "Sorry I can't remember the name of the color. It might be cream or even oyster."

"I know which one it is." Frank grinned and left the room.

"Monroe changed your tire?" Strickland asked.

"Insisted on it. I didn't think it was necessary, but he nattered on and on about the consequences of poor car maintenance, so I finally let him." She leaned forward and put a hand on his blotter. "I'll tell you one thing, Eugene. If you ever want to know anything about rims, he's the man to ask." She gave the desk a light pat before scooting back in her chair and tossing her hair over her shoulder. Strickland made a choking noise. "You okay, Eugene? I mean Sheriff? Want me to get you a glass of water?"

He raised a hand. "I'm fine, Livvy. What happened next?"

"He followed me home. Kind of a sweet gesture if you ask me. I thanked him and he waited for me to go inside before leaving."

"Do you have any idea what time that was?"

Olivia squinted at the ceiling, then looked at the Sheriff. "I'd say around one."

"Are you fuzzy on the times, Olivia? Just say so if you are."

She shook her head. "When I got to my room it was five after one. You can check that clock, too, but Dad's picky about our clocks. He says they should all be set according to Greenwich Village time. Why he cares what time it is there is beyond me."

"You mean Greenwich Mean…never mind." Strickland got to his feet, and Olivia heard a chair scrape behind her.

Frank came back to the room, nodded at Strickland, and handed Olivia her keys. "Her clock's right."

"We'll take a look at the clock in your room later on today. Don't touch it until we give you the okay."

"I won't even go in there."

"Thanks for coming in, Livvy."

"What's this all about, Sheriff Eugene?" Olivia stood, and noticed something on Eugene's desk. She stared at it a few seconds before reaching for her coat and turning toward the door.

"Just tying up loose ends." He looked at Frank and Ben. "I guess we let Monroe go. Looks like he's got an alibi."

Olivia was fascinated at the way her day was turning out. "You mean I'm an alibi, too? Like Tanya?"

Strickland motioned to his door. "I'm afraid so."

Olivia led the way, stopping in the squad room. "Is Tucker in trouble?"

"Maybe, maybe not. Cheryl Mecklenberg is dead. Mr. Monroe is the last person we know of who saw her alive."

"She can't be dead! She was at my house just last night!"

"She is."

"How?"

"Not sure yet, but it wasn't natural."

"She was murdered?" Olivia's voice rose as she spoke.

"That's another thing we're not sure of." Strickland paused, then scratched his chin and stared at her a moment. "People talk to you, Livvy. You've probably heard more secrets than any one else in town. Someone knows something. They may not be aware they know it, or maybe they don't want to get involved. Either way, you'll hear about it. When you do, no matter how insignificant you think the information, I want you to tell me. Keep your ear to the ground."

Olivia placed a hand over her racing heart. "Mercy." Eugene *needed* her. "Consider my ear already at the grindstone."

He patted her lightly on the shoulder. "Take care, Livvy."

Olivia watched Eugene cross the bustling room, stopping and talking to other officers as he went. She held her hands out to keep Ben and Frank from following him. "When was she killed?"

"She talked to her sister around midnight, and the coroner says the outer limit on the time is three this morning," Ben answered. "That's just a guess, though. He has to run tests to be sure."

"And you thought Tucker did it?" Olivia asked, aghast at the notion.

"He was with her last night. But Monroe couldn't have gotten to Old Mill Road in the six minutes between her phone call and the time he came across you. Not even in a Porsche. He went to the truck stop on 12 after leaving you. That's why we had Tanya in. She waited on him last night."

"That's enough, Ben," Frank said. "Keep this under your hat, Livvy."

"It'll all be out soon," Ben told him.

"Yeah, but Strickland may want to control when."

"True," Ben admitted. "Frank's right, Livvy. Keep the details to yourself."

Olivia nodded somberly. "You can count on me. Who found her? Did she have a roommate?"

Frank shook his head. "She had a breakfast date. When Ms. Mecklenberg didn't show, her friend got concerned, went to her house, and found her." He grinned. "Eugene had a point. People talk to you, tell you things. Even Ben and me are guilty."

"I won't tell Eugene you gave me info. It'll be our little secret. I can keep a secret, fellas. In this particular instance, what goes in my ear, stays in my ear."

Strickland stopped at a door on the far side of the room. When he turned to look at them, Olivia, Frank and Ben hurried to join him.

"You're free to go, Livvy," Strickland said as he opened the door.

She peeked into the room and saw Tucker slumped in a chair, legs stretched out in front of him and hands clasped together over his stomach. Olivia heard a soft snore.

"Does he know she's dead?" Olivia asked.

"Doesn't seem to be taking it too hard, does he?" the sheriff answered.

"He's obviously distraught. Sleepiness is one of the signs of depression, you know. Will you tell me when you find out how she died, Sheriff Eugene?"

"You'll be the first."

"There's no need for sarcasm."

Eugene ran a hand along his cheek. "It's been a rough morning."

"Have a cup of tea. Chamomile soothes and calms."

Tucker opened his eyes and slowly sat up. "Am I cleared?" he asked, raking his fingers through his hair.

"You can go."

Olivia looked at Eugene in surprise. His tone tacked the words 'for now' onto the end of his sentence as if he'd said them aloud.

Tucker stood and reached for the jacket hanging on the back of his chair. "You gonna give me a ride, or do I have to hitchhike?"

"I'll drive you," Olivia said.

❧❧

Tucker pulled his coat on and walked to the door. He leaned against the frame, studying Olivia from the top of her taffy-colored hair to the tips of her black-booted toes. She wore a velvet leopard-print top tucked into black jeans belted at the waist. A bag the size of a small suitcase hung over one shoulder, and a tan, suede, fleece-lined coat was draped over her arm. Large green eyes stared back at him.

"Did they drag you away from a safari?" Tucker asked.

Olivia handed her purse to the note-taking cop, Ben, who took it with a bewildered expression. She passed her coat to the quiet cop, Frank, who appeared as baffled as his partner.

When she shoved an arm into one sleeve his face cleared, and he held the other side of the jacket for her.

"It's a good thing we ran into each other last night. I'm your alibi, or at least part of it." She looked over her shoulder. "Thanks, Frank."

"I've always been lucky," Tucker said.

"Really? Me too."

"Did you get your tire fixed?"

Olivia took her purse from Ben. "Yep. I had no idea how to go about doing it, so I went to Ducky's Automotive Emporium thinking someone there might point me in the right direction. Turns out they sell tires."

"The words 'Automotive Emporium' didn't give you a hint?"

Olivia shrugged. "I find it's best not to assume. Anyway, I got four. Ducky, that's Ducky Jenssen, owns the place. He put them on right away. Did it himself."

"Four?" A flash of irritation whipped through Tucker. He didn't like the idea of someone taking advantage of Olivia. "You only needed one, and maybe not even that. You could have just picked up a nail, which could be fixed."

"You're not going to tell me about rims again, are you?"

"No." Tucker looked at Frank and Ben. "This Ducky doesn't sound particularly ethical."

Olivia waved her hand in a dismissive gesture. "He said what you did about only needing one and the nail and all that. I told him I wouldn't feel safe unless I got new ones all around. I had to insist and I hate that. I hate being adamant."

Frank patted Olivia's shoulder. "That was sweet, Livvy. I'm sure Ducky can use the extra money right now, what with the new baby."

"Nothing sweet about it." A flush rose in Olivia's cheeks. "I needed tires, Ducky sells them. It was a simple business transaction." She put an arm through one of Tucker's and looked up at him. "You poor thing. Let's get you out of here."

Tucker couldn't argue with that. "Let's." He nodded at the police and walked down the hall beside Olivia.

CHAPTER THREE

"You must be devastated. Last night, at the party, I could sense how close you and Cheryl were," Olivia said in a low voice.

"I feel bad about what happened, but I barely knew her," Tucker replied. Whatever Olivia sensed, it wasn't closeness. Although he couldn't say why, by the end of the evening he'd wanted nothing more than to put distance between himself and Cheryl.

"Try not to dwell on what might have been."

"We didn't have plans to see each other again."

"Don't let this turn you bitter."

Tucker sighed as they left the building. Apparently Olivia heard what she wanted to. He saw her car parked in front of the station, and stopped, trying to think of a way to postpone going home. He nodded in the other direction. "I'd invite you for a cup of coffee, but the café is closed." Maybe she'd suggest another place.

Olivia looked at her watch. "No it isn't."

"It was last night."

She smiled, and it was like sunshine after a week of rain. Olivia looped her arm through his and turned toward the 24 Hour Café. Tucker strolled beside her, watching her hair bounce around her shoulders as she moved.

"If I've told the owners once, I've told them a thousand times, the name of the place is misleading. The café is open twenty-four hours a week. Monday through Saturday, eleven to three. They're closed on Sunday so the family can rest."

"I don't know why, but that never occurred to me." He hesitated, and then said, "Aren't you afraid to be with me? I could be a murderer."

"You didn't do it," Olivia said, sounding convinced.

"How can you be so sure?"

"That has to stay in my hat."

Tucker ambled along, trying to translate what she'd said. "So she was killed when I was with you, or when I was at the truck stop."

"If she was killed."

Tucker stopped and looked at her upturned face. "What do you mean? Or does that have to stay in your hat, too? They told me she was murdered."

Olivia's brows drew together, and she appeared deep in thought. "Eugene didn't say anything about not mentioning it. He told me her death wasn't natural, and when I asked if she'd been murdered, he said he didn't know. Kind of a puzzle, isn't it?"

"Yeah, it is. Maybe whatever killed her could have been an accident. Like a fall."

"Hum, that's a thought. Or..."

"Or what?"

"Nothing."

"Ah, you're thinking suicide."

"It's a possibility. Did she act differently last night?"

"I told you, I barely knew her."

"Right." Olivia tugged on his arm and started walking again. "Let's talk about something else."

The town reminded Tucker of a movie scene. Wreaths and bells hung from lampposts and storefronts. Elaborate holiday displays filled shop windows. Outdoor speakers trilled festive music, and 'Merry Christmas' banners stretched across the streets. People they passed smiled and nodded. Tucker didn't know if it was the season, or if everyone liked Olivia. He suspected the latter.

Tucker slowed his pace. "It's not every day I meet someone who has a town named after them."

"It was named after my great-great-great grandfather. I'm the last of the Chathams. Too bad I wasn't a boy."

"Yeah, that's a shame," he said with a grin. "Have you lived here all your life?"

"Except for the time I lived in Lakeville, when I was married to Victor. And the time I lived in Deerwood, when I was married to Eric. Sammy and I lived here."

Tucker cleared his throat, and hoped he could sound as blasé as she did. "How many times have you been married?"

"Just three. Dad makes a big deal out of it, but I'm old-fashioned."

Tucker glanced at her, and realized she was serious. "Old-fashioned?"

"I only sleep with men I'm married to. That's one of my rules."

"What are the other rules?" Tucker asked, feeling as though he'd just been given the verbal equivalent of a cold shower.

Olivia tilted her head and nibbled on her lower lip for a moment. "I can't think of any others. I guess that's all of them."

"If I had to live by one rule, that wouldn't be it. You might want to add a few exceptions. You could end up with twenty last names."

"I know you're making fun of me, but three exes aren't so many. My friend Josie's been married three times." Olivia stopped and turned to him, holding a hand up in the classic scout pledge sign. "Their names were Tom, Dick and Harry." Laughter bubbled out of her and she dropped her hand to her side. "I'm not kidding, they really were. 'Course now we call them Moe, Larry and Curly."

"Of course." They began moving again, but she stuffed her hands in her pockets instead of returning her arm to his. "What do you call your three?"

"I don't make fun of them. They were nice guys." She squinted up at the cloudless blue sky. "Eric was so gifted, and Victor had such great hands."

Tucker thought she sounded wistful. He didn't want to

hear about Eric's gifts or Victor's hands, and surprised himself by asking, "Why divorce them if they were so great?"

"For their own good. I was in Eric's way. He was too polite to say so, but I knew it. He was an artist. Work, work, work. Every time we went anywhere, I knew he was just itching to get home so he could paint. After a year I told him I thought he'd be better off alone. He took it well." She gazed up at Tucker for a moment, and he noticed a faraway look on her face. "He lives in Paris now. Can you imagine? Paris, France. He sent me a portrait of myself for Christmas. It's wonderful, he really is gifted."

"Was Victor an artist, too?"

"Musician. That man could pick up any instrument and make notes come out of it no one else could. Such hands. But he got it into his head that we should live in a commune outside Spokane." Olivia hesitated, then said, "Don't think I'm shallow, but I'm not cut out for commune life. It'd be nice to have people around all the time. That'd be fun. But I'd hate sharing the. . .um. . .facilities, if you know what I mean."

"Coming through loud and clear. He went without you? Why didn't he give up the commune idea?"

Olivia's eyes opened wide. "What kind of wife would make her husband give up his dream?" She shook her head. "No, I told him to follow his heart. He took it well. A few days ago he sent me a recording of a song he wrote. Don't laugh, it's called 'Sweet Olivia'. Wasn't that nice of him?"

"I'd like to hear it." She got Christmas presents from her ex-husbands? Tucker had never heard of such a thing.

"You'll hear it till you're sick of it. Some record studio gave him a contract." She smiled brightly. "See, they're both better off without me, and everything worked out just fine."

"And the other one? Sammy?"

Olivia's smile disappeared. "If he doesn't stop pestering me, I'll have to think up a name to call him." They came to a stoplight, and waited for it to change.

"Pestering you how?"

Olivia took a hand out of her pocket and waved it beside

her head. "Always buzzing around. Like a gnat. Hey, that's a good name. I'll call him The Gnat. Josie'll love it."

"It certainly paints a picture."

"You may have met him last night. He was coming in as I was going out."

The light changed and they crossed the street. "I don't remember a Sam or a Sammy," Tucker told her.

"Sammy's pretty forgettable."

"He's still invited to parties at your house?"

"He crashed. Dad would never kick Sammy out. For one thing, it would cause a scene. For another, Sammy's a banker. Dad can't bring himself to be rude to bankers. Actually, Dad can't bring himself to be rude to anyone. What about you? How many times have you been married?"

"None." He suppressed a shudder at his narrow escape.

Olivia gaped at him. "That's much weirder than three times."

"I guess I'm not old-fashioned." They reached the café and he held the door for her.

"Marie," Olivia said as soon as they were inside. "This is Tucker. He got confused by your sign last night and stopped, but you were closed."

A lady wearing a striped uniform and apron looked at Tucker. "Livvy explain it?"

"Yes, ma'am."

"End of confusion. The usual, Livvy?"

"You can skip the sandwich, but I'd love some coffee."

"Do you need a menu, sir?"

"Just coffee."

Marie disappeared behind a counter and Tucker followed Olivia to a booth by the front window. She tossed her purse into the corner of one seat. A moment later, her coat landed on top of it. Tucker took his jacket off and waited for Olivia to sit.

"Put your coat down, Tucker. I'll take you around and introduce you."

Tucker followed in Olivia's wake, feeling like a show-and-tell project. He lost track of who was who. Olivia seemed to know everything about everyone. She asked about their families, by name, including their pets, and they all smiled and cheerfully answered her questions. A radio in the background played Christmas music. Tucker wondered whom he'd have to bribe to get some Bob Seger piped in.

As they slid onto the leatherette seats, Olivia leaned toward him. "I hope this wasn't a bad time for you to meet people. With you grieving and all."

"I'm not grieving, Olivia." Two mugs of coffee sat on the table. The one in front of Tucker was filled to the brim. Olivia's was half-full.

"It's okay, you're allowed." Olivia picked up a small pitcher sitting next to her cup. She filled the rest of her mug with milk and looked at him as she set the pitcher down. "They got tired of me using up all their little plastic thimbles of cream. Now they just bring me milk."

"Wise of them." He picked up his mug and took a sip as he watched Olivia tear open white packets of sugar and pour the contents into her cup.

"Do you want to talk about it? Losing a girlfriend must be unbearably traumatic."

"I told you, she wasn't my. . .never mind." He lost count of how many packets Olivia added to her coffee. She picked up a spoon and stirred whatever it was she'd made. She'd turned a perfectly good cup of coffee into a liquid dessert.

"If you feel like crying, go ahead. It isn't unmanly or unmacho or anything. Don't try to be brave."

"I'll remember that."

"Are you sure you don't want to go home? We can leave if you're uncomfortable." She sipped her coffee. "Perfect."

"I think it's a good idea to be around people. It's best to move on."

"Healthy attitude," Olivia said with a nod. "I've been doing some thinking."

"About what?"

Olivia rummaged in her bag, and pulled out a pad of

paper. She slid the tablet over to Tucker. "Do me a favor and tear off the top sheet."

"Why?"

"Are you one of those people who needs a reason for everything?"

"Guess so."

"I'll tell you after you do it."

Tucker tore off the sheet and handed it to Olivia.

She smiled. "Good. You did it right. If I had any doubts, and I didn't, they would have just been whisked away."

"I'm glad you're happy. What did I do right, why did I do it and how did it whisk away doubts?"

"The reason concerns Cheryl. Are you sure you want to hear it?" She drank from her mug, then put it on the table and rolled it between her palms.

"Positive." Tucker enjoyed watching Olivia's changing expressions. Green eyes coupled with the leopard top gave her a feline look. He wished her head wasn't as empty as her flat tire.

"When I was in Eugene's office I noticed a plastic bag on his desk. Not a sandwich bag, but a big one." She held her hands a foot apart. Apparently thinking more explanation was needed, Olivia continued, "Suppose someone, through no fault of her own, was late for dinner and you didn't want her supper to be ruined. You could put the whole plate of Chicken Cordon Bleu and asparagus tips and rice pilaf or whatever inside a baggie this size and put it in the refrigerator and—"

Tucker held up a hand. "I get the picture."

"That's what was on Eugene's desk."

"A plate of Chicken Cordon Bleu inside a baggie?" he baited her, biting the inside of his cheek to keep from laughing.

She threw him a long-suffering look. "There was an open appointment book inside the baggie. The kind that has addresses and phone numbers and a calendar. It also had a notepad and the top of the pad, where someone had torn a page off, had a ragged edge. You aren't the person who took the page. You tear evenly."

Tucker sipped his coffee. "So?"

"The book was Cheryl's. It had her name on it."

"Again, so?"

"She didn't rip off the last page. She didn't die accidentally, she was murdered."

"You lost me." Tucker was beginning to think he'd say that every time he talked to her.

Olivia sipped her sugar concoction. "She was real persnickety about stuff like that. No ragged edges on papers you turned in to her. She even took points off for that. I ended up being persnickety myself. That's another thing I didn't like about Sammy. He'd just tear away."

Tucker shook his head. "It's a wonder you two got together at all."

"Isn't it? Anyway, I figure there was something on that page and the killer tore it off. If it had been done while Cheryl was alive, she'd have fixed it. Made the edges straight."

"Maybe she changed, got less persnickety."

Olivia looked at him the way a patient mother looks at her child. "I doubt it. Once anal, always anal." She tapped her fingers on the table. "I'd sure like to see that pad. Do you think Eugene would let us have it for five or ten minutes? We could rub a pencil over the next sheet and see if we can read what was written on the missing page."

"Sure, Olivia. He'd be delighted to let us borrow it." Tucker nodded at a pay phone on the wall. "Why don't you call him? He can send Ben or Frank over here with it and save you the trouble of going back to the station."

Olivia wrinkled her nose at him. "I'll overlook that comment and your tone on account of your recent bereavement. You're obviously under extreme emotional distress."

"Obviously. You didn't tell Eugene that Cheryl wouldn't have torn the page like that?"

"Why bother? The cops all think I'm an airhead. I'm surprised they believe I can tell time."

Tucker looked at Olivia and realized, much to his surprise, that she wasn't dumb at all. Her eyes were bright with intelligence. She came at things from a different direction, but she wasn't a fool.

"You should tell them," Tucker said as Marie came to the table and refilled his cup. She raised her eyebrows at Olivia.

"One's my limit, Marie."

Tucker could understand that. One would be the death of him. After Marie left, Tucker said, "The police should know. It could be important. You can't keep this in your hat."

"Don't get me wrong, Ben and Frank are nice guys. Salt of the earth. I mean it; they give you a ticket and feel so bad about it you end up comforting them. But they're in over their heads with murder."

"I saw other cops at the station. Ben and Frank aren't Strickland's only deputies."

"No, but they're the cream of the crop. And Eugene can't do it all himself. I'm afraid it's up to us to solve this thing."

"Us?" Tucker asked.

"Don't you want my help?"

"I don't plan on getting involved."

"Why not? She was your girlfriend."

"For the last time, she wasn't. . .I give up." Tucker resisted the urge to pound his head on the back of the booth.

Olivia drummed the table with her fingertips. "I wonder if anything was stolen." She got a pencil from her purse and wrote on the paper Tucker had torn. "I also wonder what she was wearing. Did she still have her dress on when you left?"

Tucker choked on his coffee, and wiped his mouth with a paper napkin. "What?"

"I'm not asking out of morbid curiosity. It could be pertinent to the case."

"I don't see how."

"You poor thing. You really don't want to talk about it, do you?" Olivia reached for her coat. "I'll take you home."

"I'm not done with my coffee," Tucker said. "And I don't mind talking about it."

Olivia dropped her jacket, picked up her pencil, and gave him an expectant look.

"She was wearing her dress. And her coat, and her shoes.

I left her at the door."

"Did she invite you inside?"

"Yes." He didn't add that the moment Cheryl had asked him to come in, warning bells rang in his ears and an inner voice screamed 'No!'

"Ah," Olivia said, and bent over the paper. "Now we're getting somewhere."

"Where are we getting?"

"She wouldn't have invited you in if she was expecting someone. We need to know how he got in. If he was already there, if he broke in, or if she let him in after you left."

"How are we going to do that?" Good God, he'd just said 'we'.

"I'm not sure." Olivia bent over the paper again. She scribbled for a moment, and then looked up. "It would be nice to know what she had on when they found her. If she was still dressed or if she'd gotten ready for bed. Then we'd have a better idea of when it happened. Especially if she was in the middle of something. Like if she'd exfoliated but hadn't toned. That could be real important."

"We should work out a signal for this. You've lost me again."

Olivia straightened in her seat. "I'm trying to be careful. I don't want to say something that could hurt you. I should take you home and we can do this some other time."

"I'd rather hear it now, if you don't mind." Tucker wouldn't have left if the 24 Hour Café had gotten a bomb threat. He was sorry Cheryl was dead, but couldn't remember when he'd had more fun.

"Okay," Olivia said in a reluctant tone. "Tell me when you've had enough."

"Deal."

"If I'd just gotten home from my first date with the new love of my life, I'd call Josie right away." She lifted her hands, palms up, and shrugged. "Now, I'm not saying Cheryl called anyone, not even her sister, but lots of women would have. Then they'd get ready for bed."

"Okay, I'm with you." Finally, he added silently. Cheryl called her sister after he left last night. That was one of the little items in Olivia's hat.

"Cheryl had real nice skin, but I don't need to tell you that. She took care of it. Cleaning, exfoliating, toning and moisturizing. That takes a little time."

"You do all that every night?" No wonder she'd been divorced three times.

"Sure." Olivia leaned on her forearms, and her expression grew thoughtful. "Let's say she took a quick shower, exfoliated and toned but hadn't put on her moisturizer. That would make it about twelve-thirty. If she'd already moisturized, it doesn't help us much. Except to say she was probably killed after twelve-thirty. But if one of those steps is missing we can pin the time between midnight, when she didn't call her sister, and how long it takes to get to the step she was at."

Tucker rubbed his temples. He didn't know if it felt like his head was imploding or exploding. The scary thing was that Olivia might have a point. "Let's go back to the police station and tell them all this. The ragged edges thing and the foliating stuff."

"Piffle."

"Piffle?"

Her eyebrows drew together. "This is important, Tucker. If she was still wearing her dress, maybe someone followed you from the party and she didn't have time to get ready for bed. Do you remember noticing headlights in your mirror?"

"No. What's piffle mean?"

She waved a hand. "I'm going to get a list of people at the party. We can go over it and you can tell me names you recognize. Maybe it'll jar something loose. Maybe someone Cheryl mentioned to you. Someone who didn't like her."

A song on the radio ended, and another tune began. Elvis Presley's "Blue Christmas" filled the air. Olivia tilted her head and gave him an impish grin. She leaned forward and in a low, conspiratorial voice, said, "Want to hear something funny?"

CHAPTER FOUR

Tucker rested his forearms on the table and brought his face within inches of Olivia's. "I would love to hear something funny." He did his best to imitate her tone.

"For the first day of my life, my name was January Eighth Chatham."

Stunned nearly speechless, Tucker managed to ask, "Is that your birthday?"

"Nope. Elvis Presley's. Mom and Dad loved him."

"They really named you January Eighth? That was on your birth certificate?" Tucker was convinced nothing would surprise him again.

Olivia nodded and sat back in her seat. "Then they came to their senses and changed the forms to Olivia Aron. With one A, just like The King spelled his middle name." Her voice held the hint of a giggle and her eyes twinkled.

Tucker wondered if he looked as dumbstruck as he felt. "Where'd Olivia come from? What's that name have to do with Elvis?"

"Nothing. That's the weird part. It just popped into both their heads at the same time. Don't you think that's strange?"

"I would have an hour ago. Now it seems kind of normal."

"You poor thing."

"Will you stop saying that?"

Olivia reached over to gently pat his hand. "Sammy says you gamble, but I hope you don't play poker. Your face is an open book."

"It is? I thought I had that little quirk under control."

She opened her purse and dropped her notes and pencil into it. "We shouldn't be talking about Cheryl's untimely passing. Not now, while the wound is still so raw." Looking up, she met his gaze. "You put up a good front, Tucker Monroe, but you aren't fooling me."

"I imagine that's pretty hard to do." Tucker hid his grin. Here he was, thirty-six years old, and she made him feel like a teenager trying to impress the most popular cheerleader. The one who wore fuzzy sweaters and dated all the cool guys. "When is your birthday?"

"April fifteenth. Dad says he was late getting his taxes in that year. He wishes he could have gotten an extension for me. He's a hoot, isn't he?"

"It seems to run in the family. You're kind of fun yourself."

Olivia smiled and squared her shoulders. "That's sweet of you to say. Tell me something, how'd you end up in Chatham?"

"I was just passing through and thought the town looked nice. I liked the name, too. I figured this place would be as good as the next. Maybe better."

Olivia's smile vanished. "And look at what's happened. You've lost a girlfriend and been hauled into the police station. I bet you wish you'd kept on driving."

"I wouldn't say that."

"I'd better get you home. You need some quiet time."

Tucker couldn't think of a good excuse to stall. He reached for his money and found an empty pocket. "Um, Olivia? I left my place so fast I forgot my wallet."

"No problem." She dipped into her bag again and brought out a wad of bills. She peeled off a ten and dropped it on the table. Tucker thought they'd wait for change, but Olivia stood and grabbed her coat. When he raised an eyebrow, she tilted her head toward the door. Tucker slid out of the booth and, after holding her jacket for her, put his coat on and followed her outside.

"Kind of expensive coffee, isn't it?" He hadn't been born to money like Olivia and hated waste.

"Marie's mother is sick and she's moved in with them. Every little bit extra helps. Remember that the next time you're there, okay? If you can afford to leave a good tip, you should do it. Just don't leave so much it looks like charity. Marie's got her pride."

Tucker thought he could afford it. He held his arm out, and grinned when Olivia wrapped hers through it. "If they need money, why don't they keep the cafe open longer?"

"They can't. Chester, he's the cook and Marie's husband, has a bad back. And Marie has arthritis in her knees. Four or five hours on their feet are all they can handle."

"Olivia!" a woman shouted.

Olivia pulled her arm from Tucker's as she turned to the lady hurrying toward them. "Nadine, how are you?"

"Just fine, Livvy. I wanted to tell you that Ben and Frank found Bobby's bike."

"You're kidding!"

The woman shook her head. "Nope. Now Bobby stands in the garage every morning looking at both bikes, trying to decide which one to ride."

"Well, a fella can't have too many bikes, can he, Tucker?"

"That's what I've always said." Tucker had no idea what they were talking about.

"Nadine, this is Tucker. He's new in town. Tucker, this is Nadine. Her son, Bobby, had his bike stolen a few weeks ago."

"A couple of days later we opened the door to get the morning paper and there was a brand-new bike on the porch. Had all the bells and whistles. A note taped to it said it was an early present from Santa." Nadine smiled at Olivia. "I'd sure like to thank Mr. Claus."

"That's the neat thing about him. No thanks are needed," Olivia said.

Tucker saw Olivia's cheeks flush, and knew he was looking at Santa.

Nadine hugged Olivia. "Merry Christmas, Livvy."

"You, too, Nadine."

"Merry Christmas, Tucker. I hope you like it here in Chatham."

"I think I'm going to like it just fine, Nadine."

Nadine scurried off and Olivia glanced up at Tucker. "What's the matter? You're looking at me funny."

"I thought my face was an open book."

"Right now it's a blank page."

He smiled and held his arm out to her. "Let's go, January Eighth."

Pulling on his sleeve, Olivia stood on her tiptoes. He leaned down, bringing his head close to hers. "Let's keep that January Eighth thing between us, okay?" she whispered. "A few people know, but it's not common knowledge. I don't want everyone in town to think my family is odd."

"I should keep it in my hat?"

"Yeah."

"Whatever you say." They strolled toward her car. "Why do you act like an airhead?"

"Like an airhead?"

"Yes, and it is an act."

"How do you know? Maybe I'm the most addle-pated person you've ever met."

Tucker shook his head. "Nope. I never find addle-pates interesting."

"You find me interesting?"

"Very."

The corners of her mouth lifted. "Well, what do you know about that?" She gave a little hop. "You're interesting, too, 'Marlboro Man'."

Tucker looked down at her. "Are you making fun of me?"

"Oh, no. That was a compliment." She was quiet for several moments, then said, "I think because it's expected of me. We all fall into roles, don't we? You look like a bad boy, so you act like one. Doing your best to hide your pain from the world."

Ignoring the pain comment, he asked, "I look like a bad

boy?"

"All whiskery. And if you combed your hair today, you did it with a toothbrush."

Tucker felt the stubble on his chin. "This hasn't been an average day."

Olivia turned her gaze to the ground. "I know. I'm sorry. I keep putting my foot in my mouth."

He'd just gotten her off the topic of Cheryl and now they were back on it. "Maybe I am a bad boy. Maybe it's not an act," he said, hoping to distract her again.

She looked up at him. "You really are?"

"Nah, I'm a pussycat."

"I thought so. But you never know. I mean, a gambler might be someone who gets into trouble now and then."

"That's true. I don't gamble much anymore. I invest in the market."

"Dad says it's pretty much the same thing."

"If you do your homework, Wall Street has better odds." The wind picked up, whipping Olivia's hair around her head. Tucker watched as she pushed it aside, and smiled when he saw her cheeks and nose turning red in the cold afternoon air.

"Dad'll try to get some tips out of you. I just thought I'd give you a little warning."

"I never give tips. That's a sure way to make enemies."

Olivia's eyes sparkled mischievously. "Ha! You'll see. He'll get some out of you." Her face became serious again. "You don't work? I mean at a regular job?"

"Self-employed. My hours are similar to the 24 Hour Café's."

When they reached her car, Olivia looked up at him. "Maybe you should throw yourself into your job for a few days. Nothing like work to get your mind off your troubles."

Tucker suppressed a sigh and opened the door for her. She tossed her purse on the back seat before climbing in. By the time he got into the passenger side, she had the car started and her seat belt buckled. He gave her directions to his condo.

"Nice place," Olivia said as she pulled in front of the unit he indicated.

"Want to come in?"

"I think you need some privacy right now. Hang on a sec." She reached for her purse and got the tablet and pencil. She wrote something down and handed the paper to him. "These are my numbers. My car, my room, and the house. Call if you get overwhelmed and need a shoulder."

"No cell phone?"

"Several," she replied softly. Her expression reminded Tucker of a lost kitten. "Why do they make them so small?"

Tucker eyed her bag. If all her cell phones rang at once, her purse would sound like an air-raid siren. He waved the paper and said, "You'll be at one of these numbers most of the time?"

"Hardly ever. But you can leave a message and I'll get back to you as soon as possible."

"If I'm overwhelmed with grief?"

"Right."

He folded the paper and stuck it in his pocket. "It's a comfort to know help is only a phone call away."

"Don't worry, Tucker. We'll get the perp."

"Perp?"

"Perpetrator. Guilty party. This won't go unpunished, I promise. By the end of the day, Josie'll be on the case, too. You take care of yourself, and when you feel up to it, we'll fill you in on our progress."

Tucker got out of the car, wondering if he should say 'ten-four' or 'Roger'. "Thanks for the lift, Olivia."

"Any time. And don't hesitate to call. I'm off to brainstorm with Josie. We'll think of a way to find out what Cheryl was wearing. Josie should be a big help in getting the scoop from Frank and Ben. She can get info out of a rock, if it's a male rock."

Tucker watched Olivia's car disappear around the corner before going inside. He wondered why Olivia was so intent on finding out what Cheryl had been wearing.

❧❧

Cheryl Mecklenberg left the world as naked as she'd entered it. Eugene Strickland closed the file on his desk, leaned back in his chair, and steepled his fingers under his chin. He shut his eyes and reviewed what little he knew about the case.

She'd been found hanging in her closet, nude, with her feet on the floor and her knees bent. The coroner, Max Baxter, estimated the time of death between midnight and three in the morning. He'd confided to Eugene, privately, that he thought she'd died closer to midnight than three. A menu from the party could help him narrow the time frame, and the autopsy would give him more information. Contusions on her neck confirmed she'd been alive when the noose was placed around it, but there were no signs of a struggle.

Eugene knew he wasn't going to like some of the things he'd uncover working this case. Cheryl's closet and drawers revealed interesting, and unusual, sexual habits. She'd owned outfits ranging from Brownie uniforms to leather corsets. Frayed padding on the rope around her neck indicated it had been used before. Often.

Although he was no stranger to the wide range of people's tastes, he hadn't expected to find this in Chatham. He'd worked on the Chicago police force, and had come across similar situations. He knew that some folks liked to have their air cut off during sex. They alleged it increased the pleasure and intensity. Eugene shook his head in dismay. The practice had claimed more than a few lives. People occasionally passed out while in the throes of all that pleasure and intensity. Unfortunately they did it before removing the noose. Professionals termed it autoerotic asphyxiation. Eugene termed it asinine.

Straightening in his chair, he rubbed his hands across his face. Cheryl hadn't told her sister she was expecting anyone, and her sister thought she would have mentioned it if she were. There was no sign of a break-in, leading Eugene to believe she'd known the killer and opened the door to her assailant.

Eugene reread the background file he'd requested on Tucker Monroe. No doubt about it, he'd have to talk to the man again, but that could wait. He put the Mecklenberg and Monroe files in a drawer and locked it.

He had two men interviewing Cheryl's neighbors, Frank and Ben talking to people in her address book, and another team at her house, collecting fingerprints and other evidence. Eugene assigned himself the task of getting a guest list and menu from the Chathams. He knew the list would include the most prominent names in the county. He and his people would have to be careful not to step on any toes.

Eugene made a mental checklist of questions he wanted to ask Monroe as he drove to the Chatham house. His file described a man who'd danced on the edge of the law at least once.

As he rounded the last curve in the Chatham drive, Eugene saw Olivia walking toward the house and honked his horn. She turned and waved. He hoped one of the other Chathams was home. The thought of another conversation with Olivia made the insides of his eyelids burn.

"Hi, Eugene," Olivia shouted when he got out of the car. "Do you have more questions for me?"

He strolled over to her. "No, I just wanted to get a copy of last night's menu and a list of people who were here. Are either of your parents home?"

"Doesn't look like it. Their cars are gone." Olivia moved toward the house. "It doesn't matter. I know where Mom keeps that stuff. You need the menu for stomach contents, don't you? I should have thought of that myself."

Eugene hoped he could get what he needed and leave quickly. "If it's okay, I'll check your bedroom clock while I'm here."

Olivia opened the front door. "No problem. Follow me."

Eugene watched Olivia pound up the stairs. Had he ever had that much energy? He took the steps at a more sedate pace, and reminded himself he needed to get on an exercise regimen.

She waited for him at the top landing, and pointed to a door to the end of the hall. "Go right in. I'll get the guest list and menu."

As he went through Olivia's three-room suite, he recalled the apartment he and Betty shared the first five years of their marriage. It hadn't been this large. Eugene looked at every clock. They were all correct. When he turned to leave, he saw Olivia standing in the doorway.

"Thanks, Livvy. Your clocks check out."

"I can use my room again? You're releasing it back to my custody?"

He looked for a trace of sarcasm in her expression, but didn't find any. "It's all yours."

"Good." She waved the papers in her hand. "I'll make copies of these for you."

"I appreciate it." He descended the stairs with Olivia, grateful she went down slower than she'd gone up.

"Eugene? If I tell you something, will you tell me something?"

"That's not how it works, Livvy. If you have information about Cheryl or the case, it's your duty to tell me."

"Nuts. Oh, well, it was worth a try."

Eugene followed Olivia into her father's study. She lifted the copy machine lid, placed one of the lists on the glass and pushed a button.

"What is it, Olivia? What do you have to tell me?"

Turning to him, she launched into a description of ragged edges and the way women get ready for bed that left his mind reeling. Knowing he'd need diplomacy, Eugene pulled himself together.

"That's interesting, Olivia. It might help us pin down the time of death."

"And convince you it was murder," she added, then repeated her ragged edge theory.

Eugene ran a hand up and down the back of his neck. The headache that had threatened earlier grew. "Thanks a lot for the information, Livvy. I'll share it with the officers at the station." He held out his hand. "Can I have the lists now?"

Olivia handed him the papers. "You didn't even take notes. What if you forget a detail?"

"I have a photographic memory," Eugene said, desperate to get away.

"Oh. I wish I had one of those."

Eugene moved to the entry. "They come in handy."

"One more thing before you go. You should add Sammy's name to the guest list. Sam Wallace. He wasn't invited, but he was here."

"I'll do that right away." He hustled outside, hoping to make his escape before she remembered something else she deemed vital to the case.

Olivia stood in the doorway. "I'll call if I come up with any more leads or developments."

"You do that," Eugene said with a wave of his hand. He got into his car and shut the door firmly behind him. His temples pounded until he reached the end of the drive. He opened his window and took a deep breath. The pressure in his head lessened.

Eugene pointed the car toward town. He didn't need ragged edges to tell him that Cheryl had been murdered. His gut told him this wasn't a sex game that had gone wrong. Could Olivia be on to something with the torn page from Cheryl's notebook? Would he have to go door to door, asking people to tear a page off a tablet? The thought brought a smile to his face.

What had she said about getting ready for bed? His smile turned to a frown as he remembered Olivia's words. Eugene thought of Betty and her nightly routine. No matter where they'd been, what they'd done, or when they got home, Betty always spent at least twenty minutes in the bathroom before going to bed. He rubbed his neck as he drove. His forehead throbbed.

The sheriff had planned on stopping at Monroe's place to ask a few more questions. He decided that could wait, and called the station to ask if the crime scene people were still at the Mecklenberg house. If they'd left, he'd need a key to get in. He was told the team was finishing up, but they'd wait for him. Half an hour later he put a plastic evidence bag filled with lotion bottles on the coroner's desk.

"Do me a favor, Max. Can you check Ms. Mecklenberg's face for any of these things?"

Max picked up the bag and looked at the labels. "No problem. I'll get to it right away."

"And can you give me some aspirin?"

Max looked at him sympathetically. "How many do you want?"

"Eight?"

"Three."

"I was at the Chatham house earlier. It was the second conversation I've had with Olivia today."

Max grimaced. "Ouch." He reached for a bottle and tumbled four tablets onto Eugene's palm.

Chapter Five

Josie opened the front door of her sprawling ranch-style house, navy blue eyes sparkling, and pulled Olivia inside. "I'm dying of curiosity. What took you so long? Were you at the police station all this time?"

Olivia followed Josie down a short hallway. Josephine Bookman moved like a model, probably because she'd been one. Her straight, pale-blonde hair cascaded halfway down her back. Olivia thought, not for the first time, that it was lucky she wasn't the jealous type. If she were, she'd hate Josie, who'd changed clothes since their morning cleaning session, and now looked perfect in designer jeans topped with an indigo cashmere sweater.

"We've got trouble." Olivia tried, and failed, to match Josie's long-legged stride.

"What do you mean?"

They entered an enormous living room done in bold colors and a southwestern motif. Bright paintings and festive throw rugs made the large space warm and inviting. Olivia shrugged out of her coat and dropped onto one end of the supple leather sofa. She pulled two copies of the guest list from her purse, rummaged in it again until she found pencils, and then put her bag on the floor.

Josie sat on the other end of the couch and curled her legs under her. "Spill it before I explode."

"Cheryl Mecklenberg died last night." Olivia passed one of the lists and a pencil to Josie.

"Who?"

"The woman who came to the party with Tucker Monroe. I told you about her."

"Oh, yeah. How did she die? I haven't heard anything." Josie's eyes opened wide. "What about Tucker? He's too gorgeous to die. Tell me it wasn't a car wreck."

"He's fine. Or as fine as can be expected for someone whose girlfriend was murdered last night. Such a brave little soldier."

"Murdered!"

Olivia filled Josie in and held up her copy of the invitation list. "We have to go through this and look carefully at every name. If there's anything hinky about someone, make a note."

"Are you saying someone at the party killed Cheryl?"

Olivia looked at her friend. "Keep up, Josie. It's a place to start. Someone could have followed her home and killed her after Tucker left. Later, when we get more info, and if we haven't already solved it, we can look at her friends and so on."

"How are we going to get more info?"

"I'll tell you later. Right now we have to go through the names. It probably won't lead anywhere, but it goes with the territory. You plod along and hope you get lucky."

"What are you talking about?"

"Cracking a case. Catching the perp and putting him behind bars."

"You've been reading detective novels again, haven't you?"

Olivia nodded. "Good thing, too. We're going to need all my skills for this caper."

"If you call me 'doll', I won't help."

"When have I ever called you 'doll'? Look at the list. Anyone jump out at you right away? Anyone suspicious at first glance?"

Josie studied the paper in her lap. "Oh, God. This is terrible."

Olivia's heart kicked up a beat. "Find anything? Already?

Who?"

Josie held up the list. "Look at these names. What do you see?"

"Don't go all muddly on me. Who got your attention?"

"All of them. Everyone on the list is boring."

"I *know* that."

"No, Livvy. You don't get it." Josie poked the paper with an index finger. "We're looking at us in ten or twenty years. We'll be as boring as they are. We don't *do* anything. We don't have any scandals, not one darn thing to hide." She shoved a magenta throw pillow behind her back. "I am so pissed. I want to have something to cringe about in my golden years. Some escapade that makes me blush when I'm eighty."

"Good grief, you're right. We're so clean we could run for office. As soon as this is over, we'll figure out a way to get some skeletons in our closets."

"Something fun, right?"

"That goes without saying. The list, Josie. Focus. See any potential killers?"

Josie slowly shook her head. "No, but give me a few minutes, okay?"

"Sure. I'll look it over again, too."

After a long moment of silence, Josie said, "This guy groped me. This one, too."

Olivia moved toward Josie to see the names.

"And him. And him," Josie added, tapping the paper.

Olivia slid into her corner of the couch. "As soon as you find someone who hasn't groped you, give a holler. Any man who hasn't made a pass at you is obviously deranged. That's our killer." Olivia didn't understand why she was being Miss Snippy Mouth. Josie couldn't help being beautiful. It wasn't her fault the "Marlboro Man" fantasies tiptoeing through Olivia's mind would soon disappear in Josie's cloud of flaxen hair.

Josie looked up from the list. "Do you want my help or not?"

"I definitely want it. You're a big part of the team. An

important cog in the wheel."

"Who else is on the team?"

"Just you and me for now. Tucker will be with us as soon as he's over the initial shock of Cheryl's sad demise."

"Why are you talking like a funeral parlor brochure?"

Olivia wondered if that was an insult. "These are sobering times, Josie. A fox is in the hen house. Are you sure you're ready for what we may find?"

"Oh, I'm ready." Josie rubbed her hands together. "How long do you think it'll take Tucker to get over Cheryl?"

"Go easy on him. He's taking this very hard." Olivia suspected he'd get over Cheryl the moment he met Josie.

"I'll be good."

Josie's smile reminded Olivia of Mona Lisa's. "The list, Josephine, the list."

Josie pointed at a name. "He drinks. Every time I see him, no matter what time of day, he smells like alcohol and breath mints."

"Terry Palmetto? He drinks? I didn't know that. He's such a…I don't know…such a Terry. I never saw him act different or anything."

"Probably because you've never seen him sober."

"Good catch, Josie. There's no predicting what a drinking man will do." Olivia made a note on her paper. "Reverend Conroy dyes his hair."

"So what?"

"Don't you think that's peculiar? He's supposed to worry about souls and the like, not appearances. Who's he trying to impress? The congregation? We figured it out right away. God? If the congregation figured it out, God can."

Josie snorted. "You're putting Reverend Conroy on your suspect list because he dyes his hair?"

"It's indicative of a person who hides things."

"He's hiding gray hair. Aren't you planning on dying your hair when it turns gray?"

Olivia rolled her eyes. "Of course I am. But I'm not the one running around preaching that spiritual things are all that matter and acting like God's my uncle. I think he bears watching." Olivia lifted her chin and added, "It won't hurt to check him out. Otherwise we'd be derelict in our duty."

"Okay, but if we're calling things like dying hair suspicious, we're going to have a lot of people to check out."

"Like I said, it goes with the territory."

Half an hour later they compared notes. "We've got nineteen names, Livvy. How are we going to check out nineteen people?"

"But only six that we both marked as possibles. We'll start with them and Sammy."

"Why Sammy?"

"He annoys me."

Josie threw up her hands, then dropped them to her lap. "Annoys you? You have some strange criteria for finding a murderer. If that's all it takes, we can add Tom, Dick and Harry to the list."

"Piffle. They're harmless." Olivia drew her eyebrows together as she studied the names. "Josie, neither of us made a note by any of the women at the party."

Josie looked at her list. "You're right. I wonder why."

"Because we made a stupid assumption. Back to work."

"How was Cheryl killed? Maybe a woman couldn't have done it."

"I don't know. That's another thing we have to find out. In the meantime we can't overlook anyone, regardless of gender or sex or if they're a man or a woman. We have to be equal opportunity detectives."

Josie nodded. "Back to work."

꙳꙳

Eugene had scheduled a late afternoon meeting with the investigators to bring everyone up to date at once. He looked at his watch, then picked up several files as he stood. Six people rose from their chairs when he exited his office.

"Conference room," Eugene said. He closed the door after the team filed in, then put his stack of folders at the head of the wood-laminated table. The unimpressive room, decorated with economical furniture and inexpensive paneling, afforded privacy. At least someone had made the effort to give officers more comfort than the prisoners, who were interrogated in a gray cinderblock room while sitting on metal chairs.

"Hear anything from Max?" Frank asked when they were all seated.

Eugene nodded. "Just spoke with him. He isn't done yet, but he did have a few things to tell me. Ms. Mecklenberg ate a macadamia nut brownie within an hour and a half preceding death. The Chathams had those at the party. Unless she brought one home and ate it later, she died between eleven-thirty and one. We know she talked with her sister around midnight. We now have a time of death at between midnight and one."

Frank frowned. "But we can't be sure she didn't bring it home with her. My wife would have taken all she could stuff in her purse."

Eugene rubbed his stomach and pulled a roll of antacids from his pocket. He popped one in his mouth. "True. Her sister said Cheryl told her she was tired and going to bed. But she didn't finish her nightly routine. You know, all that stuff women do before turning in. Max couldn't find a trace of toner or moisturizer on her face. But she had some, right with all her other paraphernalia."

The men nodded knowingly. Even Ben, who Eugene knew hadn't been on a date in over a year, bobbed his head up and down. Sylvia Farley, the one woman in the room, scowled at Eugene.

"Max found no sign of intercourse," the sheriff continued. "Since the only bruise was a contusion around her neck, he says she didn't struggle. She'd received a blow to the back of her head, and was probably unconscious when hanged."

"Wasn't leaving her like that taking a chance?" Frank asked.

"You're right, it would have been risky. Maybe the killer thought she was dead and wanted to make it look like an accident, a kinky game gone south. If she'd come to, she could have easily removed the noose and identified her attacker." Eugene put his hands flat on the table. "We sent her notepad to a lab in Chicago for processing. Our people don't have the equipment needed to examine the sheet under the torn one. That's it from me, what do you have?"

"Not much," one of the crime scene investigators, answered. "We got a lot of fingerprints, and we're running them, but no hits so far."

"That matches what the neighbors told us," another officer said. "None of them knew her other than to say 'hi', but said she had visitors at all hours."

A third man looked at his notes. "No one remembers seeing anyone, but it was late and dark and the assailant probably kept to the shadows. He or she wouldn't want to attract attention."

"You didn't find anything other than fingerprints at the house?" Eugene asked, turning to Sylvia.

"Her bedroom was messy, like it was searched by an amateur. The rest of the place was tidy. We didn't find anything remarkable. Nothing to incriminate anyone."

"Did you take the friend who reported it through the house?"

"Yes," Sylvia replied. "She didn't notice anything missing. Cheryl's family lives in Pittsburgh. They haven't visited her in years; she usually went there. The sister is arranging for Cheryl's body to be shipped home. She doesn't see any reason to come here, and wouldn't know if anything was missing."

"Okay," Eugene said, then took a closer look at Sylvia. "Something you want to add?"

Sylvia's shoulders rose and fell. "I noticed most of her things were expensive. More than she should be able to afford on a teaching salary. I brought her bank records to the station and I want to go through them. It's a shot in the dark, but when you add the pricey furnishings to some of the outfits in her bedroom, you've got to ask yourself what she was up to."

"Follow your instincts," Eugene told her. "I've found there's almost always a reason for them. Frank, you and Ben come up with anything?"

Frank shook his head. "She was new to the area. Her book didn't list many people from Chatham. Want us to try in Deerwood tomorrow?"

"Hold off on that. I'll need you here. Eugene handed everyone a sheet of paper. "This is the Chathams' guest list. I've marked the names of people I want to talk to. Divide the rest between you however you like. While you're at it, go back to her neighborhood and re-interview people. Ask if they've remembered anything they'd like to add to their statements. Track down anyone who wasn't home today." He stood. "The state boys are joining us soon. We will cooperate fully. I'm not saying you should sharpen their pencils for them, but you will help in any way you can. We want to bring this to a speedy conclusion."

Eugene left the station before anyone had a chance to intercept him. He'd intended to pay a visit to Monroe earlier in the day, and didn't want to be diverted a second time.

Chapter Six

Tucker watched the monitor, studying a spreadsheet filled with more than thirty standard ratios every serious investor ran on a corporation's financial records. After changing the screen to the company's last five annual income statements, he tapped a few equations he'd developed on the keyboard, then sat back and analyzed the results. Research and development funding, while substantial, had steadily declined to a small percentage of revenue. He made a note in the file and closed it. Sinking money into a business more interested in short-term gains than long-term growth would end up biting him in the ass, and his ass had enough tooth marks.

Moments later a bell chimed and he glanced at the clock. It was after six. Wondering if Olivia had decided to check on him, he went to the front door and found Sheriff Strickland on his porch.

"You want me to come to the station again?" Tucker asked, thinking he'd call a lawyer this time.

"It's your decision, but we could talk here."

Tucker motioned the sheriff inside. "Coffee?"

"If it's no trouble."

"Just made a pot. We can talk in the kitchen." Tucker led the way to the cheerful room overlooking the back yard.

"Nice place." Strickland draped his coat on a chair before sitting.

After putting two mugs of coffee on the table, Tucker took

the seat across from Strickland. "I hired one of those interior experts, or whatever you call them. Fabric swatches and paint chips give me hives." Tucker cared more about comfort than décor, but had to admit he liked the conveniences in his modern kitchen. The over-sized hunter green corduroy sofa and chairs in the living room suited him. His office held sturdy, practical furniture and his feet didn't hang over the end of the large bed in his room. A man couldn't ask for much more. "What can I do for you?"

"Anything you want to change about your story?"

"It's not a story, it's what happened."

"Do you remember if Ms. Mecklenberg took anything from the party?"

"Is something missing from the Chatham house?"

Strickland shook his head. "I meant food, something to snack on later."

"Not that I noticed. She grabbed a brownie before we left and ate it on the way home, but she could have had something else in her purse. Trays of food were everywhere. Why? Did she die from some kind of poisoning? Is anyone else sick?"

"Not that I know of."

"You could at least tell me how she died. If she was murdered, people deserve to know."

"And they will, when I'm ready to make it public." Strickland lifted the cup to his mouth.

Tucker studied his visitor, and saw that he was being watched with equal intensity. "What is it you want, Sheriff?"

"I ran your name through the computer."

"Kind of thought you would."

The sheriff set his mug on the table. "Got some interesting data. You were involved in a pyramid scheme in Chicago."

"If involved means I lost money, then yes, I was." The money was nothing compared to the beating his self-respect took.

"You were accused of more involvement than that."

"Did you happen to read that the charges were dropped before it came to trial?"

"Yep, but it got me wondering how a smart fella like you

could get bamboozled so bad."

"I wonder about that myself." Refusing to back down, Tucker held Strickland's gaze.

"You were engaged to the ringleader, and you didn't know about the scam? You were just an innocent victim?"

"Afraid so."

"How could you live with her and not know what she was up to?" Strickland rested his forearms on the table.

Tucker saw the other man's wedding ring. "How long have you been married?"

"Twenty-seven years."

"Where's your wife right now? What did she do today? Yesterday? Last week?"

The sheriff grimaced. "Right now she's probably making her special fruit cake, but I take your meaning."

"I'm not going to rehash all that. If you have a question about Cheryl, ask it. If not, I have work to do."

Tucker hated reminders of what an idiot he'd been. Danielle Rousseau, born Dixie Lynn Root, made a fool of him and he'd let her. She'd used him in every way, and he hadn't even known her real name. He hadn't seen or spoken to her in over a year. Now, when he tried to imagine Danielle's face, it came to him in shadows with indistinct features surrounded by auburn hair.

"Just so happens I do have a question or two." Strickland looked at Tucker with dark, expressionless eyes. "Why didn't you go inside with Ms. Mecklenberg last night?"

Tucker stared into his mug. Having met good and bad cops, he had mixed emotions about them. One had saved him; another falsely arrested him. His intuition told him that under the bluster, Strickland was a good man. Something in the way he carried himself, how he worded questions and listened intently to answers, reminded Tucker of the officer who'd helped him. Jonathan Vicknair, the closest he'd come to having a father. He met the sheriff's gaze. "You ever have a gut instinct? Being a cop, you must have."

"Sure, all the time."

"I had one last night. Every warning system I have went off like gangbusters. I just wanted to get away from her." He hesitated, but the sheriff didn't fill in the silence. "I wonder if I should have, if I could have done anything. I wonder if the killer was in there, waiting for her."

"That's understandable." Strickland sounded sincere. "Wish I could ease your mind, but I can't. Do you remember something that caught your attention? Something that made your alarm system go off?"

"I've tried, but I can't think of anything. I wasn't attracted to her, and that may have been part of it. But nothing that could have caused such a strong reaction stands out."

"If you weren't attracted, why did you go to the party with her?"

"Like I said, she invited me. My social calendar isn't packed these days, and I thought it might be a good way to spend the evening."

Strickland pushed his chair away from the table but didn't stand. "You planning on sticking around town?"

"Is that your way of telling me not to leave?" Tucker straightened and crossed his arms over his chest.

"Just an innocent question."

"I don't plan on going anywhere."

"Mind telling me why you picked Chatham in the first place?"

"I was looking for a small town. A quiet place where I could live in peace. Somewhere with little or no crime."

"Doesn't exist," Strickland said with a sad smile.

"Probably not, but this is the only place I've ever lived where bikes magically appear on porches. Doesn't happen in Chicago."

"Who told you about that? Olivia wouldn't."

"The boy's mother."

Strickland rubbed his chin. "Nadine. Olivia thinks no one knows she's behind their windfalls. Hang around long enough, you'll hear lots of similar stories. They're all true."

"Do people take advantage of her? Cry on Olivia's shoulder just to get something?" Tucker reached for his mug.

Strickland shook his head. "Everybody likes Olivia. Anyone taking advantage of her would find himself real unpopular real fast."

"Message received."

"And another thing, just so you know. It makes Livvy happy, too. She likes to think she helps. That girl would give you the shirt off her back."

Strickland smiled, the first real one Tucker had seen from him. Tucker compared what Strickland said about Olivia to what he knew about Danielle. No need to give Danielle the shirt off your back. If she wanted it, she'd take it.

"Speaking of Olivia," Tucker said, "she's got some notions about Cheryl's death."

Strickland's smile faded, and his face took on a pained expression. "I know, she told me. At length."

"Good. I don't think I could explain her theory and do it justice. She has a different way of looking at things, doesn't she?"

"You could say that."

"Was she on to anything?"

Strickland stood and reached for his jacket. "No comment."

"Damn. She was." Tucker got to his feet and grinned, not sure if his smile was in spite of, or because of, the other man's obvious discomfort. "Did she help with time of death or the torn page or both?"

"We do have a few scientific methods, Monroe. We don't rely entirely on face creams and ragged edges to solve crimes in this little backwater town."

"That's good to know. I'm sure Olivia will appreciate having her theories confirmed." Tucker followed him to the entry and leaned against the wall.

Strickland opened the door and turned to Tucker. "Welcome to Chatham."

"Thanks. I think I'm going to like it here."

Tucker waited for the sheriff to drive away before making his phone call.

＊＊

Tucker came in the door feeling relaxed and mellow. Earlier in the day he'd thought nothing would surprise him again, but he'd been wrong. Hunger had driven him to brave the one restaurant in town he'd avoided. The place specialized, according to their sign, in 'Mexican, Italian and Chinese Quisine'. Tucker knew if he was ever going to try it, this would be the perfect night. He'd ordered spaghetti, thinking if it tasted like a Chinese tamale he could fill up on salad and bread. He'd never had better pasta, and decided to go there at least once a week and work his way through the entire menu.

Ignoring the flashing light on his ancient answering machine, he went to the kitchen and took a beer out of the refrigerator. He brought it to the living room and dropped onto a chair next to the phone table. After taking a swallow of Old Style, he hit the machine's play button. The first messages were instantly forgettable. Then his mother's voice rose from the speaker, and dread filled Tucker's stomach.

Drunk as usual, she made little sense. He listened to her incoherent rambling, and thought of ketchup mixed with hot water, passed off as tomato soup. Not big on nurturing, his mother. After he'd made enough money, he bought her a house in the Chicago suburbs, far from the slums of his youth. He'd arranged a line of credit with a supermarket near her home, which kept her in food, but not booze. That, he'd told them, he wouldn't pay for. Not wanting to give her too much cash at one time, he sent weekly checks for incidental needs. If she wanted more, she could sober up and get a job. The meandering ended, and he decided not to return the call. She wouldn't remember anyway. He'd send a small check in the morning, and she'd wonder what prompted her good fortune. Then she'd drink the proceeds.

As he brought the bottle to his mouth the final message began. His tension eased and he lowered his hand to the armrest.

"Tucker? Are you there? This is Olivia. Olivia Chatham. We met last night at my parents' party. And later you helped me with a flat tire. But I suppose you could have changed more than one tire, and if you did, telling you that you changed mine doesn't help much, does it? I'm the one who gave you a ride home today. We met at the police station. I was one of your alibis, and we went out for coffee. At the 24 Hour Café. Remember? That's me. I'm the one you had coffee with and who drove you home. Anyway, I'm returning your call.

"Oh! This'll help. I'm the one who was named January Eighth for a day. Where was I? Oh yeah, I'm returning your call. It's eight-thirty and I'm in my room. I'll be here all night so call whenever you feel like it. Or don't call if you don't feel like it. 555-1221. That's my room number.

"I could just come over to see how you're doing, but I don't want to intrude uninvited at a time like this. You're probably having a rough night and need some kind of warning before someone drops in and rings your bell. But I'll be here the rest of the night if you need comforting. In case you forgot since the beginning of this message, I'm Olivia Chatham. O-l-i-" The machine ran out of tape.

Tucker's laughter echoed in the large room. He picked up the receiver, half expecting to hear Olivia still talking. When he heard the dial tone he hung up and played the message again. Looking at his watch, he tried to stop chuckling. If she heard, she'd probably think he was having a breakdown. After a few moments he picked up the phone and dialed.

"Hello?"

"Olivia? This is Tucker Monroe. We met at your parents' party last night and later I changed your tire. I'm the person you had coffee with. The one—"

"Don't be ridiculous, Tucker. I know who you are. How do you feel?"

"I'm fine. Is this a bad time? Did I catch you in the middle of something? Like toning or foliating?"

"It's exfoliating, and no, you didn't. I haven't started yet. I wanted to be ready to jump in my car if you need comforting. Do you?"

It was tempting. "No, I'll be okay."

"Were you hitting a bad patch earlier? Is that why you

didn't answer when I called?"

"I'd gone out for dinner."

"Good for you. You need your strength. Where did you go? Were you able to keep it down?"

Tucker grinned. "I managed. I don't know the name of the place. It just said Restaurant. Specializing in Mexican, Italian, and Chinese food."

"I know the one you mean. The name is Restaurant. I've been trying to get them to call it The El Toro Marco Polo Lotus Garden, but the owners are stubborn. Some people don't like changes, even those for the better. They're eccentric, but there's nothing wrong with being a bit different and their food is good. Are you okay, Tucker? You sound like you're strangling."

He swallowed his laughter. "Fine, Olivia. I just had to clear my throat. Maybe you'll go to the El Toro whatever with me some evening."

"Whenever you feel up to it. If you're doing okay, why did you call?"

"Because the sheriff stopped by earlier. It seems you may have been on to something with your edges and nightly routine theories."

"Really? Did Eugene say that?" Her voice rose as she spoke, sounding ecstatic.

"Not in so many words, but when you're a gambler you get used to reading people. I asked him if he'd talked to you and he said he had. He wouldn't say if it did him any good, but I read his body language, like you read my face. I could tell you'd been a big help."

"Well, how about that? I told you, Tucker. We'll solve this case. Just as soon as you're on the mend you can join the team. Josie and I spent the afternoon together and we're coming up with a doozie of a plan."

"I'd like to meet Josie."

"She's skipping the memorial. Says they're too depressing. But I'm going and meeting her after. You can come with me."

Memorial? "What time is the service? Sorry, but it slipped my mind."

"Nothing to be sorry about. You've had to process an awful lot in one day and you can't be expected to remember everything. Six o'clock."

"On Tuesday, right?"

"You poor thing, so much to absorb. It's a wonder you're coping as well as you are. Wednesday. At the Methodist church on Lombardi Avenue."

"I'll see you then, Olivia."

"Call if you need anything. Don't be shy about asking for help."

"I'll ring you if I get too low. Olivia?"

"Hum?"

"If you phone me again, you can just say your name. I remember you."

"Okay. I wasn't sure you would."

"I got that impression."

"I'm not surprised. You're very intuitive. You want some advice? Take a sleeping pill. You have to take care of yourself and you need your rest."

"I'll do that. Goodnight, Olivia."

"Night, Tucker."

Tucker knew he shouldn't be flattered by her attention. Kindness was automatic with Olivia. But something in him wanted to believe her concern was personal. Then he remembered her 'rule'. What woman in her right mind only slept with men she'd married? Would she buy a car without a test drive? Thinking of Strickland's comments about her earlier, Olivia's guileless emerald eyes popped into his mind, and he realized she probably would.

Using Cheryl's death to lure Olivia to his place would put him beneath Danielle on the measure-of-a-human-being scale. Looking forward to a memorial wasn't a stellar quality, either, but having someone fuss over him was a new experience. He might as well enjoy it while he could.

CHAPTER SEVEN

Sitting between her parents on the front pew, Olivia tried to concentrate on Reverend Conroy's sermon, but her mind wandered. Sunlight streaming through stained glass windows reflected off the minister, at times making his too-black hair appear blue. He reminded her of a crow. Even his nose looked like a beak. Olivia missed Reverend Newton's merry smile, and wondered how long Lawrence Conroy and his wife, Rose, would stay in Chatham.

Rose, plump and round-faced, her iron-gray hair pulled into its customary bun at the nape of her neck, sat at the organ. A fireplug of a woman, she resembled a Rottweiler. Olivia noticed the devotion on her face as she watched her husband speak. She wondered if Rose thought he'd written the book he held. Rose glanced at Olivia and scowled, as if reading her mind. Olivia turned her attention to the sermon.

As the warmth of the church, combined with the drone of Conroy's voice, were about to lure Olivia into a nap, the organ wheezed the closing hymn's first chords. Her eyes snapped open and she straightened. Time to go to work.

She smoothed the skirt of her red and black plaid dress and waited for her mother to lead the way down the aisle. As usual, people grouped in clusters outside the sanctuary. Some shrugged into coats, looking eager to leave. Others appeared to be settling in for long conversations. Olivia spotted her prey.

Anne McClain was the only woman Olivia and Josie had added as a suspect. She made it to their list for the same reason she was included at most functions, her husband. Luke McClain owned the largest construction company in the area. Outgoing and jovial, he was one of the town's most prominent citizens. Luke went to college in Michigan, and returned to Chatham with a new wife. Anne was on his arm at every public event. Rumors had it that was the only time he spent with her. His roving eye was legendary.

If Luke had set his sights on Cheryl, and she rebuffed him, he may have gotten angry enough to kill. He was used to getting what he wanted. On the other hand, if she hadn't rejected him, Anne may have learned of the affair and decided enough was enough. Her husband had treated her badly. Every woman has her limit, and one more rival may have been hers.

Olivia strolled over to Anne, resolving not to let sad eyes and a defeated expression lull her into sympathizing with a possible killer. She'd been friendly with Anne over the years, but didn't know if they could be called buddies. Contact with her usually left Olivia feeling depressed, and she tried to limit her exposure to negativity.

"Olivia, it's so nice to see you. We didn't get a chance to talk at the party. You disappeared too fast."

Olivia had never seen Anne look so alive. Her face glowed and her posture oozed confidence. "I had another party to go to. How have you been?"

"Never better. And you?"

What had happened to Anne? Did she think she'd gotten away with murder? "I'm fine, just fine." Staggered by Anne's new vitality, Olivia couldn't remember the approach she'd decided on. "Um, you look different. Have you done something new to your hair?"

She patted her short, dark bob. "I had a bit cut off. Easier to take care of, now that I'm a businesswoman. I won't have time to fuss."

"A businesswoman? I didn't know. What business?" Olivia expected to hear she'd decided to work for her husband, and smelled disaster.

"Flowers. I'm opening a florist shop next to Hendricks' General Store."

"Your own business?" Olivia sputtered. "I had no idea."

Anne grabbed Olivia's hand and squeezed. "I could hardly wait to tell you. You're my best friend, you know, Livvy. I wanted to tell you in person. It's all happened so fast."

Best friend? They went out to lunch once a month. Anne must be the loneliest person in town. "What's going on? You look like a kid at a magic show."

"I left Luke."

Olivia brought her hand to her mouth. "Oh, no. I'm so sorry."

"Don't be. It's the best thing I could have done. Luke went crazy. He came to my parents' house in Michigan and begged me to come back. No more chasing women. No more treating me like an accessory. He said he needs me. Can you imagine?"

Olivia couldn't. "When did all this happen?"

"Two weeks ago, and he's been living up to his end of the bargain." Anne looked over Olivia's shoulder and blushed. Olivia turned to follow her gaze and saw Luke wink at his wife from across the room. Anne leaned close and whispered, "He's a new man, Livvy. We left your house early Friday night. Luke said he wanted to show me something. It was the store! He bought it for me."

"I can hardly believe it," Olivia said, still stunned at seeing Luke McClain flirt with his own wife. First murder in Chatham, now this. Had the world gone mad?

"Then we went home and...well, you know. We're getting along like newlyweds. Better than newlyweds. I feel like a different person. He's never been so attentive. I should have left years ago."

Olivia hugged her. "Maybe it wouldn't have turned out like this. Sometimes timing is everything."

Anne hugged Olivia back, then pulled away. "You're right, of course. I can't dwell on the past. You'll come to my grand opening, won't you? I hope to open before the end of January."

"Wouldn't miss it. So you and Luke were together all Friday night? Never out of each other's sight?"

"Or reach," she said with a giggle.

Olivia was thrilled for Anne, but worried she'd soon hear details. "Be sure to let me know when you open the store. I'd better go tell Reverend Conroy what a brilliant sermon he gave this morning. Can you remind me what it was about?"

"Haven't a clue. Ask Rose. She looked like she was memorizing it."

Olivia's jaw dropped. "Good one, Anne. I think I'm going to like the new you even better than the old you."

"Will you help me think of a name for the shop? You're good at things like that."

"That's easy. The store is helping your marriage, right?"

"Right."

"Flower Power."

"Oh, that's perfect!" She gave Olivia a bright smile and turned toward Luke.

Two names off the list, Olivia thought. Husbands and wives weren't the best alibis for each other, but Anne had been telling the truth. She'd been miserable for so long she wouldn't know how to fake happiness. Olivia scanned the room, looking for a place to accomplish the task she needed to do during the memorial. Nothing looked promising.

She moved down the hall toward the office and saw a closed door. After making sure no one was watching, she opened it and peeked inside. She quickly closed it, then opened it again. On the plus side, it was a closet and she could use it. On the minus side, it was a very small closet.

A string dangled in front of her eyes. She pulled it and an overhead light went on. Olivia took a deep breath and slipped into the cramped space. Unless she could find something else, and she doubted she could, this would have to do. When she opened the door to leave, her damp palm slipped on the knob and she tightened her grip. Her face felt clammy and her vision blurred. Once in the hall, she fought the desire to bend over and get more blood to her head. Olivia didn't know how she'd manage to stay in that tiny closet long enough to accomplish her mission, but she didn't have a choice. It might work if she could leave the door open a crack.

Olivia made her way to the nearly empty vestibule. She heard shouts from the parking lot and engines revving as people headed home to their pot roast or fried chicken. The door opened and another family left the church. The cold air revived her. She noticed Reverend Conroy standing by himself. Might as well get it over with, she thought, and walked toward him.

Olivia plastered a smile on her face. "Wonderful sermon, Reverend. I don't know when I've heard anything like it."

Conroy beamed. "Did you like my metaphor?"

"Oh, my, yes. You sure have a wide vocabulary. It's quite voluptuous. You must have worked a long time on that meteor."

He blinked. "Metaphor. I don't really work at them. They come to me all the time and I jot them down."

"It was a lulu. By the way, Mom said you left their party early Friday night. I hope nothing was wrong."

"Rose got one of her headaches. When that happens, there's nothing for it but to get her to bed and give her a pill. Those little things are strong, knock her out for hours."

"I'm sorry to hear that." A sleeping spouse wasn't much of an alibi. "Of course, you could have come back to the party after she was settled in for the night."

"And leave her alone? I wouldn't dream of it. One never knows when one will be needed, does one?"

Olivia wanted to grind her teeth. "When one does something nice for another one, one would hope one's sacrifice is appreciated by the one for whom one is making it." She saw him grimace, and bounced on the balls of her feet. *Take that, you hair-dying phony.* "I don't want to monopolize your time, Reverend. You keep coming up with those matadors and I won't miss a single Sunday." Olivia turned to the coat rack.

"Metaphors. Not meteors or matadors, metaphors."

She pulled her coat off a hanger and smiled at him. "You betcha."

⤧⤧

Late that afternoon Olivia stopped her Lexus in front of Josie's house and tooted the horn. She hoped to corner Ben at Country Lanes. The one thing Deputy Ben Appleby never missed was his Sunday bowling league.

"Where were you an hour ago?" Olivia asked when Josie opened the passenger door. "I called, but you weren't home and I thought you might have forgotten about today."

"I had to follow the lead to the end." Josie slid into the car, closed the door and reached for her seat belt. "Terry Palmetto has been sober since the day after Thanksgiving. He's also been without a driver's license since the day after Thanksgiving. DUI. He got a ride to the party with Toby Hendricks."

Olivia drove toward town. "Did he ride home with Toby, too? What time did he leave?"

"He got a lift back to town with the mayor, who dropped him off at an AA meeting. Scootie Greenwald took him home from there."

"Did you get any times? Must have been early if there was an AA meeting."

"Over the holidays they have extra meetings. The mayor dropped Terry off at the church at eleven. After the meeting they had coffee and cookies and talked. Scootie says he took Terry home around twelve-thirty."

"You talked to Scootie, too?"

"I'm thorough, Livvy. I'll tell you one thing; I never want to hear another word about twelve step programs. If you ever have kids, I don't want to hear about their first twelve steps. I mean it."

"Are you in a bad mood?"

"Kind of. I spent most of the day hearing lectures and now you're dragging me to Dusty Lanes."

"Don't let them hear you call it that. Remember, Country Lanes. Just keep saying it over and over to yourself."

"Country Lanes, Country Lanes."

"When you talked to Scootie, did he stutter?"

"Not once."

"Darn. When he's lying he sounds like Porky Pig." Olivia slowed as she reached Chatham's city limits.

"He was telling the truth. Terry Palmetto is off the suspect list." Josie flipped her visor down and looked in the mirror as she finger-combed her hair.

"Oh, well. We had to expect it. A drunk probably couldn't pull off a caper like this. We can cross off the McClains, too. Reverend Conroy is still in the running, though." Olivia told Josie what she'd learned at church. When she turned a corner, she heard a thump.

Josie looked behind the driver's seat. "You have a bowling ball, Livvy? How did you get one so fast? You just decided to do this last night." She turned back to the mirror.

"I already had it. When you went off to be a cover girl, I got lonely and took up bowling. I have some dandy shoes, too. The kind that don't have to match your purse and belt, because no purse or belt would ever match those shoes."

"Ah, you missed me." Josie pushed the visor up. "That's so sweet."

"I told you I missed you."

"Yeah, but I didn't know how much. Okay, so what's the plan?"

"Ben's our best hope, but we need a ruse. We'll pretend to need help with our swings, then kind of segue into the case."

"No problem."

Olivia pulled into the bowling alley parking lot and nosed her way into a spot. She shifted to park but didn't shut off the engine. Turning to her friend, she said, "Go easy on him, Josie. Ben's kind of a babe in the woods."

"We need the info, don't we?"

"Yeah, we do. But don't lead him on or anything, okay? You know how you can be sometimes. I'm well aware that justice often has a price, but what price justice? I'd hate to see Ben get his hopes up only to be disappointed." A wave of melancholy washed over her. "Unfortunately, murder is like an onion, with layers and layers. There are people in those layers, innocents who just want to live in peace. Keep in mind, Ben's a little lamb. Try not to hurt his onion layer."

Josie tucked her hair behind her ears. "I'll be careful, but I'm not smart like you, Livvy. I have a few physical advantages and I have to use what I've got. You're the lucky one. In a few years my looks will fade, but you'll always be an intellectual."

Olivia slapped her palm against the steering wheel. "I hate when you say things like that. You're bright as a button, you just need to apply yourself."

Josie reached for the door handle. "Right now I'm going to apply myself to Ben. Don't worry, Livvy. He'll be singing like Celine Dion in no time."

"I think I've created a monster," Olivia muttered as she shut off the engine.

CHAPTER EIGHT

Olivia trailed Josie into Country Lanes. At the desk, she was assigned an alley and given a score sheet. Josie went to another counter for shoes. A group of men near the center of the room watched every move Josie made. Olivia saw Ben among them.

After laying the paper on the table at the end of their lane, she sat on a plastic bench, plunked her purse beside her and dropped the heavy bowling bag at her feet. She unzipped the case and pulled out an iridescent purple ball. Tilting it under the florescent lights, she admired the shifting colors and the way it glowed. Why didn't she bowl more often? She looked at her name, written in large italic script around the finger holes, and gave a satisfied nod. No doubt about it, the ball was a vision. She set it on the seat next to her and reached into the bag again.

When she pulled turquoise bowling shoes out of the case, tiny bells she'd tied to the laces tinkled merrily. Bowling was such a fun sport. Anyone could do it. If you didn't worry too much about the score, it could be a terrific way to spend an afternoon. The colors alone made for a good time. After church she'd changed into blue jeans and a lime green sweater. Purple, green, turquoise and blue. Horseracing was the only other activity she could think of where such a combination would not only be acceptable, but expected.

Olivia tied her shoes and looked for Josie. She spotted her near a rack. Ben stood next to her, hefting a ball and talking animatedly. Josie's eyes focused on Ben with an intensity Olivia felt halfway across the room. Poor Ben, this was probably a very bad idea.

Deciding to take a few practice shots, she stood at the end of the polished alley and held the ball in front of her nose. Her aim must be rusty; the ball fell in the gutter an instant before straying to the neighboring lane. "If at first you don't succeed..." she muttered. Olivia lost track of time, and was startled when Josie dropped onto a seat at the table.

"What were you and Ben talking about? Why did it take so long to find a ball?"

Josie slipped her feet into red and green shoes, tied the laces and slapped her hands on her legs. "That's what I'm about to tell you, little buddy. I've got a ton of info!"

"Already? Wow." Olivia put her ball down and slid onto the seat beside Josie.

"When I'm assigned a job, I do it. Okay, first, Cheryl was naked and hanging in her closet."

"No!" Olivia brought her hand to her chest. "She hung herself?"

"Not so fast. It looks like a sex game that went bad. Auto-erotic asphyxiation."

"Huh?"

"Remember the article I sent you from New York? The one about the guy I worked with who died that kinky way?"

"Oh, yeah. Automatic fixation, choking during sex. I have to admit something, Josie. I still don't quite understand it."

"That's okay. You don't need to."

"Good."

"It looks like Cheryl was into that big time. But," Josie added, raising a finger in the air, "she'd been hit on the back of her head before being strung up. She wasn't dead, but probably unconscious, when someone put the noose around her neck. Definitely murder. And, there was no sign of intercourse. The cops think the hanging was an attempt to throw them off."

"A wild herring," Olivia said, shaking her head in wonder. "You amaze me, Josephine. Anything else?"

Josie fluffed her hair. "She died between midnight and three in the morning. She was in the middle of getting ready for bed. There are about a million fingerprints in her house. And Ben's going to help me learn the art of bowling when he's done with his league. We'll know lots more before we leave here tonight, Livvy. Just don't cramp my style. Don't look at me like that. Ben wants to talk about it."

"How do you know?" Olivia felt terrible. Pumping Ben for information was one thing. Making him believe he had a chance with Josie was another.

"Because I barely had to ask and the words just tumbled out of him. Your job is to listen, okay?"

Olivia nodded, resigned to what was about to happen.

"One more thing before he gets here. Ben said Cheryl lived way beyond her means. Sylvia Farley's going through her bank accounts, but she hasn't found anything yet. Cheryl had all kinds of things she couldn't possibly afford on a professor's salary. Furniture, clothes, jewelry. But her credit card balances are zero. No sign of any loans either. They found a safe deposit key and the police plan on checking it out tomorrow."

"Good grief, Josie. Five more minutes with Ben and we'll know her height, weight, and if she had any allergies."

"All in a day's work." Josie looked up as Ben came toward them. "Careful now, let me do the talking."

"Hi, Ben," Olivia said as she stood. "Josie says you're going to help us with our swings."

Ben tossed his jacket on a chair and placed his bowling bag on the floor. "I'll do what I can, but I can't promise you'll be on the tour next week."

"We just want to break sixty," Olivia told him.

"Show Ben your style, Livvy." Josie patted the seat next to her and raised her eyebrows at Ben.

Olivia retrieved her ball. "Okay, this is how I start." She stood at the end of the aisle with her feet close together. "Then I do this," she said and took a step. "Then this." Another step.

She made her way to the line, announcing every movement.

Olivia tried to swing the ball in slow motion, but couldn't manage it on the down slope. Her ball went into the gutter two feet from her outstretched hand. When she turned toward the table, Josie and Ben had their heads together.

"Hey, you missed it."

Josie waved a dismissive gesture. "No we didn't. You were fabulous. Show us again."

"Okay, but this time I'll go my normal speed." Olivia went through the motions, the bells on her laces ringing cheerfully with each step. Her ball inched down the lane, barely making it to the end and knocking over a pin. Olivia clapped as she turned. Her audience didn't seem impressed. Her audience didn't seem to notice. She shrugged and took a seat behind Ben and Josie.

"Some of those outfits," Ben said with a shake of his head. "Things a little girl would wear. Ruffles and short, wide skirts. And others that were no better than being naked. She had a leather outfit, I tell you I can't figure out how a person would get into it."

"Interesting," Josie said in a low voice. "I never knew police work was so fascinating, Benjamin."

"It usually isn't. Did I tell you about her shoes?"

"No, what about them?"

"Same as her clothes. A pair of boots that make no sense at all. I mean they're practical in a way. They'd have come all the way up her leg and kept her warm. But the heels, no one could walk in snow on heels that high. Another pair of shoes were shiny, with a round toe and a little strap across the top. My niece has some like that. She's six. Cheryl had the strangest taste. We found a leather flyswatter in her closet. Who'd want a leather flyswatter?"

"Oh my," Josie said. Her round eyes made her look mesmerized. "What do you make of it?"

Ben moved closer to Josie, but Olivia still heard him. "I think she had an alternative source of income, if you get my drift."

Josie nodded soberly. "I think I follow you."

A trust fund, Olivia thought.

"We'll know more after a few days. We're studying her calendar now."

Olivia leaned forward. "What about her calendar?"

Ben scratched his head and rested an arm on the back of his chair as he turned to look at her. She resisted the urge to pat his checkered, flannel sleeve. With his unruly brown hair and bewildered chestnut eyes, he reminded her of a lost little boy.

"Lots of dates, some repeats. The funny thing is, none of the names match any in her address book."

"What do you mean?" Josie asked.

"There was a Charles and a Kurt and a Mark on her calendar once a month or so. But none of them were listed in her address book. Two, Edgar and Ezra, were regulars. Edgar every Monday and Ezra every Wednesday. Up until a few weeks ago, that is. Edgar still showed up, but Ezra's name isn't in there after the first of the month."

"Edgar? Ezra?" Olivia said. "Charles and Kurt and Mark are common. Even Edgar maybe. But Ezra?"

"I've never met an Ezra. Have you?" Ben looked at Josie.

"Never. Not even in New York, and in New York you meet all kinds of people with funny names."

"The only Ezra I've ever heard of was the writer." Olivia sat back in her seat and cupped an elbow in her palm. She raised her other hand to her face and tapped a finger on her chin. "Mark, Mark, Charles, Charles, Kurt, Kurt."

"What're you doing, Livvy?" Ben asked.

"Stream of consciousness," Olivia replied. "Something's clanging in my head."

"Excellent! Leave her be, Ben. When Livvy gets on a stream of consciousness roll, she's the best."

"Ezra, Ezra. Lunatic or genius or both? Poet and traitor. Edgar, Edgar. Crow. Raven." What was nibbling the edge of her mind? "Raven. That's it!" She snapped her fingers and leaned forward. Ben and Josie bent their heads toward her.

"What do you have, Livvy?" Josie whispered.

"Ben, you can say you came up with it. Eugene will probably give you a raise."

"What?"

"It's code. Ezra Pound. Edgar Allan Poe. Charles Dickens. Mark Twain. Kurt Vonnegut. We had to read all those guys in her classes. She said she wanted us to be well-rounded in literature. Frankly, I could never understand a word of Ezra Pound and Poe lost me a few times, too. But Ms. Mecklenberg could go on forever about all those guys. Edgar was spooky and Ezra was just plain nuts."

"You mean she marked down in her calendar when she read stuff by them?" Ben asked.

Olivia shook her head. "Nope. I mean she gave her dates nicknames. I'll bet she liked Mark, Charles and Kurt. Edgar and Ezra may have irritated her, or they'd have better names. My guess is those two, whoever they are, turn out to be a couple of sticky wickets. I wonder why she bothered with them if she didn't like them."

Ben sat back and whistled softly. "I better write those names down so I don't forget them when I talk to Eugene. Can you say them again, Livvy?"

"Sure thing, Ben. Better find something to write on." She chewed on her lip. "Now all we have to do is match the code name to the real person."

"How do we do that?" Josie asked.

"Plod along like we have been. I already have an idea who Edgar is."

"Who?"

Olivia shook her head and looked significantly at Ben, who was tearing a piece of paper from the score sheet. "I'll tell you when I know more. I'd hate to accuse an innocent person. Let's just say that today, while I was looking at someone, the word 'crow' popped into my head. Crow, you know. Like a raven. Like Poe wrote about." She lowered her voice and said, "Nevermore."

"I see," Josie said, looking baffled.

"How about her friends and colleagues in Deerwood? Are you getting any info from them?" Olivia asked Ben.

"Nothing so far. Her neighbors say she kept to herself, but seemed to have a lot of friends. At least she had a lot of company. We haven't found anyone who claims to have known her well." Ben looked at Josie and squared his shoulders. "We put an ad about the memorial in the Deerwood paper."

"Good thinking," Olivia said. "That'll get the attention of her friends and co-workers. It'll be their last chance to say goodbye." And it saves me the trouble of placing the ad, she thought. Perps like to come to funerals and memorials to see the result of their handiwork.

"Can you tell me the names of those writer fellas again, Livvy?" Ben held a stubby pencil poised over the torn score sheet.

After she'd recited and spelled the authors' names, Ben stuffed the paper in his pocket and left, saying he had a lot to memorize before morning.

"He's kind of cute," Josie said as they watched him leave.

"He's not your type."

"No, but my type haven't worked out so well, have they?"

Olivia stared at the empty doorway, deep in thought. After a moment she shook her head and looked at Josie. "Those children's clothes Ben described are weird. I wonder what her boyfriends thought of them."

"Livvy, they weren't boyfriends. They were clients who paid for her time and attention. Know what I mean? The outfits were for them."

"Oh." Her mind raced. "Oh...you mean...oh. Why would they want her to dress like that?"

"Different strokes for different folks."

"What about the other stuff? Do you think Ben was confused? Those boots do sound peculiar."

"It's kind of hard to explain," Josie said. "Some people like their sex rougher than others."

"Tough love."

"Not exactly. They just like a little pain."

"For Pete's sake, why would someone want to be hurt?"

"Kiddo, some men, and Sammy's probably one of them, would stick their little willies in a bear trap if they thought they'd get a charge out of it."

Olivia gasped. "Mercy, how you talk sometimes. I think you got out of New York in the nick of time, before you got jaded."

"No argument here."

A stab of guilt hit Olivia. "This could turn unsavory, Josie. If so, I apologize in advance for involving you in sordidness."

"Don't worry, we won't uncover anything I haven't heard of. I'm a little concerned about you, though. You may be in for a shock or two. Let me think about this. I may need to prepare you. Maybe someday we'll go to Madison. I'm sure a city that size has a few specialty shops and I could show you some of the items people buy. We could use our computers on the Internet, but I don't want to leave a cookie at any of the sites."

Olivia stared at Josie, wondering what she was talking about. What did computers have to do with cookies? She leaned forward and pressed the back of her hand against Josie's forehead. "You aren't feverish. Are you getting enough sleep? Eating right?"

"I'm fine. Don't worry about me, Livvy."

"You'll tell me if the stress of the case gets to you?"

"I promise. Actually, it's kind of fun. Apart from someone dying, that is. We haven't had this much excitement in years."

"Know what I think?" Olivia asked.

"What?"

"Remember when I said there was a fox in the hen house?"

"I'll never forget it," Josie replied.

"I think the fox may have been Cheryl."

"I think you're right."

Olivia straightened in her seat. "It's a good thing Tucker just dropped her off and didn't accept her invitation to go inside. He could have gotten in way over his head."

"Must have smelled a rat."

"Could be. He's got finely homed instincts. I could tell that right away. He positively hums with homing instinct." Olivia reached for her bag. "This case is going to keep us on our toes. I have a feeling something big is going to break."

"What's our next move?" Josie took off her shoes.

"Tomorrow I have to go to Madison. We need a few things we can't get in Chatham. I don't know how long it'll take. You can try to find out if Bruce Littlejohn has an alibi."

"Another name on our list. Is your Edgar suspect on our list, too?"

Olivia nodded. "You bet he is. I do believe we have a knack for this, Josephine."

"What's in Madison?"

"Special equipment. I'll need some of it when I go to the memorial on Wednesday."

"Sounds intriguing." Josie looked at her hands and twirled a ring around her finger. "Livvy, don't think I'm crazy, but I might ask Ben on a date."

Olivia dropped the shoe she'd been putting in her bag. It jingled when it hit the floor. "Why would you do that? We can get the info we need without going that far. You're going to break his spirit."

Josie stared at Olivia. "You know my letch test?"

"That thing you do where you take something like ten minutes to stretch and cross your legs?"

"Yeah, that one." Josie smiled dreamily. "When I tested Ben, his eyes never left mine. The way he looked at me gave me the feeling he was listening."

"Wow, has that ever happened before?"

"A couple of times, but not like this. There were guys who didn't gape at my legs, but they didn't act like they heard a word I said, either. Livvy, try to understand. I'll be careful with Ben's onion, but I have layers, too."

"I know you do. You're very deep, Josie." She saw a clock on the wall. "Good grief, look at the time! Mom and Dad won't be home for dinner, so Dorothy's making my favorite. I'd better not be late."

"Hot dogs and beans?"

"You betcha. Want to come for dinner? I warn you, it'll be a working supper."

"Sure. How could anyone refuse hot dogs and beans?"

Olivia retrieved her purple bowling ball. "And candy cane ice cream. Don't dawdle, Josie."

CHAPTER NINE

Olivia couldn't recall what occasion had prompted her to buy a simple beige dress, but as she'd gotten ready for the memorial Wednesday, she'd been happy to find it hanging with her other clothes. Pearl earrings and necklace added the final demure touches. Now, standing in the church vestibule watching people enter, she knew she looked the part of respectful citizen. No one would guess she was on duty. She didn't strike up a conversation with anyone, needing to keep her attention on the guest register. To her relief, everyone signed it. Her nutmeg brown heels began to pinch, and the matching purse grew heavier by the moment. Soon the service would begin and she could sit down. She wondered what was keeping Tucker.

When he arrived a moment later, her heart skipped a beat. He wore a charcoal suit and a dove gray shirt that matched his eyes. His tie combined both colors. He'd had his dark hair trimmed. It looked as if he'd parted it on one side, then been caught in a gust of wind. Why did tousled hair make her look silly and him look like a GQ cover? She watched him scan the room. *Good grief, it shouldn't be legal to be that handsome.*

More than his appearance, she admired the decency he radiated. Tucker took her breath away, and she knew by the end of the evening he'd belong to Josie. For a moment her chest felt filled with lead. Olivia told herself they'd make a good couple, and both deserved happiness. *Maybe he has a brother and when Tucker marries Josie his brother will come to the wedding and we'll meet and fall in love and I'll be happy, too.* When his gaze met hers, he moved in her direction. His smile could thaw an iceberg.

"Do you have a brother, Tucker?" she asked when he stopped in front of her.

His eyebrows drew together. "What the…no, I don't have a brother."

"Oh." She'd ask about cousins another time. "How are you holding up? You should have worn a coat. We can't have you catching a cold."

"I'm fine, Olivia. How have you been?"

"Busy. Right now I'm on the job. Will you do me a favor?"

"I'll do my best."

"It's pretty easy. You just have to stand guard at a closet door while I'm inside."

Tucker scratched his cheek. "I can probably do that. Want to tell me why?"

"I need some time alone with the guest register. It looks like the service is about to get started. I'll explain later."

They sat at the back of the church so Olivia would hear if someone arrived late and remained in the lobby. "Everyone here is from Chatham," she whispered in Tucker's ear. "Hardly anyone's come, and no one from Deerwood. There was a notice in their paper. Wouldn't you think at least one person would have come?"

He shrugged. "Hard to say. This is a busy time of the year. Lots of people are out of town for the holidays."

"No one, not one friend or colleague in Deerwood, is in town and saw the notice? That doesn't make sense. It defies practicality." Part of Olivia ached for Cheryl. She must have been a lonely woman. Another part of her wondered if Cheryl's lack of friends had anything to do with what Ben had told her and Josie.

The service was brief, or as brief as anything could be with Reverend Conroy at the podium. As soon as he finished, Olivia stood and headed for the register, towing Tucker behind her.

She plucked the book off its stand and went down the hall, chattering nonstop in an effort to calm her nerves. Stopping at the closet, she said, "I'm going to be in there for a few minutes, but I don't want to close the door all the way. That's where you come in. If someone comes around, give me a signal."

"What kind of a signal?"

"Clear your throat or snap your fingers. Something that warns me, but doesn't draw any attention."

Olivia felt moisture on her brow. Her pulse raced. She took a deep breath, then opened the door and slipped inside. She left the door slightly ajar and turned on the light. Crouching, she put the register on the floor and dug in her purse.

"Tucker, you there?" she asked.

"I'm here. All clear."

"I'll just be a minute." She found her wallet and turned the register to the first page. Only three sheets had names on them. "Won't be long now. Still clear?"

"Uh huh."

"Try not to draw attention to yourself."

"If someone sees me talking to a door, it might look a little odd."

"Oh, of course. I didn't think of that. You sure keep your head on your shoulders." She closed the book and stood, then turned off the light. "I'm done, is it still clear?"

Tucker opened the door. Olivia slid out of the closet and leaned against the wall. He smiled and looked as if he was about to say something. Then his grin evaporated and he frowned as he reached for her arm.

"My God, Olivia. Are you sick? I've never seen anyone so pale."

She waved a hand in front of her face. "I'm fine. I've got to get the guest register back to the stand."

He took it from her. "Forget the damn register, you need—"

"Don't swear in church, Tucker. We have to get the—"

"I know, I know. Wait here." He strolled down the hall, the guest book clutched in one hand.

Olivia patted her face with a hankie she found in her

purse, did her breathing exercise, then bent at the waist. When she straightened Tucker stood in front of her, hands in his pockets and concern written on his face. His gray eyes reminded Olivia of twilight on a summer evening.

"All taken care of. Want to tell me what's going on?"

"I needed to know who showed up tonight."

"I gathered that much." He gestured at the closet door. "Are you claustrophobic?"

"Maybe a little."

Tucker mumbled something and raked his fingers through his hair. "The next time your 'job' includes close quarters duty, I'll do it for you. Would that be okay?"

"Oh, thank you. Yes, you can do all our closet investigating." Happy to have the task behind her, and knowing she wouldn't have to do it again, she looped her arm through his and tugged him toward the coat rack. "We're meeting Josie at The Mill. Have you been there? It really was a mill at one time, but now it's a restaurant and bar."

"It's on my list of places to go."

"Well, then, this is your lucky day. Want to go together or take our own cars?"

"Why don't you ride with me?"

"Good idea. We can talk on the way."

After saying their goodbyes, Tucker led Olivia to his Porsche. He held the door for her, and she got in the way she'd seen Josie do. *Sit first, then swing your legs in together.*

Tucker went to the driver's side and settled in. "Buckle up," he said as he started the powerful engine and put on his seat belt.

Olivia did what he said, then turned to him. "Christmas is a week from today. You're invited to our house."

"I don't think that's a good idea. Christmas is a time for family."

"Might as well give in, Tucker. If you don't, Mom will just pack a huge basket full of food and send me over to your place with it. We're having roast turkey with all the trimmings and pumpkin pie. It's a tradition, but if you'd rather have ham or something else, just say the word. Traditions are made to be broken."

"Turkey's fine. Are you sure about this?"

"Positive. Come around eleven, we eat on the dot of noon. This way we'll have time to chat first."

"I'll be there."

"This car sure goes fast."

"Too fast?"

"Kind of." Olivia gripped the edge of her seat.

Tucker slowed. "I should go car shopping. You said I'll need something better when it snows."

"Ducky's Auto Emporium sells SUVs. Don't buy a red one. You don't want to draw attention to yourself. We may need to be incognito at times."

Tucker pulled into The Mill's parking lot. "Gotcha."

❧❧

He'd planned on buying a winter vehicle before he'd met Olivia. Now Tucker made a mental note to buy a red one. There may be occasions when he'd need to be the boss. This might be a good time to introduce her to that fact.

The Mill lived up to its name on the outside, rustic and unimpressive, but the inside was obviously someone's pride and joy. Dark wood had been polished to a glow and crisp linen-covered tables sat discreet distances apart. A bar stretched the length of one wall. Olivia handed her jacket to the coat check boy.

"Grab a seat wherever you want, Livvy," the bartender called.

"Thanks, Ron," she replied, and led Tucker to a corner booth. "I don't see Josie. She must be running late."

A woman in a black dress and frilly white apron dropped menus on their table. "Karen just loves her flute, Livvy. Plays it all the time."

"That's great!" Olivia clapped her hands. "Yvonne, this is Tucker. He's new in town. Tucker, this is Yvonne. Her daughter wants to join the high school band."

"Nice to meet you, Tucker." Yvonne put a hand on Olivia's shoulder. "We were having trouble coming up with the money for a flute. This is an expensive time of year and we have six kids. Livvy was garage saling in Madison, and found a flute for five dollars! I'd swear it's new. Looks like it's never been out of the case."

Tucker raised his eyebrows at Olivia. "You go to a lot of garage sales?"

"Now and then. They're good places to find things you didn't know you needed."

"I see." Tucker saw color rise in her cheeks and she wouldn't meet his gaze.

"What can I get you to drink? The usual, Livvy?"

"Yes, please. We're meeting Josie, so we'll order dinner after she gets here."

Yvonne turned to Tucker. "What'll it be?"

"Old Style. Draft if you've got it."

"Isn't a bar in Wisconsin that doesn't have Old Style on tap." Yvonne swept away.

"You just happened to find a new flute at a garage sale? I wonder what the odds of that are." Tucker watched her closely. Olivia would make a terrible liar. She was too fidgety to pull it off.

"I never said I got the flute at a garage sale. I said I went garage saling in Madison and that I bought a flute. Yvonne must have misunderstood and thought I got it at a sale. Want to know why I was in Madison?"

"I'm sure you'll tell me soon enough. So this brand new instrument only cost you five dollars?"

"I didn't say that, either. It wasn't new when I sold it. I'd owned it. I figured five dollars was fair market value for a hand-me-down flute."

Tucker leaned against the plush backrest of his bench seat and smiled. "I like you, Olivia. A lot."

"I like you, too, Tucker." She beamed across the table at him.

Yvonne returned with a tray. She put a glass of white

wine in front of Olivia and set an oversized shot glass filled with cherries next to it, then placed a frosted mug of beer on the table. "I'll keep an eye out for Josie and tell her where you are," Yvonne said, then moved away.

Olivia dropped a cherry into her wine, then popped another one in her mouth and closed her eyes as she ate it. "Yummm." She opened her eyes. "How rude of me. Help yourself to my cherries, Tucker."

He bit back a smile. "No, thanks. I've always thought they go better with wine than beer."

"True, but you never know. People have strange tastes sometimes." She plopped three more cherries into her glass and took a sip. "Needs one more."

Tucker watched in amusement, then saw someone coming toward them. The tall blonde woman wearing a simple navy dress moved like a ballerina. Heads turned as she passed. She glided to their table, and Tucker stared dumbfounded as the definition of drop-dead gorgeous sat next to Olivia. Whoever this lady was, he wanted nothing to do with her. In his experience, beauty often came with a high price. Too high. He pushed himself against the back of the booth, putting as much distance between them as possible.

"Have you ordered yet?" the newcomer asked.

"We were waiting for you. Tucker, this is Josephine Bookman. Call her Josie. She's my best friend in the whole world and she's going to be a big help in landing our perp. Josie, this is Tucker Monroe. I've told you about him."

Josie held out her hand. "At last we meet."

"A pleasure," Tucker said, shaking her hand. He glanced at Olivia and wondered why she looked sad. A moment ago she'd been savoring cherries in wine.

"Let's get the ordering out of the way, and then I'll bring you both up to speed." Olivia's voice had lost some of its perkiness.

"What's their specialty?" he asked.

"Everything's good."

"I'll trust you to choose for me," he said. Why had the

appearance of her best friend deflated Olivia?

"Do you have a cholesterol problem?"

"No."

"Good," she said with a nod. "You need something nourishing. The He-Man filet should be just the ticket. Medium, of course. I know you'd probably prefer rare, but beef needs to be cooked longer to get rid of all those cow germs."

"Sounds good to me." It was exactly what he'd have chosen.

Minutes later, their dinners and Josie's wine ordered, Olivia reached into her purse and brought out two small bags. "I got us all the same equipment. We may need more, but this was all I could think of at the time." She handed one bag to Tucker and emptied the other onto the table. Picking up a silver tube, she said, "This is a tape recorder. There may be times we can't take notes." She put it down and picked up another object. "A miniature camera." The last item was a cell phone.

"I thought you had trouble keeping track of cell phones," Tucker said.

"These have clips. We can wear them on our belts. The tape recorders do, too. I didn't get belts because Josie and I'll use our own. We need to accessorize. I didn't know what kind of belt to get you, Tucker. Do you have your own?"

"A few. What about the cameras? They don't have a clip."

"They're the size of a credit card, so we can keep them in our wallets. I just used mine at the memorial. Handy little thing."

"That's what you were doing in the closet? Taking pictures of the guest book?"

"Yep. I didn't want to trust my memory. As they say, knowledge is power. Perps often show up at their victims' funerals. Since Cheryl is being buried in Pennsylvania, our only chance to lure the killer was the memorial."

"You went into a closet, Livvy?" Josie asked, her voice barely above a whisper.

"I had to, I needed the four-one-one."

"Four-one-one?" Tucker asked.

"Slang for information."

"You never cease to amaze me," Josie said. "You sure know a lot of things."

"I try to keep abreast." Olivia swept the equipment into the bag and handed it to Josie. "They were out of night vision goggles, but I ordered three and they should be here next week. I said I needed them by Christmas."

"Livvy, you are so smart." Josie dropped the bag into her purse. "You think of every little detail."

"Just trying to plan ahead. You never know what you might need or when you might need it." Olivia sipped her wine as Yvonne approached and set Josie's drink on the table. When they were alone again, she said, "Here's what we've got so far, Tucker."

Olivia filled him in on the suspect list and the people she and Josie had eliminated. She also told him what they'd learned from Ben. Cheryl had a kinky streak. Tucker felt a surge of relief that his internal alarm system had gone off the night she invited him in. Thank God that still worked. He'd worried Danielle had stolen it, too.

"Josie eliminated Bruce Littlejohn yesterday. She did some fine work."

"He was out of town that night. Vegas," Josie said.

"On a junket," Olivia added. "Are you ready to join the team, Tucker?"

"Absolutely."

"Good, because we're going to need you to check out two of the suspects."

"Who?"

"Mitch Long for one," Josie answered. "You can usually find him at that bar on Packer Avenue. Spud's Suds. He spends a lot of time there."

"A misproportionate amount of time," Olivia added. "Josie and I don't want to talk to him. He's oily. Be careful, Tucker. Just brace him, get the skinny, and get out."

"Ten four."

"Brace? Skinny?" Josie asked.

"Cop lingo for questions and answers. Q and A." Olivia took another sip of wine.

"Cool," Josie said as their dinners arrived.

Tucker picked up his fork. "Who's the other suspect I'm supposed to check out?"

"Harvey Pierce, a clerk at First National. Sammy's bank," Olivia replied. "He's very sweet, but shy. We put him on the list because Josie and I figure waters still run deep. He's an unknown quality, and we don't want any loose threads. We think he'll be more open with you because you're a man." She dug into her walleye almandine.

"Roger," Tucker said.

Olivia's hand froze, fork midway to her mouth. "No, Harvey. Are you sure you're up to this?"

"I'm fine. I need to keep busy."

"Oh, Tucker, you have such a strong spirit," Olivia said, a note of sadness in her voice. She glanced at Josie, then back to him. "We're down to four suspects. Your two, Sammy, and Reverend Conroy. If nothing pans out, we'll throw a wider net. Josie's handling Sammy and I'm covering Conroy like flies on rice."

"Sounds like a good plan."

"Are you busy Saturday, Tucker?" Olivia asked. "We thought we'd meet here around six and rendezvous."

"I'm free. By then I should have something to report vis a vis my two."

"Wonderful. Everything's coming together neat as a pin."

Tucker watched the two women as they ate. Olivia tackled her fish with the abandon she seemed to bring to everything, while Josie daintily nibbled on a broiled chicken breast. He saw genuine affection between them, the type of kidding and nudging that comes from a close bond. But Olivia seemed to have lost some of her vitality, and he couldn't understand why. As they lingered over coffee, Olivia's filled with sugar and cream, Josie straightened in her chair.

"Look at the bar, Livvy. Ben's here."

"I wonder why. This doesn't seem like his kind of place."

"I might have told him I'd be here tonight. I think I'll go over and say hello." Josie smoothed her dress as she stood and moved toward the bar.

"Ben the deputy?" Tucker asked.

"Yes. He's been helpful to us with the case. That stays between you and me and Josie, though. We don't want him to get in trouble."

"I take it Josie's getting the info, I mean the four-one-one, from him."

A busboy cleared the dishes, and Olivia didn't answer until he'd left. "I told you she could get answers from a stone, if the stone was male. Josie's quite beautiful, isn't she?"

While watching Olivia, less animated than he'd ever seen her, realization struck. She'd assigned Josie the role of his next great love, probably to help him 'recover from his loss', and sensed his apathy toward her friend. He'd have to use caution navigating this female minefield. "Some men might be attracted to her. I prefer cute and sweet."

"Have you ever seen hair like that? And it's natural, no one could get that color from a bottle."

Tucker glanced at Josie, sitting next to Ben at the bar, then back to Olivia. "I guess it's okay. Too blonde for me, though. I like darker hair. The color of sand on the beach when the sun is bright. It looks soft and sparkly."

Olivia lifted a lock of her hair and held it in front of her nose, eyes crossing as she examined it. She waved the tress, then released it and looked at him. "My hair is kind of sandy blonde. It doesn't sparkle, though."

Tucker pretended to study it. "Now that you mention it, your hair is my favorite color. I think I see a bit of sparkle there, too."

"Really? Well, wake me up and call me Doogie." She wiggled in her seat. "Have you ever seen eyes like Josie's? They're navy blue, and it's not because of contacts. They're honestly navy blue."

"I've always been partial to green."

"You have?" She opened her eyes wide and half stood as

she leaned across the table. "My eyes are green, and I don't wear contacts."

Tucker moved forward and stared into her eyes. "You're right, green as emeralds."

Grinning hugely, Olivia sat again. The smile left her face. "Josie's tall. That was a big asset when she modeled in New York City, New York."

Tucker settled into his corner of the booth. "She's a long drink of water, that's true. I tend to like women a little smaller. It brings out the macho protectiveness in me." He raised a hand. "Now don't get your feathers ruffled because I said something chauvinistic. It's the truth, and I believe honesty is the best policy."

"It surely is. I feel the same way about wanting to take care of those smaller than me, and I'm not a chauvinist."

"Anything but."

She tilted her head. "The funny thing is, I feel protective toward a lot of big people, too. So many seem to think their size keeps them safe. But we know that's not true, don't we? Sometimes they fall the hardest, and need help getting back on their feet."

Something inside Tucker melted. "I guess you want to protect everyone. That sum it up, January Eighth?"

"It's one of my foibles."

As Tucker looked at her pixie face, a door in his heart opened and he knew he was in trouble. He didn't need the kind of complications a woman brought, but sometimes life didn't offer a man any options. He had the feeling this was one of those times.

CHAPTER TEN

Early Saturday evening Tucker entered The Mill and scanned the room. An arm waved from the corner booth he'd shared with Olivia and Josie after the memorial. He crossed to the table and felt a stab of disappointment when he saw the arm belonged to Josie.

"Evening, Tucker," she said as he slid onto the seat across from her.

"Hi. Olivia running late?" He pulled off his coat and placed it beside him.

"She called and said she was at the Crow's nest. Didn't say which one."

"Crow's nest?"

"Code name for Reverend Conroy. He's either at his church or home. Livvy worries someone will listen in on our calls, so we use codes. Sammy's the Gnat. Will we need names for Mitch and Harvey?"

"No," Tucker replied with a shake of his head. "They're off the suspect list."

"No doubt?"

"Not on my end." He looked at his watch, then out a window at the bleak winter sky. Pulling his new phone from a pocket, he said, "I'm calling Olivia. She shouldn't be following suspects alone after dark."

Josie waved a hand. "Livvy's fine, just caught up in the chase. Tell me why you cleared Mitch and Harvey."

After five rings, Tucker drew his eyebrows together.

"Something must be wrong. She's not answering."

"Maybe she's busy."

"She's the one who insisted we carry the damn phones. If she's not answering, I'd like to know why. She could be in trouble."

"Honestly, Tucker. You sure get worried easy. You sound like her mother."

Tucker disconnected and put the phone away, then reached for his coat. "Her mother may have a point. Where does Conroy live? If she's not at the church, I'll go there."

"The corner of Green and Bay Streets. Want to hear what I found out from Sammy?"

Sammy the Gnat, one of Olivia's exes. The only one she didn't like. "What?"

"Not much really," Josie replied with a shrug. "When I asked, he told me he didn't know Cheryl. Then he had about a thousand questions. How did she die? Exactly when did it happen? I said I didn't know, and he asked me to tell him if I found out anything. Livvy thinks that's a mighty odd way to react to a stranger's death."

Tucker agreed. He got to his feet. "We'll have to meet and rendezvous etcetera another time. Right now I better find super sleuth."

"Aren't you going to tell me what you found out about Mitch and Harvey?"

"I'll wait till Olivia's with us. That way I only have to tell it once."

❧

Tucker spotted Olivia's Lexus a block away from Conroy's church. Light blazed from the building's windows and a sedan sat in the lot. He parked behind her SUV and walked to the driver's door. When he saw no one inside, he looked up and down the avenue. Converted gas streetlights cast a glow, but shadows filled the areas between them. Someone had shut off the speakers, and the air didn't hum with ubiquitous Christmas carols. It was quiet for a Saturday evening, and the stillness added an eerie dimension to the night. Breath vaporing around his head, he crossed to the church and tried the front door. When it wouldn't open, he knocked. No one answered. He moved to a window and peeked in. Empty.

Looking down the street, Tucker saw an open store and walked toward it. As he neared the combination video/bait shop, Reel 'Em In, he heard a noise. He stopped and cocked his head, listening.

"Psst! Tucker! It's me, Olivia. Olivia Chatham. I'm right here, behind the wiggling bush."

Tucker swiveled to gaze at a row of shrubbery, and saw one limb vigorously shaking.

"Get on your hands and knees and crawl back here, but don't draw attention to yourself."

"For the love of…" Tucker mumbled, walking to the bushes. He wondered if the branch would break off before she yanked the plant from the ground. The moment he came within reach, Olivia grabbed his arm and pulled. He thumped down beside her.

"Do you think anyone saw you?" Olivia asked. "You didn't sneak."

"I have news for you, Olivia. Crawling around on all fours would draw more attention than…" He stopped when he saw her red cheeks and nose. Her teeth clattered together. "What are you doing? How long have you been here?" Catching her hand, he started to rise. "We need to get you warm."

"No," she said, tugging free. "Tucker, there's some she-nanigans going on. Conroy went into the church, but he must have gone out the back door because right away I saw him scamper down the alley to the video store. That's not normal, not one little bit normal. What do you suppose he's up to?"

He rubbed her hands. "Don't you have gloves?"

"In the car."

"Hell of a place for them." He cupped her face, and she lifted her chin and closed her eyes, tempting him more than he liked when she made a contented sound. "It's cold, Olivia. You're cold."

"It is a bit nippy." Her voice wobbled in rhythm with his palms massaging her cheeks.

"Let's go meet Josie. We'll talk about the state of our investigation over coffee. I'll try some the way you like it, filled with sugar and cream." God help him.

"You go ahead, I'll catch up later."

Frustrated, Tucker scooted behind her. He pulled her back to his chest and wrapped both sides of his open jacket around her, hoping his body heat would add warmth. "Okay, tell me what's going on. Why didn't you answer your phone?"

"It's in my car, I'm not wearing a belt today. I saw Conroy and decided to tail him. When he went in the church, I figured he was going to work on tomorrow's sermon. I was about to leave when I saw him in the alley. Why sneak to a video store?"

"Maybe he's buying bait. Is fishing against your religion? He may have to get worms on the sly."

She shook her head and picked a pad and pencil off the ground. "No. Besides, the lakes aren't frozen enough for ice fishing. That side of the store isn't even open. Crow left his house at oh-seventeen-thirty-hundred hours, then went in the front of the church and out the back. Erratic behavior, there's no denying it."

Translating the time to five-thirty, Tucker rolled his eyes. "Who cares if he goes to a video store?"

"It's not *that* he went, it's *how* he went."

"Scampered?"

"No moss on you."

Tucker pressed his lips to the top of her head and inhaled the fresh smell of shampoo, detecting a hint of coconut. Combined with her exotic perfume, the scent brought a tropical paradise to mind. Something inside him stirred. He looked over her shoulder at the pad in her hand. Streetlights made her notes visible, but he couldn't decipher them. They looked like something an archeologist would find on the walls of a cave. "Any new developments? Other than the fact that Conroy scampers to video stores?"

"I checked out the pictures of the memorial service guest

register. No new names to add to our suspect list. Fruitless venture, but it comes with the territory."

"You can scratch two names off your list. Mitch and Harvey are clean."

"That leaves Sammy and Conroy. If they are somehow cleared, we'll branch out and investigate in Deerwood. Undercover. Incognito."

"How did those two make your suspect list?"

"Reverend Conroy dyes his hair. He seems like a man who hides things, even going to a video store. He's not ministerly."

"And Sammy?"

"He wants something from me, but I don't know what. He says he wants to try again, but he didn't really try before. The way he acts, kind of shifty at times, makes me think he has secrets. I doubt we ever loved each other; he just wore me down until I married him. Then he ignored me."

"Clearly an ass." Her reasons weren't scientific, but Tucker had faith in instincts, and thought Olivia's were good. Maybe this wasn't a game. Maybe one of her suspects was dangerous. "I'd appreciate it if you don't go tearing off by yourself. If you need to follow someone, or go incognito, call me."

She turned and rested her head on his shoulder, looking up at him. "I can't interrupt you every time Crow or Gnat is on the move."

"I don't mind. It beats worrying about you."

Eyes opening wide, she said, "You worried about me? Why? I told you I'm lucky."

"Luck can run out."

Olivia laughed. "What a silly thing to say. Tell me about Mitch and Harvey. Was it hard to brace them?" She squirmed, and her breath feathered his cheek.

Tucker cleared his throat, grateful for the layers of clothes between them. She seemed oblivious to his physical reaction, but another part of him he'd thought Danielle killed rose from the dead. "Not hard to brace Mitch at all. I didn't even have to ask anything. I found him at Spud's Suds, complaining the police had checked his alibi with the owner and other customers. Called it harassment. He said he'd done some handy-man jobs for Cheryl, and they'd had some good times together. Coming from him, that could mean anything. But he claims he didn't care about her one way or another. What he thought of her doesn't matter. He closed the tavern that night, and he has witnesses and the bar tab to prove it."

"He's a prize, isn't he? See why Josie and I didn't want to question him?"

Tucker shifted position. If there had been snow on the ground, it would have melted. "Anyway, he's cleared."

"Mitch is kind of an odd duck, so I'll bet he's Kurt."

"Here I go, saying it again. You lost me."

"Kurt was in her calendar a couple of times a month. We figure she gave her dates authors' names to protect the inno-cent, whoever they are. Kurt would be Vonnegut. What about Harvey?"

Tucker pushed a strand of hair from her cheek. "Harvey is a kind man, but a lonely one. He admitted knowing Cheryl. They met when she opened an account at the bank. But he says they just went for coffee and talked. I believe him, he seemed genuinely sad she's dead. Apparently his wife isn't the easiest of women, but I'm just guessing on that. He didn't com-plain, just said Cheryl was knowledgeable on a variety of sub-jects and a good conversationalist. She also listened when he spoke. He seemed to appreciate that."

"Bessie Pierce does like the sound of her own voice." Olivia grew quiet and tilted her head. "Now that I think about it, I've never seen her when she wasn't talking. Poor Harvey. I bet he's Mark." She tapped the pencil on her pad and stared across the street.

"Another author?"

"Mark Twain."

Tucker nodded. "That fits. Let's go now, Olivia. We need to warm you up."

"Not until Crow leaves. What do you suppose he's up to?" She gazed at him again.

Tucker looked into wide green eyes, then stared at parted

lips. Without thinking, he tightened his hold and kissed her. Someone sucked all the air off the planet. Tucker had spent quality time with many women, but this was the first time a kiss left him breathless. He forced himself to relax his arms and pull away.

Olivia didn't move. She kept her eyes closed and her face tilted up. "You can do that again, Tucker."

He coughed. "It's probably not a good idea. We're on the job."

Opening her eyes, she turned to face the store. "Oh darn, I forgot about Crow. You certainly have a distracting affect on me."

"Ditto." After a moment he added, "You taste sweet."

"I had a peppermint before you got here."

Tucker inhaled her scent again. "I have the feeling you always taste sweet."

"You're a nice man."

A foolish one, he thought. "Here's the plan. I'll go into the store and check out what Conroy's up to. You stay here. Don't move. I'll be back in a few minutes."

"What are you going to say if you see him?"

Tucker got to his feet. Painfully. "I'll play it by ear."

"You have the makings of a good detective." Olivia pulled her knees to her chest and wrapped her arms around them.

"Stay put." Tucker crossed to the store and went inside.

A bell over the door rang and an acne-scarred face popped around a rack of videos. "Can I help you find something?"

Stuffing his hands in his pockets, Tucker shook his head. "Just browsing." He roamed from drama to comedy, animated to history. He was the only customer. Stopping in front of the mystery section, he grinned and picked up a tape.

"That's it for you?" the clerk asked when Tucker brought it to the counter.

Going on a hunch, Tucker said, "Unless you have something for more mature audiences."

"I'm not sure what you mean."

"Movies rated with Roman numerals." When the clerk didn't answer, Tucker added, "As in X's."

"Ah," acne face said with a wink. "Adult rodeos. Ride 'em cowboy! Give me a second."

He disappeared behind a blue curtain at the rear of the shop. After a few moments a gust of cold air blew the fabric and wafted through the room. The clerk shoved the cheap drape aside and motioned Tucker to enter.

Five minutes later Tucker stood behind the bushes, one video and a package of microwave popcorn inside his jacket, and looked at empty space. Turning right and left, he saw Olivia trotting down the sidewalk, hair bouncing around her shoulders. He cursed and followed, catching up with her in front of the church.

"I told you to stay put. What part of that didn't you understand?"

"You sound grumpy, Tucker. That's not like you. You must still be out of sorts because of Cheryl. Maybe you cared for her more than you want to admit."

He held up a finger. "We had one, count them, one, date. I've seen you more than I ever saw Cheryl, and that suits me fine. Why didn't you wait by the bushes?"

"Crow was in the alley again. I had to follow."

"No, you didn't. We just had this discussion. You aren't going to take off on your own following potentially dangerous people. Isn't that what we agreed?"

She scraped the toe of her boot on the cement. "Technically, no. You suggested, but I don't recall agreeing."

"Agree now."

"It doesn't make sense. I can't call you every time Crow moves."

"Yes, you can."

"What if you're busy? I can't dawdle. The dog that moves around gets the bone."

Tucker filed that away to ponder later. "We'll figure something out. If you don't agree, I won't tell you the skinny."

Her face lit up. "You found out something about Conroy?"

"You won't tail a suspect without letting me know, right?"

"I'll call."

"And you'll let the phone ring more than once, right?"

"Are you trying to irritate me? It won't work. I have a very high threshold of annoyance. Mom says that's an excellent trait, one of my good ones."

He ran his fingers through his hair and blew out a puff of air. "It must be one hell of a lot higher than mine. Okay, here's the skinny. The Reel 'Em In has a back room, filled with the kind of movies I'm sure you've never seen and never will. Sex videos."

"No!"

"That's where Conroy was. He went out the back door when I asked if they had anything X-rated."

"You're sure about that?"

"Did you see him in the alley a few minutes ago?"

"Yes."

"Then I'm sure. I don't know what he rented, but there were a few empty slots. One had *Kitten With a Whip* written on the shelf. Another was *A Beautiful Bind*."

"Oh dear." Color rose in her cheeks and she stared at the ground for a moment before meeting his stare. "Wonderful detecting, Tucker. Very perspicacious of you."

Her wide smile told Tucker she'd been dying to trot that word out in a conversation.

He'd look it up when he got home. With a flourish, he whipped the video and popcorn from under his coat. "I got this for you. You're off duty, Conroy will be in front of his television the rest of the night."

Olivia peeked at the tape. Clapping her hands she bounced on her toes and grinned. "Miss Marple! Brilliant! My favorite!"

"Why did I know that?" he said as he handed it to her.

"We can watch it at your house. You even got microwave popcorn. Smart move. Did you know that if you make popcorn the old fashioned way, on an electric stove, you can start a fire? And pouring water on it doesn't help one little bit."

"You don't say."

She nodded emphatically. "I do say, but you'll just have to believe me. I'd rather not go into the details of how I came by that information."

"I believe you." Tucker made a mental note not to leave

her alone in his kitchen.

She touched his arm and looked up at him. "Can we watch Miss Marple now?"

"I'm afraid I'll have to pass. I'd probably end up kissing you again."

"That'd be okay."

"Then I might be tempted to do more. Remember your rule?" Just his luck. He'd finally found a good woman, one who made him feel alive, and she had the world's dumbest rule. "I'm not going to marry you, Olivia."

"I'm not going to marry you either, Tucker." She nibbled her lower lip. "Maybe I should reassess, become more of a free spirit."

"Don't make any hasty decisions." He bent and kissed her forehead, then walked her to her car and opened the door. "Enjoy the movie."

She hopped onto the driver's seat and started the engine, but didn't close the door. "Can I ask you a question?"

"I don't know how I could stop you."

"I've noticed you never call me Livvy. Why not? Everyone else does."

"I don't want to be like everyone else."

"No worries there. You're very unique in your oneness." She reached for the door. "Have you looked at SUVs?"

"Bought one. It should be ready on Tuesday."

"Just in time for Christmas. Don't forget, you're due at my house at eleven a.m. in the morning."

"I'll be there."

Tucker watched her taillights disappear. He'd never considered himself a bad man, but he hadn't thought of himself as an overly disciplined one, either. If he was offered something he wanted, he took it. What the hell had come over him? What man in his right mind would turn down Olivia because he didn't want her to break an asinine rule she shouldn't have in the first place? Why had he picked tonight to be noble? Turning to his car he muttered, "Probably because I'm so damn unique in my oneness."

CHAPTER ELEVEN

Olivia threw the door open before Tucker had a chance to knock. The sight of her took his breath away.

"Merry Christmas, Tucker! You're right on time. I knew you'd be punctual. And you have presents! Is one of those for me? You're so handsome today! Of course, you're handsome every day, but even handsomer today. That coat is perfect for your coloring, but you'd look good in anything. Isn't this a beautiful…" She stared over his shoulder.

"Mind if I come in?"

Her hands flew to her cheeks, then she backed up and opened the door wider. "Good grief, where are my manners? Come in. Let me take your jacket."

Tucker stepped into the entry and shrugged out of his coat, balancing two gifts with one hand. Olivia stared out the door, then turned to him and closed it.

"Is that yours? What is it?"

"An Expedition," he said, handing her his coat. "I can go through damn near anything with that. Snowstorms, mudslides, avalanches, you name it."

She disappeared into an enormous closet. "It's a lovely vehicle, but it's red."

"Just like your outfit."

Olivia came out of the closet. In her scarlet dress, made of some kind of fuzzy cheerleader-sweater material, she looked like a princess. A matching headband held her hair off her face. Tucker watched her, mesmerized.

"I thought we agreed you wouldn't get red."

"Technically, no, we didn't. You suggested another color, but I don't recall agreeing."

Her brows drew together as she looked up at him. "But red will draw attention to you."

"I'm sorry, January Eighth, but if I did everything you asked, I wouldn't be unique in my oneness."

"I guess that's true enough." She looked down, tapping the toe of one high-heeled shoe on a marble floor tile. After a moment she met his gaze. "You're right. You have to follow your own balloon."

"I like your headband."

She gave him a huge smile, reached up and felt the bow at the top of her head. "You're supposed to tie it at the waist as a belt, but I wanted to be different for once, so I improvised. I'm glad you like it."

"Being unique in your oneness?"

Clapping her hands, she laughed. "Yes! Just like you!" She took his arm and led him down a wide hallway.

Mouthwatering aromas of roast turkey and pumpkin pie filled the air, making Tucker's stomach growl. They passed the vast room where the party had been held, another that looked like an office, and several more before stopping near the back of the house.

"We're in here."

Tucker paused. He'd expected something opulent and formal. This room was large, but the cozy atmosphere took him by surprise. A fire blazed in the hearth. Expensive comfortable-looking furniture was scattered in groupings, as if people had carried seats around the room, stopping now and then to join in conversations. The rear wall, floor to ceiling glass, looked over a brick patio and extensive grounds. In summer, when the rolling lawn filled with color, the view would be spectacular. He wondered if he'd get to see it.

In contrast to the elaborate white and gold tree in the party room, the one in here was smaller and real. Tucker savored the smell of fresh pine. The tree held a montage of decorations, some shiny and new, others old and faded. Many looked as though a child had made them. Olivia tugged his arm, and when he glanced at her, he knew many had been made by a child. He pictured Olivia as a little girl, bending over a table covered with glitter, paper and glue, diligently making stars and angels.

"Tucker," Richard said when they crossed the threshold. "Good to see you." He shook Tucker's hand.

"How nice of you to come." Her mother began to rise from her seat on a sofa.

"Don't get up, Eleanor." Tucker moved to the couch and bent to lightly peck her cheek. He didn't know how anyone could see this lady and not want to give her a hug or chaste kiss. "Merry Christmas. Thanks for including me today."

Eleanor patted the seat next to her. "Sit beside me. It's wonderful to see you again. We're so pleased you're sharing Christmas with us."

He sat and held out one of his packages. "This is for you. I hope I didn't get it all wrong, but when I saw it, I thought of you."

She took the present and placed a hand over her heart. "How thoughtful of you. I'm sure it will be perfect. We have something for you, too. Livvy, get Tucker's gift."

Olivia skipped to the Christmas tree and dove under it. She reappeared with two packages in her hands. Before handing them to him, she asked, "Is that other present for me?"

"Honestly, Livvy," Eleanor said, then turned to Tucker. "She got us up at five-thirty this morning to open gifts. Livvy always did love presents."

"What're you drinking, Monroe?" Richard asked. "We're having Kir Royales."

"Sounds good." Tucker had no idea what it was. Richard moved to a bar on one side of the room. Stacks of folded wrapping paper, boxes, and a pile of bows lay next to an entertainment center near the bar. No wonder Olivia got excited at Christmas. He worried about his gift for her, and wished he'd bought something better. There was nothing he could do about it now. Holding up the remaining present, he gazed at the tag. "Yes, I think this does say 'Olivia'. Must be for you."

She handed him the gifts she'd pulled from under the tree, and snatched hers. Paper flew. A moment later her eyes opened wide.

"Oh, Tucker, this is the most gorgeous hat in the history of the world." She reached for the faux leopard fedora and promptly put it on. "How did you know I've been needing something exactly like this? I wouldn't have gotten such a perfect one, though. I'd probably have gotten something ridiculous and impractical."

"I remembered your leopard top the day you were my alibi. I thought this might match. You may need a hat on stakeouts."

"Excellent thinking on your part. It's important to keep your head warm. This is one of my best presents ever." She settled on the floor by his feet and elbowed his leg. "Open yours. The little one first. That's from all of us. The bigger one's just from me."

Richard crossed to them, handed Tucker a glass, and sat on a chair facing his wife. Tucker sipped appreciatively.

"What is in this, sir?"

"Call me Richard, son. No need for formality. It's champagne, a touch of Cassis and a twist of lemon. Gotta be careful not to use a heavy hand with the Cassis. Like it?"

These people knew how to live, Tucker thought. "Kir Royale, the name fits. It tastes like something for royalty."

"No toffee-noses here. Just us normal folk." Richard nodded at the gift in Tucker's hand. "Open your present."

Tucker set his glass on the end table at his side and carefully unwrapped the smaller of the two packages. Olivia squirmed and nibbled her lower lip. Tucker took the lid off the box and stared at an elegant pen and pencil set. Marbled in different shades of gray, he recognized the name. Mont Blanc. Tucker knew he held at least one thousand dollars worth of writing instruments. He blinked and a lump formed in his throat. When was the last time someone had given him such a generous present? When was the last time someone had given him anything?

Glancing at Richard, Olivia and Eleanor, he said, "I don't know what to say. Thank you doesn't seem enough."

"Just tell us if you like them, dear," Eleanor said, touching his arm. "If you don't, we can exchange them."

"I wouldn't trade these for anything."

Olivia clapped. "Good! We guessed right, Mom. Open your other gift, Tucker. The one just from me."

"First things first." Tucker reached into a pocket of his suit coat and pulled out a small ivory envelope, then passed it to Richard. He'd written one word on the otherwise blank card inside.

Richard opened it. After looking at the card he gazed at Tucker, eyebrows raised.

Tucker nodded. "It's not a sure thing, but damn close."

Richard leaned forward and clamped a hand on Tucker's shoulder. "Good man. I'll get my broker on it first thing in the morning."

"If you don't open your gift from me, I will," Olivia said.

"Yes, ma'am." Tucker unwrapped the last box and had no idea what he was looking at. His best guess was two misshaped hockey pucks, but knew that was wrong when he lifted one. It was soft and had some kind of handle on its side. "I'm speechless. Thank you, Olivia."

"I made them myself." Olivia sat primly on the floor, legs curled under her and hands clasped in her lap. She still wore the hat. "I didn't follow the instructions to the letter, which is why they don't match. I always think of knitting directions as merely guidelines. Where's the creativity in doing exactly what thousands of other people have done?"

"None that I can think of." Tucker still didn't know what the two black disks were.

"I hope you're not disappointed they aren't fancy. I wanted them to be personal."

"They are that."

"Being a manly man, you would have probably preferred

leather gloves, or at least knitted ones. But, Tucker, all those fingers can be a bit much, so I made mittens."

At last, Tucker thought with relief. The things he'd thought were handles must be thumbs. He slipped them on and stared at his hands. He'd have to put rubber bands around the wrists or they'd fall off. She must think he was the size of a gorilla. He couldn't detect a consistent pattern in either mitten, and other than the color, they looked nothing alike.

He gazed at Olivia's upturned face. "These are the finest mittens I've ever seen. Every time I wear them, I'll think of you. When did you find time to make them? Between crime solving and flute buying, you've been mighty busy. Don't overdo. You don't want to burn your candle at both ends."

"Knitting is relaxing, but thanks for the candle tip." She beamed at him, then stared open-mouthed at her mother. "You didn't open yours yet, Mom. Hurry!"

"Mercy, Livvy. I'm glad Christmas only comes once a year." She opened Tucker's gift and held up the teal, turquoise and navy Hermes scarf he'd spent an hour picking out. "Thank you so much, Tucker. It's beautiful." She handed it to Olivia. "Won't this be perfect with my new pants suit?"

"Brilliant, Mom! You'll be the belle of the boat." Olivia returned the scarf to Eleanor and looked at Tucker. "Mom and Dad go on a cruise every year. Next week they're off to Hawaii."

Tucker picked up his drink and raised the glass in a toast. "If I don't see you again before you leave, bon voyage."

Olivia reached for a glass on an end table and clicked it against his, then her mother's and father's. "That either means have a nice trip or eat well. My French is rusty."

"In this case, it means both." Tucker sipped, feeling as if he'd fallen into a Norman Rockwell painting.

"You about ready to eat?" came a voice from the doorway.

Olivia jumped up. "Starving, Dorothy."

"No hats at the table, dear," her mother said.

"Nuts," Olivia muttered, removing the fedora.

Tucker put his mittens in their box and stood.

Olivia wrapped an arm through his and they followed her parents out of the room. "Dorothy's been slaving away for hours, but she says she likes cooking." She lowered her voice. "She calls the kitchen her oasis of sanity. I always thought an oasis was a water hole, so I'm not sure what she means. Between you and me, Dorothy gets a tad confused at times, but she's such a dear, no one tells her. She doesn't like any of us to go in the kitchen. Since an incident last summer, I'm banned completely. I don't want to go into details, but Josie and I had a bit of a snafu when we were watching movies one night and went to the kitchen to make a snack."

Tucker patted the hand on his arm. "I understand." He imagined popcorn burning, and wondered how many fire trucks had been needed to put the blaze out.

He wasn't surprised when Dorothy joined the family at the table in the formal dining room. He was surprised at his reaction to the festive meal and atmosphere. Something about this family warmed him. It felt as if he'd come home, as if he'd spent Christmas here all his life.

❧❧

An hour later, Tucker wondered how he'd manage to get out of his chair. He'd eaten two helpings of everything. Dorothy had watched him closely at first, then seemed to thaw. Clearly protective of Olivia, she let him know without saying a word that if he upset Olivia, he'd answer to her. Tucker didn't want to answer to her, and made an effort to find her good side. A hearty appetite and praising every dish had softened her expression. He patted his stomach and said, "If I lived here, I'd weigh three hundred pounds."

Dorothy made a clucking noise, but Tucker saw the corners of her mouth lift before she ducked her head.

Olivia placed her linen napkin next to her dessert plate. "Perfect as usual, Dorothy." She looked at her mother. "May Tucker and I be excused? We have to go over a few things related to the case. I'm afraid this has to be a working holiday for us."

"You aren't getting into anything dangerous, are you, Livvy? I don't know if you should keep nosing around. It doesn't sound safe. That's what we have Eugene and his officers for," Eleanor said with a frown.

"I'm only searching for answers to a few questions, Mom. And Tucker looks out for me." In a stage whisper she added, "He's a worrier, just like you."

"Good, I'm glad to hear it," Richard told him. "Sometimes a firm hand is called for with Livvy."

"Piffle." Olivia took Tucker's arm and led him from the room. She stopped at the bottom of the staircase. "Wait here, I'll be right back."

She scurried down the hall and returned wearing her leopard hat and carrying his gifts. "Can't have you forgetting these," she said, waving the boxes and starting up the stairs. "The night vision goggles got here. Wait till you see them!"

CHAPTER TWELVE

Once again Olivia led the way, chattering nonstop. She reached the end of the hall and opened the last door. Tucker followed her into the room and came to a halt. Elegantly decorated in pastels, everything from the overstuffed sofa and chairs to most of the paintings on the walls spoke of privilege. Some of the art looked like she'd bought it at a garage sale. She probably had, trying to help an artist. He glanced at Olivia, looking for some sign of pride in the gracious suite. Was it possible to take so much for granted?

She closed the door behind them. "This is my sitting room. I know it must look girlie-girl to you, Tucker, but I adore it. This is my own personal little corner of the world, if you know what I mean."

He knew exactly what she meant. "It's a bit girlie-girl, but since that's what you are, it suits you fine."

"Somehow I knew you'd understand." She pointed at another door. "My bedroom's in there. I'd show you, but I can't remember if I made the bed this morning. I was in kind of a hurry, and I'd hate you to see it at less than peak condition."

"Maybe some other time." He nodded at a painting propped against a wall. "That's you. It's terrific. Is that the one your ex did? Eric, right?"

Grimacing, she said, "I don't know where to put it. If Mom and Dad saw it, they'd hang it in the entry where everyone would notice it the moment they came in. I'll just stick it in my closet or under my bed. It doesn't look one bit like me. Artists are exotic creatures, aren't they? Some can look at a garden and see a dump. Others look at a dump and see a garden. Eric always thought I was prettier than I am."

"It looks just like you," Tucker said honestly.

She tugged him to the sofa. "You must have an artistic side you haven't tapped into. I should have known; you're a very sensitive soul. Make yourself comfortable."

Tucker sat at one end of the couch, Olivia the other. She dipped a hand into a box on the coffee table and pulled out two pairs of goggles. After giving one to him, she pulled off her new hat, slipped the glasses on, and replaced the fedora. She turned to him with a thousand-watt smile. Tucker had never seen a more ridiculous sight, and tried to restrain his laughter. It came out an uncontrollable cough.

Olivia jumped up, tore off the glasses and hat, and hurried to an ornately carved door on one side of the room. When she opened it, Tucker saw a wine rack with several glasses dangling underneath by their stems. Shelves held tumblers. She grabbed one and set it on a small counter next to a tiny sink. Bending over she opened a miniature refrigerator under the counter and pulled ice cubes from the freezer compartment. She plopped them into the glass, filled it with water, and brought it to Tucker. He quickly drank half, praying she wouldn't put the hat and goggles on again.

Olivia sat next to him and patted him lightly on the back. "Whatever came over you, Tucker? Are you sick?"

"No, just swallowed wrong. Thanks for the water. It was just what the doctor ordered."

The phone rang. Olivia moved to the end of the sofa and answered. After listening a moment, she said, "Merry Christmas to you, too, Sammy. What do you want?"

She tilted her head and gave Tucker a mischievous grin. "Of course people can call just to say Merry Christmas. What do you want?" Her grin widened. "Don't be such a goose, Sammy! You're a banker. Give yourself a loan." She shook her head. "I can't touch that unless it's an emergency, and you're not one. The rest of my money is tied up in cash."

She held the phone away from her ear for a moment. Tucker heard sputtering from the receiver.

Olivia glanced at him, and turned on her megawatt smile. "No can do. I'm preparing to invest it in the stock market! Bye, Sammy." She disconnected.

Groaning, Tucker dropped his head to his hands. "I'm not going to help you invest, Olivia."

"I didn't plan on asking you to, but I wanted to understand your world a little better. I talked to Ducky Jenssen, you know, from Ducky's Automotive Emporium? Where you got your red Exhibition? He's also a broker. Ducky has several business interests, his fingers are in more than one pie. He's quite an epicure. He agreed to help me. It'll work out for everyone. I'll learn about bulls and bears and selling shorts and he'll get a commission. He's usually in need of extra money, what with the new baby and all."

"A broker who sells cars? Why don't you find someone with more experience?"

"And take my business to a stranger? Away from Chatham? Nope, it's here or nowhere. I believe community spirit should start in your own town. Besides, I won't lose money. I've always been lucky, remember?"

"Do me a favor, invest a small amount at first. See how Ducky does with that before you dive in whole hog." Good God, now he was talking like her without trying.

"Will do."

"I take it Sammy wanted to borrow money."

"Three thousand. That's a lot, don't you think? Sammy always liked things with Gucci or Pucci or Mucci or whatever written on them. He never shops here; he goes to Chicago and Madison. He's very materialistic. No deeper than a rain puddle. He'd disagree with that assessment, but a monkey never sees its own tail."

For a moment, Tucker could only stare at her, wondering if a monkey really couldn't see its tail. "That sounds kind of hypocritical coming from someone who woke her parents at five-thirty this morning to open presents."

She turned in her seat to face him. "It's a family tradition. They'd have been crushed if I hadn't. I had to set my alarm, but they were already awake and waiting. They just pretended to be asleep."

Tucker thought of the pride in Eleanor's voice when she'd told him Olivia had wakened them, and knew Olivia was right.

She tilted her head and drew her eyebrows together. "I like things well enough, but I can do without most of the stuff. They say money doesn't buy happiness, but I'm not so sure about that. When I have kids, and they get the sniffles, I'll be able to whisk them to the doctor right away and not fret about the bill. Money frees you from a lot of worries."

Since her comment was among the wisest observations he'd ever heard, Tucker's admiration for her grew. "You'll be able to replace stolen bikes and buy new flutes."

"Exactly. I can enjoy seeing my kids peddle around and toot in the band. I can watch them open gifts first thing Christmas morning and laugh and not concern myself with how I'll pay for everything. That seems like happiness, doesn't it?"

"It certainly does," Tucker replied, stumped by his reaction. She'd used the 'k' word, twice, and the urge to bolt out of the house hadn't struck him.

Olivia crossed to another cabinet and opened it. Tucker saw a television and sound system inside. She pushed a button and Christmas music filled the air.

"Do you have any Bob Seger?" Tucker asked.

"I surely do." Olivia looked through a stack of CDs and pulled one out. A moment later Seger's gravelly voice sang the praises of old time rock and roll. Tucker leaned back in his seat and grinned. Just the ticket. His face froze. Now he was thinking like her. If he wasn't careful, he'd soon be foliating every night.

"I'll make a point to get all Seger's CDs, and I'll stock the fridge with Old Style. We may need to tryst here from time to time." Olivia took her seat on the other end of the sofa and kicked her shoes off.

Please don't put the hat and goggles on again.

Folding her legs under her, she turned to him. "I'll bring you up to speed, but before I start, I have to tell you what a magnificent job Josie's been doing. It wouldn't surprise me if Eugene tried to hire her away from us. She found out Cheryl had a safe deposit box stuffed with cash. There were other things in there, too, but Ben is being a nun about it. Josie doesn't want to press him. She has to be careful of his onion."

Tucker translated 'a nun' to 'mum', but the rest lost him. He cleared his throat. "His onion?"

"His feelings. People are complex, with lots of layers. Like an onion. When Ben's ready to tell Josie what else was in Cheryl's box, he'll open that next onion layer."

"I see." Tucker pinched the bridge of his nose.

"Josie and I figure all that cash is ill-gotten. Why else put it where you can't get to it other than during banking hours? This way there's no paper trail. We can't wait to get to the layer of Ben's onion that knows what else was in her box."

Tucker rubbed his temples.

"Crow, Reverend Conroy, is still a suspect. You saw the dodgy way he rented a dirty movie. And Gnat isn't out of the picture either. He told Josie he didn't know Cheryl, but his curiosity about her passing was highly suspicious. If she was kinky, they could have crossed paths."

Tucker straightened. "Was he kinky with you?"

"No, but I wouldn't put anything past him. I caught him with another woman doing… well…I'd rather not say. I doubt she was the first. Josie says he'd stick his…never mind." Her cheeks grew bright pink. "Josie can be earthy at times. I think she changed a little when she lived in New York City, New York, but she's still my very best friend and I'm sure she'll be her old self in no time."

"That's very perspicacious of you. Insightful. I looked that word up after you used it."

A smile lit her face. "Don't you love learning new words?"

"I'm starting to love a lot of things. Kir Royale, Christmas traditions and small town life, to name a few."

"Good! Then you'll stay a while." Her face took on a serious expression. "Don't you have Christmas traditions? Where is your family?"

"We had one tradition. Mom got drunk. It was more a daily event than a tradition. I have no idea who my father is. Neither does my mother." The song changed to Still The Same, and Tucker thought of the irony. As usual, in her holiday phone call, his mother slurred her words. "I grew up on the south side of Chicago. It was not a nice place. There were times I was not a nice person."

"I don't believe that. About you, I mean. I believe the rest."

Leaning forward, he took her hand and looked her in the eyes. "It's true. I skated on the edge of the law for years. Oddly enough, it was a cop who rescued me. For some reason he took an interest, paid attention to me, and taught me right from wrong. After a while, he became the most important person in my life. I worried more about disappointing him than doing exactly what I wanted exactly when I wanted. He died some years ago, but if I had to say who my father was, I'd say Jonathan Vicknair."

Thinking of his mentor stopped Tucker for a moment. He dropped her hand and gathered himself. "Anyway, I pulled my head out of my ass, went legit, and fell in lust with a woman who really gave me an education. I wanted someone who was the opposite of my mother. She dressed nice and looked pretty, but inside she was just like dear old Mom. There was no good in her, none at all." A new tune began. Beautiful Loser, that says it all, Tucker thought.

"If you loved her, I'm sure there was. And in your mother, too. Maybe no one ever gave them a chance."

"You might find some redeeming value in those two scavengers, but no one else would. Danielle, my fiancé, fooled me and too many other people. After she stole a lot of my money, I wanted to get away. To disappear. Here I am."

"I don't want to open a kettle of worms by bringing up something painful, but how did she steal your money?"

"Stock swindle. Paid old investors big dividends using

capital from new investors. Greed drives people to do stupid things. I was among the dumbest. I trusted her and didn't do my homework. I'll never make that mistake again."

"You poor thing. You've been through so much. What happened with the swindle and Danielle?"

"The authorities thought I was involved, but dropped the charges before it came to trial. Danielle was convicted."

"How could they have thought you were crooked? You're no scofflaw. Except for having a bit of a lead-foot, you're very law-abrading."

"That's why they dropped the charges. I was innocent, which made it tough to prove I wasn't. They finally realized I'd told them the truth." The haunting opening notes to Turn the Page came from the speakers. Good idea, Tucker thought, wondering if life was playing some cosmic musical joke on him.

"Okay, Danielle was a bad apple, but I'm sure your mother has good in her."

"You wouldn't say that if you knew her."

"I don't need to know her, I know her son. A bad person couldn't have raised someone as wonderful as you."

After what he'd just told her, what a fool he'd been, she thought he was wonderful? He'd need time to mull that over, and decided to change the subject. "What's next on your detective agenda?"

"Josie and I are going to tail Conroy and Sammy until we can eliminate them, or go to Eugene and tell him we've got the killer. We'll follow them, go through their garbage, learn their habits. Before long, we'll know them better than they know themselves. If one of them killed Cheryl, he'll slip and we'll be there to witness it."

Tucker shook his head. "I don't like the sound of that. Don't follow them to places that aren't public without taking me with you. Don't go through their garbage."

"But it could hold a bonanza of clues and info."

"It could get dicey. If one of them is the killer, and finds you rooting in his trash, you could be in very hot water. Even if neither of them is guilty, if they find you going through their garbage, they won't like it."

"If frogs had wings, they wouldn't bump their little behinds when they hopped. 'If' is a mighty big word."

A sputter similar to Sammy's tickled the back of Tucker's throat. "It's illegal. Haven't you heard of the Rubbish Privacy Act?" He hoped she wouldn't check that out.

"I've never heard of it."

"It's been on the books for quite some time."

"Well, what a bother," she said with a scowl. "Every time I'm about to take a step forward, something holds me back. I'm starting to feel repressed."

"It'll pass. Keep me abreast of what you're up to, so I'm in the loop, or I'll worry. You don't want me to worry, do you?"

She patted his arm. "Of course not. Josie's in Arizona, visiting her folks for Christmas, but she'll be back by the end of the week. We're reconnoitering on Friday to compare notes again. One of us will call and let you know where and when."

"You call with the recon details, January Eighth. I like the sound of your voice."

"Oh, Tucker. You say the nicest things."

He'd never met anyone like Olivia. The tiniest, easiest things, like a kind word, seemed to fill her with joy. She beamed at him and, right on cue, Seger launched into You'll Accompany Me.

"I'm not going to marry you, Olivia."

He didn't realize he'd said the words aloud until she replied.

"I'm not going to marry you either, Tucker."

❧

Eugene Strickland sat in his favorite chair, digesting his holiday meal. He heard rattles and clinks in the kitchen as Betty put away the dishes she'd washed and he'd dried. His thoughts turned to the Mecklenberg case and the latest disappointment. He'd heard from the lab in Chicago, and the tablet in Cheryl's address book yielded no clues. Whoever tore the top sheet also took several beneath it. No one could decipher what had been written.

The state police, already stretched thin with the holiday upsurge in crime, had arrived. They wanted to focus on Deerwood, believing the victim hadn't lived in Chatham long enough to forge a murderous relationship. In Eugene's experience, that kind of rage could spring up in minutes.

Upon learning Eugene was a veteran of the Chicago force, and a highly decorated one at that, the state boys were happy to let his department handle Chatham interviews, which suited Eugene just fine. In fact, he'd suggested it. In this way they could make the best use of resources. Eugene and his people knew the residents. Folks tended to clam up with strangers.

As much as he'd like an outsider to be the culprit, he doubted that wish would come true. For reasons he didn't understand, Eugene liked Monroe, and was thankful he had a solid alibi. Reverend Lawrence Conroy and his wife, Rose, hadn't lived more than a year in Chatham. That made him almost an outsider, and the good Reverend wasn't cleared. Neither was Sam Wallace. Eugene needed their fingerprints to compare with those found in the victim's house.

Cheryl's safe deposit box had been filled with cash and a few other interesting items. Digital photos of Conroy in compromising positions with the deceased filled one envelope. Eugene didn't care what consenting adults did behind closed doors, but being handcuffed to a headboard wouldn't give him the response it gave Conroy. He doubted the snapshots would amuse Rose. The thought of marriage to Rose made Eugene shudder. She reminded him of a prison guard, and if she were his wife, he might stray, too. Conroy was a man as well as a minister. If Cheryl had threatened to upset Conroy's comfortable world by exposing the photos, he might have become desperate and killed her. Men of God were supposed to be above reproach. Men of God had inflicted untold damage on innocents. The collar didn't impress Eugene. Conroy had to be seriously considered a candidate.

Another envelope held evidence that Wallace was in debt

up to the knot in his Pierre Cardin tie. One tape, labeled 'Sam Wallace, 11/20' contained pillow talk. If the man on the tape was Sam, and experts would probably be able to ascertain if it was, Sam had committed a serious federal crime. He'd tried to cover his debts by raiding dormant accounts at the bank. Unfortunately for him, the bank was due for an audit in the spring. On another tape, labeled 'Sam Wallace, 11/27' a man pleaded for the first tape. Whoever the man was, he sounded desperate. Bankers had inflicted more damage on people than men of God. Eugene knew he'd be busy next week.

CHAPTER THIRTEEN

Tucker pulled on his leather bomber jacket and patted its pockets, making sure they held his new mittens. He'd stuffed rubber bands inside them, and would put them on and secure the wrists before entering the restaurant. Thinking of Olivia brought a grin to his face. He climbed into his Expedition and recalled the conversation they'd had yesterday afternoon.

"Tucker? It's Olivia. Olivia Chatham, remember? I'm the one—"

"I remember you, Olivia. How are you?"

"Just dandy! We've hit a bit of a snag, but not much of one. I know I said we'd meet tonight, but Josie just got home and she's too pooped to pop. Is it okay if we get together to-morrow, or is Saturday bad for you?"

"Saturday's fine." Like last week, it felt good to face Saturday night with anticipation instead of dread. "Where and when?"

"The place you like. Restaurant. The one that should be the El Toro Marco Polo Lotus Garden. Do you remember how to get there, or is that day still a blur to you?"

"I remember. What time?"

"Six sharp. Oh-eighteen-hundred o'clock."

"Got it."

"One more thing. Be sure to tell the owners how much you like their food. They're the sweetest people, but some-times I get the feeling they need more positive feedback. Folks often forget to compliment, especially at busy times like around

Christmas. Praise is always welcome."

"I'll write that down."

"I'll introduce you, but just so you know, their names are Paul and Judy Fenster. Everybody calls him Punch."

"Punch and Judy? Like the old television show?"

"I don't know. Everyone's always called him that. I thought he may have been a bit of a scrapper when he was younger. During his salad days. You know, one of those fellas who enjoys fisticuffs."

Tucker grinned. When was the last time he'd heard the words 'salad days' and 'fisticuffs'? *"If he's one of those, I'll make sure to praise his food. Wouldn't want fisticuffs."*

"Oh, he's a lamb now. I imagine Judy put the kibosh on his youthful rascalities. Sat him down and said, 'No more rowdy dow!' Besides, only a fool would try any shenanigans with you, Tucker. You'd give them a paddling!"

"I already told you. I'm a pussycat."

Olivia made a noise suspiciously like a snort. *"Right. I have to run, but I'll see you tomorrow."*

"At oh-eighteen-hundred."

Wondering what outrageous antic she'd come up with next, Tucker smiled. A car pulled out of a spot in front of the restaurant, and he took it as a good omen. He parked, ran his fingers through his hair, and got out of the truck. Before he went to the door, he tugged his mittens on and wrapped the rubber bands in place.

Inside, he stopped for a moment, letting his eyes adjust to the darkness. Red and white checked cloths covered the tables, each holding an empty wine bottle in a basket. Candles stuck in the bottlenecks glowed and sent shadows scurrying around the room. Bulls' horns decorated the walls. Delicate paper, folded into different shapes and embellished with Chinese letters, hung from strings attached to the ceiling. They swayed and twirled gently. Tucker spotted Josie in a booth, sipping a cocktail, but didn't see Olivia. A glass of wine, and a smaller one filled with cherries, sat on the table. They didn't look like they'd been touched.

He slid onto the seat across from Josie. "Where's Olivia?"

"Hi to you, too." Josie gave him a cool gaze.

"Sorry. Good evening, Ms. Bookman. It's lovely to see you again. Do you perchance know where Ms. Chatham is?"

"She had to stop at Eyesore, but didn't think it would take long. That's why I ordered her drink. Maybe she ran into someone there and got to gabbing and lost track of the time."

"I know I'm going to regret asking, but what's Eyesore?" He stuffed his mittens into his pockets.

"It's Livvy's nickname for Ivy's Store, a boutique. She set up shop next to Spud's Suds. One day they played the jukebox so loud, Ivy complained. That night Ben chased off some vandals throwing rocks at her sign. Before he got there, they'd broken a few lights. The 'v', 'y' and 't'. Now it spells I-S-S-O-R-E. Wonderful police work, if you ask me. Crime doesn't have a chance against Ben."

Tucker rubbed his temples. "Why is she at a boutique? I thought we were solving a murder. Does Nancy Drew think Ivy is involved?"

"She needed a new dress for the opening of Anne's flower shop. But that was over an hour ago. She should be here by now. She never tries on clothes at the store. The dressing rooms are too small. Ivy doesn't mind letting her bring a few outfits home. Olivia takes care of things, and besides, she always buys everything she borrows."

Tucker checked his watch. A few minutes after six. "What time does Eyesore close on Saturday?"

Josie's eyebrows drew together. "Good question. It closed at five. I wonder if Livvy talked her into staying open a bit later." Her brow cleared. "But they'd be done by now for sure. Livvy's probably on her way."

A waiter approached and Tucker ordered a beer, then pulled his cell phone from his pocket. Josie told the man she wasn't ready for a refill, and he headed toward the bar. Tucker called Olivia's cell, but received no answer. Looking at Josie he asked, "Do you know the number at Ivy's?"

She pulled an organizer from her bag and rattled off seven

digits. Again Tucker's call went unanswered.

"I don't suppose you have Ivy's home number in there." He nodded at Josie's address book.

"Nope. Her last name's Jenssen. I'm sure she's listed."

Tucker got her number from directory assistance. This time he got an answer.

"Ms. Jenssen? You don't know me, I'm new in town. I'm Tucker Monroe, a friend of Olivia Chatham."

"Hello, Mr. Monroe. I saw you at the Chathams' Christmas party. How nice to have a new face in town. What can I do for you?"

"Was Olivia in your store today?"

"Why, yes. Not long before closing."

"Did you happen to notice when she left? Or what direction she went?" Tucker nodded his thanks at the waiter when he placed a frosted glass of Old Style on the table.

"Lord, no. It was a madhouse today. I barely had time for lunch. Everyone in town wanted to exchange a gift or buy something on sale." She dragged out the last few words, then paused. "I'd forgotten, but one strange thing happened. Livvy said she'd try the dresses on in the shop. She usually takes a few home and decides which she likes there. But today she said she might forget if she didn't pick something out right away. 'Things are popping, Ivy,' she said to me. I had no idea what she meant, but she was wound tight as an eight day clock."

"Do you remember what time she paid for whatever she bought? Or how long before closing?" A sick feeling formed in Tucker's stomach. If Olivia was excited, how could Ivy forget selling her a dress? Olivia would have been in full chatterbox mode.

Silence weighed on the line. After several moments Ivy said, "I don't recall her buying anything. And that is a first. It's never happened."

"Do you remember seeing her leave the dressing room?"

"She didn't use a regular one. Poor dear is a bit claustrophobic. My sister suffers with that. Insists on being cremated.

She says she could never breathe in a coffin. She—"

"Olivia and the dresses?" Tucker interrupted.

"Oh, yes. Sorry. I let her use my fitting room. It's larger and brighter." Again Ivy's words trailed away. Then she gasped. "Mr. Monroe, I didn't check that room before I left. I was so tired, I just grabbed my coat and purse and closed the shop. Livvy could still be there." She spoke so loudly, Tucker pulled the phone from his ear.

Josie, sitting across from him, widened her eyes. "Livvy's stuck in Eyesore?"

"Sounds like it," he whispered. While concerned Olivia might be locked in a boutique, some of his unease left Tucker. At least she was safe. "Calm down, Ms. Jenssen. I'll meet you at the shop in a few minutes."

After he disconnected, Tucker's disquiet returned. If Olivia was locked in a boutique, why didn't she call someone for help? If her phone was broken for some reason, she could use the store's. "Who knows Olivia is claustrophobic?"

"In Chatham?" Josie replied. "There aren't many secrets here. I'd guess everyone knows."

"Seems to me there are plenty of secrets." He almost knocked his beer over as he got to his feet. Throwing five dollars on the table, he looked at Josie. "We may have to meet another time. If Olivia isn't at Ivy's, I'll have to look for her."

Josie waved a hand in the air. "Ben's working tonight, so I've got nothing planned. I'll wait in case Livvy shows up."

"Call me if she does," he said, then hurried to the door. "And keep her here. Take her keys if you have to," he added before dashing to his SUV.

Tucker tried to calm himself as he drove to Spud's Suds, remembering Josie had said it was next to Ivy's. Olivia had a tendency to go in several directions at once. She could have met someone at the store and left with them. A sob story would distract her, and she'd listen as long as necessary if she thought it would help. She could have had another flat. There were any number of reasonable explanations for her missing their appointment and not answering her phone. Hell, with Olivia the explanations didn't need to be reasonable. Maybe she spotted a colorful bird and followed it. Still, he'd feel a lot better once he knew she was okay. He wanted to hear her voice. If she wasn't at the store, where could she be? He considered possibilities as he parked behind a car a block from the boutique. Spud was having a banner night, and vehicles filled the street. He didn't see Olivia's among them. A diminutive lady with stylishly coifed gray hair closed the driver's door of the car in front of his and waited as he approached.

"Mr. Monroe?"

He held out his hand. "Tucker. And you're Ms. Jenssen?"

"Ivy." She shook his hand. "I surely hope I didn't lock Livvy in the shop."

Walking toward the store, Tucker said, "I know you were busy today, but do you remember if Reverend Conroy stopped in?"

"Yes, he did. The reverend's wife exchanged a sweater and he helped her pick out a new one. They weren't here long. Rose always does what he says, so I imagine she wears what he tells her, too."

"Were they here while Olivia was?"

"I'm sorry, Tucker. I can't recall."

"That's fine. What about Sam Wallace?"

"Livvy's ex? Oh, yes. He popped in as she was going to the alteration room. Gave me a fright, I don't mind saying. I didn't want them to run into each other. He can be a bit of a pain. He mumbled something about needing a late Christmas present, then poked around and ended up buying a pair of earmuffs. Earmuffs of all things. Who would want earmuffs for Christmas? I was glad to see him go."

A strange feeling came over Tucker at Ivy's words. His internal alarms fired again. "How long was he here?"

"Not long, just a couple of minutes." She harrumphed. "Earmuffs."

Music greeted them the moment Ivy opened the shop door. Her hands flew to her cheeks. "I was in such a hurry, I forgot to shut off the tape." She went behind the counter and ducked below its top. Silence filled the air, followed by pounding and mumbled words.

Tucker ran toward the rear of the shop. "Olivia! Where are you?"

"In here!" Her voice came from behind a door to his left. "Please get me out!"

Ivy scurried to his side as Tucker turned the doorknob. It didn't move. He looked down and saw a key sticking out of the lock. He turned it and threw the door open. Olivia flew out, hitting him square in the chest and nearly knocking him over. His breath left in a whoosh.

She buried her face on his shoulder and wrapped her arms around him. "Oh, Tucker. I thought I'd be locked in there for all eternity."

Hugging her, Tucker said, "Didn't you know I'd look for you?"

"With Josie at the restaurant, I didn't think you'd notice I wasn't."

He heard a sniffle and whispered, "I always notice when you aren't around, January Eighth. You brighten a room like no one else. I promise, if you're missing again, I'll look for you."

"You say the nicest things. I promise to look for you if you're missing, too."

"That's a comfort." He kissed the top of her head.

Ivy reached out and tapped Olivia's arm. She pulled away from Tucker and hugged the shop owner.

"Thanks so much for letting me out, Ivy. You must be tired after all the customers today."

"I'm so sorry, Livvy. I should have checked the store before leaving. But I swear, I didn't lock you in that room. I never would have done that to you. Never."

"I know." Olivia leaned back and looked Ivy in the eyes. "You wouldn't, and you didn't. I heard someone outside the door. Heavy footsteps. That's who did it."

"But who? Who would do such a thing?"

"It's a puzzlement."

"Did they say anything?" Tucker asked.

Olivia shook her head. "I heard something click. Later, I tried to get out and couldn't. Whoever it was didn't say a word, but it was a person full of meanness. I sensed evil. It made the hair on my neck stand on end."

"We have to go to Strickland with this," Tucker told her.

"With what?"

"Someone locked you in a room. That's enough."

"No, it isn't. He'll say someone could have bumped it, or Ivy accidentally turned the key. He's got too much on his plate to bother with this."

Tucker decided to table the discussion. He could convince her later. "Why didn't you answer your cell phone? Why didn't you call me or Josie?"

"My phone broke." Olivia unclipped her cell from her belt and handed it to Tucker.

He put it to his ear. Nothing. "Did you charge it?"

"No, I wrote a check. What does that have to do with anything?"

Tucker rubbed his forehead. "Do you have the box and all the stuff that came with it?"

"Oh, my, yes," Olivia replied. "I'm a responsible consumer. Some of that equipment could be important. One of these days I'll read all the instructions."

He handed her the phone. "One of those important pieces of equipment is a battery charger. Plug it in when you get home, okay? Do that every night."

Olivia's mouth formed an 'O'. "Who'd have guessed? How do you know all these things, Tucker? You're so worldly."

"That's me. Worldly." For the first time since she bounded out of the closet, Tucker took in Olivia's appearance. She looked fine, with bright eyes and a big smile, but he knew she'd had an ordeal. "I can drive you home, Olivia. You've been through a lot today."

"Oh, no. We have to meet Josie and I'm starving. There's just one thing I need to do before we go." She turned to Ivy. "Um, I need to…I was in there a long time and…"

"You know where the washroom is, honey," Ivy said in a motherly tone. "Tucker and I'll wait at the front of the store. Take all the time you need."

Olivia's hat and coat hung from a hook on the door. Her purse sat on the floor. She reached for them, then turned toward the rear of the boutique.

Ivy took Tucker's arm and led him to the counter. He trusted Olivia's instincts, and if she said she'd sensed something, he had no reason to disbelieve her. Someone in the store had locked her in a room. Whether or not Strickland got involved, Tucker wanted to know who had done such a cruel thing to Olivia.

"I know I'm asking a lot, but could you go through your receipts and list everyone who was in the store today?"

"Of course. Some people didn't buy anything, or paid cash, and I'll list those I remember, too. I'd do anything for Livvy. She's practically family." She leaned against the front counter. "Last fall my grandson, Ralph, had problems in third grade. They wanted to send him through second grade again. Other kids called him stupid, and he was the saddest little boy. Sylvester, my son, everyone calls him Ducky, was beside himself."

Tucker thought Sylvester was a cat, and Daffy was a duck, but supposed no man would want to be called Kitty.

"Livvy heard the story and went to their house," Ivy continued. "She stood right there on the front porch and announced Ralph was no dumber than she was. That meant the world to Ralph. He loves Livvy, and that was the nicest thing she could have said. She took him to the park and they played on the swings. I guess he opened up to her."

"I wouldn't be surprised."

"All the kids in town love her. Most adults, too, now that I think about it." Ivy drew her eyebrows together. "I think part of Livvy never grew up, and that's good. She never became untrusting like so many do. People are drawn to her innocence. She makes us all feel a bit younger, a bit happier. It's amazing what a difference one person can make, isn't it?"

"I hadn't thought about it, but you have a point."

Ivy's expression softened. "Sometimes Livvy seems oblivious to the real world. Other times she seems to understand it better than anyone." She shook her head. "Anyway, it turns out Ralph is nearsighted. He told Livvy he had trouble seeing the chalkboard. She took him directly to Dr. Shultz's office and sure enough, Ralph needed spectacles." Ivy looked past Tucker. "Here she comes. Are you okay, Livvy?"

Olivia reached the counter and stood beside Tucker. She held three dresses up. "I'm fine, Ivy, but I can't make up my mind. I'll just take them all."

Tucker detected a sparkle in Olivia's eye, and wondered what put it there.

Ivy took the outfits and hung them on a rack. "I'll bag these up for you. No charge, Livvy. I feel awful for leaving you in that room."

"Oh, no, you don't," Livvy replied. "It's not your fault I get woozy in cramped spaces. You just put that on my bill like always."

"But—"

"Please, Ivy. I'll be miserable if you don't. Really. Miserably miserable. That's a lot of misery over a few dresses."

Ivy patted Olivia's shoulder. "All right, dear. If you insist." She pulled a large plastic bag from under the counter and slid it over the tops of the hangers. "I was just telling your young man how you solved Ralph's school problem."

"Oh, piffle. That was nothing."

"Nothing?" Ivy tied the bag at the bottom and faced Tucker. "Livvy arranged for the eyeglasses and examination payment, too. She got Dr. Shultz to agree to set up an exchange program. Livvy and Ralph put it together. Ralph goes around town picking up old glasses people don't need anymore. It'll pay his debt to the doctor, and provide spectacles to people who need them at a fraction of the cost of new ones."

Tucker grinned at Ivy, then Olivia. "Pretty smart thinking."

"That's not all. She gave Ralph a new wagon to use on his

rounds. You've never seen a prouder boy."

Olivia's face reddened. "That was one of my old wagons. From when I was a kid."

"Really? It's so shiny."

"Mom and Dad gave me several. I used the pink one to tote dolls, the red one for stuffed animals, and the blue one for rocks. The green one was for everything else."

Tucker beamed at her. He had no idea why a little girl would want to carry rocks in a wagon, but knew she'd had a purpose. Probably one no one else could fathom, but a purpose all the same.

"But there's only so many wagons a girl can use before she moves on to other interests. I guess they have a shelf life." Olivia plopped her hat on her head, then looped an arm through Tucker's. "We better get to the restaurant. Josie will be having a fit."

Tucker took the bag. "Thanks, Ivy. We'll wait for you to lock up and walk you to your car."

"What a nice man you are. I'll call you with that info tomorrow, Tucker."

Olivia looked at him. "What info?"

"I don't want to bother you with it yet. It may be nothing."

They escorted Ivy to her car, then Olivia pointed down a side street. "I'm parked over there."

No wonder he hadn't noticed her Lexus when he arrived. "It was nice of you to arrange for Ralph to get glasses," Tucker said as he strolled beside her.

"I'm going to tell you a secret."

"If you're sure you want to."

Olivia nodded. "I can trust you. Sometimes I help people with little things. Nobody knows that."

"Ah. You do it anonymously." Tucker thought back to his conversation with Strickland. Everyone knew.

"Right. Plus, I don't want anyone to know it's me. I've been lucky. I have the best parents in the history of the world, and I've always gotten everything I want or need. And I've never done one darn thing to earn any of it."

"You're being kind of hard on yourself."

"I'm being honest. I wish everyone could be as lucky as me, but they aren't. So sometimes I help their luck. But it's tricky. If you just hand things over to people, they could think it's charity. Or worse, think it's owed them. If they don't do anything to earn it, they could end up as worthless as me."

Tucker frowned at her. How could she think she was worthless?

"Is something wrong?"

"I'm pretty mad at you right now."

Olivia's mouth fell open. "Why? For giving things away? Please don't be mad, Tucker."

"For calling yourself worthless. I never want to hear you say anything like that again."

"But it's true."

"It's complete bullshit. If I hear words like that from you again, I'll spank your little behind." Not in this lifetime. "That'd be a first wouldn't it?"

"No, you wouldn't," Olivia answered with a shake of her head. "You're too kind. But it did happen. A day that will live in antiquity."

"What happened?" Who would strike Olivia?

"Mom gave me a paddling. It was well-deserved. I'd been a little dickens, that's for sure."

He stopped and turned to her. "I can't imagine your mother raising her hand to anyone."

"It hurt her terribly. She cried and cried. We'd been to the library, and Glory Bea Carter had a pimple on the end of her nose. I couldn't stop staring at it, even though Mom nudged me a couple times. Finally I said, 'All that makeup doesn't hide your pimple, Miss Carter.' Mom gasped and apologized and hurried me out of there. She told Glory Bea we were going home to play 'Hide and Seek'. That was our code. When I was bad, she said that and it meant we were going to look for my manners. But Mom was especially upset that day.

"On the way home she said, 'Livvy, I swore I'd never do

this, but you're getting a spanking today. Next time you feel like being rude, maybe you'll remember and you'll stop and think.'" Olivia rubbed her rear end. "She was right."

Tucker shook his head and they began walking again. "I still don't believe your mother would do that. She must have put a pillow over your behind before spanking."

"No, she took me to her hobby room and sat me on her lap. She was crying and I was crying and she hugged me and whispered, 'Paddle, paddle, paddle' in my ear. Then she stood me in front of her and said I'd never forget that day, and she was right. I never want to make Mom cry like that again. She couldn't take another ballyhoo of that magnitude."

"Ah, that makes more sense. A verbal spanking is more your mother's style." They reached Olivia's car and Tucker hung her dresses on the hook in the back seat.

Olivia's eyes widened. "You didn't think I meant a physical spanking, did you? Mom couldn't do that."

"True. I lost my head for a moment." Tucker stuffed his hands in his pockets.

"Where are your mittens? It's cold, and we can't have you coming down with a bug."

Shit. He pulled them out and waved them under her nose before tugging them on. "Right here."

"What are those for?" She nodded at the rubber bands he snapped around the wrists.

He'd prepared for this. "I worried someone would try to steal them, take them right off me. Won't be so easy with rubber bands as anchors."

Olivia raised her hands to her cheeks, then her hat. "Mercy, you like your present as much as I like mine."

"My best ever." He watched a blush spread across her cheeks, again struck by how easy it was to make Olivia happy. Then he remembered her ordeal this afternoon. "Are you sure you're up to dinner?"

The sparkle came back to her eyes. "You bet I am. And I have a clue! I want to tell you and Josie together so I can see your faces when you hear. It's a doozie!"

Chapter Fourteen

Olivia stopped at a convenience mart on the way to dinner. Puzzled, Tucker pulled into the slot beside her.

"I'll just be a minute," she called when he lowered his window.

She bounced into the store, and reappeared a few minutes later. Waving at him, she returned to her car and climbed in. Once again he followed her taillights. After parking in front of the restaurant, Tucker walked to Olivia's SUV. He noticed she didn't bother to lock it.

"You've got new dresses in there," he nodded at her car. "Don't you think you should lock the door?"

"Whatever for?" she asked, looking up at him with a baffled expression. "There's hardly any theft in Chatham."

"Crime is limited to murder and trapping people in small rooms?"

She dismissed him with a shake of her head. "You are a worrywart at times, Tucker. Anyone who needs clothes bad enough to steal is welcome to them." Wrapping an arm through his, she said, "Are you sure you aren't interested in Josie? You once said she wasn't your type, but have you changed your mind?"

"No," Tucker replied without hesitating. "Josie's nice, but she lacks that extra pizzazz I like."

"Well, you're about the only man I've ever met who would say such a thing, but I'll take you at your word. It's a good thing she lacks your extra pizzas, because I'd hate to see you hurt again. She seems to really like Ben. They were together earlier this afternoon. Josie was supposed to get info, but when I talked to her later, she said it was a dry well. If you ask me, they got to canoodling and she forgot her mission. Don't hold it against her. She deserves some happiness, so if she got distracted, it was probably a good thing."

"Distractions can happen to the best of us."

She tugged his arm and they moved toward the restaurant. "True, but we need to keep them to a minimum. The first hours after a crime are the most important. After that chances of solving the nefarious deed decline like a sled going down a steep hill."

Cheryl's murder had been two weeks ago. Tucker wondered how Olivia defined 'first hours', but didn't want to ask. Her eyes sparkled and she practically skipped as they walked. Something had wound her up, and he decided to relax and enjoy the show.

Inside the restaurant Tucker bumped into Olivia when she abruptly stopped.

"Josie! What's gotten into you?" she said, sounding aghast.

Josie, coming toward them from the back of the room, shrugged as she reached the table. "Whatever do you mean, Livvy?"

"Jeepers, Josie." Olivia scrambled to the table, Tucker right behind her, and slid onto the seat across from her friend. She removed her coat and hat, placing the fedora beside her, on top of her purse.

Tucker settled next to Olivia. *Jeepers? Had anyone said 'jeepers' since 1955?*

"You're wearing white," Olivia told Josie in a loud whisper. "White white. Not winter white. In your face white. It's months until Memorial Day. Are you ill?" She leaned across the table and put the back of her hand to Josie's forehead.

Brushing Olivia's hand aside, Josie said, "I'm fine, Livvy."

"I've got to admire you." Olivia resettled in her seat. "We said we needed to get some skeletons in our closets, and you start with a fashion gaffe. Besides wearing white in December, your purse doesn't match your shoes. It's red. Brilliant!"

Josie met Olivia's gaze, completely ignoring Tucker. "You know how Ben decides what to wear every day? He reaches into his closet and puts on the first thing he finds. He makes me think about things, Livvy. I'm not going to follow all the fashion rules anymore. I'm my own woman. I felt like wearing white jeans and shoes today, so I did."

"Are you going to break fashion rules all the time?"

"If I feel like it." Josie picked up her cocktail and took a sip.

"Good grief, you're growing up right before my eyes. I'm so proud of you."

"I do believe you're right, Livvy. I'm starting to feel my age. Hard to believe I'll soon be thirty. The time for shallowness is over."

"You are thirty. You'll soon be thirty-one."

"Baby steps, little buddy. I'm growing up in baby steps."

Olivia lifted the glass of wine still sitting on the table. "Here's to maturity." She and Josie clicked glasses.

While Olivia plucked cherries from the glass next to her wine, Tucker raised an arm and motioned for the waiter. He asked for menus and ordered a beer. The waiter returned with another frosty mug of Old Style and, with a huge smile at Olivia and Josie, made a production of placing menus in front of them.

When he took a step away, Olivia stopped him. "Wait, Scootie. We'll be ready to order in a second." She glanced at the menu, then said, "I love Judy's tacos. And her rice is the best ever. Five hard shell beef tacos and a double order of rice."

"I'll have the same, only make mine one soft shell chicken and a single order of rice." Josie handed Scootie her menu.

They looked expectantly at Tucker. He trusted Olivia, and echoed her order.

When they were alone, Olivia said, "Sorry to rush you, but we've got business to attend." She reached into her oversized purse and pulled out a small box of sandwich bags and her notepad. "This is what I stopped for," she said to Tucker as she ripped the box open. "We need baggies. I should have thought of that before." She handed a stack to Tucker, then Josie, and kept several for herself. "Would have come in handy earlier," Olivia added as she shoved the empty carton aside.

"How?" Tucker asked. What was she up to?

"For evidence. We may come across important evidence getting to the bottom of this skullduggery. Like I did today." Olivia took a sip of wine, added another cherry, and sat back looking enormously pleased with herself. "Mom and Dad leave on their cruise Monday. I'll have even more time for investigating. Plus, we can use my house as a meeting place. Our own little lair."

"What happened today, Livvy?" Josie asked.

Olivia wiggled in her seat, then opened the notepad she'd placed on the table. She shook it, and a loose piece of paper fell out. "This, my friends, is evidence. Whoever locked me in the closet slid it under the door." She picked it up by a corner and gently put it in a plastic bag before letting Tucker and Josie read it.

Curiosity killed the cat.

"What on earth…" Josie muttered. "How awful."

Olivia reached over and patted her arm. "No one's really going to kill a cat, sweetie. It's an old saying, and a warning to me to butt out. Like I'm a Nosy Parker, for heaven's sake. We're just solving a crime, and getting close if I'm not mistaken. Why else would anyone give me a message like that?"

"Why did you have it in your notebook? And why did you put it in a baggie now?"

"Fingerprints, Josie. This could be full of clues. Well, it already has a big one. But it could have more, like the kind of paper it's typed on and prints and who knows what all? I had to protect it for Eugene. Eventually we'll show it to him. When that jackanape slid it under the door, I faced a juggernaut, no doubt about it. Then I thought of my tablet and pushed it between sheets, hardly touching it at all."

Tucker stared at the note. "What's the big clue?"

"See the 'i'?" Olivia pointed at all of them. "They're raised, uneven with the other letters. Plus, you can tell the paper's been hit. This was done on a typewriter, not a computer. And typewriters can be matched. All we have to do is find the owner of this one, and we've got our perp."

Tucker sat back in his seat. "Jeepers." She actually had a point. Whoever wrote that note was either a killer, or had information. And they didn't want Olivia poking around. He shook himself from his thoughts and reached for her hand. "We're going to Strickland."

"Not yet." Olivia pulled from his grasp. "We need to study the note first."

"'Curiosity killed the cat.' What's to study?"

Olivia's eyes widened. "You recited that without reading the note. Tucker, you're eidetic."

That stopped him.

"What's that?" Josie asked, looking at him as if he carried an epidemic.

"Photographic memory," Olivia answered. The smile she turned on him would thaw the coldest heart. "You are one surprise after another."

Tucker felt caught in the warmth of her gaze. Then, remembering someone had not only threatened her, but trapped her for hours in a closet, reached for her hand again. "Strickland has to have this."

Once more she pulled away. "Don't be a fly in the ointment. I'll give it to him. First we have to have dinner and study it and try to figure out our next move."

"We are going to Strickland." He got to his feet.

"Of course we are. That's what I've been saying. But Scootie's bringing our dinners, and if we don't eat, Punch and Judy will be crushed. What do a few hours matter?"

Tucker ran his fingers through his hair and sat. "Christ. I thought you said time is important now. While we're sitting here eating tacos, we could be giving Strickland valuable information."

Olivia straightened and nearly glowed when he said 'valuable information'. Feeling he'd been kicked in the stomach, Tucker relented. They'd eat, then go to the sheriff. She wasn't in immediate danger, not with him around. And he'd be with her until the note was safely in Strickland's hands.

The waiter put plates in front of them, then passed out silverware wrapped in red checkered napkins. "Anything else?"

"No thanks, Scootie." Olivia held her nose over her dish and inhaled deeply. "Smells fabulous. Judy's best batch."

The waiter stared at Josie, looking like a kid eyeing an ice cream sundae.

"Thanks, Scootie. We'll give a shout if we need anything," Josie said with a smile.

Tucker had to admit, she seemed to have lost some of her haughty attitude. Maybe the meek little deputy really was good for her. Stranger things were known to happen.

"Okay, gang," Olivia said. She unfurled her napkin and put it on her lap, then leaned forward. "First, we tell no one, and I mean no one, except Eugene, about the note. Remember, a closed mouth gathers no feet." She dug her fork into the massive pile of rice on her plate. "We also have to act a bit dumb. That'll be hard." She held her loaded fork an inch from her mouth. "But if we say too much, we could give Ben away. That can't happen. Our source will dry up faster than my skin in October. Ben's loyalty to the uniform can't come under scrutiny."

Tucker had never met a woman who ate with such relish. She closed her eyes as she chewed her rice, then reached for a taco. Most women he knew would run from that plate. Olivia embraced it. A rush of joy raced through him. Olivia savored life, not just food. She wasn't too thin, or too heavy. She was curvy and soft and healthy. Considering her love of food, that was an accomplishment. Tucker guessed tearing around finding bikes and flutes and wagons burned a few calories.

"Thanks for that, Livvy," Josie said. She picked half the meat out of her taco and pushed it into a pile on the side of her plate. "I'm glad you're thinking of him. If he got into trouble, I think I'd die."

"Don't be dramatic, Josie. But I get your point. We'll take care to safeguard our mole."

"Mole?" Josie's eyebrows drew together.

"Spy talk for source. Not a real mole. That's a varmint. This is a compliment."

"Oh. Good." Josie went back to dissecting her dinner.

"We have to figure out who belongs to this typewriter. I can tell you one thing. It pretty much lets Sammy off the hook."

Tucker sampled his food, surprised how hungry he was and pleasantly reminded of the quality of this little hole in the wall. Everything tasted like a bite of heaven.

"How does it get Sammy off the hook?" Josie asked.

"He wouldn't have a typewriter. Not in the computer age. Not with his ego. Not with his need for the newest and the best. Nope, Sammy and typewriters wouldn't get along any better than Sammy and anyone else."

"But wouldn't that be why he'd use one?" Tucker interjected. "He couldn't be trapped by one he didn't own."

Olivia shook her head. "Even if he did find one to use, he'd mess up. That note doesn't have any misspelled words."

"There aren't many to misspell."

"Doesn't matter," Olivia said around a bite of taco. "He can't help himself. He messes up even the smallest things. He didn't type this." She drummed her fingers on the table, then pulled her new tape recorder from her bag. Holding it close to her mouth, she said, "Note to self: Sammy could have an accomplice."

Josie pushed her plate aside with a sigh. "I'm growing up. I really am. But after so many years of calorie counting, it's hard to moose food like you, Livvy."

Olivia stared at her empty dish, then beamed at Josie. "It'll get easier. We just have to stretch your tummy."

Tucker, who'd inhaled his dinner, marveled that someone could leave food like this untouched. "Unless anyone wants coffee, I vote Olivia and I go to the police station."

"Oh, not tonight, Tucker," Olivia told him. "I need until tomorrow. My magnifying glass is at home, and I have to study the paper with it."

"Nope. We're going to Strickland now. No ifs, ands, or buts."

"Nuts." Olivia scowled at him. "What would one night matter?"

"Tonight. Now. We're going. This isn't a suggestion, Olivia Aron Chatham. It's a fact."

"Okay," she said with a dramatic sigh. "Let me out of the booth. I need to use the powder room and thank Punch and Judy for dinner. Don't forget, you should do that, too."

"As long as I can do it on the way out the door. Hurry."

Olivia reached for the baggie with the note.

"You can leave it, Olivia. It's safe with us."

"No, I can't Mr. Smarty. Chain of possession." After grabbing the plastic bag she flounced away.

Tucker watched Olivia, then looked at Josie. "Has she always been so headstrong?"

"She's always been Livvy, if that's what you mean."

He supposed he did. When Olivia returned he stood and held her coat for her.

"I'll call you tomorrow," Olivia said to Josie. "We need to plan something for New Year's Eve. I'd almost forgotten about it." She donned her fedora.

"Sounds good to me." Josie slipped into her jacket and stood.

On the way out, Tucker told the waiter he'd be back. It was the best food he'd ever eaten. Then he took his mittens from his pockets and settled rubber bands around his wrists. Spring couldn't come soon enough.

After walking Josie to her car and watching her leave, Tucker turned to Olivia. "Why don't you ride with me? I'll bring you back after we see the sheriff."

"Good thinking. It'll give us time to strategize." She stood beside the open passenger door and stared inside his Expedition. Her eyebrows drew together.

"Something wrong?" He moved a Bob Seger CD off her seat.

"How does a person get into this gracefully? It should come with stairs."

Tucker laughed and helped her into the SUV. "I'll go to Ducky's next week and get some."

"Mercy me. It's so tall, I'm afraid I'll get a nosebleed."

"Now you know why I bought a red one." Tucker closed her door and went to the driver's side.

Olivia chattered all the way to the police station. Between telling him items on her murder-solving agenda, and leaving notes to herself on her tape recorder, she barely stopped for air. When he parked in the nearly empty lot, she hopped out of his truck and marched into the building with a spring in her step. Tucker hurried to keep up. For someone who'd hesitated going to the police with the note, she seemed remarkably eager.

"Hiya, Randy," Olivia said to the officer at the front counter.

"Hey, Livvy. Something wrong?"

"We've come to assist Eugene in his inquiries. Has he left for the day yet?"

"Nope, but I'll need to tell him more than that. Exactly what inquiries are you talking about?"

Olivia leaned forward and, in a quiet voice, said, "Just between us, Tucker and I are here in an undercover capacity regarding the most recent Chatham homicide."

Tucker hid his laughter behind a cough. *Most recent Chatham homicide?*

"Eugene asked me to keep my ears on full alert, and report anything that may help solve this dastardly deed directly to him." She straightened and adjusted her hat. "It just so happens I am currently, at present, holding a piece of evidence."

Randy reached for his phone and hit a button. A few moments later he hung up and said, "He told me to send you back."

"Good work." Olivia nodded at Randy, turned, and took Tucker's arm. "This is turning out to be quite a day, isn't it?"

"Oh, yeah."

❧❧

Eugene heard footsteps and looked up to see Olivia and Monroe approaching his door. She wore the most ridiculous hat he'd ever seen. He half rose and motioned to the chairs in front of his desk. "What can I do for you?"

"It's lucky you're still here, Eug…Sheriff. Working on our murder?"

Our? "Every day until it's solved. What's up, Livvy?"

"We're here to report malfeasance."

Eugene opened a desk drawer and grabbed his antacids. He glanced at Monroe and saw his mouth twitch.

"Can you report it to one of the deputies?" He tapped a stack of papers on his desk. "I've got a lot of reading to do tonight."

Olivia reached into her purse and withdrew a plastic bag, then placed it on top of the papers. "Here's one more thing to read. After you finish we can plan our next move."

"'Curiosity killed the cat.'" He looked at Olivia and Tucker. "So?"

"I think you should hear her out, Sheriff," Monroe said. He seemed more serious than a moment before.

Eugene popped an antacid into his mouth, then settled back in his chair. "You've got the floor, Livvy." When she looked down, then back at him with a confused expression, he felt the onset of a headache. "Why don't you just report your malfeasance? You have my full attention."

"Oh. Okay. For a second there I thought you wanted me to stand or something."

She scooted forward in her seat and regaled him with a saga about dressing rooms and paying for a cell phone with a check instead of credit card, and being locked in Ivy's Store. Eugene found his bottle of aspirin and swallowed two, chasing them with cold coffee. When she got to the note, he listened closely. Glancing at Monroe, he saw the man's expression had sobered considerably.

"So you can clearly see we need to go door to door and

ask for people's typewriters," Olivia said. "It sounds a bit daunting, but my bet is most folks don't have them anymore. From there on, it's just a case of elimination. Whoever owns the typewriter is our killer." She beamed at him, then pointed at the door. "Would you mind if I ran out there and got a glass of water, Eugene? I declare, all that talking dried me up."

"Go ahead, Livvy."

She stood. "Do you want some, Tucker? Eug…Sheriff?"

Both declined. When she'd left his office, Eugene stared at Tucker. "Are you encouraging her? Because I've got to tell you, I don't like what I just heard. I don't like it at all."

"We agree on something. I'd be happy to get Olivia off the case. Want to tell me exactly how I go about doing that?"

"I don't know." Eugene rubbed his forehead.

"I've made her promise to tell me what she's up to. I never liked Olivia involving herself in this, but now the stakes have risen. If anyone tries anything, I'll be there. In the meantime, the faster you solve this, the better for everyone."

Olivia breezed into the room, carrying a plastic cup. "Much better." She took her seat again. "Now, as I said, we need to check typewriters. But let's go about this logically. Reverend Conroy and Sam Wallace are prime suspects, so we'll start with them. Do you want me there when you serve the warrants, Eugene?"

Good Lord. "Why would I serve them warrants, Livvy?"

She sighed like a mother grown tired of chasing a toddler. "To get their typewriters. I don't think Sammy would have or even use one, but we have to keep our ducks in the water and cross all the letters that need crossing. Who knows? Maybe he had an accomplice. It's a whacky world at times."

"What makes you think either of them are involved?"

"Did I forget to tell you that part? It's simple really. Reverend Conroy dyes his hair and Sammy's not nice." She raised a hand, as if to stop him from interrupting. "Please don't tell me Conroy's a minister and wouldn't do such a thing. He's still a person, and people are capable of anything. It's something I've learned the hard way these last few days." She looked at Tucker and put a hand on his arm, then faced Eugene again. "I do believe I may have lost my faith in people if Tucker hadn't come along. He's a wise and kind man with all sorts of talents. So you see, it all works out. I find out someone in our midst is evil, and meet someone new who's good. Things seem to even out."

Eugene noticed Tucker's expression, and if he'd had any doubts about the man, they would have evaporated. He'd bet Monroe would move heaven and earth to live up to Olivia's assessment. No one would harm her, not while Monroe was around. He focused on Olivia again. "Hair dying and not being nice aren't going to get me a warrant, Livvy. Is there anything else you know?"

"Sammy needs money. A lot of it. He wanted to borrow three thousand from me. He wouldn't tell me why he needs it, but I told him no dice. I think he's got his fingers in some shady pies. Conroy sneaks to the Reel 'Em In and rents dirty movies. Now, I'm a live and let live kind of gal. I know there are different pokes for different folks. But that just doesn't seem upstanding behavior for a man of the cloth."

Eugene felt the stirring of unrest. He needed to take a deep breath and think. "Strokes," he said, buying time.

"What?"

"Strokes," he repeated absently. "Different strokes for different folks."

"Oh." She gave her head a shake. "This isn't the time for grammar, but we can discuss it later if you like. The point is, poking or stroking, it isn't ministerly."

Eugene tapped a finger on his desk. "Anything else, Livvy?"

"Not so far. I think you've got enough to get started. Maybe you can lift prints from the note or match the paper to the store that sold it. That and the typewriter are all I have today."

"I'll get right on it. You've done all a sheriff can hope for, Livvy. I think it's time you retired from law enforcement."

"Not while I'm on a roll, Eug...Sheriff."

"Do what he says, Olivia," Tucker said. "He can take it from here."

"But he asked for my help, didn't you, Eugene?" She turned to Tucker. "He said to keep my ears wide open and I have and now we've brought him suspects. I know Sammy's iffy, because of the typewriter, but I like him for the perp. He's duplicitous. Same with Conroy."

Eugene pushed his chair back. "I appreciate all your hard work, but it's time for you to let go."

"Nuts," Olivia said as she rose. Looking at him hopefully, she said, "If a person doesn't break the law, they can do whatever they want, can't they?"

"It's illegal to interfere in a police investigation."

A huge smile crossed her face. "Interfere? Me? Piffle. When have I ever interfered?"

Tucker stood as she trotted out of the room. "I'll keep an eye on her, but solve this. Fast."

Eugene waited a few moments, giving them time to leave the building, before unlocking and opening a bottom drawer. He pulled a tablet out and set it on his desk. He'd always kept private notes during a case. Things he needed to look into, inconsistencies or nuances he couldn't explain. When he found answers, he jotted them on the pad.

—What prompted Mecklenberg to move to Chatham? Neighbors in her Deerwood apartment building had complained of too much activity in her unit and she'd been asked to leave. A private home would suit her 'second job' better than another apartment, and prices were cheaper in Chatham than Deerwood. College towns can be expensive. It also put some distance between her daytime and nighttime careers. Plus, she may have had clients in Chatham.

—Who were the people on her daily calendar? There were no clear answers yet, but Ben had come up with an idea staggering in its simplicity. Literary pseudonyms for clients. Eugene didn't believe for a second that the notion was Ben's alone. He'd probably gotten it from an episode of Columbo. It didn't matter where he got it, the suggestion had merit. Ben had mentioned Edgar Allan Poe and Ezra Pound. The moment Olivia said Conroy's name, Eugene had thought of 'The Raven'. Conroy had always reminded him of a crow. Could Edgar be code for Conroy? Nothing could be ignored at this point. Olivia didn't know about the photographs of Conroy in Cheryl's safe deposit box, yet she'd singled him out.

Olivia brought Sam Wallace's name up as a suspect as well. Eugene wasn't familiar with Ezra Pound's work, but did know the man was widely disliked. Wallace would hardly be considered a town favorite. If folks knew what Eugene did, he'd be run out of town. Wallace had been threatened with a rape charge. When the victim decided against taking action, Eugene had no choice but to drop the case. But he'd believed the woman and had kept an eye on Wallace. Tapes, labeled 'Sam Wallace', found in Cheryl's bank box, made it clear the speaker had money problems. Olivia confirmed that and fixed a dollar amount. The man lived beyond his means. He also, according to his victim, had a fondness for rough sex. Items found in Mecklenberg's house revealed a woman not opposed to filling that need.

The bottom line was inescapable. The victim had dirt on at least two men. Enough dirt to kill her? Maybe. But not before getting the evidence of their deeds. Was something missing from her cache at the bank? Could she have been a threat to someone else? Someone who destroyed whatever she held over him?

Eugene grunted. The address book may not have revealed any physical evidence, such as notes or prints, but it might turn out to be what cracked the case. That and Ben's theory and Olivia's…whatever she used. Instinct? Logic from a parallel universe? Would he end up going door-to-door, asking for fingerprints and typewriters? He would if he had to.

After glancing at other questions on his list, he locked his papers in the drawer, stood, and took the note Olivia had brought. It had to be logged and stored. 'Curiosity killed the cat'. Eugene's gut told him somehow this message would be the key. Olivia's prying may have opened the door enough for him to see inside the case. Monroe's parting words resonated in Eugene's ears, and he agreed with them. Solve this. Fast.

CHAPTER FIFTEEN

"Did your parents get off okay?" Josie asked when Olivia climbed into her car late Monday morning.

"Right on schedule. Mom's as giddy as a kid going to Disneyland and Dad's worried the stock market won't survive without him. Mom says he'll relax as soon as they're on the boat. She's an optimist." Olivia buckled her seatbelt and hoped Josie wouldn't drive too fast. "You sure you don't mind working on New Year's Eve?" They'd decided to forego parties in the interest of society. A murderer was on the loose, and New Year's Eve could garner insights. Josie's assignment was to follow Sammy. Where he went, who he went with, and what he did, could be a fountain of information. Olivia would tail Reverend Conroy. If either man did something hinky, it would be documented. The women might even foil a second crime. Holidays were rife with danger.

"Ben's coming with me, so I'll still have fun."

"Josie," Olivia said on a heavy sigh. "This is work, an obligation. You can't let hanky-panky distract you."

"I'll have you know I'm legendary for being on time and ready. Photographers loved working with me. I'll do my job, Livvy."

"I surely hope so. This isn't a photo shooting. This is a murder. You can't stand around woolgathering while someone takes your picture. You have to observe and record what you observe and analyze and make decisions and—"

"Whewy!" Josie waved a hand in front of her face. "What

wound you up? I'll observe and record and analyze." She patted Olivia's leg. "Don't worry, little buddy. I want Ben to see the serious side of me. I'll be on the ball like you wouldn't believe. Is Tucker going with you?"

"Insisted on it. He wants this murder solved as much as we do, poor thing. Since I got that note, he's always asking where I'm going and who I'm meeting. I think he worries tragedy could strike again. I keep reminding him, I'm lucky. But he needs reassurance or something." She stopped, thinking of what little she really knew about him. Instinct told her he was good to the bone. A kind and decent man. But his life hadn't been easy. Tucker carried an air of distance, keeping him a smidgen too far from people. Yet the smallest thing, like a pair of handmade mittens, thrilled him to pieces. Tucker was a tortured soul, she decided. It would be her job to heal him. "I think I'll knit Tucker a pair of slippers when I get time. He loves his mittens."

Josie looked at her and raised a brow. "I doubt he'd be so attached to them if someone else made them. If you'd use your feminine wiles, you'd have him eating out of your hand."

"What do you mean?" *Feminine wiles?* Olivia looked at her hand. She approved of Josie's decision to grow up in baby steps, but she could be a tad enigmatic at times. Like she knew a secret and it was a lulu.

"I think he has a crush on you, Livvy. You take care with him. He's got an onion, too."

"Good grief." Olivia slumped in her seat. She'd have to remember to buy more yarn. Tucker must like red, he'd bought a truck that color. Red slippers might make a terrific gift.

"I'm serious. He likes you."

"He's friendly."

"I mean like as in *like*."

"Don't exaggerate, Josie. He only kissed me once." Would she ever get over that kiss? She doubted it.

"*Kiss?*" Josie sputtered. "He kissed you and you didn't tell me? Wow. Tell all."

"Nothing more to tell," Olivia said, trying to ignore the

tingle in her stomach. Doggone it. Why couldn't she talk to Josie about this? They shared everything. But for some reason Olivia held her silence, as if speaking of Tucker's kiss would diminish its magic.

Josie smiled impishly. "When you're ready to talk, I'm here. Did you tell Tucker about Cheryl's other life?"

"You mean that she was a bit bawdy?"

"She was a prostitute."

"We don't know that for sure."

"Get real."

Sometimes Josie made her feel like an unsophisticated rube. "I didn't see the need to go into too much detail, so I just said the police believe she had eclectic tastes in boudoir activities." With a shake of her head, Olivia pushed thoughts of Tucker aside and reached into her purse. Pulling out some papers, she said, "Whenever you see a typewriter, stop and use it. Copy this exactly. Remember to have blank paper with you at all times. Then put the date and time and location on the sheet and bring it to me."

After a glance at the paper Olivia handed to her, Josie said, "How did you get that? Did Eugene give it back to you?"

"Nope. I copied the note on their machine when I told Punch and Judy goodbye. It's almost as good as having the original. I can still compare the 'i'."

"I never would have thought of making copies. Does Tucker know you did that? He'd be impressed."

"I'll tell him on New Year's while we're tailing Crow. If Rose and Conroy go out, I have to find a way to get into their house and look for a typewriter. I checked the church earlier today. Nothing but computers there." Olivia saw a sign and bolted upright. "Pull off at the next exit!"

"What's wrong?" Josie's face paled.

"There's a starving artist show at the Holiday Inn."

"You gave me a heart attack over *that*?"

Twisting in her seat, Olivia watched the exit as they passed it. "Why didn't you turn? I need to buy some paintings."

"We've got a lot to do today. If there's time, we'll stop on the way home." A smile quirked Josie's lips. "You don't need paintings, Livvy. You just want to help some artists. Probably con artists."

"Whatever medium they use, they're starving. And I do need paintings. I'm tired of some of the ones in my room."

"Whatever you say." Josie laughed, then her expression sobered. "I have sincere doubts about what we're doing, Livvy. But you need to learn what kind of people we're dealing with. When we get to Leather and Lace, I want you to behave. No screeching or carrying on. This is serious business."

"You already told me fifty times. I'll behave."

Josie had told Olivia she needed a lesson on the underbelly of the world, and they'd decided to visit a shop in Madison. Leather and Lace had a nice ring to it, but Josie said Olivia was in for a shock. Olivia doubted anything would shock her again.

In Madison Josie expertly navigated busy streets and pulled into a small strip mall. Olivia unhooked her seat belt. Before she could hop out of the car, Josie put a hand on her arm, stopping her.

"Don't buy anything. If you simply have to make a purchase, pay with cash. Don't tell anyone your name. Or mine."

"For Pete's sake, Josie. You're scaring me."

"Good. Remember, stay out of trouble. We won't be here long, but sometimes trouble seems to find you."

Olivia muttered under her breath as she climbed out of Josie's car. "Sheesh, she spends a few years in New York City, New York, and thinks she knows everything."

"Leave your hat in the car. It's too noticeable."

She hated taking it off, but had to admit Josie was right. Tucker's gift was a beauty. She tossed it on her seat. "Lock the doors."

The front windows of the store were black, with white lacy scrolls painted on them. A sign on the door prohibited anyone under eighteen from entering. A chill ran up Olivia's spine. Inside the store, she let her eyes adjust to the darkness. Josie told a man behind the counter they were just browsing, and he left them alone.

Tugging Olivia's coat, Josie said, "This way." She led the way to the back of the store and pointed at a row of closed doors in a dim hall. "Let me tell you what goes on in those rooms."

Josie's description left Olivia breathless. People actually did those things? In a store in a strip mall? She wished they'd stopped at the Holiday Inn. Starving artists needed her, and she was stuck in a shop hearing things she didn't want to know.

Next Josie took her on a tour. Books and magazines, all with lurid covers, stood on shelves and lay stacked in piles. Movies sat in racks. One wall displayed leather garments Olivia could imagine no use for. Who would wear pants that didn't cover their behind? Bras without centers? Pinned next to these items, sexy lingerie wafted in the breeze of a heat vent. Other garments, many of them uniforms, hung on a clothes stand. Why in the world would a nurse come here for a working outfit? The uniform came with a stethoscope. Olivia held it to her ears, but heard nothing. Her head swam.

A jumble of colorful packages captured her attention. Olivia went to them, picked up a box and motioned Josie to join her. "Edible panties? How on earth would you serve them? In a cone? Puff pastry?" Would her mother hear of this and have them at her next party? She could be quite a trendsetter.

"I'll explain later."

On a shelf below the panties, a pile of handcuffs caught Olivia's eye. Finally, something she could identify and use. Taking three, she said, "I'm getting a few of these. We may need to make a citizen's arrest. Not the cuffs with fur on them, though. They're just an ostentatious display of wealth. Even that's fake. The fur isn't real. Thank goodness no animals were hurt making those tacky things."

Josie took a handcuff from Olivia and opened it, then dangled it between them. "Worthless for arrests, Livvy. They don't need a key."

"Then what are they good for?" Olivia tossed the cuffs back on the pile.

"Games."

"Games? Like cops and robbers?"

"Something like that."

A crate next to the panties held whips. Another contained riding crops. Olivia blew out a puff of air. "I don't understand this store, Josie. Not one little bit. Nothing goes together. Are you sure this isn't some kind of Salvation Army shop?"

"Everything here has a sexual use. Everything."

Holding the box of edible panties to her chest, Olivia said, "Not these. These are fun, silly unusual gifts. I'm buying them. Someday I'll be happy I have a unique present for someone."

Josie rolled her eyes. "Pay cash. Before we go, I have one more thing to show you."

Olivia followed Josie to a row of what looked like exercise equipment. When Josie explained their uses, Olivia slapped a hand over her mouth to hold in a squeak. "Are you *sure*?"

"I'm sure. Ready to go?"

Olivia nodded and moved to the counter to pay for the panties. Pink, yellow, green, blue, purple, turquoise and red. Enough for an entire week. She wondered if they were really to eat, or to wear. If a person wore edible panties, how would she wash them? It was all too much to consider right now. She wanted to get out of Leather and Lace as quickly as possible. Looking at Josie, she asked, "Can we go see the starving artists now?"

An hour later the women exited the Holiday Inn, a man following them carrying three wrapped parcels. He fit the packages into Josie's trunk, tipped his hat, and left.

"Your bedroom is going to look like a flea market," Josie said as she got behind the steering wheel.

"Diamonds in the rough," Olivia replied. She shut the passenger door and grinned at Josie. "Little pieces of coal waiting for their value to develop."

"That's half right." Josie pulled onto the highway. "They should be burned."

"I hope Tucker likes the one I ordered for him."

"What's not to like? It's not every day a fella gets a gift

that tacky."

"How could a drawing of two of Tucker's favorite things be tacky? He can hang it on his wall and it'll make his house feel more like a home. Plus, thanks to his commission, a starving man will eat tonight. It's a win win situation." Olivia felt a twinge of worry. The artist said he could finish the project by the following afternoon, but she'd be happier once the future masterpiece was in her hands. She wanted to give it to Tucker before they set out to follow Crow on his New Year's activities.

❧❧

When he left the barbershop Monday afternoon, Tucker caught a glimpse of Olivia leaving a store on Main Street. He quickened his pace, but lost sight of her. How had she disappeared so fast? Her hat should make her easy to find. Retracing his steps, he looked into windows he passed. No sign of her. As he crossed an alley entrance, the hair on his neck rose and his blood felt icy. He stopped and stared down the narrow space, then took a few steps. The frost in his veins turned into white-hot anger. A man held Olivia against the side of a building, one hand at her throat. Her purse and a shopping bag lay on the ground beside her. The man had one foot planted on her fedora, crushing it.

In three long strides Tucker reached him, jerked him by the collar, and threw him to the ground. He cupped Olivia's head in his hands. "Are you okay?"

Her mouth opened and closed, with no sound coming out. Finally she nodded and looked at him with a sad and bewildered expression. Seeing her face, knowing chatty Olivia was speechless, filled every cell with rage. It felt like he was looking at the world through a red mist.

Tucker turned to the man, struggling into a sitting position, and grabbed the front of his shirt. He pulled an arm back, hand forming a fist, and hesitated long enough to savor the fear in the thug's eyes. A gentle voice spoke in his ear, and a soft touch caressed his shoulder.

"Don't, Tucker. If you hit him, you'll hate yourself."

"If I don't, I'll hate myself." He didn't take his eyes off the cringing bastard who'd manhandled Olivia.

"Please."

The simple word and tender tone broke though his furious haze. Tucker released the goon, flexed his fingers, and turned to Olivia. He took her by the shoulders. "Are you sure you're okay?"

"Positive. Sammy scared me for a moment, but then you came to my rescue."

"That's Sammy? Your ex-husband?" Tucker glanced at the pile of human shit sitting on the dirty cement.

"One of them. The bad one."

Tucker looked into her eyes. "Did he do this while you were married? Did he ever hurt you? If he did, I'll kill him right now."

She put a hand on his chest and shook her head. "Never. I think he's been drinking. And he must need money pretty bad, because that's what he wanted from me. I'm so glad you came along, Tucker."

He wrapped his arms around her and she buried her face in his chest. "Me, too."

"Now will you believe I'm lucky? You got here in the nick of time, just like a hero on a white horse."

Tucker fought a ridiculous surge of macho pride. "You're pretty resourceful. You'd have thought of something."

She raised her head and looked at him. "I don't know what. In a way it's good this happened. Sooner or later, you and Sammy would have crossed paths."

"Why would we have crossed paths?"

"Yin and yang. It was inevitable. Sammy's not good at much of anything. He can be a smooth talker if necessary, but that's about it. You're a manly man, and he's probably jealous of that. He'd have to act the rooster and goad you. Now he knows better."

Tucker heard sounds of movement, and turned to Sammy as he got to his feet. "Pick up Olivia's things," he growled.

Ignoring him, Sammy took a few steps toward the front

of the alley.

Gritting his teeth and trying to tamp his anger, Tucker grabbed him by the arm and spun him around. "I told you to pick up Olivia's things."

Sammy made a show of ambling to the items, then swooped them off the ground and held them out to her.

"Wipe the dirt off," Tucker ordered.

After a sideways glance at Tucker, Sammy swiped her purse and bag with the hem of his coat. He slapped her hat against the side of his leg, then bowed and held out the items as if offering a gift. Without a word, Olivia took them. She blinked several times, and Tucker thought her eyes looked suspiciously bright.

"See you around," Sammy told Olivia before strolling down the alley. He looked like a man without a care in the world. Tucker's stomach knotted and he took a deep breath before speaking to Olivia.

"What's in the bag?" he asked, hoping to distract her.

"A gift for my friend Anne. The one opening a flower store," Olivia answered in a small voice.

"Can I see it? Why don't we go for coffee, and you can show me what you bought her? Better yet, we'll go for wine and cherries. I'm in a mood for Chardonnay and cherries."

"Can I take a rain check, Tucker? Right now I just want to go home." Her eyes brimmed with tears.

"Sure, January Eighth. Any time you want."

She brushed her hat, then fingered a rip on its top. The tear looked like a large comma. "Look what he did."

"I'll buy you a new one."

"It wouldn't be the same. I'll take it to Pincushion Cleaners. They work miracles with mending and cleaning."

He reached for the fedora. "Let me do that for you. I know where the place is."

"Thank you, Tucker. I owe you one."

Her crestfallen expression was a knife in his gut. She didn't owe him a thing. If pressed, he'd say it was the other way around. He watched as she walked away, shoulders drooping, and felt helpless. Olivia, the epitome of sunshine and happiness, was going home to cry. He caught up and escorted her to her car, then stood on the sidewalk long after she was out of sight.

Two hours later Tucker stared at his computer screen. Instead of spreadsheets, he saw Olivia's disconsolate image. "Crap," he said as he stood. He grabbed his coat and slammed the door when he left his house.

Tucker marched across the bank floor to an office in a rear corner of the building. He stormed into it and saw a woman behind a desk jump. "Tucker Monroe to see Sam Wallace. No need to announce me," he told Sammy's secretary, then moved to the door behind her. It crashed against the wall when he threw it open.

Sammy, sitting behind his desk with his phone held to his ear, squinted at him. "I'll call you back," he said and hung up. "What the hell do you think you're doing?" He got to his feet and glared at Tucker.

"Olivia Chatham is the only genuinely good person I've ever met." He tried to keep his voice even, but the red mist was back. He moved to Sammy and grabbed him by the shoulders, slamming him against the wall behind his desk. "If anything happens to her, if she so much as breaks a fingernail, I'll kick your ass from here to Milwaukee before I even ask a question. Is that clear?"

Sammy looked over Tucker's shoulder. "Call security and the police."

Tucker assumed the secretary had followed him. "Do that. Then I'll tell them I saw you do this to Olivia earlier today. You'll be as welcome around this town as the bird flu."

He heard a gasp, then the sound of footsteps. The secretary came to a stop beside them.

"You pushed Livvy around? Sam Wallace, you're slimier than my sister-in-law's Lima Bean Surprise Salad. Just so you know how slimy that is, the last time she served it, her mother had to have her stomach pumped." She kicked Sammy in the shin with the toe of the sharpest pointed shoe Tucker had ever seen.

Sammy's yelp echoed in Tucker's ears, bringing a grin to his face.

"I've got to admit, Lima Bean Surprise doesn't sound very appetizing," Tucker told the woman.

"No one in that family can cook," she said, taking her gaze off Sammy for a moment to glance at Tucker. "Orville says I have beautiful eyes, but he really married me for my pot roast."

Sammy struggled against Tucker's grip. "Can we end the Martha Stewart moment? Get your hands off me."

Tucker released him, then picked an expensive-looking pen off Sammy's desk and broke it in half. Waving it under the other man's nose, he said, "Touch Olivia again, and you'll look just like this. Deader than Hoffa."

Wallace pointed at him. "Get out of my office." He swiveled to point at his secretary. "You're fired."

"Suits me right to the ground," she said with a sniff. Grabbing Tucker's arm, she gave it a tug and led him out the door, closing it behind her. "Whiny little pissant," she muttered.

"I'm sorry you lost your job." Tucker wondered what he could do to help her find a new one.

She gave a snort and held out her hand. "Joellen Poteet's my name. And don't you worry about my job, young man. I was leaving the end of the week anyway. Got a better job at another bank. Sam Wallace can make his own coffee from now on. He sure won't have much luck finding someone to take my place."

Tucker shook her hand and grinned. "In case you missed it earlier, I'm Tucker Monroe."

"I know who you are." She patted her hair, then crossed her arms and stared at the top of her desk. "Guess I better get this packed up."

"I'll help you and see you to your car." He grabbed a pencil off her desk and jotted his number on a piece of paper. "If Wallace does anything to get back at you, anything at all, I want you to call me right away."

"He won't do anything, Mr. Monroe."

"Tucker."

She smiled. "Tucker. And you call me Joellen. My Orville is a big man. So are my boys. Sam wouldn't dare try anything." She moved to a closet and pulled out a box. "Shouldn't take long to pack up the rest of my things. I've been taking personal items home since I took the other job." She picked a framed photo of three giant men off her desk and put it in the crate.

Tucker cleared his throat. "Um, Ms. Poteet, Joellen, I'd appreciate it if you don't mention this to anyone."

She dropped a vase of plastic flowers and gaped at him. "I got to kick Sam Wallace and you want me to keep it to myself?"

He tugged on an earlobe. "See, the thing is, it would get back to Olivia. She's not one for violence, and might get mad at me." He dropped his hand and met Joellen's gaze. "I'd truly hate to have Olivia mad at me."

"You've got a point." Joellen put one hand on her hip and rested the other on the box. Brightening, she asked, "Can I say I kicked the fool, but not why? That way I'll still be the envy of Chatham and Livvy won't be upset."

Tucker thought for a moment. He doubted Wallace would tell anyone. "Sure, that'd be fine. Just be careful my name stays out of it."

She rubbed her hands together and a look of mischief crossed her face. "This could even be better. Everybody will try to guess why. Rumors will fly and that's when things really hop around these parts."

Tucker laughed, enjoying her enthusiasm. Then another idea hit him. He nodded at her computer. "I suppose everyone here uses those."

"Oh, my, yes."

"So there aren't any typewriters at the bank?"

"Nope." She drew her eyebrows together. "Well, there are a few downstairs. It's hard to throw things away, and no one wanted to buy them. We put them in the offices that auditors use."

"Mind showing them to me before we leave?"

"No problem. I need to check those rooms anyway. Auditors are due in a month or two, so I should tell Susan if anything needs restocking."

"Susan?"

"The office manager. She usually handles auditors' comfort."

"I thought audits were a surprise." Tucker's warning system began humming. Could it be coincidence that Wallace was desperate for money right before an audit?

"Some are, some aren't. This one was arranged by the board. They do it every year."

"Interesting. Always at the same time?"

Joellen closed the box on her desk. "Usually in the spring. When they have a firm date, they let us know so we're sure to be on our best behavior. This year the audit is much earlier than normal. Ready to see the typewriters?"

Fifteen minutes later Tucker carried Joellen Poteet's box to her car and waved goodbye. He held five sheets of paper in one hand. A simple sentence was typed on each. 'Curiosity killed the cat.' He'd also noted the day, time, location, and model number of each machine. Olivia would be thrilled.

Chapter Sixteen

At six o'clock Tuesday evening, Tucker answered the knock on his door to find Olivia beaming at him. "Right on time."

"Of course. I'm very punctual. Can I come in?"

Tucker's cheeks warmed. He took a step back and ushered her indoors. Even though he'd expected her, seeing Olivia made all other thoughts evaporate. "Maybe we should play Hide and Seek. I must have lost my manners."

Her eyes widened. "You remembered my code with Mom."

"It should be our code, too. Let me take your coat."

"I need to get something from my car first. You have to turn away when I bring it in. But before I get it, I have news." Her green eyes sparkled and she looked like a kitten with a new toy.

"I can't wait to hear it."

"Joellen Poteet, down at Sammy's bank, kicked him yesterday." She clapped her hands and gave a tiny hop.

Something heavy filled Tucker's stomach. "Why did she kick him?"

She put a hand on his arm, and lowered her voice as if she didn't want to be overheard. "Joellen's being real secretive, but Mavis Waters was at the bank when it happened and says she saw it all. I don't know how because she's blind as a mat, poor dear, but she says it's true. Sammy groped Joellen's behind regions, the cur, and she hauled off and kicked him." Her voice rose as she talked, and she ended by demonstrating a kick.

The weight left Tucker's belly. He didn't remember seeing anyone in the lobby. Thankfully, this Mavis person must not have seen him, either. She sure as hell hadn't seen what happened. Maybe Tucker's luck was changing. "You don't say."

"I'm just reporting the facts."

"Wallace should have stayed in bed yesterday. It wasn't a good one for him."

"I just heard all this and thought I'd pop like a balloon before I got here to tell you. Now, I need a favor. You stay here with the door closed. Don't peek. When I knock again shut your eyes and open the door. Promise?"

"I promise."

"This is going to be the best surprise ever. Don't forget to close your eyes tight." Olivia dashed outside.

When she returned he shut his eyes and held the door wide open. He heard something land with a soft thud on the carpet. She closed the door and turned him away from it.

After nudging him a few steps, she said, "You can open your eyes now, but don't look behind you."

Tucker did as she asked. "You sure are being mysterious."

"You'll know why soon enough. First, why don't you show me around? I'd like to see your bachelor pad." In the living room, Olivia took off her coat and tossed it and her purse on a chair. "I sure miss my hat."

"You'll get it back soon. The Pincushion girl said two weeks, three tops."

Tucker showed her the condo, listening to her ohs and ahs as they made their way through his house. When they returned to the living room, Olivia stopped in front of the sofa and gazed at the wall behind it.

"It's your decision, of course, but I think this is the perfect spot."

"Perfect spot for what?" He'd never seen such barely contained excitement. Olivia had clearly recovered from Wallace's attack the day before.

"Wait here." She hurried to the entry and returned carrying a large package that had to be a wall hanging of some sort. "It's a housewarming, welcome to Chatham, gift," she said, holding it out to him.

Was she giving him the portrait one of her exes had painted? He hoped so, but felt compelled to say, "You just gave me Christmas gifts. I'm not sure I'd feel right taking more from you."

Olivia's face fell. "Oh, please, Tucker. I had it done especially for you. The poor artist worked like crazy to finish by today. It's not much, really. Just a little something to help feed a starving person and make your house more a home."

Obviously it wasn't the painting of Olivia. What could it be? Who was starving? Tucker reluctantly took the parcel and tore off the paper. Speechless, he stared at a colored chalk drawing of Bob Seger holding a bottle of Old Style. He coughed and tried to think of something to say.

"Do you like it? I thought it would be nice to have two of your favorite things to look at whenever you want."

"It's amazing, Olivia. The contrast is very creative." Tucker tried to imagine this hanging on his wall, and couldn't.

"Are you interested in art?"

"Not really, but I know what I like." That much was true.

"The frame blends real nice with your tables. I thought it looked like something you'd like."

"You know me pretty well." Tucker admired the heavy oak. "I'll need to get a special kit to hang this."

"Over your couch?" Olivia's cheeks were flushed and her eyes glittered.

He gazed at the blank wall behind his sofa. Keeping things stark had been his objective when he moved in. But if Olivia wanted the drawing up there, that's where it would go. He could avoid looking at it, or get used to it. He couldn't disappoint her. "That's the perfect spot for it."

Olivia leaned over her purse and reached into it. After pulling a paper from it, she crossed to him. "This is for you, too."

"What is it?" Tucker gazed at the paper, then at Olivia. "Where did you get this?"

"I copied it at the restaurant before we went to the police station with the original."

Tucker nodded. "So that's why your mood changed. I wondered why you were reluctant one minute and raring to go the next. Pretty clever."

Olivia straightened her shoulders and lifted her head. "Dad always says, 'Don't think harder. Think smarter.' He's a wise man. Mom says, 'When you run into trouble, make lemonade.' I'm not sure where she read that, but it's true. I take it to mean you have to find a way around obstacles."

"Well, you did a good job of that. I assume we're supposed to go around comparing this to typewriters all over town."

"Starting tonight with Crow. If we get the chance. Josie has a copy, and she'll try to get into Sammy's place to look for a typewriter. Fat chance of that, but we have to cover all our bases and home plate."

"Hang on. I think you'll be pretty pleased with me." Tucker went to his office and got the papers he'd typed on at the bank. Returning to the living room, he held them out to Olivia. "Our first five samples."

"Tucker," Olivia squealed, taking the sheets from him. "How fabulous! Where did you get these?"

"At Wallace's bank."

She stared at him. "How did you manage that?"

"Um…" He hadn't thought of a way to explain it. "I was making a deposit and an idea hit me. I told the teller I was looking for a typewriter and asked if they had any. I said I had a couple forms I needed to fill out. She took me to the basement and I got those," he nodded at the papers in her hand.

Olivia narrowed her eyes. "She took you to the basement and left you there? Which teller?"

"They were kind of busy. I think she just wanted me out of her hair. I didn't catch her name."

"Was she a bit of a stocky gal? With short hair and sensible shoes?"

It sounded good to him. He snapped his fingers. "That's her. How did you know?"

"Zelda Blumgarden," Olivia answered with a sigh. "Poor thing. She's so gullible. A real people pleaser. She'd do anything anyone asked. I worry that trait will get her into a tight spot of hot water some day."

Tucker could relate. "Should we compare the samples to your copy?"

"Oh, yes," Olivia said and turned toward his office, walking with a spring in her step. "We may crack this case tonight, Tucker."

Tucker watched her turn on his desk lamp, then lean over the papers with her nose practically pressing on top of them. She wore a black sweater tucked into black jeans. A belt, with her phone and tape recorder clipped on it, circled her waist. The sweater was made of some fuzzy material that hugged her curves. Her hair fell past her shoulders. He reached out to touch it, wondering if it felt as soft as it looked, but stopped when she turned to face him. Her eyes reminded him of emeralds, and he felt trapped in their gaze. A horse galloped in his chest.

"Is something wrong?"

Tucker cleared his throat. "Nope. Just wondering if I'm dressed okay for the mission."

She took in his blue jeans and navy sweater. "Just fine. Perfect garb for a clandestine, recon sauce gig."

"Any matches?" he asked, pointing at the papers.

"No, darn it to pieces. But at least we've eliminated a few typewriters. Do you have a file we can store these in? Eugene may need them when he closes the casebook on this miscarriage of justice."

Tucker reached into a drawer and pulled out an empty file. Olivia stuffed the samples in it, then folded her copy of the original note.

"I checked the church yesterday morning, and all they have are computers. Tonight, if Rose and Crow go out, I'll sneak into their house and look for a typewriter."

With a shake of his head, Tucker said, "Uh-uh. That's breaking and entering. Not gonna happen."

"How am I supposed to solve this without evidence? The Conroys aren't as easy as Zelda. We can't just go to their door and ask if they have a typewriter we can use."

"You'll have to put all your brainpower into finding another way. Don't think harder. Think smarter."

Olivia put her hands on her hips. "Am I going to wish I hadn't told you that?"

"Probably," Tucker said with a snort. "I'm not going to let you do anything illegal."

"You wouldn't be a stick in the fudge if I had a badge." She drummed her fingers on her belt. "I wonder if Eugene would give me one. Just until we solve this dreadful incident."

"You can always ask. But tonight you don't have a badge, so you aren't breaking into anyone's home."

"If they don't go out, it'll be a mute point anyway. We'll play it by ear."

Tucker decided not to argue. He'd tackle the problem if it came up. "Ready to go?"

"Whenever you are. Dorothy made sandwiches for us. They're in my car. That way we won't have to break surveillance for supper."

"Good thinking."

"Are you sure you don't mind spending New Year's Eve following Crow?"

"It'll be fun. By the way, you owe me a kiss."

"I what?" Olivia yelped.

"You don't have to do it now, but I expect one at midnight. Tradition and all that."

"Oh, my." Olivia's hands flew to her cheeks.

Tucker moved closer and put a finger under her chin, tipping her head up. Then he gave her a chaste kiss which made his toes curl. What was it about her that got him worked up so easily? Any contact seemed magnified a thousand times compared to touching other women. "That's for my gift," he said around the lump in his throat.

"What gift?" Olivia's eyes looked glazed, and he wondered if she felt what he did.

"The picture."

"Oh, yeah. That. You're welcome. Don't forget, I gave you a frame, too."

Tucker kissed her again, harder this time. He had trouble stopping. "Thanks for the frame."

"Tucker? Remember when I told you Ben and Josie got distracted?" She sounded like she'd just run a quick sprint.

"When they canoodled?"

"Yeah. I'm feeling like that now."

"You feel like canoodling?"

"No. I mean yes. I mean I feel distracted and I feel like canoodling."

Tucker took a deep breath and tried to steady his pulse. This was Olivia, not some woman of the world. He'd like to canoodle her better than she'd ever been canoodled, but that wouldn't be fair. "I'm not going to marry you, Olivia."

"I'm not going to marry you, either, Tucker."

"Then we'd better not canoodle. You've got rules."

"Doggone it. Another thing I never should have told you."

Tucker smiled and turned her toward the door. "Time to get on the job, Officer Chatham." He liked the sound of her giggle.

Staring at the picture in his living room, Tucker wondered what visitors would think of it. He didn't care, but did wonder. That reminded him of something. "I forgot to tell you, I'm having company Friday night. Can you join us?"

"Sure." Olivia reached for her coat. "Who's coming?"

"Jack and Amanda Lindsey. My attorney and his wife. They're passing through town and called to say they'd like to see my new place. I'd also like you to meet them."

"Are you and your lawyer friends?"

"We knew each other before my case, but not well. We found we have a lot in common while we prepared for court. I like him and Amanda. You will, too."

"Super," Olivia said with a big smile. "I can hardly wait. What time?"

"Come over around six. You can make sure everything looks okay before they get here. I'd hate them to see my socks lying on the floor."

"Don't be silly." Olivia moved to the door. "Remember to hang the picture before then. It'll be the first thing they see when they go to the living room. Isn't that wonderful?"

"Fabulous." Tucker grabbed his coat and followed Olivia to her car. "Sure you don't want me to drive?"

She stopped and stared at him. "Your car is red, red, red. Mine's better for this line of work. Besides, the back seat is full of our dinner."

Tucker climbed into her car and looked behind him. She'd said Dorothy made sandwiches. From the looks of it, enough to feed a boy scout troop. Heavenly scents filled the car, and he inhaled the aromas of spices and meats and other items he couldn't name.

Olivia snapped her seat belt. "Dorothy made a few side dishes and desserts for us, too."

"Bless her."

༄

Eugene sat in his office, putting finishing touches on his reports. One of his officers had uncovered new information on Reverend Lawrence Conroy. It seems he left his last position under a cloud of suspicion. Rumors, unproven, abounded that he'd had an affair with a parishioner. Armed with the incriminating photographs of Conroy and the deceased found in Ms. Mecklenberg's safe deposit box, and the negative reports of his past behavior, Eugene had him brought to the station for questioning earlier.

The interview went much as Eugene had predicted. Conroy admitted being in Cheryl Mecklenberg's house, and even gave fingerprints when asked. He and Rose had made a courtesy call on Cheryl when she'd moved to Chatham. They did that with many newcomers. Churches could always use fresh blood. He hotly denied the rumored affair which caused him to relocate. Questions about his relationship with the victim met arrogant disdain. Getting to his feet, and looking down his nose, he'd told Eugene he refused to answer any more 'unfounded, baseless and scurrilous innuendo'. Then Eugene showed him the pictures, and he folded onto the chair like a rain-soaked newspaper.

After assuring Conroy the conversation and photos would remain confidential, unless murder charges were brought, the good Reverend couldn't talk fast enough. Words flew from him like water from a downspout.

He and Cheryl had enjoyed a lusty relationship. Rose was hardly a passionate partner, and Conroy had preferences she would never consider. Their intimate moments were fast and predictable, like she had their sex life on a time clock. Cheryl, on the other hand, was open to experimentation and agreed to every act he suggested. For a price. Conroy considered the money well spent.

Conroy also admitted going to Cheryl's house the night of her murder. Rose had taken medication for a headache, and he hoped for a quick roll in the hay before she woke. But he didn't have much time, and Cheryl wasn't agreeable. Rather than try to persuade her, or offer a bonus, he'd left. She'd been aloof and haughty, not unlike Rose at times. Conroy's ardor vanished, and he returned home. He recalled that Cheryl had answered the door wearing a robe, but said he didn't know what, if anything, was under it. He hadn't known about the explicit photos. Cheryl had never told him about them, and certainly never attempted any kind of blackmail. After a pensive moment the minister paled and wondered aloud if she'd planned to.

Conroy estimated his time of arrival at twelve-fifteen, and departure no later than twelve-twenty. He hadn't seen anyone but Cheryl at or near her home. Eugene had no reason to hold the man, and let him go. Once cornered, Conroy appeared beaten. His voice had been soft, but clear. He'd met Eugene's eyes and didn't fidget as liars often did. Of course, he could be an accomplished liar and less likely to show signs of deceit. But Eugene felt he'd been honest. He wasn't eliminated as a suspect, but he'd moved down a notch or two on the list. Eugene set the report aside and took another blank form from his desk.

Sam Wallace's interview had not gone as smoothly. He'd arrived at the police department grumbling about wasting taxpayers' money and muttering insults regarding Eugene's competence. The sheriff took it in stride and left the petulant banker alone in the interrogation room for half an hour.

When Eugene entered the room and sat across from him, the whining began again. Ignoring him, Eugene put one of the tapes found in the safe deposit box into a recorder on the table. Wallace's complaints came to an abrupt halt. Eugene played both tapes and showed him the markings on their cases, identifying the speaker as Wallace.

"You can't prove that's me," Sam said. But his voice lacked conviction.

Unfortunately, that was true. He'd gotten the report from the lab in Chicago, and their findings were inconclusive. The tapes were of poor quality. Eugene saw no need to confirm Sam's statement, and had let that comment pass, instead telling Wallace he knew about the three thousand dollars he'd asked to borrow from Olivia.

Wallace's bravado returned and he informed Eugene borrowing money was hardly a crime. He refused to be fingerprinted. Undaunted, Eugene speculated that Sam's prints were on file with the bank. At that comment, Sam's face turned ashen, and he agreed to let the sheriff take them before he left the station.

"You say the man on the tapes isn't you. But mentioning your boss brings out a suspicious turn-around. Suddenly you're willing to cooperate." Eugene studied the man across the table.

Wallace shrugged, but his attempt at nonchalance fell flat. "Who would want their boss to know the police want his fingerprints?"

"Seems like more than that to me." Eugene went in for

the kill. "How cooperative would you become if I said your boss should listen to the tapes?"

"Please don't do that." Wallace wilted, seeming to shrink in front of Eugene's eyes. He wiped his hands over his face and looked into the distance.

Knowing people are generally uncomfortable with silence, and often feel the need to fill it, Eugene waited him out.

"If I talk, can it be confidential?" Sam asked.

"Depends on what you say." Eugene had already spoken with the bank's chief executive officer. He'd called immediately after hearing the recordings, and been told the man was in Florida. His secretary gave Eugene his phone number. Thanks to a whistle-blower, the banker already knew about Sam's theft. He planned an audit as soon as possible. An announcement to employees was in the offing, and steps had been taken to catch anyone attempting to return the money.

"I don't know what to do." Sam looked on the verge of tears. "Maybe I should call my attorney."

"If that's what you want." Eugene stood and stared down at Wallace. "But think about this while you wait for him to get here. I can't arrest you on theft charges. I don't have any evidence. Only a voice on some tapes. You can confess, and there's still nothing I can do. People confess all the time. We also need proof, and I don't have any. I'm after a murderer. If you didn't kill Cheryl Mecklenberg, it'd be wise to clear yourself."

"I didn't kill her."

Eugene reclaimed his seat.

"I got in over my head and borrowed from those dormant accounts. But I plan on replacing it. Why else would I ask Livvy for money? She's got that in her sofa cushions. I need to return it before the audit, and I've heard a rumor they're moving it up."

Eugene didn't want to listen to his self-justification. "Tell me about Cheryl."

He admitted a relationship, if you could call it that, with the victim. He also said he'd visited her that night. In fact, he'd arrived as Conroy was leaving. If he'd gotten there two min-

OBLIVIOUS • 177

utes earlier, the men would have run into each other on her doorstep. He'd gone to her place to plead for the tapes. At the party, Cheryl had offered to sell them to him, hinting if he didn't buy them, she'd turn them over to the bank.

"How dumb can a broad be?" Sam had said to Eugene. "I'm desperate for cash, and she tries to squeeze money from me. She was a fool."

"Now she's a dead fool."

Wallace had the decency to look ashamed. "I'm sorry she's dead, but I didn't kill her. She showed me her day-planner, and my boss' name and number were written on the top page. I shoved her away, tore the paper from the planner, and left."

"She could have just looked the number up again."

Sam's shoulders slumped. "I know, but I wasn't thinking straight. I was so mad I wanted to get out of there before I did something stupid."

He claimed he'd left her alive, calling him every name imaginable as he ran into the night. According to Wallace, he arrived around twelve-twenty, corroborating Conroy's time of departure, and left about fifteen minutes later. Wallace saw no one at or near her house except Cheryl and Conroy.

As with Conroy, Eugene didn't have one piece of evidence tying Wallace to the murder. After taking Sam's prints, Eugene reluctantly let the man go.

He finished his official paperwork, feeling something had finally been accomplished. He'd narrowed his list of suspects. Wallace had supplied Conroy with an alibi, but Sam still didn't have one.

He made one extra note on his private list of questions and observations. Although Wallace hadn't fidgeted in his seat, as liars often do, his eyes moved constantly. Never landing on anything for long, his gaze jumped from one spot to another like drops of water in a hot skillet, and rarely met Eugene's stare. Sam Wallace moved to the top of Eugene's suspect list.

CHAPTER SEVENTEEN

Although they'd had no luck with Crow on New Year's Eve, Tucker couldn't remember having more fun on that holiday. He usually spent it at a party, surrounded by booze-sodden revelers. This year he and Olivia had sat in her car, outside Conroy's house, and devoured every scrap of food in Dorothy's picnic baskets. They saw the bluish flicker of a television inside the minister's home. Wisps of smoke curled from the chimney. When a few snowflakes drifted from the sky, Olivia laughed and pressed her nose against the car door window. Tucker watched her, knowing no matter how snug and comfortable Conroy was inside his cozy house, no one could possibly feel warmer than he did at that moment. Olivia's enthusiasm brought him nothing but joy.

"Maybe we'll get a blizzard. Maybe we can go sledding tomorrow." She turned to him and rubbed her hands together. "Don't you just love the first real snow of the season?"

"Can't say I ever paid much attention. And I've never been sledding."

Her jaw dropped. "You've never been sledding? How about ice skating?"

"Never did that either. I'm willing to try a sled, but you'll have a tough time convincing me to lace on a pair of skates."

"We'll take winter sports one at a time, Tucker. Not to worry."

Unfortunately, the snow melted by the next morning. He imagined Olivia's disappointment, and felt its tug himself.

Damn global warming. Now, three days later, he heard her puttering in his kitchen as he looked out the window, waiting for his guests. When a car pulled into the driveway, he hurried to the entry.

Grinning and feeling like a kid, Tucker threw the door open and made a sweeping gesture, inviting Jack and Amanda Lindsey in. "'Bout time you got here. You used to be prompt, Lindsey."

Jack followed his wife inside. "One thing you should know about marriage, Monroe. Time becomes relative when women are getting ready to go somewhere."

"Don't believe him, Tucker," Amanda said as she shrugged out of her coat. "He kept me cooling my heels while he played with his Christmas present."

"What would that be?"

"An intercom system for the house. He's trying to figure out all the bells and whistles, and driving me nuts."

Tucker took their jackets and moved to the closet. "I can't believe you're still with this bum, Amanda."

"He's a work in progress."

"It'll take the rest of your life to whip him into shape." Tucker hung up their coats and turned to his friends.

"That's the plan," Jack said. "Every time she fixes one of my flaws, I develop another to keep her around. How have you been, Jailbird?"

"Not bad, Shyster. You?"

"Never better."

"Oh, that's so sweet." Olivia peeked around the corner. "The part about keeping her, not the part about Jailbird and Shyster."

"Don't give him too much credit for being a romantic. When we're alone, he calls me Brat."

"What do you call him?" Olivia stared wide-eyed at Amanda.

"Smart ass."

"You're small, but scrappy. I like that." Olivia clapped her hands and grinned.

Amanda's laughter filled the air. "You must be Olivia. I've been dying to meet you. Tucker sings your praises. It sounds like you're the bee's knees, as my mother would have said."

Wanting to stop this before it started, Tucker led the way to the living room and said, "Make yourselves comfortable. Can I get you something to drink? Glass of wine, Amanda? Beer, Jack?"

"Perfect." Amanda chose a chair facing the sofa.

Jack sat on the chair next to her and Olivia plopped onto the davenport. Tucker couldn't read Olivia's expression. He'd seldom seen her at a loss for words, but there was always a first. Amanda, a petite redhead, and Jack, the ultimate golden boy, could make quite an impression.

"What's it like to have a town named after you?" Amanda asked Olivia.

"Not me, a great-great-great grandfather. I don't have any brothers, so the name dies when I do. Isn't that a shame? I should have been a boy."

Tucker rolled his eyes, and Amanda winked. He went to the kitchen for their drinks, but still heard the conversation.

"That's a lovely drawing," Amanda said.

"I had it done for Tucker. He loves Bob Seger and Old Style."

"How thoughtful of you. No one else in the world has a picture like this, and it includes two of Tucker's favorite things. No wonder he thinks you're special."

"Mercy me." Olivia sounded flustered.

Tucker hurried to put their drinks on a tray and brought it to the living room. "Here we go," he said, handing the women their wine. Olivia beamed when he passed her a small glass of cherries, making him pleased he'd thought to buy them. He put Jack's beer on the coffee table and settled on the sofa next to Olivia with his mug.

"Thank you for keeping Tucker out of the hoosegow, Jack. He told me how clever you are."

"It helps to have an innocent client. One who cooperates. His case was every lawyer's dream. A slam dunk."

"Oh, my. I'll have to remember that. Slam dunk. That's a doozie of a saying."

Jack grinned and sipped his beer. His gaze traveled to the wall, then back to Olivia. "I agree with Mandy. That drawing is very distinctive. Truly one-of-a-kind, Olivia."

"You can call me Livvy. Everybody but Tucker does. He says he doesn't want to be like everyone else, and calls me Olivia. He's very unique in his oneness."

Jack coughed and set his beer on the table. "We have a lot in common. I'm the only one who calls Amanda Mandy. I guess I'm unique in my oneness, too."

"Definitely," Olivia said with a nod. Then she put her hand to her mouth as if surprised. "Where are my manners? We should bring your bags in. Do you want to freshen up or anything?"

"No, thanks," Amanda said. "We're booked at the bed and breakfast and already dropped our suitcases there."

"Bed and breakfast?" Olivia's eyebrows drew together.

"The B&B, Fluffy Pillows and Pancakes. You have to love a place called Fluffy Pillows and Pancakes."

Olivia straightened and grinned. "I named it for them. Only it's not a bed and breakfast. B&B is for bed and brunch. Scootie Greenwald's folks own it. I'm afraid they aren't morning people. Lance and Rhonda say if their guests can't wait until eleven to eat, they can go to the truck stop. I hope that's okay with you."

"It's fine with us," Jack told her. "Mandy and I like to sleep in, too."

Tucker saw laughter in Jack's eyes, and felt the need to defend Olivia. He couldn't let anyone, even a friend, snicker at her. "Olivia takes a personal interest in everyone. She's the most popular person in Chatham."

Olivia's cheeks flushed. "Tucker, you do run on at times." Turning to Jack, she added, "Just ignore him. I'm like everyone else. No better or worse."

"I have the feeling you're much better than most," Jack said, his tone sincere.

Tension left Tucker's shoulders. He should have known Jack would appreciate Olivia. Tucker admired the man. Always polite, always a gentleman, Jack had never lacked female companionship. Happy-go-lucky, love 'em and leave 'em Lindsey. Then he met Amanda, and nobody else mattered. When they looked at each other, Tucker felt the warmth they shared and fought a pang of envy. Maybe there really was one perfect mate for everyone. He glanced at Olivia, who watched him with a smile that could eclipse the sun. Something soothing crept under his skin, and he wanted to hug all three of his guests. Without understanding where the notion came from, he felt part of a unique club.

"I'm going to make snacks. Want to keep me company, Amanda?" Olivia stood.

"Love to." Amanda got to her feet.

"Do you like popcorn?"

Tucker's pulse jumped. "Use the microwave."

Amanda looped an arm through one of Olivia's, and they left the room.

Tucker turned to Jack. "Did you know if you make popcorn the old-fashioned way, on an electric stove, you can start a fire? Pouring water on it doesn't do any good."

Jack laughed. "Better hang on to her, Tuck. You look more relaxed than I've ever seen you."

Tucker thought for a moment. "Now that you mention it, I feel more relaxed than I've ever been."

"Olivia's not much like Danielle, is she?"

Tucker's back stiffened. "She's nothing like Danielle. Thank God." He paused, then continued, "After Danielle, I didn't want anything to do with women. Ever. But Olivia is a force of nature. She won't rest until everyone she knows is happy." He shrugged. "I guess that includes me."

"You're a lucky man. Don't blow it. For a great love you need to take great risks."

"Christ, where did you read that? On a greeting card?"

Jack grinned. "I don't remember. Sounds kind of catchy, don't you think?"

"Do you have to talk all flowery to Amanda?"

"If I said that to Mandy, she'd laugh for a week."

"Wise woman. She knows bullshit when she hears it."

Jack leaned forward and picked up his beer. "What's going on? A minute ago you were epitome of laid-back. Now you look tense. Legal trouble? Can I help?"

Tucker shook his head. "No, nothing like that. There's been a murder, and Olivia is playing super sleuth. I worry about her. People get hurt snooping the way she is. But she won't listen to me and butt out." He raised his mug and drank.

"Can the authorities do anything about it? Make her stop interfering?"

"So far she hasn't done anything illegal. She got a threatening note, and we turned it over to the sheriff. He's a good man. Smart. He knows more than he lets on. He also understands what Olivia doesn't. Someone who's killed once probably wouldn't mind killing twice. Not if it's to cover their crime. Eugene, that's his name, Eugene Strickland, is doing the best he can to solve this fast. Until then, I keep an eye on Olivia as much as possible."

"She means that much to you? Thinking of settling down?"

Tucker plunked his mug on the table. "No way. I just don't want to see her hurt."

"Sounds like more than that to me."

Feeling cornered, and desperate, Tucker rubbed his temples. Was it too much to want what Jack and Amanda had? Probably. Still, he had to ask. "How do you know?" He stared intently at Jack. His friend watched him with a somber expression, encouraging Tucker to continue. "How do you know you've met the right person? The one great love, as you'd put it?"

Jack shifted position. "It took me forever to figure this out. You'd better thank me for saving you a lot of time. All you have to do is ask yourself one question. Can you imagine your life without her? If not, she's the one."

"It's that easy?"

"It's that complicated." Jack smiled and finished his beer. "As you will soon discover, nothing involving your great love is ever easy."

"A monkey never sees its own tail," Tucker muttered.

"Excuse me?"

"Nothing."

☙❧

Clutching her package, Olivia raced to the back door and entered the kitchen. In her excitement after the starving artist show, she'd forgotten the panties she'd bought, and left them in Josie's car. She'd picked them up on her way to Tucker's house this evening.

"Sorry for deserting you," she said to Amanda. "I needed to get something from my car. I'm hoping you can help me."

"I'll do what I can."

"Josie, my best friend in the whole wide world, took me to a specialty store in Madison. They had the strangest merchandise. You're an innocent, so I won't shock you with details. Suffice to say, that place isn't for everyone. Hardly anyone. But that's beside the point." She pulled the panties from the bag and placed them on the counter.

Amanda stared at the box. "Oh my."

"Exactly," Olivia said with a nod. "Some of their inventory was very odd, but these were intriguing. I can't figure them out. They're supposed to be edible, but it doesn't say how to serve them. What do you think? An ice cream cone or puff pastry? I'd like to surprise Tucker with them one night."

Amanda cleared her throat. "I'd love to be a fly on the wall when you do. Hummm…let me think." She drummed her fingers on the counter. "Have you tasted them?"

"What?"

"Just a nibble may help decide how to serve them."

Olivia snapped her fingers. "You are so smart, Amanda. I never would have thought of that." She opened the box and pulled out the yellow ones. "I'm not partial to yellow. Are you?"

"Heavens no. Should we just tear off a chunk?"

"Why not? I wouldn't even know what utensil to use with these." Olivia tugged the panty, which ripped easily. She handed half to Amanda. "Here goes."

Amanda tore a shred off hers and popped it into her mouth. Olivia did the same. Then they tried a second piece.

"What do you think?" Olivia asked.

"Maybe I'm crazy, but I think it tastes like cauliflower."

"Me, too." Olivia stuck out her tongue. "Why would they make something so pretty taste so bad? Do you know anyone who likes cauliflower?"

"Jack."

"You're kidding."

"I told you, he's a work in progress. He actually likes cauliflower."

Olivia pushed the box toward Amanda. "You can give these to him. I'm so glad I asked you for help. If we hadn't tested them, we wouldn't have known how awful they are."

"Hold on a sec," Amanda said, raising a hand. "Maybe Tucker likes cauliflower."

"Mercy, what a thought." Olivia wished she'd never bought the panties. What a dilemma. "Even if he does, I don't want to watch him eat these. Jeepers, I thought I was buying a neat gift. It turns out to be a poke in a pig."

Amanda picked up the box and handed it to Olivia. "Run out to your car and stick these in the trunk. Put them in a dumpster on your way home."

"Excellent idea." Olivia clapped her hands. "This will stay between us?"

"Absolutely."

Olivia ran to her car, feeling she'd escaped a terribly embarrassing scene. Something had changed in Tucker tonight. He'd seemed more peaceful, more content than she'd seen him. He'd looked at her funny. Not bad funny, just different funny. Like they shared something private and special. She wasn't sure what caused the change. Only that it happened after Amanda and Jack arrived. Maybe their happiness had rubbed off on him. Whatever the cause, Olivia didn't want to do something silly and ruin everything.

When she returned to the house, she found Amanda finishing a glass of water. Olivia drank one, too. Gathering her courage, she turned to Amanda and asked a question that was probably rude, but she couldn't contain. "How did you and Jack get together? You're very pretty and he's very handsome, but how did you end up married? I'm messing this up. I mean, how did you…what did you…is there any one extraordinary thing you did to make him love you?"

Amanda's smile was warm and comforting. "I have no idea. It just happened. Are you in love with Tucker?"

"I think I might be. He's a wounded bird right now, due to a recent tragedy in Chatham, which is a tad difficult to explain right now. But underneath all his gruffness is a wonderful man. I just know it. And I love his courage and strength and kindness. But I'm not much, certainly not enough for a person like him." She fought tears. "I think I'm just dreaming to hope he'd fall for me. Josie says I should use wiles on him. Feminine wiles. But I don't know what they are or how to use them."

"They're different things for different people. In your case, I think Josie means just be yourself."

"Oh," Olivia said. A flutter of hope grew in her chest. "I can do that." She felt a bit awkward and wrung her hands. "Thank you for agreeing to keep this experiment our little secret. I've never been in a store like that, and only went for research. The edible undies were an impulse buy."

"Research for what?"

"A case I'm working on. With the police." Olivia heard footsteps coming toward the kitchen. "I'll tell you and Jack about it together."

Tucker and Jack entered the kitchen. "No popcorn?" Tucker asked.

"Good grief." What kind of hostess was she? "We got to gabbing and I completely forgot. I'll get right on it."

"No need. Jack and I decided to treat you ladies to dinner at the El Toro Marco Polo Lotus Garden. Feel up to it?"

"Oh, yes." Olivia gave a hop and turned to Amanda. "You'll love it."

"I'm sure I will." Amanda crossed to Jack and he draped an arm across her shoulders. "We love trying out new restaurants and foods."

"Tucker?" Olivia asked. "Do you like cauliflower?"

"No. Why?"

"I just wondered." Relief washed over her like a summer rain. Thank heaven she'd asked Amanda about those darn panties before serving one to Tucker. Looking up at Jack she said, "I hope this doesn't sound brassy, but you're very good-looking. I bet if the cauliflower people used you as their poster boy, more people would try it."

"That's not brassy. It's a lovely thing to say." Amanda gazed up at Jack, who looked perplexed. She patted his arm and smiled.

"You have such nice friends, Tucker," Olivia told him. "And don't you worry yourself over cauliflower. You're plenty handsome without it."

"That's good to know." Tucker looked like her father had when they'd gotten lost on the way to the Wisconsin Dells.

Olivia winked at Amanda. "Shall we go?"

⟿⟿

Tucker wondered what Jack and Amanda would think of the restaurant. It wasn't your everyday establishment. They seemed to take its eclectic décor in stride. Both sniffed appreciably, and said they were famished.

"Scootie," Olivia said when the waiter bustled over to seat them. "These good people are staying at your mom and dad's place tonight. Isn't that wonderful?"

He bobbed his head up and down. "I'll call and tell them to be extra nice, since these folks are friends of yours."

"Oh, piffle," Olivia made a dismissive gesture with her hand. "Lance and Rhonda are kind to everyone." Pointing at a corner booth, she asked, "Is it okay if we sit there?"

"Wherever you want, Livvy. I'll be over in a sec to take

your drink orders."

They made small talk while waiting for their drinks and examining menus. After Scootie put glasses in front of them, and took their orders, Amanda said, "You mentioned a police case you're working on, Olivia. Must be fascinating."

"Oh, it is." Olivia's voice held a quiver of excitement. "That was why I did the research I told you about earlier. It was in the line of duty."

"What research?" Tucker asked.

"Just a little something I had to do. Josie went with me, so you don't need to get all questiony." To Amanda and Jack, she said, "Tucker doesn't want me going places alone or without telling him. Honestly, my own father wasn't so persnickety about my comings and goings."

"From the sound of it, Tucker has reason to worry. He told me about the note," Jack said.

"Well, phootie. He's sure making a big deal out of that little thing."

"What note?" Amanda asked.

Olivia regaled them with all that had happened since the night of the Chathams' Christmas party. She told the story in great detail, albeit taking a few side streets along the route. Occasionally Jack or Amanda would interject a question or comment. Olivia's tale paused only when their meals arrived. When Scootie was out of sight, she picked up the narrative.

Tucker groaned when she mentioned his 'bereavement'. "I went out with the woman once, and didn't plan on dating her again. Olivia's turned Cheryl and me into a Shakespearian tragedy."

"I have not. I admit, at first I thought you two were having a glorious love affair. But then you explained and I learned more about Cheryl and realized I'd misjudged. Still, her death had to have been hard on you. Naturally you'd grieve. It's human nature." She rolled her eyes at Amanda. "Don't you get tired of men refusing to admit when they're sad or upset? Sometimes they can be difficult to read."

"So true." Amanda raised her wine glass to click with

Olivia's. "Do you mind if I take one of your cherries? I don't believe I've ever had them in a white merlot."

Tucker admired the way she accepted Olivia's quirks. He saw the corners of Jack's mouth twitch. Tucker wished the evening would never end.

"Help yourself, Mandy." Olivia slid the small glass closer to Amanda.

When Olivia related her theory of Cheryl using literary codes for clients, Amanda interrupted to say she thought her conclusions were brilliant. Olivia glowed at the praise, and Tucker wanted to reach across the table and give Amanda a hug.

"I don't remember when I've eaten so well," Jack said and rubbed his stomach. "Don't tell Hannah I said that. She'd probably quit."

Tucker knew Hannah was their housekeeper/cook. "Tell her I said 'hello'. I'd pay serious money for one of her peach cobblers."

"It'll make her day," Amanda said. She glanced at Olivia, and added, "Maybe I can talk her into sharing the recipe with Livvy."

Olivia bounced in her seat and flashed a grin filled with mischief. "Oh, that would be super. One more thing, would you mind telling the owners you liked the food?"

"Olivia's big on complimenting people."

"Helps keep their spirits up. So many people have problems we never know about. A kind word can go a long way. I'll take you to the kitchen and introduce you."

Jack got to his feet. "I'd be happy to tell them. Mandy?" He held a hand out to her.

"Would you mind telling them for me? I haven't had a moment alone with Tucker, and I'd like to catch up with what's new in his life."

"Sure. We won't be long."

Olivia nudged Tucker, and he stood to let her out of the booth.

After he sat again, and they were alone, Amanda said,

"She's quite a gal, your Olivia."

Tucker bristled, wondering if Amanda was being sarcastic. Snapping at Amanda would cost him Jack's friendship, but he couldn't let anyone insult Olivia. "Have you ever known someone truly good? When you scratch the surface, you find more gold beneath?"

"Just Jack. Until tonight. Now that I've met Livvy, I know two people like that. If I could bundle her up and take her home with me, I would. But I have the feeling you'd be on our doorstep before I could get her inside."

Tucker grinned. "You don't miss much, Amanda."

"She's lovely. Olivia's kept the fresh innocence so many of us lose. We become cynical, but not Livvy. Because of that, she sees things the rest of us miss. Her thought process may be unconventional, but that doesn't mean she's wrong. Suspecting someone of murder because they dye their hair probably isn't taught at any police academy. Yet she could be onto something. This minister has exhibited erratic behavior. She added Sammy to her list because she doesn't like him. Again, not the most logical reason, but her instincts are good. He's shown he's capable of violence. Both Wallace and Conroy were in the store the day she got locked in the dressing room. Either of them could have slipped her that note. Don't underestimate her intuition."

"I'm starting to believe her intuition is better than a lie detector." At times he'd wondered if his concerns were foolish. When Jack and Amanda took them seriously, he knew they were real.

It felt like a spider was walking up his spine.

CHAPTER EIGHTEEN

When Tucker answered his phone the following Monday morning, Olivia's voice brought a smile to his face. He'd tried to think of an excuse to call her all weekend, but couldn't come up with a convincing reason. Inviting her for dinner or a movie crossed his mind. He dismissed the idea before acting on it. That would be too much like a date. He wasn't sure he was ready for a step that big.

"I'm sorry, can you repeat that? I was distracted."

"Sure. Happens to the best of us. I asked if you could make it to my house for lunch today. Dorothy's going to be gone most of the afternoon, so Josie and I decided to meet for a strategy session. We need to wind up a few loose threads."

"What time?"

"Oh-thirteen-hundred-o'clock."

"I'll be there." The thought of Dorothy's food made his mouth water.

"Excellent. Josie and I'll make sandwiches. See you then!"

Olivia hung up before he had time to say good-bye. Where did she get so damn much energy?

Josie appeared when Tucker knocked, and he felt his grin fade. She waved him inside.

"Don't tell me Olivia's taken off again. It seems every time she makes arrangements for us to get together, she ends up missing." He stuffed his mittens in his pockets.

"She's here. Follow me." Josie hung Tucker's coat in the closet and led the way down the hall.

They reached the dining room as Olivia came through the swinging kitchen door. She carried a plate of bread and two bowls; one filled with raisins and another with mini-marshmallows. "Hi, Tucker. Great timing, we're just ready to eat. Can you find a place on the table for these?"

Tucker made room and Olivia set the dishes down. Somehow she'd managed to squeeze three empty plates, a bowl of potato chips, another of pickles, jars of peanut butter and jellies, napkins, three glasses of milk, one half full, and a gravy boat filled with what looked like chocolate sauce between more stacks and scraps of paper than Tucker had ever seen in one place. A notepad sat beside the partially filled glass.

"Spoons," Olivia said with a snap of her fingers. "Be right back. Make yourselves at home. Tucker, you're at the head of the table."

She swept away, and returned a moment later. A spoon went beside each glass of milk.

After taking her seat, she filled the half-empty glass to the brim with chocolate sauce and stirred. "Dig in before it gets cold."

"It's already cold, Livvy. They're peanut butter and jelly sandwiches," Josie said from the other side of Tucker. She faced Olivia across the table.

"Figure of speech. Help yourselves."

Olivia sampled her milk, now as dark as coffee, and nodded before setting the glass down. Tucker watched as she slathered two slices of bread with peanut butter and topped them with raisins. She sprinkled marshmallows over the raisins before dropping one slice of bread on the other. Tucker doubted even Elvis would eat that sandwich. He reached for the bread and peanut butter.

"You can use as many raisins and marshmallows as you like."

"I think I'll skip them and use jelly."

"Really? Josie likes her sandwiches that way, too. Frankly, I think it seems like a strange combo, but to each their own." Olivia took a big bite as she slid the gravy boat toward Tucker.

He offered it to Josie, who declined.

"Nobody else wants chocolate?"

"Not me," Josie said.

"I'm watching my figure," Tucker told her. Seeing how much Olivia used gave him enough of a sugar rush.

Olivia giggled and poked him in the arm. "You goose."

They passed jars and bowls until everyone had what they wanted.

"I'm so glad you could make it on short notice," Olivia said. "I looked through my case file last night and it made me kind of dizzy. I felt pixilated."

Looking at the pile of notes, which he assumed was her 'case file', made Tucker dizzy, and probably pixilated, too.

"I'm here to tell you, I barely slept a blink worrying about everything. So today's order of business is organizing. It's time to hone our skills and whittle all the data down to workable pieces of info. Then we'll tie it all together, put the pieces in order, and assign final tasks if they're needed."

"We're going to do all that this afternoon?" Josie asked.

Olivia wrinkled her nose. "Sounds daunting, doesn't it? We'll do as much as we can. Then we'll play Monopoly or something. All work and no play isn't healthy."

Olivia examined a pile of notes as she ate, then waved most of them in the air. "Good news. These are lists of things to do, but we've already done most of them." After aligning the edges, she sat them at the end of the table. "I'll hang onto everything until the perp's trial is over and he's locked up in the clink. Just in case Eugene needs documentation."

Tucker made another sandwich and watched Olivia sift and sort. Occasionally she'd mutter something unintelligible and make a note on her pad. Josie and he held a whispered conversation about the weather, shopping in Chicago, and her stories about the modeling rat race. She seemed content to let Olivia do whatever she was doing. Tucker didn't know what had made him stop in Chatham that day months ago, but sent up a prayer of thanks that he had.

He didn't know how much time passed, but the food was

long gone when Olivia set the pages aside and looked up.

"I can't thank you two enough. You've been an enormous help today, and I don't think I'd have gotten nearly this far without you."

"You know me, Livvy. I'm always here for you."

Olivia reached across the table and patted Josie's hand. "I know you are."

"Glad I could help." Tucker was rewarded with a sweet smile.

Olivia stood and began arranging stacks at the end of the table. "As much as I hate the thought of a murderer in our midst, I surely hope we find the killer here. The very idea of going through all this again in Deerwood, where Cheryl used to live, gives me a headache something chronic." She ran a hand up and down her neck.

Tucker stood and moved behind her chair. "Let that go for a few minutes and sit down. I'll rub some of the kinks out."

Olivia plopped on her chair and he massaged her shoulders, gently digging his thumbs into some of her knots. No wonder she wore a pained expression. Her back felt like a gravel road.

"Know what I think?"

She tilted her head back and looked up at him. "What?"

"You should retire from the force. This case is making you too tense. It's not good for you."

"Nope, we're almost there." She lowered her head. "There's time enough for relaxing once children and women and men are safe walking the streets of Chatham. Anything new from Ben, Josie?"

"Not really. They're going back and re-interviewing some of Cheryl's neighbors. One of them, Quetzi Miller, hasn't returned any of their calls."

"She's so shy."

"I know, but she should stop dodging Ben. It'd make his job easier." For a moment, Josie took on a thoughtful expression. "Did you know Quetzi's dating Scootie Greenwald?"

Olivia straightened. "No. You're kidding."

"Uh-uh. For a couple weeks now."

"I'm surprised I hadn't heard. Usually tongues wag with that kind of news." Olivia pulled Tucker's hands from her neck. "Thanks so much. I feel rejuveniled."

"They're keeping a low profile. I only know because Ben and Scootie bowl together."

"I haven't seen her in a while. Maybe I should pop over there some day soon." She looked at Tucker, who'd reclaimed his seat at the head of the table. "Would you like a dog?"

Now Tucker knew what pixilated meant. He could think of no other word to describe his reaction to this conversation detour. "Excuse me?"

"A dog. Would you like one? Quetzi owns The Cat's Meow, but she has dogs, too. And birds and turtles and gerbils. A cute little Yorkie would keep you company."

"Why don't we solve the case first? I have to be mobile until we get the perp sent up the river to the big house."

"Good thinking. A pet is a lot of responsibility." She slapped her hands on the table. "Okay, back to work. Here's where we are. Everyone but Conroy and Sammy have been eliminated as suspects."

"Ben says Crow's pretty much cleared, but won't say why. Eugene had him and Sammy on the hot seat. I guess Crow somehow convinced Eugene he's innocent."

"Piffle. I imagine Eugene's mighty weary by now. He's probably not at his peak performance level, and Conroy took advantage and droned on and on with some flimsy alibi. Crow's not eliminated for us. We need to get into his house and look for a typewriter. It all comes back to that note and who typed it."

"Ben says Crow told Eugene he doesn't have one. He and Rose got rid of theirs when they bought a computer. Sammy says he never had a typewriter."

"They can say whatever they want. We need to know for sure. A lies goes around the world while the truth is still pulling its boots on. Did Eugene or Ben search their houses?" Olivia made a note on her pad.

"No. They didn't have warrants and neither man consented to a search."

"Why no warrants?"

Josie made an exasperated noise, put an elbow on the table and propped her chin in her hand. "Both suspects deny typing the note. They deny knowing about the note. They deny seeing you in the store that day. Even Ivy doesn't remember if they were there when you were. How can Ben and Eugene get a warrant based on nothing?"

Leaning forward, Olivia said, "That note is important. I know it is. The case may hinge on it. One way or another we have to search those houses." She sat back in her chair. "Did Ben mention anything more about Sammy? How he reacted to being questioned?"

"He reacted like a sniveling little brat."

"And it's working. A squeaky wheel gathers no moss. He whines and the police back off and Sammy gets his way. No search."

Tucker finished his milk, wishing it were an Old Style. "What if you hadn't gotten the note? What would be our next step?"

"Good question. I don't know, but it doesn't matter. I did get the note and it does have an uneven 'i' and we have to follow the trail." Olivia tapped a fingernail on her notepad. "Josie, are you sure Ben's told you all he can? Have you used wiles on him?"

"Some, but not too much. His onion, you know. He says one of their problems is too much information. Cheryl had a lot of visitors, and any of them could have left a fingerprint or a hair or whatever at any time. Her sideline probably earned her a lot of enemies. Their suspect list is a lot longer than yours. It includes darn near everyone."

"What sideline?"

Tucker saw Josie subtly nod in his direction and look pointedly at Olivia. Ah, something he wasn't supposed to know had come up.

"Remember when I explained it, Livvy? That day we bowled and again last week. When we went to that store in Madison."

"Oh, yeah. No, I guess she wouldn't make many real friends with that kind of tomfoolery." She gazed at Tucker. "Josie and I learned a few things it's best you not be privy to. There are times it's best to let sleeping dogs rest."

"If you mean her prostitution, it's all over town."

Olivia's jaw dropped. "Really? Everyone knows? Egads, I'm out of the loop lately."

"My barber told me."

"News like that travels, no matter how hard the police try to keep it quiet," Josie told her. "You haven't been making your usual rounds, so it's understandable you wouldn't have heard the gossip. Neighbors suspected because men came and went at odd hours. It just takes one person from Eugene's office to slip, and the rumor's confirmed."

"Quetzi lives on the same street Cheryl did. When's Ben going back to interview her?"

"He's trying to do that today. I'll ask how it went when I see him tonight."

"Good." Olivia began doodling. "Can you also ask what, besides tons of cash, was in her safe deposit box? Whatever it was could be a hot potato. Yes indeed, a very hot potato."

"I'll ask, but I won't push. I don't want Ben to think I'm using him. He might drop me."

"Phootie." Olivia set her pencil on the pad. "He's not going to drop you, but I see your point. Just do your best. Any rumors about her box?"

"None that I've heard."

"The police must have a really big clamp on that info." Olivia stood and began stacking empty dishes. "Eugene and the boys can track down her customers and follow that purple herring all they want. I'm sticking to my plan until Conroy and Sammy are nailed or cleared." She looked at Tucker. "Would you like an Old Style?"

He got to his feet and lifted the remaining plates and bowls.

"I'd love an Old Style."

"You, Josie?"

"Sure."

"I'll be right back."

Tucker followed her into the kitchen. The outside door opened as they set their dishes on the counter.

"What are you doing in here?" Dorothy asked, coming into the room.

"Tidying up. We had a long lunch."

"You let me do the tidying up. Shoo now." She sat a grocery bag on the kitchen table.

"I was just trying to help." Olivia looked crestfallen.

"I know, sweetie. But it's my job and I want to keep it. If you do my work, I could get fired."

"Never," Olivia said with a giggle.

"You run along and I'll get this place back to normal in no time."

"We're low on raisins."

"Not anymore." Dorothy moved to the door.

"I'll help bring your bags in, ma'am," Tucker said.

Dorothy looked up at him, gratitude in her eyes. "None of that 'ma'am' stuff 'round here."

"Yes, Dorothy."

When they returned to the kitchen, arms full of grocery sacks, Olivia was gone. Tucker found her and Josie in the dining room, three frosty mugs filled with beer in front of them.

Olivia looked up and stood as he approached the table. "Let's go to my room. Dorothy will want to clean in peace."

In her suite, Olivia turned on the CD player, and Bob Seger's voice came from hidden speakers. She and Josie sat on the sofa. Tucker took the chair nearest Olivia.

"We're almost done for the day," Olivia told them. "We just need a plan to get into Crow's and Sammy's houses."

"No," Tucker said firmly. "I won't have any part in illegal activity. If you do that, I'll leave Chatham and never come back." *Right.*

Olivia's face paled. "It's the only way," she argued. "We

have to search for that typewriter."

Tucker slid forward and took one of her hands. "Listen to me, Olivia. You've done all you can. In the meantime you're missing out on local gossip and not making your normal rounds, whatever those are. You said you had trouble sleeping last night. Your neck is so knotted, I almost broke a couple fingers massaging it. And what do you have to show for it? Two suspects and no evidence. Let the police do their jobs."

Her eyes pleaded with him. "I know it's Conroy or Sammy. I know they're Edgar and Ezra in Cheryl's book. Sammy needs money. Apparently Cheryl had a lot. According to Ben, she lived above her teaching wherewithal. Conroy hasn't been in town long enough to know much about him. But he's oily. He's more fake than Tammy Faye Bakker. There's not one ministerly thing about him. Just a load of hot air. Why would someone like him, a man so full of himself he doesn't have room for anyone else, marry a woman like Rose? He'd want a trophy wife. She looks more like his mother. It makes no sense."

"There's no law against owing money or putting on a false front."

"I know, Tucker. Sammy's always spent too much money. But he's never been violent. Something's changed, made him careless. Maybe careless enough to kill. What if he asked Cheryl for money the same way he asked me? Without you to stop him, he could have killed her.

"Why should a minister put on a false front? A man of God should be more accepting of all people and their flaws, including his own. Why try to hide them? Why scamper around renting dirty movies? He's pretending to be something he's not. Maybe he's killed before and Rose knows. Maybe all this minister stuff and his marriage to her is his cover, his disguise."

"Tell all that to Eugene, then get back to your normal life. What about Kiwi? You said you haven't visited her in a while."

"Quetzi. It's pronounced Ketzee. Isn't that a beautiful name?"

"Adorable. I bet she misses you. And what about your

other friend? The one with the flower shop. Doesn't she need help getting ready for her grand opening?"

"It's been delayed. Some problem came up with the contractors and supplies. Isn't that always the way?"

"I'm begging you to drop the investigation, Olivia. Jack and Amanda invited us to visit. Why don't we plan a trip there? You'll love their house. It's almost as big as this one."

Olivia bounced in her seat. "That would be super! As soon as the case is solved, we'll go."

Tucker groaned. "What am I going to do with you?"

She grinned and leaned toward him, giving him a hug.

"Aw," Josie said. "You're so cute together."

Olivia pulled away. Her cheeks grew pink and she ducked her head. "I forgot you were still here, Josie."

"Well, I am." She sipped her beer and winked at Tucker. "Want me to go?"

"No, that's okay. We're about finished with work and then we can play Monopoly." Her gaze passed between Tucker and Josie, landing on each for a long moment. "The end is so close. When I went through my notes today, I felt it. I'm missing something. One tiny piece that'll wrap all this up in a big bowtie. I'm going to find it. But Tucker's right. I'm not being me. Rumors swirl, and I'm unaware. People I used to see regularly feel like strangers. I'm losing touch with those I love, and they may need me. I have to make my rounds. That's where I'll find the last piece. Somebody knows something. Murders don't happen in vacuum cleaners."

"Does this mean you're not going to break into Conroy's and Sammy's houses?" Tucker asked, feeling as if a boulder had been lifted off his back and replaced with feathers.

"It means I'm going to spread my wings. If an opportunity presents itself, I'll grab it. In the meantime, I'm going to mingle and keep my ear to the grindstone. Just like Eugene asked in the beginning."

"I guess that's some progress." Tucker shifted in his seat and put an ankle on his knee.

Olivia beamed. "After church next Sunday, I'll ask Crow

if I can study his sermon. He always reads them from typed pages. I should have thought of this earlier. He may write them at home. An uneven 'i' is an uneven 'i', no matter what word it's in. Is that legal enough for you, Tucker?"

"Be subtle." *If you can.* "Don't raise his suspicions."

"I'll tell him I was mesmerized by his metaphors. He won't suspect a thing."

⁂

Olivia was drifting off to sleep when her phone rang. She rubbed her eyes and lifted the receiver. "Hello?"

"It's me," Josie said. "Ben just left. Quetzi agreed to see him tonight, so we stopped on the way to the movies. I waited in the car. But he told me what she said."

"What did she tell him?" Olivia sat up and turned on a light, then pulled a notepad and pencil from her nightstand drawer.

"She was home the night Cheryl was murdered. Nursing a sick puppy. The dog was all she talked about."

"She's a gentle soul."

"Whatever. Now Ben knows all about that pup, but nothing more about Cheryl. Quetzi didn't pay much attention to the neighbors that night."

"Is the puppy okay?"

"Oh, for heaven's sake. Yes, the puppy is fine. Am I off duty now? I need to get some sleep."

"Don't let the bedbugs bite!" Olivia hung up and turned out her light. If she were an animal, she'd want to live with Quetzi.

⁂

Olivia spent the next three days making her rounds. Ivy merrily sold her several scarves, at Hendricks' General Store she bought red yarn for Tucker's slippers, then went to Ducky's Automotive Emporium to arrange tutoring for the stock market. Her father and Tucker took investing so seriously, but Olivia thought bulls and bears sounded fun. Anne was thrilled when she stopped at Flower Power and admired the improvements. When Anne began praising her husband, Luke, Olivia made a hasty retreat before too many details were revealed. Some things she didn't need to know. She had coffee at the 24 Hour Café, and caught up on local gossip.

No one mentioned Cheryl's safe deposit box, but most people were full of other tidbits about the woman. Her wide array of costumes was a hot topic. Everyone knew the police found Cheryl naked, hanging in her closet with her feet touching the floor. They agreed it was a horrible way to die, but took solace in the theory that Cheryl was unconscious when the murderer put the noose around her neck. At least she hadn't felt pain.

Olivia hadn't realized how much she missed her friends. There was comfort in belonging to a community. She decided she must be one of those people who need a routine.

Knowing she shouldn't set foot in The Cat's Meow, or she'd end up taking at least one four legged ball of fur home, she called Quetzi instead of visiting. Quetzi's voice, always soft, grew more timid when Olivia asked if she'd known her ex-neighbor. The change in tone put Olivia's instincts on alert, and she made arrangements to have dinner with Quetzi the following week. Deep in her bones Olivia knew this was important, but the other woman's schedule was too full to meet sooner.

By Thursday night Olivia was exhausted and ecstatic. She felt like herself again, and intuition told her she'd made progress on the case. When the phone rang, she answered hoping to hear Tucker. She had so much to tell him. Her heart plummeted when the caller spoke. It was Sammy, and he wanted to see her. Alone.

His wheedling didn't break her resistance, but his tears did.

CHAPTER NINETEEN

Olivia thought about calling Tucker to tell him she was meeting Sammy. She knew he'd insist on going with her, or veto the appointment altogether. How could she make him understand she had to go? Tears probably didn't move Tucker like they did her. She couldn't remember seeing or hearing a man weep before last night. Whatever bothered Sammy must carry enormous weight.

On the other hand, she couldn't go without letting anyone know where she was. What if someone needed her or an emergency reared its ugly head? Knowing Josie ran errands every Friday morning, Olivia left a message on her home voice mail. By the time Josie heard it, Olivia would be back in her room.

Olivia drove to Lake Nowthen and, after getting lost on the winding roads, finally found the cabin. Sammy said the owners were from Chicago, and left a spare key with the bank. It wasn't breaking and entering if he had a key. She parked beside his car, grabbed her purse, and climbed out of her SUV. The gray sky promised snow, and cold air made her breath vapor around her head. She hurried to the front door. Sammy opened it before she knocked and hustled her inside. She stuffed her gloves in her coat pockets and rubbed her hands together to warm them.

"You'll have to make this fast, Sammy. It's freezing in here."

"I just turned on the space heater. It'll warm up in no

time. Thanks for seeing me."

"Were your tears real?"

His eyes misted. "Yes, Livvy. They were real. Have a seat. I've got a lot to tell you."

Olivia looked around the dusty room. She imagined it was a wonderful vacation home in the summer, filled with people and laughter, but today it looked sad and lonely. Light filtered through the curtains. Rather than cheer the place, it accented the deserted atmosphere. She moved to a chair by the front window, next to the space heater, and sat.

Sammy settled himself on the sofa, as close as he could get to her. Their knees almost touched. "I have a confession to make."

Olivia's heart skipped a beat. She needed to get this on tape. Luckily, she'd clipped her miniature recorder to her belt before leaving the house. She reached under her jacket, as if scratching her back, and turned it on, hoping it would pick up sound through the coat. "I'm listening."

"I told you I need money, but not why. I'm afraid I've done something bad, Livvy. I could get into real trouble."

"You've already asked, and I said 'no'." Olivia wished he'd forget about the money and get on with the real confession. How he killed Cheryl.

"Let me explain, and you may change your mind. I went a little overboard after our divorce. Spent too much."

"You always spent too much."

Sammy ran a hand through his hair and took a deep breath. "I know. Will you let me finish?"

"If you hurry. That heater isn't doing much good." Olivia leaned over to look at it, making sure it was set as high as possible.

"Like I said, I overspent and got myself in a jam. The bank has dormant accounts. That means money people haven't touched in years. To pay my debts, I borrowed from them."

"Then everything's hunky dory. What's the problem?"

"By 'borrow' I mean took. That's illegal. I thought I could replace it before the next audit, but the board decided to schedule it earlier than usual this year. I need three thousand dollars as soon as possible. I'll sign a note. We'll do this all on the up and up. But I have to get that money back into the accounts. If I don't, I'm looking at unemployment and possibly jail." His voice shook, and he ran a hand across his eyes.

What a conundrum. On the one hand, she didn't want innocent people to lose money. On the other, she wanted Sammy out of her life for good. A loan would mean contact. He'd call monthly, explaining why he had to miss another payment. And he still hadn't mentioned Cheryl. Olivia wondered if she was wasting precious time.

"Did you know Cheryl Mecklenberg? The lady who was killed a few weeks ago?"

"No. Why do you ask? What's she got to do with this?"

"Don't lie to me, Sammy. You did know her. You were a customer."

"What do you know about her?"

"Enough. You saw her once a week until the first of December. Why did you stop seeing her? Did she break it off? Did your checks bounce?"

He sat back as if she'd slapped him. "I don't know what you're talking about."

"Fine." Olivia grabbed her purse. "You want money, I want truth. We may have reached an agreement, but you'd rather lie. Good luck with your dormer accounts."

He reached out to stop her, and she gasped, thinking he meant to strike her. Pulling his arm back, he turned his palm out in a gesture of surrender. "I'm not going to hurt you, Livvy. I'm sorry about the other day. You know me. I'm not usually like that. I'm sneaky and a cheat and just about every other rotten thing, but I've never intentionally hurt anyone before. That shows how desperate I am. Don't go. It won't happen again."

Olivia saw desolation in his eyes. "Will you tell me the truth? All of it?"

Drawing a cross over his chest with his finger, he said, "I swear I will. You'll loan me the money?"

She placed her handbag on the floor again. "If you answer my questions honestly, yes. Admit you knew Cheryl."

"I knew Cheryl quite well." He sagged in his seat. "It started last summer. After what happened with us, I needed someone. But I didn't want attachments. A man's got urges, and I'm no different. She took care of me, for a price."

"Why did you stop seeing her?"

"She found out I borrowed from the accounts."

Olivia narrowed her eyes and held his gaze. "You mean stole."

"All right, all right. Call it what you want."

"It was theft." She reached for her purse again. "By truth I meant you offer it with honest answers. Not admitting it when caught in a half-truth or lie or whatever that word is that means putting a nice spin on a naughty deed. Organism? Euphonium?"

"Euphemism."

She snapped her fingers. "Yeah, that's the word. No more of those. Just call a spade a shovel and we'll finish our business and be on our way. You get one more chance. One."

Sammy took another deep breath, seeming to collect himself, and nodded. "The truth, and nothing but the truth, from now on."

Finally, she thought. Good grief, what would she do if the tape recorder wasn't working? She couldn't worry about that now. "How did she find out about the accounts?"

"I told her. Dumb, I know, but I did. It was on my mind all the time. Still is. We were in bed, and like an idiot I forgot who and what she was. I spilled my guts. The bitch taped it." He snarled the last words.

Olivia tamped down the fear his tone sent through her. She told herself he wouldn't find her recorder. "How do you know she recorded it?"

"She told me the following week. I begged her to give me the tape, but she laughed and said she'd rather hang onto it. She liked the idea of having something on me. Cheryl loved making people miserable. I stopped seeing her and hoped she'd drop it." He snorted. "Like I said, I'm an idiot. She didn't drop it. She recorded the second conversation, too. Me pleading like a child. Listening to them made me want to puke."

"When did you listen to them?"

"The other day in Eugene's office. The police found the tapes and brought me in for questioning."

Ben told Josie they'd questioned Crow and Sammy, but hadn't given many details. Olivia assumed the tapes were the items in Cheryl's safe deposit box. Heavens to Betsy, those cops were a clever bunch.

"Does he suspect you of her murder?"

"No. Yes. I don't know." Sammy rubbed his head as if he were trying to get lice out of his hair. Then put his elbows on his knees and leaned toward her. "Listen to me, Livvy. This is the truth. Eugene knows some of it, but not all. That night, the night she was killed, was the same evening your parents had their Christmas party. You were leaving when I got there, so you didn't see any of this. Cheryl taunted me. She did it with a smile and made it look like we were having a civilized conversation. But what she said wasn't civil. It was the making of a nightmare. She wanted money or she threatened to go to my boss. That would have been the end of it for me."

Olivia's heart thudded and she placed a hand over it as if to hold it in her chest. "My God, Sammy. You killed her."

"No! I swear I didn't! You have to believe me. I did go to her house that night. Reverend Conroy was leaving when I got there. He didn't see me. Cheryl let me in, but only laughed at me more. She even showed me where she'd written my boss' phone number in her day planner. I tore it out."

"Mercy, the ragged edge."

"What?"

"Nothing. Go on with your story. What happened next?" If Sammy had left her alive, Cheryl would have straightened the edge of the paper. Olivia kept a close watch on him. Could he really be a murderer?

His eyes grew wet and it took him a moment to speak. "I pushed her. If she'd just shut up, stopped laughing, stopped threatening, I'd have left her alone. But she kept on and I went a little crazy. She tripped and fell and hit her head. But she was alive when I left. Knocked out on the floor, but alive. That's the God's honest truth."

Olivia couldn't speak. Words stuck in her throat. Tension filled the room.

"If I did it, why did Eugene let me go? Why didn't he arrest me?"

"Maybe he can't prove it. Yet." Her mind raced. "You left her on the floor?"

"Yes. She was breathing, but there was a knot on her head. I got out of there as fast as I could."

According to local rumor, and Ben's comments to Josie, Cheryl was found hanging in her closet, not on the floor. Sammy wasn't liked in Chatham, and probably hadn't heard the scuttlebutt. Testing the theory, Olivia said, "Maybe she died later. Maybe that bump on her head broke something inside and she passed away, lying where you left her."

Tears spilled down his cheeks. "Don't say that, Livvy. Don't even think it. I can't be a killer. I'm every kind of rat imaginable, but not that." He stood and walked to the window, pulling the curtain aside to look out. "I check the paper every day, trying to find out how she died. There hasn't been a word. I can't figure out why the public isn't entitled to know. Why are the cops being so quiet about it? What would it hurt to tell us what killed her?" He flicked the curtain closed and hung his head. "I can't be a murderer." It came out a whisper.

This was no act. Sammy's pain was almost tangible. Olivia got to her feet. "I believe you Sammy. I think you left her alive on the floor."

His head came up and he turned to her. "You believe me?"

"Yes. I'll come by the bank tomorrow and drop off the money."

He crossed to her and caught her in a bear hug, lifting her off her feet. "Livvy, you're the best. How could I have cheated on you?"

A tinkling sound rang out. Olivia's heart sank, and Sammy

set her down. He bent and picked a tube off the hardwood floor.

"What's this?" he asked, holding it in front of her face.

She reached for it. "Just a decoration from my belt."

Sammy pulled his hand away and examined the silver tube, then looked at her. His eyes held a strange mix of curiosity and rage. "Is this a recorder?" He wiggled its base, and his voice came from the device. It echoed in the room, seeming to bounce off the walls.

"Sammy, it's your turn to listen. When I came here, I thought you might have been the killer. After the other day, don't you think I have the right to be suspicious? Now I know you aren't the murderer. I was just being prepared, but we can erase the tape."

He threw his head back and cackled. "Women and recorders are going to be the death of me." His shoulders shook with his laughter.

Worried he was near the edge, Olivia wanted to reassure him before he went completely crazy. "She wasn't found on the floor, Sammy. She was hanging in her closet."

"Right."

"It's true. Have I ever lied?"

"You're a woman. Have you ever told the truth?" He looked at her through eyes filled with mirth. He tossed her recorder in the air and caught it, the smile leaving his face. "Want to know what jail feels like, Livvy? Want a sample of what you're trying to do to me?"

"What are you talking about?" Olivia took a step back, but he was quicker.

Bending at the waist, Sammy pushed into her stomach and straightened, holding her over his shoulder like a bag of cement. Olivia kicked and screamed, but knew no one was near enough to hear. He went through a doorway and into the kitchen. After moving the table with one hand, he kicked a throw rug aside.

"Ever see a storm cellar, Livvy? Or don't you have one up at your place? Nah, probably not. What self-respecting storm would dare hit Chatham manor?"

"Let me go, Sammy. Please." Dread and fear made it nearly impossible to speak.

He lifted a trapdoor, then carried her down a short flight of steps before dropping her on the cold ground. She scrambled to her knees, but was too slow. He climbed the stairs and looked down at her. "I'll be back in an hour or two. You just sit there and ask yourself one question. Do you really want me to go to prison?"

The door slammed shut, leaving Olivia in darkness. She heard the scrape of the table being pulled into place above her. Fighting panic, she reminded herself to breathe. The door didn't budge when she pushed on it. Something hard and cold bit into her thumb, and she stuck it in her mouth. She tasted blood and felt the wooden surface with her other hand. After locating a nail, she avoided it and turned on the stair, pressing her back against the door. Using all her strength she pushed, and thought the trapdoor moved a fraction. Hope blossomed.

She didn't know how much time passed before she detected a scent that didn't belong. An odor familiar, yet out of place and alien. When she identified it, terror threatened to overcome her.

Smoke.

❧❧

Tucker finished his burger and pushed the plate aside. He took a sip of water and turned the page of the newspaper lying in front of him. Someone stopped beside his table in the 24 Hour Café, then slid onto the other bench. Tucker looked up to see Sam Wallace staring at him.

"Sit somewhere else." He returned his attention to the paper, pretending to be fascinated by an article announcing the cancellation of Chatham's annual ice fishing contest.

"Let me give you one piece of advice," Wallace said. "Don't let Livvy catch you cheating."

Tucker didn't look up. "You still here?"

"What are you going to do? Beat me up? In front of all

these people?"

"Not if you leave. Now."

"You should thank me. I'm helping your future ex-wife."

"Olivia doesn't need your help." Tucker folded his paper and reached for his coat. Sitting close to Wallace made him want a shower. Snide comments about Olivia made him want to shove a fist into Wallace's nose. The shower seemed wiser.

"She's getting it anyway. I'm curing her of one of her fears."

"She has no fear." Didn't that say it all? He'd feel better if she did.

"You've never seen her in cramped quarters. That gal is so claustrophobic she's contagious with it."

Tucker released his coat and dropped all pretense of politely conversing with Wallace. "What did you do to her?"

Wallace leaned back and crossed his arms over his chest, a smug grin on his face. "They have storm cellars wherever the hell you're from, Monroe?"

Tucker moved faster than he thought possible. Before anyone could react he hauled Wallace out of his seat and followed his earlier instinct. Sam fell to the floor, blood flowing from his rearranged nose. He struggled to lean on an elbow and brought a hand to his face.

"You son of a bitch," he snarled. "You'll pay for this." Glancing up he called, "Someone bring me a towel."

"Oh look," came a voice from the next table. "Sam Wallace tripped."

"He should be more careful," another patron commented.

Other than positioning chairs for a better view, no one moved.

Tucker grabbed a fistful of Sam's jacket and hauled him to his feet. Bringing his face close to the other man's, he growled, "Where is Olivia?"

A siren broke the silence, seeming to send an electrical current through the café. The atmosphere felt charged, and Tucker's pulse kicked up a notch. He shook Wallace. "Where is Olivia?" he repeated through clenched teeth.

"Got your scanner on, Chester?" someone yelled.

"Yep," a man behind the counter replied. "Fire out at one of the lake cabins."

"Summer people." The tone made it sound like they carried a disease.

"Space heater," Wallace whispered. Color leached from his face. "I didn't shut it off."

A fire truck lumbered past the restaurant. Tucker shoved Wallace aside. His heart beat so hard it felt like an entire orchestra played in his chest. "Tell them Olivia's in the cabin, in the storm cellar," he shouted as he raced to the door.

CHAPTER TWENTY

Olivia heard footsteps above and called out. A moment later scratching sounds came from overhead.

"Hang on, Livvy. I'm here," Josie yelled.

"Hurry! What's burning?"

Something thudded and the door opened. Josie reached a hand down to Olivia. She squinted against the bright kitchen light and lunged out of her prison, landing on her belly on the floor. Josie looped an arm under one of hers and tugged.

"Move, Livvy. The cabin's on fire."

Ben appeared in the doorway to the living room. "It's burning fast. We've got to get out of here." He lifted Olivia from the other side and together he and Josie half carried, half dragged her outside.

When they were safely clear of the building, all three dropped to the ground and stared at the flames. Olivia didn't know if it had started snowing, or if the specks flying everywhere were ashes.

She hugged Josie, then Ben. "You saved my life." Emotion choked her voice.

"We sure did, little buddy." Josie put an arm around her.

"I'm no expert, but the front drapes are almost gone. I think that's where it started," Ben said.

Olivia shivered. "Sammy had a space heater near them."

Ben lifted a leather strap from around his neck and gave Olivia her handbag. "You women go a little crazy when you lose one of these."

"Oh, Ben. You thought to grab my purse. Even in the face of a blazing fire." She looked at Josie. "He's a treasure."

"You can say that again. Hands off, Livvy. Ben's mine."

Olivia glanced at Ben and stifled a laugh. She'd never seen a deeper shade of red on anyone's face. Who'd have thought Josie and Ben would become the perfect couple? She supposed a pairing like theirs was one of those mysteries of the heart.

They sat on the frozen earth, arms around each other, and watched flames crawl up one side of the cabin and lick at the roof. Olivia heard sirens in the distance, closing fast.

"How did you know I was here?"

"You left a message saying you were meeting Sammy at a bank customer's cabin. I called the bank and they told me which keys were missing. I guess it's common for folks to leave keys with the bank. In case maintenance is needed or there's an emergency."

"Pretty smart, Josie."

"Damn straight. I'm starting to think like you."

"It's a good thing." Olivia squeezed Josie's shoulder.

"Then I called Ben and told him to meet me here. We didn't even have to break in. Sammy left the door unlocked."

"That saved precious time." Olivia shuddered at the thought of dying in that cramped cellar. Of suffocating on smoke while gasping for air.

"What got into you, Livvy? Why would you agree to meet Sammy?"

"He cried, and I couldn't take it."

"You could have met him in a public place."

"Sammy wanted to meet here, and I agreed because I thought he'd talk more if we were alone. Jiminy Cricket, I was right! He told me everything and it's all on ta…" She stared at the fiery cabin. "I have an excellent memory."

Eugene's cruiser screamed to a stop, two squad cars and an ambulance right behind it. Fire trucks brought up the rear of the impromptu parade. In minutes the area filled with people. Ben got to his feet. Olivia and Josie followed suit.

"Who's injured?" someone asked as he approached. He

and his companion carried medical bags. Eugene trotted up to them.

"No one," Olivia replied. "Josie and Ben saved my life, Eu...Sheriff."

"Ben did most of it." Josie elbowed Olivia, and she nodded approval at her friend. Let him take the credit in front of everyone. He'd be the town hero.

"Nah," Ben said, blushing from his neck to his hairline. "Josie's the one who saved the day."

More people arrived. "Keep them back," Eugene told the other cops before turning to the medics. "Take Livvy to the ambulance and check her over."

"I'm fine," she said.

"Procedure," he told her, a gentle expression on his face. "I'm surprised you didn't know that, being an honorary officer and all."

Olivia's heart nearly stopped. It was the nicest thing he could have said. She blinked away tears and wished Tucker had heard. She looked at the growing mob, wondering if he was among them. "Oh, yeah. I forgot that rule."

Eugene patted her shoulder. "I'll need to talk to you later, honey. You go with these men and let them do their jobs."

Olivia walked between the medics, who she now recognized as Mike and Archie Simpson, brothers as well as best friends. When they reached the ambulance Mike opened the back doors and patted the vehicle's floor. "Hop up, Livvy. You look okay, but we need to check you out. What's wrong with your hand?"

Olivia looked at her bloody thumb. "A nail pricked me. No biggie."

"You'll need a tetanus shot."

"No, thanks. I hate shots."

"Sorry, but you have to get one."

"Nuts."

"My nickname is Painless." He smiled at her and opened his bag. "I'll do the injection last." He held a light to one of her eyes and squinted as he studied it.

Wanting to forget the shot looming in her immediate future, Olivia surveyed the scene. Lights from official vehicles twinkled overhead, bathing the area in an almost festive glow. Thankfully the cabins were spread well apart. Flames leaped to a few trees, but were quickly doused by firemen carrying hoses. The air grew thick with smoke, and the scent was musty and dank. Nothing like a bonfire.

The little cottage was ruined. No one would laugh or cry or play games or share family moments in it again. Maybe the owners would rebuild.

Town folk straggled up to the site. Police kept them at a distance from both the cabin and her, but Olivia had a smile and a wave for everyone. If not for the smell and the smoke and the water, it would feel like a party. A breeze carried wet mist across the scene, and Olivia lifted her face to it, enjoying its refreshing spray.

Mike tapped her on the arm. "It's time. Can you take off one side of your coat and roll up your sleeve?"

Olivia did as he asked, saying whatever popped into her head as she tried to focus on anything but the needle he held. She didn't know what she said, but appreciated the way he nodded and pretended she made sense.

≈≈

Tucker stood on his brakes and shifted into park. The car rocked when he hopped out. He shoved his way through the crowd, eyes on the inferno in front of him. Loud noises filled his ears, like the screams of men in war movies. When people backed away, and looked at him with alarm, he realized the sounds came from him. One sentence repeated over and over in his mind, rising to a crescendo. *Olivia's in there. Olivia's in there.* A window shattered and a tongue of fire shot out. Tucker ran toward the building. He ignored hands grabbing at him, trying to hold him back. Then a familiar voice broke through his haze.

"Tucker," Josie said. "Wait."

He looked down to see her standing in front of him, hands

on his chest. Gently moving them away, he said, "Olivia's in there. I have to get her out."

"No, she isn't. That's what I'm trying to tell you. She's fine." Josie pointed at the ambulance. "She's over there."

Tucker's gaze jumped around until he saw Olivia. His knees nearly buckled. She sat on the floor of the vehicle, legs dangling over the edge, merrily chatting as someone gave her a shot.

Ben waved him through the police line and he walked to the ambulance slowly, savoring the sight like a parched man eyeing a clear stream. Relief and anger battled inside him. How many times had he told her not to go running around without telling him? What in the world was she doing in a cabin at Lake Nowthen? How the hell had Wallace gotten involved? Questions tumbled in his mind. By the time he reached Olivia, his patience had evaporated. If one of the medics stuck a thermometer in his mouth, the back of it would explode and mercury would fly out the end.

Olivia saw him and broke off mid-sentence. Then she grinned and began swinging her legs, nearly kicking one of the men beside her. "Tucker! You won't believe—"

"What the hell is going on?" he interrupted.

"Quite a lot. The best part is Eugene called me an honorary officer. Isn't that wonderful?"

"I'm so happy, I could wet myself."

Her smile disappeared. "You almost sound angry."

"You were specifically told not to go off on your own. What part of that didn't you understand? You owe me an explanation and I want it now."

"Told? Specifically told? I owe you an explanation?" She pulled her coat up her arm and looked at the man who'd given her a shot. "Thank you very much, Mike. Now I know why they call you Painless. You're very gifted with a needle." After hopping off her perch, she stomped away.

"That's not the way to handle Livvy," Mike said.

"Enlighten me. What is the way to handle her?"

"I don't know, but that ain't it." He snapped his black bag

shut.

Tucker followed her, calling her name. She kept moving forward, never giving a backward glance.

"Olivia!" Tucker quickened his pace and caught up with her, stopping her by gently taking her arm.

She turned to him. "I'm not speaking to you."

"Then listen."

"I've done nothing but listen to men all the live long day."

"Put yourself in my place. How would you feel? I thought you were in there." He pointed at what was left of the cabin.

"I'd be happy you weren't in there. That you're okay. That's how I'd feel if I were in your place."

"I *am* happy you're okay."

"Then why are you acting so mad? Why did you yell at me?"

"Because I asked you nicely not to go off by yourself, and you did it anyway. That could have gotten you killed."

A small smile quirked her lips. "Don't be silly. You know I'm lucky. I've told you that several times."

Tucker made a strangled noise and pulled at his hair. He took her by the shoulders and turned her toward the cabin. "Look at that. I thought you were *in* there. I didn't think of luck. All I could think was how to get you out."

Facing him again, she said, "Oh, Tucker. You were worried about me."

"Yes, Olivia. I was worried about you. Don't ever scare me like that again."

"I won't."

"Right. Until the next time."

With a sigh, he wrapped her in a hug. His spirits soared when he felt her arms circle his waist. "We may have to get married."

"What?" she squealed and tried to pull away.

He held on. "It's probably the best way to keep you out of trouble."

"I think you're just feeling frisky."

She had no idea. He'd love nothing more than to canoodle

that very moment.

"Are you turning me down? You've married every other Tom, Dick and Harry. What's wrong with me?" He couldn't figure out why he'd said that. He had no intention of marrying. The words popped out of his mouth without permission.

"That's Josie. I married Eric, Victor and Sammy."

"Forget about them. Why not me?"

"Phootie. A worldly man such as yourself wouldn't want to be stuck with the likes of me."

What was she talking about? "You think there's something wrong with you? I promise, except for your tendency to ignore those concerned for your safety, there isn't one darn thing wrong with you."

"Marriage without love is wrong."

"Don't you love me?"

"Of course I do."

He barely heard her whispered words, but he did, and wanted to shout with joy. She pulled her head back and looked at him expectantly. He couldn't say what he knew she wanted to hear. How could he when he wasn't certain it was true? "Then what's the problem?" This was the most ridiculous conversation he'd ever had.

"You only want to be married for one night, and I don't want to get a divorce in the morning." Soot covered her cheeks and she looked on the verge of tears. "I don't want to talk about this anymore. Can I go home? All this smoke is making my eyes leak. You probably think I'm crying, but I'm not."

He kissed her forehead. "Sure, January Eighth. I'll drive you. We'll come back for your car later."

She sagged against him. "That sounds heavenly. I'm tired and cold and hungry and dirty. Will you find Eugene and tell him I'll answer any questions he has tonight or tomorrow?"

"Yep. You go wait in my car." Reluctantly, he let go of her.

"Don't tarry, okay? This place is pandemonium." She looked more closely at him. "Wait a second. Where is your coat? Your mittens?"

Tucker held a hand to his ear, as if he hadn't heard her.

"I'll be right back," he called.

Rather than dispersing as the fire weakened, more people arrived in a steady stream. Tucker found it difficult to comprehend so many folks lived in Chatham. He saw Scootie, who seemed to be looking for something or someone. Ivy stood next to Ducky, both of them searching the area. A small boy between them kept pushing his glasses up his nose. A lady he recognized from the day he'd had coffee with Olivia, Nadine, surveyed the crowd. A boy on a bike waited at her side. Yvonne, the waitress from The Mill, examined the scene. Beside her a young woman holding a flute did the same. He recognized Lance and Rhonda from the B&B, Fluffy Pillows and Pancakes. Punch and Judy, owners of the Restaurant, were also in attendance. Many more he didn't recognize filtered up. Most glanced at the ruined cottage, then explored the area.

"There she is," someone called.

As if choreographed, the large group moved toward Olivia. Within moments they'd surrounded her, gathering her into their fold. Dumbstruck, Tucker stood frozen in place. He'd never seen anything like this. How many people would turn up if he needed help? Only one. Olivia. That, he decided, said it all.

"I told you everyone likes Livvy. Under any other circumstances, you'd have to serve free food and booze to get all these people together in one place. Word got out she was in danger," Eugene said.

Tucker hadn't heard him approach. "Until today, I never believed one person could make much difference. I may have to change the way I live."

"One person can make all the difference in the world." Eugene cleared his throat. "Got time to answer a few questions?"

"Sure. By the look of things, I've got plenty of time. Olivia won't leave until she's had a word with everybody. Wouldn't want to hurt anyone's feelings."

"The way I hear it, you punched Sam Wallace around the time the alarms sounded. You shouted that Livvy was in the storm cellar here and ran from the café like a bat out of hell. That right?"

Taking his gaze off Olivia's bright smile, and the happy group around her, Tucker turned to Eugene. "He came in and sat at my table, all pleased with himself. I told him to go away, and he said he was curing Olivia of one of her fears. She only has one that I know of. Claustrophobia. I convinced him to tell me what he'd done."

Tucker told Eugene the rest of the story, ending, "I wanted to kill him. I wanted him deader than Hoffa. As if claustrophobia weren't bad enough, she was trapped in a burning building. Can you imagine the terror? It's a wonder she can function at all right now."

"People do amazing things. You can't predict them. Not really. But I better warn you, this will probably catch up to her in an hour or two. Once everything settles down, and she has time to think, she'll feel like a mule kicked her."

"I know. I'm taking her home. Dorothy and I'll stay with her. Can one of your boys drive her car to the house?"

Eugene glanced at the people still milling about. "We'll have so many volunteers we may have to hold a raffle. First prize, drive Livvy's car home for her."

Tucker smiled, his first in what felt like years. "Is Wallace locked up?"

"Not yet." Eugene scratched his cheek. "He took advantage of the hubbub at the café and took off. We'll find him, though. The bulletin went statewide."

"Probably find him under his bed, crying like a little girl."

"I'll remember to look there," the sheriff said with a chuckle. "Listen, can you tell Livvy I'll be out to see her in the morning? No need putting her through the ordeal again tonight. Besides, I'll be busy finding and booking Wallace. Now I've got a reason for a warrant, I can go through his apartment and car. Maybe find evidence for the Mecklenberg murder."

"Will do." Tucker took a step away, then stopped. "Eugene?"

The sheriff looked at him with raised eyebrows.

"I just wanted you to know, calling Olivia an honorary officer was about the best thing you could have done for her. After all that happened today, that's the first thing she told me."

"I'll be damned." A grin spread across Eugene's face and he shook his head. "Sometimes I accidentally stumble onto the right words."

"You can put the hick cop act away, Sheriff. You know exactly what you're doing all the time, and my wager is it's almost always the right thing." Tucker brought a hand to his brow, as if saluting, and grinned.

Eugene's face reddened, and he quickly strode away, barking orders in a gruff tone.

Tucker found Ben and Josie. He felt he owed them more than a thank you, but couldn't find the words to even say that. He sputtered and started over. Then gathered his thoughts and tried again. "About today…what you did…I can't imagine…if not for you…"

"You're welcome, Tucker," Josie said with a laugh. "We love her, too."

Tucker bobbed his head up and down, afraid if he spoke his voice would catch and give him away.

"Take Livvy home. We'll see you tomorrow."

He hoped Josie read the gratitude in his expression, since he'd lost the ability to speak. He suspected she understood. Over the past few weeks, he'd watched Josie change from a self-involved beauty to a giving, levelheaded beauty. Other than inside himself, he'd never seen such a dramatic change in so short a period. Odd that their growth came about because of other people. Ben, without even trying, had changed Josie for the better. Olivia, completely unaware, had done the same for him.

He made his way through the people around Olivia. Her face lit up when her gaze fell on him.

"My driver's here," she told the crowd. "If I don't get home and get a bath soon, I think I'll look and smell like this forever. Will you forgive me if I leave?"

"Sure, Livvy. You go on."

"Take care of her, young man."

"A bubble bath, Livvy. A nice long soak will do the trick."

"Come to the café tomorrow. I'll get more raisins for your sandwich."

"Stop by The Mill after that. Wine and cherries on the house."

More offers came as they made their way to Tucker's car. Olivia seemed oblivious to the affection in their tones. Maybe she was used to it. No, that implied she expected it and took it for granted. She believed they'd do that for anyone.

"Isn't it odd so many of my friends happened to be in the neighborhood this afternoon? How wonderful to see them all."

Tucker stared at her little pixie face, and silently admitted defeat. No matter how hard he fought it, he loved Olivia Aron Chatham with all his heart.

"Must be that luck of yours."

CHAPTER TWENTY-ONE

Dorothy hurried outside as Tucker stopped under the portico. She wrung her hands and looked frantic. Tucker could relate. Olivia hopped out of the SUV and was enveloped in the other woman's arms. After squeezing her tight, Olivia stepped back. A hand flew to her cheek.

"Jeez Louise. Look what I've done to your clothes. Now you're as dirty as I am."

"Not quite." Dorothy took her arm and led the way into the entry. Tucker followed and closed the door behind him.

"I've got to get cleaned up, if that's even possible." Olivia kicked off her filthy shoes and started up the stairs, Dorothy at her side.

Tucker wasn't sure what to do, and wondered if they'd forgotten him.

Olivia came to a halt and looked over her shoulder. "Come on up, Tucker. You can fill Dorothy in on everything while I shower. Then I'll tell you both the rest of the story. The parts you don't know."

The twinkle in her eyes told him words would soon bubble out of her like a waterfall. He'd have to keep a watchful eye on her. Eugene was right. When everything hit, she'd feel like she'd been kicked by a mule.

When they reached her suite, Olivia threw the door open and held her arms out, as if embracing the rooms. "There's no place like home," she said. "Oh, look. It's snowing."

Tucker glanced out one of the windows and saw puffy

flakes falling on the other side. Some hit the glass and left wet trails as they slid down the pane. "Looks like it'll stick this time."

"Goody. New snow always makes everything look fresh and happy." She turned to them. "I won't be long."

"There's no rush, honey. We'll make tea and have it waiting when you're done."

"Excellent idea, Dorothy." Olivia disappeared into another room.

"Come on, Tucker. You can help me."

He followed Dorothy to the kitchen and sat on the chair she pointed to. She raised herself on tiptoe and reached into a cupboard over the refrigerator. After pulling out a bottle of whiskey, she took glasses from another cabinet and set them on the table. She poured two fingers into one and moved it in front of him. Tucker swallowed it in a single gulp. Dorothy refilled his glass and poured into the other. She sat across from him, placed the bottle between them, and raised her drink. They clicked glasses, then sipped. Neither had said a word since leaving Olivia's quarters.

Dorothy broke the silence. "Why don't you tell me what happened? I'll get Livvy's version, but it'd be nice to have one without a lot of detours first."

"Somehow Wallace convinced Olivia to meet him at one of the lake cabins. He locked her in the cellar and left. If that isn't bad enough, he'd turned a space heater on. Apparently the drapes caught fire."

"My God," Dorothy mumbled. "That poor girl. How did she get out?"

"Josie and Ben rescued her. I don't know much beyond that. Wallace is loose, but Eugene has people looking for him. Hell, everyone who knows Olivia is probably looking for him."

"I never did like that man. He always seemed slippery to me. Snake charmer."

Tucker finished his drink and stared at the empty glass in his hand. Once again the enormity of events smashed his composure. "I saw the building, saw all the flames, and knew she was inside. Or thought she was." He rubbed his eyes, then met Dorothy's gaze. "Damn."

She reached across and patted his arm. "I've lived with Livvy all her life. Let me tell you, there have been more than a few scares. I love her like my own, but she's a handful. None of her husbands were strong enough to manage her. Think you are?"

Tucker shrugged. "Guess we'll find out."

Dorothy rose and filled a teapot with water, then put it on the stove. "You've decided to stick around?"

"This is as good a place as any to settle."

Dorothy's laugh boomed in the kitchen. Warm and throaty, it seemed to come from deep inside her. "Welcome home, son."

Ten minutes later Tucker followed Dorothy into Olivia's room again. He set the tray he carried on the coffee table, then settled on the sofa. Dorothy dropped onto an overstuffed chair. They made small talk about the weather, guessing how much snow would fall.

Olivia emerged from her bedroom, wrapped in a fluffy pink robe. With her rosy cheeks and damp hair, she looked clean and scrubbed and bright as a summer day. Tucker wondered why the sight of her always turned his thoughts flowery. He'd have to get over that.

"Super," she exclaimed. "What a treat to come out of the shower and find both of you and a pot of tea waiting. It must be my lucky day." She plunked down beside Tucker and reached for the teapot.

Tucker and Dorothy exchanged a glance. He took the mug Olivia held out to him. Dorothy did the same. Olivia took the third mug and settled into her corner of the couch. She sampled her tea and made appreciative noises.

"This has a nice twang to it," she said to Dorothy. "Is it a new brand?"

"Something I mixed myself."

"Be sure to remember how you did it. It's your best ever."

Tucker sipped, and tasted whiskey. Dorothy winked at

him.

"Did you do all that foliating stuff?" he asked. She looked pretty, not covered in grease.

"Of course."

"I guess it's not so bad." He sipped his tea, enjoying the peaceful camaraderie surrounding him. "How did Josie and Ben find you? What made them go to the cabin?"

Olivia told them the story, heaping praise on Josie and Ben. Tucker listened carefully, knowing he'd hear the saga several times over the next few days. He wanted to be certain she didn't leave out a detail when she told Eugene what had happened.

"Wallace got away, but he'll be caught before long." Tucker placed his mug on the table. "The sheriff will have him behind bars tonight, if I don't miss my guess."

Olivia straightened. "Why?"

Astonished, Tucker could only stare at her for several seconds. "Why? He damn near killed you."

"He didn't set the fire. I admit, he wasn't prudent with the space heater, but being careless isn't illegal."

"Olivia," Tucker said, trying to control his temper. There was such a thing as being too nice. "He locked you in a cellar, then left. You were his prisoner. Don't you think that deserves punishment? It's kidnapping."

"It was wrong of him, and I plan to give him a good piece of my mind. But jail? He shouldn't do hard time for that."

"What about Cheryl?"

"He didn't kill her."

"How do you know?"

Olivia rolled her eyes. "Weren't you listening? I just told you everything he said." She launched into her conversation with Wallace again, ending with, "So you see, he's innocent."

Tucker decided against arguing. Dorothy remained quiet, and he assumed she'd come to the same conclusion. This wasn't the time or place, and they weren't the people. Eugene could explain the legal intricacies to Olivia. He watched her eyes flutter, and knew the combination of whiskey and excitement were taking their toll.

Olivia raised a hand to her mouth and yawned. "I know it's early, but I could use a short nap."

"Good idea," Tucker said. "I'll be here when you wake up."

Olivia got to her feet. "Good. We'll need to get on with catching the killer. Now that we've eliminated Sammy, Crow will get our full attention." She went to her room, leaving the door ajar.

"With any luck, she'll sleep until morning. Do you have a pillow and blanket I can use?" Tucker asked Dorothy. "I'll sleep on the sofa."

"Who do you think you're fooling?"

Exhausted, Tucker rubbed his forehead. Events of the day were catching up with him, too. "I'm not trying to fool anyone. I'm trying to do right."

Dorothy's expression softened. "I know. After hearing what happened, I'm overprotective. I'll get you that linen."

When she reached for the tray, Tucker picked it up. "I'll take it down."

Dorothy left the room, muttering something about the surprise Olivia's parents would find when they returned from their cruise.

Half an hour later, Tucker lay on the sofa, watching snowflakes drift down. Red streaked across the sky as the sun dropped below the horizon. Wind blew against the house, but didn't rattle the windows like it did where he grew up. Cold air didn't seep through cracks. Rodents didn't scurry in the walls, and drunken curses didn't carry from the street to his ears. He didn't have to ignore sounds coming from the next room. He realized Olivia had a precise and accurate grasp on one aspect of her life. She'd always been lucky.

What would Olivia think of him if she knew the squalor of his childhood? Dumb question. It wouldn't change her opinion, no matter what she thought of him. Olivia didn't pass judgment on people's upbringing. But who he'd been in his youth would bother her. If she knew he'd stolen and fought and got into more trouble of his own making than ten other kids, her view of him would take a nosedive.

It was too early to sleep. He turned Olivia's wide-screen television on, careful to keep the volume low. Sometime after seven Dorothy reappeared, carrying soup and grilled cheese sandwiches on her tray. Tucker quickly relieved her of the burden, taking it from her hands and placing it on the table.

She went to Olivia's room, but soon returned. "Out like a light. No sense waking her just to eat. What she needs now is sleep."

They ate dinner and passed the remainder of the evening watching what Dorothy called 'my programs'. Tucker had never seen any of them, but enjoyed the companionship he and Dorothy shared. She yawned and got to her feet after the ten o'clock news ended.

"I'm going to bed," she told him. "It's been a long day."

He noticed she left the door to the suite open. Wise woman. He shut the television off, spread the sheet and blanket Dorothy had dropped off earlier, and stretched out on the sofa.

Tucker woke, alert in an instant. A sniffling noise brought him to his feet. He knocked on Olivia's door.

"Come in."

He turned on the light, crossed to the bed and sat next to Olivia. Reaching for a tissue box on her nightstand, he said, "What's wrong?"

"Nothing." She ducked her head and fumbled at the box.

Tucker took a tissue, then put a finger under her chin and pushed until she looked up. Tears glittered in her eyes. He softly blotted moisture from her cheeks. "Something must be wrong."

"I dreamed about it. About being in the cellar and smelling smoke and being so afraid. If I'd died, I never would have seen you again."

"But you didn't and I'm here now."

"Will you stay?"

"As long as you need me. I'll be in the next room."

"No." She shook her head. "I mean stay in here."

Tucker grew still. What a conundrum, as she would say. "I better not. What about your rule? I'm only human, and a pretty weak one at that."

"I've reassessed my rule. Time to move on, so to speak."

This was steamrolling from conundrum straight into juggernaut. He cleared his throat. "I've reassessed your rule, too. Now I think it's a damn fine one. If I stayed, you'd hate yourself, and me, in the morning. I'd probably hate me, too. I'll just go back to the sofa and we can both hate me now."

She giggled. "Don't be silly. I could never hate you."

He studied her face, blotchy and damp from tears. She was rumpled and sniffling and so kissable he bit his lip to keep away from hers. "Your rule inspired me, Olivia. From now on, I'm only sleeping with women I'm married to."

Her eyes widened. "Good grief, Tucker. You'll have way more ex-wives than I have ex-husbands."

"Maybe I'll just become a monk."

She gave him her impish smile. "You're not at all monkish."

"It'll be an interesting experiment, though." He kissed her forehead and tucked the covers around her shoulders. "I'll be in the next room if you need me."

When had he turned so damn noble? Tucker tried to comfort himself with the truth. He hadn't lied to Olivia. If he took advantage, he would hate himself in the morning. It was better to hate himself now.

❧❧

Something burned his eyelids, and Tucker raised them to see sunshine streaming through the windows. He rose from his makeshift bed and looked outside. Nearly blinded by rays reflecting off pristine snow, he stretched and rolled his shoulders, trying to work out kinks. Immaculate powder flowed across fields and hugged trees, looking like someone had thrown a soft white blanket as far as the eye could see.

"Good morning, sleepyhead," Olivia said. She stood in

the doorway leading to the rest of the house. "We held break-fast for you. Dorothy's making her special strawberry and chocolate chip waffles. She's out of potato chips, thanks to our lunch the other day, but she'll find something crunchy for them. Maybe cereal. Hungry?"

Not anymore. "Does she have coffee? I'm not real big on breakfast."

"Of course she has coffee. But you should reconsider the breakfast thing while you evaluate becoming a monk. It's the most important meal of the day."

Clad in blue jeans topped by a colorful sweater, and with her hair shimmering in the sunshine, he thought she looked like an exotic bird. He wouldn't have been surprised if she stood on one leg, and wondered if peacocks did that. He didn't know where the image came from. Probably some television show about rare animals.

"Mind if I use your bathroom?"

"Right through there." She pointed at her bedroom. "Come downstairs when you're finished. I'll pour your coffee, and once you smell Dorothy's waffles, you'll beg for break-fast."

❧❧

Olivia paused on her way to the kitchen. Sometime dur-ing the night her Lexus had been parked behind Tucker's Ex-hibition. She liked seeing them together, and wondered how daffy she was if just observing their vehicles lined up gave her a thrill. A tinge of sadness weighed on her. She knew she'd made a fool of herself the night before, asking Tucker to stay with her. Of course he wouldn't want to do that. Yet he man-aged to reject her gracefully, obviously trying not to hurt her feelings. What a wonderful man.

"He'll be down in a minute," she told Dorothy when she entered the kitchen. "He says he just wants coffee."

"You know where the mugs are. Give him a glass of juice, too."

Proud to be given a kitchen job, Olivia brought Tucker's

coffee and juice to the dining room and set them at the head of the table, beside an empty plate. She left it there in case he changed his mind, and made sure the butter and jellies were within his reach.

"Beautiful day, isn't it?" Tucker said when he entered the room. He took his seat and lifted his mug, inhaling appreciatively before sipping.

Dorothy came through the swinging doors, carrying a plate of toast, a platter of waffles, a large bowl of hash browns, and a small pitcher filled with syrup. The doorbell rang as she placed the food on the table. "Dig in while it's hot. I'll get the door."

Olivia's stomach growled and she forked two waffles onto her plate, then added a huge spoonful of potatoes and a piece of toast. "I'm starving." She topped her waffles with butter and syrup.

Dorothy and Eugene came in from the hall.

"Eu...Sheriff." A burst of joy filled Olivia. He must need her for something to come over so early in the day. "Or should I call you boss?"

"Sheriff is fine." Eugene sat across from her and put a notebook and pencil on the table.

"I'll bring you some coffee," Dorothy told him.

"Bring him a plate, too," Olivia said. "He'll want some of your strawberry chocolate chip waffles. Did you find cereal for crunch?"

"There was an extra bag of potato chips."

"Excellent." Olivia ate a forkful and smacked her lips. "Sure you won't change your mind about breakfast, Tucker?"

He had a strange expression on his face. Kind of like he'd just seen a magic trick and couldn't believe his eyes. Eugene wore the same visage.

"None for me," Tucker said.

"Me either," Eugene echoed.

Dorothy snickered and left the room. Olivia ate, feeling Tucker's and the sheriff's scrutiny. She wondered if they were waiting for her to do something.

"Do those waffles really have potato chips in them?" Eugene asked.

"Yep. They add a special zing. Do you need me to work today, Sheriff?"

He shook his head, like a puppy waking up, and said, "No, Livvy. You're off duty until further notice. Procedure again."

"Darn procedure. It's pesky."

"I just have a few questions."

"Fire away."

"We picked Sam up last night. He only got about thirty miles. A trooper saw him buying gas. He told me his version of what happened. Why don't you tell me yours?"

Olivia wondered if she'd have to tell her story every day for the rest of her life. Goes with the territory, she thought. Police work had to be repetitive at times. Dorothy came and went as she detailed the events of yesterday. Olivia paused when both men happily took the scrambled eggs and sausages Dorothy offered. They spooned potatoes on their plates and dug into the food like famished vagabonds. She wondered if she'd been too enthusiastic over her breakfast. They'd probably left all the waffles for her as a gentlemanly gesture.

Eugene waved his fork. "Go on, Livvy. The recorder fell off your belt. Then what happened?"

She finished the tale and her food. Pushing her plate aside, she eyed Tucker's. "For a man who doesn't like breakfast, you sure managed to swallow a mighty big one."

"I was told it's the most important meal of the day." He leaned back in his chair with a contented sigh.

"Your version agrees with Sam's for the most part," Eugene said. "We went through his apartment and car and sent evidence to the lab. No typewriter, though. Hopefully we can close the case and get back to normal soon."

"Any chance of him confessing?" Tucker asked.

Eugene shook his head. "Swears he didn't kill her."

Aghast, Olivia's jaw dropped. "Are you talking about Cheryl? Sammy didn't kill her. He shoved her, and she was knocked out. But she was alive when he left."

"So he says."

"I believe him."

"You can be a character witness at his trial. In the meantime, I've got some loose ends to tie up."

Olivia reached across the table and touched Eugene's arm. "Please hear me out. There's still another suspect. Crow, I mean Reverend Conroy, was there that night. Sammy saw him leave."

"He's one of my loose ends. But Wallace is the one who admits hitting her."

"If Sammy did it, why alibi Crow? Why admit pushing, or even seeing, Cheryl? Why not let Conroy take the blame? He could say he saw Conroy leave, and that Cheryl didn't answer when he went to her door. Sammy's a ne'er-do-well and a skunk. But he's not a killer. Maybe Crow went back later. Did you consider that?"

Eugene stared at her and she remained quiet. He seemed to be having a conversation with himself. Finally he nodded and said, "You're a brave girl, Livvy. You've earned a little more information. Hell, it'll be all over town soon anyway. I'm surprised it hasn't gotten out yet. Wallace told you about the victim's safe deposit box. What he didn't tell you, what he doesn't know, is that it held more than the tapes."

Fascinated, Olivia leaned forward. "What else was in there?"

"I have to keep that close to my vest. Let's just say it raises a few questions about someone other than Wallace and leave it at that."

Olivia gaped at him. What was he talking about? He wasn't even wearing a vest. Sympathy almost overwhelmed her, and when he lumbered to his feet, she had to fight the urge to go to Eugene and give him a hug.

"I know you believe Wallace, and I'm not saying you're wrong," Eugene said. "I'm just saying he's a strong suspect. It's true that Conroy could have gone back. The same could be said of Wallace. Maybe he told you half the story. One thing is certain. Cheryl didn't die from a head wound and she didn't die lying on the floor. Someone took her clothes off and strung her up in the closet. I'm going to find out who."

"I know you will, Eu…Sheriff." Olivia and Tucker walked him to the door.

When they were alone, Olivia said, "He looks tired. We have to solve this soon so the poor lamb can get some rest."

She wondered if it were possible to arrange a free cruise for Eugene and Betty. Her parents always came home so relaxed. She'd have to think of a way to get some tickets into Eugene's hands. Maybe she'd hold a contest of some sort, and rig it so he'd win.

"I'd better go, too," Tucker said. "I could use a shower and clean clothes."

"Of course. Thanks ever so much for all you did."

"It was my pleasure, January Eighth. I'll come back later. Maybe we can go out to dinner and a movie. Would you like that?"

"There's nothing good showing in town. Why don't I rent a movie and bring it to your house?"

She noticed his hesitation and her cheeks grew warm. Fiddlesticks. She must have made a colossal fool of herself. Now he was afraid of her.

"I'm not sure that's a good idea," Tucker said.

"I'll bring supper." If she could pull this off, convince him to let her in his door, she might be able to save the situation. She'd behave like a perfect lady and he'd know she'd learned her lesson. He wasn't interested in her. He'd rather be a monk than be with her.

"Um…it's just that…"

Her heart went out to him, trying so hard to put her in her place without causing hurt. "It's okay, Tucker. I know you want to be a monk, and I understand."

His expression changed, and she couldn't read it. He looked surprised and amused. She wondered if there was something wrong with her makeup. Had she smudged her mascara again?

"I'll ask Dorothy to make her special ham." Get his mind

on food, she told herself. It seemed to work. Now he looked pleased. He clearly liked a good meal, and that gave her an inspiration. With her kitchen privileges returned, she'd ask Dorothy to teach her to cook. If she learned how to make a decent supper, he might change his mind about her. And about becoming a monk.

"I'll get the movie. Anything special?"

"Seabiscuit." She clapped her hands. "Don't you love that movie? It makes a person feel so happy."

"I haven't seen it."

Stunned, Olivia could only gawk at him for a moment. Mercy, he'd missed out on an awful lot in his life. "You're in for a real treat. Ham and Seabiscuit. Is seven okay? Or should I come later? Or earlier?"

"Seven is fine. Try to stay out of trouble until then."

Olivia returned to her rooms and folded Tucker's blanket and sheet. She held his pillow to her nose before placing it on top of the bedding. There wasn't much she could do until church tomorrow, when she'd have the chance to get her hands on Crow's sermon. She looked outside and got the germ of an idea. Josie would love it.

CHAPTER TWENTY-TWO

Hendricks' General Store began as a small outfit, filled with odds and ends. People said it was like the old Five and Dime. Olivia had no idea what they were talking about. Now the shop was the size of a warehouse. A person could get lost in a place like that, going from aisle to aisle finding treasures galore. She and Josie decided if Hendricks' didn't have what Olivia wanted, no place would.

Late Saturday afternoon they entered the vast building and got their bearings. Josie took off in one direction, and Olivia followed. Josie had a knack for knowing where to look for things she wanted. Olivia thought she had some kind of homing instinct, like a dog that finds its way back to its master after being separated.

They made their way deeper into the store, and Olivia began to doubt her friend. Surely they wouldn't stick her hoped-for prize in a spider web-filled corner. It should be near the front, with a light shining on it. Josie stopped at a back wall festooned with life preservers.

"What are we doing here? These aren't what we're looking for." Olivia wondered how Josie had gotten so confused.

"They're what I'm looking for. Ben bought a boat last fall. Did you know that?"

"I heard something about it."

"It's adorable, Livvy. One of those cute things you can zip around in. Or go slow and sip a pina colada and wave at other boaters. He says it'll go up to thirty miles an hour, and on the water that can feel like you're flying. I can hardly wait." Josie's face was never more gorgeous, and that was saying quite a lot.

"If you're going to go that fast, I don't blame you for wanting a few life preservers. I'll help you carry them. Do they only come in orange?"

Josie pointed. "I think I see some blue ones over there. They'd match his boat better."

"What's the boat's name?" Olivia reached for a life preserver and looked for a size tag. "This just says 'adult'."

"We'll buy four. That way you and Tucker can come with us on our maiden voyage. Or maybe our second outing. The first will probably be special, just between Ben and me."

Olivia grabbed another preserver while Josie picked two more. "You didn't tell me the boat's name."

"I don't think it has one yet."

"'Titanic'."

"*What?*" Josie looked horrified. She put a hand on her hip and glared. "Are you trying to jinx us? To give Ben's boat bad karma?"

"Of course not, you goose. It's for insurance. Lightning doesn't strike the same place twice."

"Titanic hit an iceberg."

"I think the saying goes for all catastrophes. Never mind. Ben will probably name it 'Josie' anyway."

"Do you think so? Really?" she asked in an awed voice. She looked past Olivia, as if watching something only she could see.

"Wouldn't surprise me one little bit. We done here?"

Josie shook her head and glanced at Olivia. "Oh, right. Let's leave these by a register and we'll get what we came for."

On the way to the checkout area, they met Toby Hendricks, son of the owners. He told a clerk to hold the preservers, then led Olivia and Josie to an exhibit that took Olivia's breath away. Shiny new sleds in cheerful reds, blues, greens, pinks, and violets were displayed on a large piece of fabric made to look like snow. How would she ever pick two? Should she get one in each color and let Tucker choose the one he liked best? Good grief, life was becoming too complicated. How many decisions should one gal have to make?

Something caught her eye and she pointed at it. "Eureka! Take a gander at that! What is it?"

"Toboggan," Toby answered.

"It looks big enough for two. Or even three."

"It is."

"Oh, my. This is too good to be true." Olivia couldn't believe her luck, and doubted it had ever run so strong. There was only one problem. The toboggan was brown and not one bit cheerful. She could hang balloons on it, but blowing them up would become tedious. "Do they come in any other colors?"

"Just brown. What color do you want?" Toby asked.

"Every color of the rainbow."

"Let me think a minute." He rubbed a hand across his five-o'clock shadow. Brightening, he said, "I think we have some rainbow decals in here somewhere. Would that do? I could stick them all over the toboggan."

"Oh, happy day! That'd be absolutely perfect. We hit the jackpot when we came in here, Josie."

"Don't I know it."

"Pick one out and I'll have it ready for you tomorrow," Toby told Olivia.

She eyed each toboggan, looking for splinters or other flaws, and settled on what was clearly the most beautiful of them all. Toby nodded and made a note on a pad he pulled from his pocket.

A clerk hurried to the group. "I have to talk to you, boss."

"I'm listening."

"Well, um…" He looked at Olivia and Josie.

With a heavy sigh, Toby tucked his paper in his pocket. "Will you excuse me a moment, ladies? I'll be right back."

Olivia and Josie admired the toboggan, trying to imagine it with rainbow decals scattered across its surface.

"It'll be a sight for sore eyes, that's for sure," Olivia announced.

"One of a kind," Josie agreed.

When Toby returned, he looked upset. "I'm in a jam, Livvy. I should say a friend of mine is. Can you do me a favor?"

"Name it."

A few minutes later Olivia and Josie left Hendricks'. They climbed into Josie's car and Olivia unclipped her phone from her belt. "I've got to let Tucker know what's going on. This could turn into a can of beans and put a fly in our ointment tonight."

"It's me," she said when Tucker answered. "Olivia. Olivia Chatham."

"Is something wrong? You sound stressed."

"I'm not sure. It could end up being nothing, but I might be a tad late tonight. Sorry, but it can't be helped."

"What's going on? Where are you?"

"I'm with Josie and we're just leaving Hendricks' General Store." She thought of the toboggan, and smiled. "We found a sled, Tucker. It's a real lulu. It may be plain now, but Toby's going to put rainbow stickers on it. Here's the best part. Two people can fit on it. Isn't that super?"

"I can hardly wait to see it. Why does a new sled mean you're going to be late? Do you need help getting it home?"

"No, nothing like that. While we were there, Toby got some upsetting news. Turns out Scootie Greenwald fell off the wagon. He's at Spud's Suds, and acting strange. Very morose. He was doing so well with his AA meetings. I don't know what set him off, but once again he's fallen victim to that old devil, John Barleycorn." It sounded like Tucker was strangling. "Are you okay?"

"I'm fine. I take it you're off to save Scootie from himself."

"Toby can't leave the store, so it's up to us."

"I'll meet you there."

"No need. By 'us' I meant Josie and me. We can handle things. He probably only needs to sit with someone and have a little chinwag. Just please don't start the movie without me."

"Piffle. What if he gives you trouble? Don't go in until I

get there. It's hard to know what a man under the Barleycorn influence will do."

"Honestly, Tucker. You're such a worrier. We'll think of some way to get him out of there peacefully. Necessity is the mother of intervention."

"Wait for me." It sounded like he was choking or coughing.

"Are you sure you're okay? Are you coming down with a cold?"

"No. I'm on my way."

"Too late. We're here. Stay put and I'll be there soon. If you leave, and we miss each other, I won't be able to get into your house."

She ended the call before he could argue. "He can be a bit of a mother hen, but his heart's in the right place."

Josie pulled the key from the ignition and opened her door. "His heart's in your back pocket."

"Good grief." Olivia got out of the car. "You say the daffiest things sometimes. I think Ben's got your head in the clouds."

"Yep. Want to know something?"

"What?"

"It feels damn good." Josie looped an arm through Olivia's. "Let's take Scootie home and get on with the evening. I've got plans."

Olivia didn't doubt that.

They entered the bar and had no trouble finding Scootie in the crowd. He sat alone at a table cluttered with empty glasses. He held on to a full one, and Olivia saw his lips move as if he were having a conversation with it. She and Josie crossed to him and dropped onto chairs.

"Hey, Scootie. How are you?" Olivia asked.

He looked up. "Livvy, Josie. Let me buy you a drink."

"That'd be nice. I'll get them." Olivia got to her feet and hurried to the bar. If Scootie ordered drinks, he'd surely get another for himself.

When Spud asked what she wanted, she told him to fill

two beer mugs with ginger ale. "Make sure the top is fuzzy like beer is."

"Will do. You here for Scootie?"

"You bet we are. But getting him out of here will take some finesse. No more beer for him."

"Gotcha. Your drinks are on the house, and if he orders another, I'll give him your version of a tall frosty."

Olivia thanked him and took the mugs he placed in front of her to their table. She winked at Josie when she handed her a ginger ale. Josie nodded.

Her phone chirped and she plucked it off her belt.

"Everything okay?" Tucker asked.

"Right as reindeer. The situation is well under control. See you soon. Don't start—"

"The movie without you," Tucker finished for her. "I won't."

Olivia returned the phone to her belt, then directed her attention to Scootie. "What's going on? You look down in the mouth." Olivia took a long drink, then wiped the back of her hand across her lips the way they did in cowboy movies.

"It's Quetzi. We've been seeing a lot of each other, and I'm pretty sure she's the one. No, I'm positive. She's the only girl for me, Livvy."

"Are you the only guy for her?"

"I thought so. But she broke up with me." He lifted his beer and drank, then set it on the table again.

"Did she say why?" Josie asked.

Scootie glanced at her as if he'd forgotten she was there. Josie sat back and gave Olivia a significant look. Olivia knew that meant she was in charge of questioning from now on.

"Did she say why she wanted to break up?" Olivia asked.

His gaze returned to the table. He made wet circles on it with the bottom of his mug. "It's that woman. The one who was killed."

Stymied, Olivia tried to figure out what Cheryl had to do with Quetzi. "Were they friends?"

Scootie snorted. "Hardly. Quetzi barely knew her. But now

the rumors are swirling and she's heard them. She's upset."

"Cheryl's activities could have a powerful impact on a delicate person like Quetzi. She's a dainty flower of a woman."

"Exactly." Scootie nodded. "She's in her own little world most of the time. Her and her pets." He looked at Olivia, despair in his eyes. "Now she thinks that's what all men are like. That we all want to treat women the way some of that lady's clients treated her. Hell, I wouldn't expect that of anyone, especially Quetzi. Wouldn't even want to do those things."

"Of course you wouldn't. Did you tell her that?"

He nodded and took another drink. "She said she couldn't risk it. We're finished." He wiped his eyes. "I've lost the love of my life because a prostitute moved to town."

Olivia leaned forward and gave his shoulder a quick squeeze. "There, there, Scootie. Don't feel so blue. She could change her mind."

"No. She was firm." He blew his nose on a paper napkin.

"Take solace that she didn't find another man. That'd be tough to overcome. But she's just misinformed. That's easy peasy to fix."

He dropped the napkin and focused on Olivia. "How?"

"I'll pop into her store tomorrow and have a talk with her." Good grief, how would she go there and get out without buying a litter of kittens or puppies or both? It would seem odd if she held her eyes closed the whole time she was in The Cat's Meow.

"You will? Ah, gee, Livvy. That's great. She likes you. She may even listen to you."

"Then stop worrying. And stop drinking. I can probably convince Quetzi all men aren't like Cheryl's customers, but I can't defend a tosspot. Climb back on your wagon and stay there. Deal?"

Scootie shoved the rest of his beer aside and shook her hand. "Deal. I can't thank you enough."

"Be good to Quetzi. That's all I ask. I'll drive you home in your car and Josie can follow us."

"Josie?" He squinted at the room.

Josie, sitting quietly beside Olivia, raised her hand. "Here I am," she trilled.

Scootie must really be pickled, Olivia thought. Or really, really in love. What else would explain not noticing Josephine Bookman?

Olivia drove Scootie's car, and made sure he got safely inside his house. When Josie dropped her at home, the clock on the dashboard read six-forty-five. She'd be late for her date with Tucker, but not by much. She thanked Josie and dashed inside, going straight to the kitchen.

The picnic basket sat on the table and plastic food containers covered the counters. Dorothy looked up from spooning au gratin potatoes into one of them.

"Everything smells wonderful," Olivia told her. "Let me help."

"You can put the ham into that one." Dorothy tipped her head toward a platter of sliced ham next to an open container.

After washing her hands, Olivia did as she was told, thrilled again at being allowed to assist. Glaze stuck to her fingers, and she licked them. "Will you teach me how to make this?"

"Nothing to it. Just honey and brown sugar."

"But I need to know exactly how." Olivia looked at the rest of the spread, taking mental notes at what went into a balanced meal. One casserole held green beans in some kind of sauce with the crunchy onions she loved so much. A loaf of bread cooled on a rack. Strawberries in red juice sat next to a platter of small, round cakes. She peeked into the basket and saw a container filled with salad. "I need to learn how to make all of this."

Dorothy snapped the lid on a storage bowl and glanced at Olivia, a knowing smile on her face. "You're learning. The way to a man's heart is through his stomach."

Olivia stared at her. Dorothy must be extra tired. That was usually when she said the most eccentric, indecipherable things. "Is that a yes?"

"It's a yes." She began loading the rest of the food into the hamper. "He can keep the leftovers and containers. I doubt he has any. Bachelors don't think of things like that."

"Thanks, Dorothy. He'll be so happy. I don't think he eats at home much."

"Go up and make yourself pretty while I finish here. Can't keep the man waiting."

Olivia pounded up to her room and looked in the mirror. There wasn't much she could do with so little time. A dab of blush and lipstick, a quick brush through her hair, and she was ready.

When she returned to the kitchen she found the basket ready to go and Dorothy loading the dishwasher. "Need help?"

"You run along, Livvy. Put the ice cream in the freezer as soon as you get there. Don't forget or you'll have a mess."

"I won't forget."

"Should I wait up?" Dorothy asked, the hint of a laugh behind her words.

"If you want. I won't be late. Tomorrow's Sunday, so I have to be up early for church." She kissed Dorothy on the cheek and waved goodbye.

≈≈≈

Olivia told Tucker what had happened as they unpacked the picnic basket. He listened with amusement. No problem was too big or too small for Olivia. From murder to flutes to the broken hearted, she made time for everyone.

"Sounds like you handled everything just right." His mouth watered at the aromas. He put the ice cream in the freezer, then set plates and silverware on the table. "What do you want to drink?"

"After seeing some of those people at Spud's Suds, I think I'll just have water."

Tucker filled two glasses with ice and water from the door of his refrigerator and set them next to the plates.

"Everything's still warm," Olivia said as she took her seat.

"It's not going to have time to cool." Tucker sat across from her and cut into a piece of ham. "Outstanding."

"Dorothy's quite skilled in the culinary arts. She's going to teach me to cook."

"How's she going to do that if you aren't allowed in the kitchen?"

"She lifted the embargo."

Tucker smiled. What a woman. He'd gladly spend the rest of his life waiting for his next surprise from Olivia. "If you learn to cook as good as Dorothy, I'll have to insist you marry me."

Olivia dropped her fork. She stared at him and put a hand over her heart. "You are a silver-tongued fox, Mr. Monroe. Now stop teasing me and finish your supper. Don't forget to eat your beans. They're full of vitamins."

"Yes, ma'am." He hid his laughter by shoveling a forkful of beans into his mouth.

Too full to have dessert, they decided to eat it later, during the movie. Olivia rinsed dishes and Tucker loaded them in the dishwasher. They put lids on the food containers and stored everything in the refrigerator. Tucker hadn't seen so much food in there, and gratitude washed over him. Dorothy was almost as thoughtful as Olivia.

Seabiscuit turned out to be a good movie. He sat in one corner of the sofa and Olivia curled up in the other. She laughed and cried and fretted and cheered. He didn't know how anyone could get so worked up over a film they'd already seen, but he enjoyed the show. Both of them.

"You could sit closer to me," he said. "We could do a little canoodling."

"I'll have to pass on that. It wouldn't be ladylike, and I've decided to be a lady."

"You're already a lady. Every inch of you."

"Then I should act like one. I'm sorry about last night."

He didn't know what she meant. "Sorry about what?"

"That I came on to you like a wanton woman. Must have scared you half to death. It won't happen again. Are you ready for strawberry shortcake?"

Christ, she sure could get things turned around. "Sounds

good." He paused the movie and stood. "About last night…you didn't scare me. I just didn't want you to do something you'd regret."

Olivia led the way to the kitchen. "You're a stronger man than I am, Tucker. Thanks to you, we can at least be friends. If I'd had my way, who knows how we'd end up?"

Tucker had a good idea, but decided not to press. He'd seen that look on her face and heard that tone in her voice before. The best word to describe them was determined. She'd made up her mind, at least for tonight. It didn't matter. He had all the time in the world, and for the next hour or two he could relax and enjoy her company. There were lots worse ways to spend a Saturday night.

After the movie, Olivia laid out her plans for the next day. She wanted to study Conroy's sermon, looking for an errant 'i'. After that she'd visit Quetzi and put in a good word for Scootie. Tucker nodded his approval. She couldn't get into trouble doing those harmless tasks. Or could she?

"Then I'll pick up our toboggan. Ready to do some sledding, Tucker?"

Good Lord.

The thought brought Tucker up short. He'd been raised with cursing all around him, and knew his language could be salty at best. He'd tried to watch what he said around Olivia. Other than asking him not to swear in church at the memorial, she'd never mentioned his expletives. But he hadn't heard her utter anything but the most mild of oaths, and suspected she wasn't comfortable around some of the four-letter words that had crept into his everyday speech. He may have tried to censor what he said, but, until now, never his thoughts. 'Good Lord' was not part of his jargon. He considered the change in him, and thought it was probably an improvement. His vocabulary could use some broadening.

"Is it true you've never been sledding?" she asked.

"There weren't a lot of hills where I grew up. In fact, there weren't any."

"You told me you came from Chicago. That's not very far.

I'd like to see where you grew up. Will you take me there some-day?"

Her request filled him with dread. He'd never take her there, but he had to be honest with her about his life. She had the right to know. "It's too dangerous, Olivia. It's a slum, one of the worst. Cockroaches the size of Chihuahuas. Rats every-where. People do drugs on the sidewalks and drink cheap booze from paper bags. They sleep in doorways and alleys. Their hair is filled with lice. They stab each other. Drive-by shootings happen every day. I'd say the people there live like animals, but they don't. Animals have some pride." He watched Olivia's expression change from cheerful to horrified, and hated be-ing the one who caused her distress. She had no experience with the worst of humanity. "I'm going to grab an Old Style. Can I get you anything? Wine and cherries?"

"No, thank you. Does your mother still live there? Don't you worry about her?"

Tucker went to the kitchen for his beer, using the time to gather his thoughts. His mother. Might as well get that out in the open, too.

He returned to the living room and took his seat. "My mother, now there's a topic." He took a long drink and set his beer on the coffee table.

"I know you have some problems with her, but I've found fences can be mended."

"My mother was, is, a drunk. She never wanted me, and didn't care if I knew it. Having a kid hanging around inter-fered with her social life. But not by much. Let's just say I had a lot of uncles." He glanced at Olivia, and she nodded, as if urging him to go on. For some inexplicable reason, he did. Now that he'd started talking, he wanted to tell her every-thing.

"She wasn't exactly a PTA mother, although she might have been if they served gin at meetings. She usually forgot to eat, which meant I didn't either. She didn't care where I was, or what I did. And believe me, I did a lot. The acorn, as they say, didn't fall far from the tree."

"You misbehaved?"

He snorted. "Yeah, I misbehaved. I stole, starting with candy and moving on to jewelry, purses, wallets and then cars. Anything I wanted, I took. Don't get me started on the fighting. I can't remember how many people I beat up."

"You were an angry young man, with good reason, and vented it the only way you knew."

"I was a delinquent and a criminal."

"Don't focus on who you were. Focus on who you are."

"Who am I?"

"A wonderful person. Kind and sensitive and patient."

He turned to her and held her gaze. "You have to face the truth, Olivia. I'm nothing. Just a pile of trash who, thanks to a good man, managed to crawl out of the dump."

"You told me about someone who was almost a father to you. Who?"

"Jonathan Vicknair. He was a cop. One day he caught me stealing a car. He nailed me, and there was no wiggle room. When he cuffed me, I knew I was going to juvie." Tucker smiled at the memory. "But that's not where he took me."

Olivia leaned forward and clasped his hand. "Where did he take you?"

"The ball park. The White Sox were playing the Twins that afternoon. I thought he was a real asshole. Figured he was into young boys. I planned on eating about twelve hot dogs and drinking six sodas, then skipping out. But it was a good game, and he was easy to be with. I ended up staying to the end, but wouldn't let him take me home. He gave me money for the train, and his card. Asked if I'd like to go to another game sometime.

"I'd see him around, and he never acted like he'd caught me hot-wiring a car. He'd just say hello and tell me what games were coming up. I finally said I'd like to go to one, and we did."

"He saw the good in you and saved you."

"Let's just say he saved me. I came to love that old man." He pulled his hand from hers and reached for his beer. "After a while his approval meant more to me than anything. I never wanted to disappoint him. That meant I had to become a model citizen. Or at least act like one. Deep inside I've always been the loser Jonathan caught stealing a car."

"Nonsense. I doubt Jonathan would have wasted his time helping a loser. If that were the case, it sounds like he had plenty to choose from. He picked you because he saw what I see. Decency and integrity. What happened to him? You told me he died a few years ago."

She'd put her finger on a puzzle he'd wondered about for years. Why had Jonathan chosen him to mentor? "Stroke. It was fast, thank God."

"You miss him very much, don't you?"

"Every day. I wish you could have met him, and he could have met you."

"What happened to your mother? Is she still in the slum?"

"I bought her a house in the suburbs."

Olivia gave him the sweetest smile he'd ever seen. "You aren't so tough after all. That was a wonderful thing to do."

"I couldn't leave her in that hellhole."

"Can I meet her?"

He should have seen it coming, but hadn't. The thought was like a dagger in his chest. "I gave her a house and arranged for food and other necessities, which is more than she deserves. But she's my mother, and Jonathan would want me to provide for her. That doesn't mean I have to visit her. Please don't ask to meet her. I never want to lay eyes on her again." He finished his beer and put the bottle on the table. "So you see, Olivia. I'm not someone you want to spend any time with. I came from nothing and I am nothing."

"You're a success story. With the help of a kind man, you pulled yourself up by the bootstraps and became the American dream. I'm so proud of you I could bust a button. I want to spend as much time with you as I can."

Tucker stared at her. "Didn't you hear me? I'm not worthy of you, Olivia."

"Piffle. I'm not worthy of you. Stop being negative,

doggone it. Be proud. You have every reason to strut like a rooster. You're a self-made man, and that's the best kind."

Tucker couldn't find his voice. She knew the worst, and still accepted him.

"Don't worry, Tucker. I won't tell anyone, not even Josie, what you've been through. I know it was hard to open up like that, and I can't tell you how much I admire you."

"I could canoodle you like crazy right now, but I won't. You're a lady, and I won't forget that."

Olivia got to her feet. "I appreciate that, Tucker. I should be going. Tomorrow's a busy day."

He got her coat and held it for her. She was quiet as he walked her to her car. She climbed in and started the engine, then lowered the window.

"I need to say something before I leave. I love you, Tucker. I love everything about you. Goodnight." She left before he could reply.

Tucker stood on his driveway, and heard his mentor's voice as clearly as if they stood side by side. "You did good, boy. Don't let her get away."

Fat white flakes began drifting down from above.

CHAPTER TWENTY-THREE

Snow crunched under Olivia's tires. The roads had been plowed, and Abe, the Chathams' outdoor version of Dorothy, had cleared the long drive, but enough white powder remained to make streets slippery. Olivia had switched her SUV to four-wheel drive before leaving home Sunday morning. She parked in the church lot and went inside. Fewer people than usual occupied pews. Olivia supposed the rest were home shoveling drives and walkways.

After exchanging small talk with several parishioners, Olivia settled in her usual spot. She missed her parents. They all went their own ways during the day, but if she wanted to talk to her mother or father, they were easy to find. With them gone, the house felt empty. Now, without one on each side like bookends, she felt their absence even more.

Her thoughts turned to Tucker and all he'd endured. She wasn't embarrassed she'd told him she loved him. It may have been forward and brassy as all get out, but it was true. He was a tortured soul, and needed to know he was deeply cared for. How could he think he was unworthy of her? He was the bravest of the brave, the strongest of the strong. After the murder case was done and dusted, she'd concentrate on Tucker and improving his self-esteem. It would take time, but she had plenty of that.

Rose Conroy's organ resonated with the rich opening chords of the first hymn, and the congregation stood. Olivia sang and observed the minister's wife. Her steel gray hair was pulled back and pinned at her nape. It looked painful, and Olivia cringed. Rose seemed to put her entire being into the music. She played with her eyes closed, face lifted toward heaven. Her mouth moved, but Olivia couldn't hear her voice above the others. Reverend Conroy, behind the podium, belted the words with gusto.

When the song ended, everyone sat and the weekly ritual began. Conroy prayed and gave his sermon and prayed again. Olivia kept a careful watch. For all she knew, he could have a wastebasket hidden behind the lectern. If he tossed the sermon, she'd need to dash up and grab it after the service. That would eliminate the need to praise and cajole the pages from him. But it wasn't meant to be. After his final 'Amen', Conroy left the papers on the stand and walked down the aisle. Olivia knew she could probably run up and snatch the sermon without anyone noticing, but stealing from a pulpit made her uneasy. A frontal assault was necessary.

Conroy stood in the vestibule, just outside the sanctuary doors, and spoke with his flock. Obsequious old goat, she thought. Olivia waited until most left, which didn't take long, before approaching.

"Wonderful sermon, Reverend. Very inspiring."

"Which part did you like most?" He squared his shoulders and beamed, appearing extremely proud of his speech.

"I enjoyed it all." In an effort to hide her dislike of the man, Olivia clasped her hands in front of her and tried to look pious. "I guess the best part was about how we shouldn't sin and all that."

He seemed pleased at her response. In fact, he gave the impression of being happy to see her. If he thought she was snooping on him, if he typed the note and slid it under the dressing room door, would he be so friendly and chipper? Probably, the sly boots. His amicable demeanor could easily be an act to throw her off balance.

"Is Mrs. Reverend still suffering from headaches?" Olivia wanted to suggest she loosen her bun to relieve some of the pressure, but decided against it.

"From time to time. She hasn't had one in a while. One hopes the trend continues."

"One certainly does." At least she'd gotten him off the topic of his sermon.

"Are you coming to the potluck dinner this evening? We'd love you to partake of the event." His smile seemed sincere.

"I'll try. You know how it goes, Reverend. Sometimes one gets caught up in one's day and all one's activities and before one knows it, it's time for one to go home and go to bed."

"Ah, to be young again." He sneaked a glance at his watch.

Olivia knew this was her moment. He was in a hurry, and wouldn't pay much attention to her request. "Before I leave, would you mind if I borrowed your sermon? I'll bring it back tomorrow."

Smug didn't begin to describe the expression that crossed his face. "I'm honored it inspired you so much, Olivia. No one's ever asked to borrow a sermon before. It's on the pulpit. You can keep it."

Olivia's pulse jumped. Would it really be this easy? "Don't you need it for your records or anything? I mean, what if someone wants to write your life story and there's an entire Sunday lecture missing?"

He smoothed his black, glistening hair, again reminding her of a crow. "Not to worry. I'll print another copy when I get home. Now, if you'll excuse me, duty calls."

Her spirits fell in an instant. He'd used a computer. Still, she ambled to the front of the sanctuary and picked the pages off the podium. With one glance she saw that all the letters lined up neatly. When was she going to catch a break? Mumbling under her breath, she strolled to her car. "Duty calls," she mimicked. "What kind of duty, that's the question. Who needs the advice of an air hose like him?"

Sitting with the heater on high, and the vents pointed at her, Olivia planned her next move. She had to talk to Quetzi, but thought it best to see Scootie first. He may have changed his mind, or could be under the weather. If everything was a go, she'd have a nice chat with Quetzi.

Scootie, looking like he'd just gotten off a roller coaster, ushered her inside his house.

"How do you feel?" she asked, noting his red eyes and whiskery face.

"No worse than I deserve. Thanks for your help last night, Livvy. Did you talk to Quetzi?"

"Not yet. I wanted to make sure you haven't changed your mind. You might want to play the field, now that you can see it without foam clouding your view."

"Nope." He shook his head, then grimaced and rubbed his temples. "She's the gal for me."

"Okay, then. I'll go have a chat with her."

"Check her house first. She might not be at the store yet."

Olivia hoped he was right. If so, she wouldn't have to look at all those cuddly little animals knowing she'd have to leave them behind when she left. "Will do. In the meantime, you clean up and have a decent meal. If she wants to see you today, you'll have to be at your best."

"Thanks again, Livvy."

Olivia drove to Quetzi's home, but she wasn't there. Before going to The Cat's Meow, Olivia sat in her car in front of Cheryl's house, three doors from Quetzi's. The place appeared innocent and normal. Its white siding, black shutters and picket fence made it look like a typical family lived there. A stranger to Chatham wouldn't have been surprised to see a couple of kids making a snowman on the front yard. If only the house could talk. Her imagination took flight, and she wondered if rumors of ghosts would crop up in town lore. The house could sit vacant for years. Who'd want to live where a murder had occurred? Sadness settled over Olivia. The world no longer seemed a safe place. Reminding herself a wily killer remained at large, she pulled away from the curb and headed for Quetzi's store. She had work to do.

Quetzi peeked around the 'Closed' sign, and broke into a grin. She unlocked the door and took a step back. "Livvy, how nice to see you. Your timing is perfect. I just finished feeding and watering the critters, and was about to call you. It turns out I can have dinner with you sooner than I thought. My evenings aren't as full as I believed they'd be."

Tiny meows and yips came from all areas of the store. Puppies jumped on the sides of kennels, and kittens sat in furry balls, as if waiting to be picked up and carried home. The cages were plastic with open tops, like children's playpens. They were painted cheerful colors, and the bright lights made the shop seem like daycare for pets. If a room could hug a person, Olivia thought this one would.

"Mercy," Olivia said and waved a hand in front of her face. "I can't do this, Quetzi. They're all so adorable, I'll end up buying every kitty and pup here. Mom wouldn't mind, but Dorothy would give me a paddling for sure."

"I understand. We can go in the back. I'll make tea."

Olivia followed Quetzi. She wore a pink and purple dress that looked like it had been made from scarves. The hem floated an inch off the floor. She pushed aside a beaded curtain and led the way into a cozy office/kitchenette. Olivia removed her coat and took a seat at the table while Quetzi filled a pot with water and placed it on the stove.

"What brings you here, Livvy? Is there something I can do for you?"

"I have a favor to ask."

"Name it." She put teabags in mugs and brought them to the table, then sat across from Olivia.

"I know it's none of my business," Olivia told her, "but I'd like you to give Scootie a second chance."

Quetzi blinked. "Oh. Oh dear. How did you know we broke up? How did you even know we were dating?"

"He was upset and told me. Please don't be mad at him. Sometimes, if a person doesn't talk, everything builds up inside them until they feel like they could explode. I don't want to meddle, honestly I don't. But he thinks the world of you. It'd be a shame to throw that away."

"Did he tell you why we broke up?"

"Something about your neighbor. The one who was murdered."

"I've heard rumors about what went on at her house. I don't want to do things like that. Men expect too much, if you ask me."

"Some do, but not most. Scootie wouldn't want anything to do with that kind of hanky panky."

"I wish I could believe that. But how can I?" The teapot whistled, and Quetzi went to it. She poured water in the mugs and returned to her seat. "I've decided to date women."

Dumbstruck, Olivia reached for sugar cubes sitting in a bowl and dropped several into her tea. Good grief, what did a person say to a bombshell like that? She stirred and added another cube. "I didn't know you were gay." She realized that sounded cold, and quickly added, "It doesn't change anything. I just didn't know."

"I'm not gay. At least not yet. I'm going to be, though." Quetzi rolled her mug between her hands.

From the mouths of babes, Olivia thought. "I'm not sure we can decide things like that. I think we're all just who we are and like who we like and there's nothing we can do about it. If dating women makes you happy, wonderful. But if you don't have that leaning, it probably won't make you happy."

"Then I won't date anyone."

"Boy, there's a lot of that going around."

"A lot of what?"

"Monkishness," Olivia replied absently, wondering how she'd get through to Quetzi. Shutting herself off from the world wasn't the best cure for relationship phobia. An idea came to her, and she held Quetzi's gaze. "When you dated Scootie, did you pick him?"

"What do you mean?"

"There are a lot of men in Chatham. Did you look at Scootie and decide to like him best?"

"No." Quetzi's brow furrowed. "It just happened."

"I think being gay or straight is like that. If we can't control who we're attracted to, how can we control if it's a man or a woman? How can we make ourselves something we aren't?" She shook her head and rested her palms on the table-top. "All we can do is be kind to each other, and accept everyone for who they are. Most people are good, and try to do right. Sometimes you run into a rascal, but not very often.

"I'm not trying to be preachy, but I want you to understand. Some folks enjoy extreme things. If they paid enough, Cheryl did what they wanted. You and I wouldn't, but that's us. Try not to think harshly of her. What makes people who they are is a mysterious process. If we haven't walked in someone else's shoes, how can we judge where those shoes go? There may be a link to Cheryl's lifestyle and her demise. I feel bad for her because I doubt she was happy. Cheryl ran with scalawags, and paid the ultimate price. But don't punish Scootie because of that. He had no control over it."

"I want to believe you, Livvy. But I'm scared."

"Because you're a gentle dove. Scootie knows that. He'll be good to you, and if he isn't, he'll answer to me. If I make sure he understands he has to treat you like the lady you are, will you date him again?"

Quetzi sipped her tea, then set it on the table and clasped her hands. "Okay, Livvy. If you think it's best."

"It's settled then. Why don't you call him now? He's one worried hombre."

"In a minute. First, I have to tell you something. I was so happy you called the other day. This has been weighing on my mind and I have to get it off my chest. I couldn't live with myself if someone else got hurt because I was too afraid to talk."

Olivia reached for Quetzi's hands. She'd known something worried the woman when they'd spoken last week. Her gut told her Quetzi knew something about the killing. Was she about to hear it? "What is it? What are you afraid of?"

"The murderer. I did see something. But I was afraid if I told the police, it would get out and I'd be the next one killed. It's shameful, but I convinced myself it wasn't my business and that I should stay out of it. Then you called, out of the blue, and I thought it was a sign. You'd never keep silent if you knew what I do."

A stampede took off in Olivia's chest. She swallowed, then croaked, "What did you see?"

Words came from Quetzi in a torrent, tumbling over one another in her haste to get them out. Olivia asked her to repeat the story, then sat still as the pieces snapped into place.

"Of course. It was there all the time, right in front of us. And we never saw it because of me. Because I made assumptions." She hopped off her chair and rounded the table, catching Quetzi in a hug. "You're wonderful! You cracked the case!"

"Livvy," she said with a giggle.

"I'm going to Eugene's office. You call Scootie. By tonight Chatham will be completely back to normal, and you'll be a hero." Olivia threw on her coat and ran to the front door, holding her hands on either side of her face, like blinders, so she wouldn't see little fuzzy creatures with wet noses, big eyes and pink tongues. Sometimes she wondered if she was becoming a softie.

Olivia raced to the police station, nearly going above the speed limit on more than one occasion. She stopped at the front desk. "Is Eugene in?"

"He's tied up with a prisoner, Livvy. Can I help you?"

"I'm sure you could, Stan. I'm sure you're quite up to the task. So don't think this is a reflection on you or your abilities, but I have to see Eugene. It's urgent. Please tell him I'm here. Please."

He stared at her, then nodded. "Something important has you wound up. I'll be right back." He crossed the room and disappeared behind a doorway.

Olivia paced and tried to organize her thoughts. Now, more than ever, she had to focus. She knew her mind wandered at times, and couldn't allow that to happen.

"What is it, Livvy?" Eugene asked as he approached. He sounded impatient.

Olivia cleared her throat, and tried to keep her voice from wobbling. "Eugene, I know who killed Cheryl Mecklenberg. Can we speak in private?"

The sheriff chewed his lip as he studied her. "Is this the

real deal, Livvy? Because if it's just another theory, I might get exasperated. You pulled me from interrogating a suspect."

"Sammy? Is he going to prison?"

"I just arrest them. Others decide the punishment."

Resigned to the facts, Olivia admitted to herself it was time Sammy took responsibility for his actions. She hoped he'd learn from the pickle he'd gotten into, and become a better person. Looking up at Eugene, she said, "It's the real deal."

"My office."

Eugene sat behind his desk and listened, asked questions, then listened again. He steepled his fingers and propped his elbows on stacks of papers. When Olivia's tale ended the third time, they both fell silent. Olivia watched him closely, looking for some sign of agreement or disapproval.

Unable to remain quiet, Olivia asked, "Is that enough for a warrant?"

"Once I confirm your story with Quetzi Miller, it'll be enough."

"Well, I'll be a monkey's uncle." A warm flush swept her from head to toe. She wanted to jump up and down, to clap her hands and dance a jig. With a little help from her friends, she and the team had solved the biggest crime in Chatham history. No one could say Olivia Chatham didn't have a place in the world. She'd found her calling. Crime buster.

Eugene leaned forward and hit a button on his phone. "Get Ben and Frank from the observation room. Send them in here."

A few minutes later, Olivia heard someone behind her. She turned in her chair. "Hiya, fellas."

Frank closed the door. "Hi, Livvy."

"Livvy," Ben said.

They sat behind her, and she was reminded of the day, not too long ago, when she'd been called in and asked about Tucker's whereabouts. Everything had come full circle. "Can I call Tucker and invite him? I know he'd want to be here for this."

Eugene rubbed his chin, like a man stroking a goatee.

"Tell Ben and Frank what you told me. Then you can give Monroe a call."

"Yes, Sheriff." She moved her chair so it faced the deputies, and told them everything she'd learned. By the time she reached the end, both men wore smiles that filled their faces.

Eugene stood. "Time to get to work, boys. Livvy, you stay here, out of sight. I'll tell Stan to send Monroe back as soon as he gets here. Don't leave this room. Don't go near the rear door."

Olivia sneaked a glance at Ben. "Can I invite Josie, too?"

"It's not a party." Eugene's eyebrows lowered.

"I know that. It's a matter of utmost gravity. But she's been a big instrument in this. Just those two, Tucker and Josie. We'll keep out of sight."

"Call her," Eugene said on a sigh.

Olivia wrapped her arms across her stomach and watched them cross the squad room and pull coats off a rack, then leave the building. Eugene had mentioned an observation room when asking for Ben and Frank. She guessed it observed the interrogation room. A two-way mirror affair, she thought. Like they had on Law and Order. Between now and the time everyone was assembled, she had to convince Eugene to let her and Tucker and Josie sit in that room and observe.

She tugged her phone from her belt and made two calls. Within minutes Tucker and Josie would join her in Eugene's office. Nearly overwhelmed with relief, she wilted onto a chair. Olivia's legs felt weak. Chatham would soon be a safe place to live again.

Olivia looked at her watch, saw it was nearly three o'clock, and gasped. In her frenzied rush to tell what she'd learned, she'd omitted one detail. She nearly tripped over her own feet as she hurried to her car, pausing only long enough to let Stan know where she was going.

CHAPTER TWENTY-FOUR

Olivia stuck her head in the door of the church kitchen and found it teeming with activity. Women scurried from the sink to the stove and to the table. How they managed to avoid running into one another was a mystery. She backed away before anyone spotted her.

As she walked down the hallway toward offices at the rear of the building, she heard a steady tap, tap, tap. She followed the sound to Conroy's office. The door hadn't latched, and when she pushed, it easily swung open. Rose looked up from her seat behind his desk. They stared at each other and Rose stopped typing on the ancient machine in front of her. Olivia noticed an empty box on the floor. It looked like a suitcase.

Forcing a smile, Olivia entered the room and nodded at the typewriter and its case. "I haven't seen one of those in years."

"My father gave this to me. I couldn't get rid of it just because everything's on computers these days. When they break down, Reverend will be glad I hung onto it."

"He doesn't know you have it?" He'd told Eugene they'd gotten rid of their typewriter when they bought a computer. Maybe he thought that was the truth.

"He told me to put it on the church raffle, but never paid any attention. I keep it in the trunk of my car and usually only use it at home when he's out."

"Mind if I take a look at what you're typing?"

"Just notes for next week's sermon." Rose put her arms across the typewriter in a protective gesture.

"You write them?" Olivia raised her eyebrows.

"No." Rose scowled, as if offended by the question. "I make suggestions. Reverend takes it from there."

"Why do you call him Reverend? He's your husband. Why don't you call him Lawrence or Larry?"

"I use his title in the company of others. He's to be respected."

"But you loosen up a little at home? Have cute pet names for him? Honey or sweetiepie or babycakes?"

"You're impertinent," Rose sniffed. She straightened and put her hands on the typewriter keys. "Reverend will be here later. You run along and do whatever it is heathens like you do on God's day."

Olivia sat on a chair facing the desk. "I'm not a heathen. What would make you think that?"

"Marrying and divorcing all the time. Like sacred oaths are just a game. Women should marry once, and stand by their man no matter what."

"Is that what you did?"

"Yes, you hussy. That's what I did. Now go. I have work to do."

"Aren't you needed in the kitchen? I can wait for your husband by myself." Olivia wanted to bamboozle the woman. Lull her into complacency.

"The ladies know what to do. When inspiration hits, I have to answer my muse."

Good grief, Olivia thought. Rose hadn't merely gone around the bend. She'd gone around several. Pretending to study her fingernails, Olivia asked, "What's the worst thing Conroy did? When was it hardest to stand by your man?"

"He's Reverend Conroy to you." She tapped a few keys, then dropped her hands to her lap and sat back. "Whatever he's done, it's none of your business."

Olivia smiled at her, hoping she looked innocent. "Curiosity killed the cat?"

Rose blanched and Olivia took advantage of her momentary shock. In one swift movement she leaned forward, grabbed the top of the paper, and pulled it from the typewriter. Settling in her chair, she looked at the sheet. It contained few words, but Olivia focused on one. In 'praise' the 'i' was out of alignment with the other letters.

"Why did you put that note under the door at Ivy's?"

"To warn you to butt out. I saw you parked in front of our house and here at the church. A stalker, that's what you are. You pull the wool over a lot of eyes, but not mine." Her complexion reddened.

"You're a tough one to fool, that's for sure. How did you know I'd be at Ivy's that day? I didn't even know until I decided to go."

Rose made an indecipherable noise, like a horse irritated with its rider. "I knew I'd bump into you somewhere. You run all over town, prying into everyone's lives. I had it in my purse, waiting for the right moment."

"Clever. Does Conroy know I've parked in front of your house and the church?"

"Not unless he saw you, too. I didn't want to bother him with trivia. He's got enough on his plate. Right now he's at the hospital, bringing comfort to the ill and feeble. He doesn't have time to concern himself with the likes of you."

Olivia waved a hand in front of her face. "Whew-ee, you sure have it in for me. What did I ever do to you?"

"I told you, you're a heathen, and a nosy one at that." She lifted her chin. "So what if I passed you a note hinting you should mind your own business? Where's the crime in that? Go away."

"Some might say it's a threatening note, using the word 'killed' as you did. The sheriff might think that's a crime. I'll ask him when he gets here."

Rose's eyes widened. "He's coming here? Why?"

"Because if Conroy is at the hospital, he isn't home. Eugene will assume he's here."

"I don't understand."

"Your Reverend is about to be arrested." Olivia hoped telling a white lie in a church wasn't too much of a sin. She consoled herself, knowing desperate times called for desperate measurements. Eugene was looking for Rose, not her husband. As soon as he discovered she wasn't home, he'd come to the church. Olivia wished she'd remembered to tell him about the potluck. He may have come here first.

Rose clutched her hands in front of her chest. "Arrested? Whatever for?" Her voice cracked.

"Murder."

Color leached from Rose's face, and her expression was one of horror. "No. It can't be."

"It can be. You didn't ask whose murder. I wonder why not."

"I didn't have to ask, you little harlot," Rose snarled. "He wouldn't harm a fly. Whoever was killed, Lawrence didn't do it." She got to her feet and loomed over the desk. "Now get out of here. I have work to do."

Rose's antagonism scared Olivia. She reminded herself there was a kitchen full of women down the hall. One scream would bring them running. Aiming for an air of nonchalance, Olivia stretched her legs in front of her. "I think I'll stay with you a while. This conversation is too enjoyable to cut short."

Rose dropped onto her chair and put her head in her hands. "Why are you doing this?" She lifted her head and met Olivia's gaze. "Why won't you leave us alone?"

"Cheryl Mecklenberg is dead. You know who killed her. Tell me what happened." She stiffened her spine and sat rigid, trying to exude authority. "Do the right thing, Rose. Spare your husband as much shame as you can."

Rose slumped, as if crumbling in on herself, and stared at Olivia. Different expressions crossed her face. Defeat came last, and took up residence. "I helped her die."

Strange way to put it, Olivia thought. "Why?"

"She was having an affair with Lawrence. After the last time, I couldn't take any more. I thought all that was behind us."

"He's cheated on you before?"

"We've had to leave several communities due to his indiscretion. It's always us who have to relocate. Never the other party. It takes two."

"It surely does. Did you kill any of the others?"

Her eyes flashed angrily. "Of course not. But they hurt me. They hurt me a lot. When he finally understood the damage his actions did to me, he promised to be faithful. This was our new start."

"What did his actions do to you?"

"They tore me apart. Made me feel I was nothing. I couldn't look at myself in the mirror. Then he carried a disease home." She wiped her fingers under her eyes. Olivia plucked a tissue from a box on the desk and handed it to her. "I had to get shots. I had to sit in a waiting room with common riffraff and get treatment for a sexually transmitted disease. All because he had an even worse disease. Sexual addiction. Like other addictions, it takes control. I understand that. But he can beat it. I keep telling myself that. With my help, he can beat it."

"So you moved to Chatham believing everything was going to be all right. What happened? What made it start up again?"

Rose sniffled and wiped her nose. She tilted her head at the computer beside her. "I was making notes for his sermon and hit the wrong key or something. I'm not sure what I did, but the screen filled with a list of places he'd gone to. Surfed I think they call it. Filthy. All of them. I looked at his email, and some of them were dirtier than the web sites." She made a scoffing sound. "Lawrence thought I only knew how to use the word processor. But I can get around the Internet a little. I know what email is. After reading those disgusting notes, and seeing those obscene pictures, I couldn't touch the computer again. I use my trusty typewriter to help spread the good word."

Olivia noticed the other woman begin to fidget. She had to keep her here until Eugene and the boys arrived. Wanting to put Rose at ease, she took a stab at a distracting question.

"How did you and the reverend meet?"

Rose's brow cleared, and she took on a peaceful expression. "We met at church. Oh, you should have seen him. Young and strong and full of vigor and righteous indignation. I think I fell in love with him five minutes after he began his sermon."

"How romantic. Love at first sight."

"For me it was. It came to Lawrence a bit slower. Sometimes I wondered if he married me for my money. But he always assures me that's not the case. He loves me. He just has a disease."

This was surprising news. "You're wealthy?"

"My daddy was. Not like your daddy, but he made a lot of money and I inherited all of it. Daddy made sure it came to me, not me and Lawrence. But I give Lawrence whatever he asks for." She looked Olivia in the eye. "He's a man of the cloth, a man of God. Worldly things don't appeal to him like they do some people. But now and then a little extra cash is nice."

Didn't the foolish woman realize she paid for Cheryl's services? If not, now wasn't the time to tell her. "Did you pay for him to receive therapy? Did he get help with his addiction?" Addiction, phootie. The man was a letch.

"I did," Rose replied with a nod. "He tried so hard. But then he met that woman on the Internet and visited her in Deerwood. In some of his emails it's clear he was trying to break it off. Then she moved here, and all was lost."

"You could have divorced him."

"Like you do? Leave when the going gets tough? My vows mean something to me."

"So you killed instead. I've always been fascinated how religious zealots manage to convince themselves the most heinous acts are fine. Yet when two consenting adults do something they shouldn't, it's unforgivable and you show no mercy. Adultery is a sin, but punishable by murder? Can you explain that to me?"

"Read the good book. Study it and learn. It has all the

answers."

Olivia heard a faint scraping noise behind her, and knew Eugene had arrived. She had to work fast, before Rose figured out there was someone in the hall. "How did you kill her? I thought you were home in bed that night. Suffering with a migraine." And that was my big mistake, Olivia thought. She'd questioned Conroy's alibi, but not Rose's. It never occurred to her that if Conroy could sneak out, Rose could, too. Of course, she'd never suspected Rose, which was another big mistake. Olivia promised herself to be more open-minded on her next case. Women were no less dangerous than men.

"I didn't swallow the pill Reverend gave me. I knew he'd leave once he thought I was asleep. It was his pattern. I faked sleep, and when he left, I dressed and went to her house. I'd just parked when he came out."

"He must not have been there long. Maybe he just went to break up with her."

Rose looked as though she'd been slapped. She grew thoughtful, then shook her head. "It was never going to end. Not while that Jezebel walked the earth."

"What if he'd checked on you when he got home?"

"He often looked in on me, but didn't enter the room. I'd stuffed pillows between the bed sheets so he'd think I was there. I had a job to do, and was determined to do it that night. I didn't know if I'd find the courage again. But before I could go to her door, your ex arrived."

Olivia nodded. "Sammy. You stood outside in the cold and waited? Not knowing how long he'd be in there? He could have spent the night."

"I wasn't cold. I was in my car and had Jesus on my side. Jesus kept me warm."

"Oh, for Pete's sake," Olivia muttered under her breath. "He didn't have to keep you warm long."

"No. That's another reason I knew it was meant to be. Sam Wallace left after only a few minutes. I went to the door, but no one answered, so I let myself in. It wasn't locked." Rose took a deep breath. "She was on the floor, and I thought your ex had done the job for me. But when I checked, I felt a pulse."

"That was a deciding moment. You could have helped her. Instead you hung her."

"I had to. By then it was a mission. Don't you see? Everything was so easy. It had to be the right thing to do. In the short time Sam was there, he knocked her out. All I had to do was finish the job. When I went through her place, looking for something Reverend might have left behind, I saw her closet. It made me ill. All those sick clothes and gadgets. I'd seen pictures on those web sites, and knew what the rope was for. The way was clear. I took her robe off and put the noose around her neck. I didn't kill her. God did. He could have stepped in and saved her at any time. If she'd woken, she could have removed the noose."

"She was unconscious."

"If she was meant to live another day, she'd have come out of it. No, it was meant to be. She died the way she lived. God took her, and used me as his instrument."

Smells of food for the potluck drifted into the room, nearly gagging Olivia. How could normal activities take place in the kitchen, only a few feet down the hall, while a nightmare of insanity unfolded in this room? "The sheriff knows you were at Cheryl's that night. Someone saw you leave. I could tell him the rest of the story, but it might go better for you if you do it. Confession is good for the soul."

Rose smiled. "When I confess, it's to a higher power than the sheriff. And you won't tell anyone anything. You're coming with me."

"I am?" Olivia looked at Rose, amazed at her self-centered piety. Was she so far gone she thought she'd get away with this?

"We're going to take a drive to the lake. Did you know they had to cancel the ice fishing contest because the water isn't frozen yet? You'll slide right in, easy as pie. Next summer someone will hook you and reel you into their boat."

"I'm not going anywhere with you."

Rose slid a drawer open. "Yes, you are. I have a…where

is it?"

"The gun?" Conroy asked from the doorway. Eugene, Frank and Ben entered the room. "I put it on the top shelf of the closet a couple weeks ago. Children come in here sometimes. I didn't want one of them hurt or even killed."

"You keep a gun in a church?" Olivia asked. What was the world coming to?

"I think you'll agree with me, Olivia. No place is safe." The reverend sounded exhausted, as if devastated with grief.

The animosity she'd felt for Conroy melted. She wondered if she'd come to like him some day. His life with Rose must have been miserable. She'd take the advice she'd given Quetzi and not judge Conroy. After all, she hadn't walked in his shoes.

"What have I done, Rose? How did I drive you to this?"

Olivia thought she saw a glimpse of the Lawrence Conroy Rose loved. When Frank put cuffs on her, the reverend reached out a hand, but Eugene held his arm and wouldn't let him move toward her. Rose stared at him with vacant eyes.

"I'll be there for you, Rose. I'll get you the help you need." Conroy trailed Frank and Ben as they led Rose from the room.

Olivia had to turn away. It was a painful scene to watch. Eugene beamed at her.

"I was prepared to rush in and take over, but you did a fine job, Livvy. You handled the situation perfectly. I told you people talk to you. She never would have told us as much as she did you."

"I'm not so sure, Eu…Sheriff. She doesn't like me. Maybe she just had to talk to someone, anyone. Maybe she couldn't live with the guilt."

"Nah. It was you, Livvy. You're the best honorary officer I've ever had. By far."

"Mercy." Olivia raised her hands to her cheeks and her breath caught. It was all so overwhelming, she didn't know if she was going to laugh or cry or do both at the same time. "Does that mean you'll need my help again?"

Was it her imagination, or did Eugene's smile fade a tad? "When I do, I'll call."

"Until then, is it okay if I pop into headquarters every now and then?"

"Sure, Livvy."

Olivia wondered if his shoes were too tight. He looked a mite uncomfortable. She glanced at the doorway and saw Tucker and Josie, grinning like a couple of loony birds. Church ladies hovered behind them.

"Looks like the potluck is cancelled," one said.

"Might as well pack it all up and take it home with us. Can't let good food go to waste." They shuffled away, whispering as they went.

By morning the rumor mill would buzz like never before.

⁂

Pride swelled in Tucker, growing and expanding until he thought he might burst. She'd done it. His Olivia had tracked down a murderer and gotten a confession. He wanted to pick her up and swing her in a circle. He wanted to hold a parade.

"Were you out there the whole time?" Olivia asked.

Tucker couldn't find his voice, and his feet refused to move. He stood rooted to the spot, like a tree growing out of the floor tiles, and watched Olivia.

"Just part of it," Josie replied. "Let's go to The Mill and you can tell us the rest. Ben can meet us later."

"Are you okay, Tucker? Why aren't you saying anything? Are you mad I came here alone? I knew the church ladies would be here."

"I'm not mad. I'm so damn proud of you I don't know what to do."

"Don't swear in church."

"Sorry."

Olivia's face took on a joyous expression. "Did you say you were proud of me?"

"You bet I am." He went to her and caught her in a bear hug, lifting her off the ground. "You're the bravest, smartest crime-fighter Chatham's ever seen. People will tell their grandchildren about this day."

"Katie bar the door," she squealed, sounding delighted. "Do you really think so?"

He sat her on her feet. "I really think so. Let's go get wine and cherries and you can tell us what we missed."

"Let's." She looped one arm through his and one through Josie's and kept up a steady stream of chatter all the way to the parking lot.

It was the most beautiful sound Tucker had ever heard. Olivia's voice soothed him like sweet music.

CHAPTER TWENTY-FIVE

Late the next morning Tucker glanced at the Bob Seger drawing as he pulled on his coat. Tucker couldn't explain it, but the wall hanging had grown on him. He nodded at Bob, then put his wallet in a pocket and moved to the entry. A chirp broke the silence in his condo.

When he heard his mother's voice, Tucker wished he hadn't stopped to pick up the phone. "What is it, Mom? I'm on my way out the door." The Pincushion girl had called, and he wanted to have Olivia's hat in his hand when she arrived.

"Can you spare a minute?" She sounded sober.

"What do you want?"

"I haven't had a drink since Christmas."

This was something new. "Congratulations. How long until you do have one?"

"I don't know. I only know I won't have one today."

"It's a start. I've got to go, Mom."

"Wait. There's one more thing. I'm sorry. Sorry for all the things I did wrong and sorry for what I didn't do right."

Tucker didn't know what to say. "You've joined a program, right? One of those groups that make you apologize to everyone you've hurt."

"I'm apologizing for us, not for any program. I'm sorry. When, if, you feel like seeing me, I'll be here. I love you, Tucker. I didn't show it, but I always loved you."

"You got one thing right. You didn't show it."

"It's no excuse, but you deserve an explanation. Sometimes it was so hard to look at you, it hurt. You're the image of your father."

Stunned to the core, he sank onto the sofa. "You know who he is? You said you didn't."

"He was the only man I ever loved. But he was married, and didn't want us. I took my sadness out on you. I just crawled into a bottle and felt sorry for myself for years. You bore the brunt of it." She hesitated, then added, "If you want, I'll tell you who he is."

"I don't want to know." After a few seconds of silence, he reconsidered. "Maybe someday, for medical reasons. I inherited his bloodline, but Jonathan Vicknair is my father."

"I'll write the name down and put it in a safe place. That way if you want to know after I'm gone, you can open the envelope and learn who he is."

"Sounds good. I've got to go."

"Remember, I'm always here and I'd give anything to see you. I don't deserve another chance, but I'm asking for one. I love you."

Tucker couldn't echo her words. "I'll talk to you later, Mom." He replaced the receiver and went to his front door. After years of neglect, she believed an apology would fix everything? Nothing could fix the past, and he'd never forgive her. He couldn't.

Olivia's voice came to him, clear and strong. "Yes, you can, Tucker. And you should."

"You were a hell-raiser," Jonathan's sonorous tone chimed in. "How many second chances did I give you?"

Tucker left his house wondering if he was losing his mind.

When his doorbell rang that afternoon, Tucker plopped Olivia's hat on his head and answered the chime.

"My *hat*," Olivia squealed. "You got my hat back!" She scurried inside and jumped up, pulling the fedora off him.

"Picked it up this morning. Looks pretty good, don't you think?"

She examined it from every angle. "It's perfect. Absolutely perfect." The top had a small flaw left from the tear. Olivia ran her finger over it. "A little scar adds to its beauty. A reminder of the fracas we experienced together. Oh, Tucker. I'm so happy."

"That's all I can ask for." He kissed the top of her head, then gently took the hat and put it on her. "Ready to do some sledding?"

"You bet I am. I called Hendricks', and Toby says the toboggan is ready."

Tucker grabbed his coat, making sure his mittens were in the pockets, and said, "What are we waiting for?"

They went to Hendricks' and loaded the rainbow decal-covered sled onto the top of Tucker's Expedition. Olivia declared the decorations a major success. Tucker watched her chatter with the clerk and smiled. Thoughts, unexpected and uninvited, came to him in a rush. What would it be like to lose someone you loved with all your heart? How much pain his mother must have endured. Alone, rejected and pregnant. If Olivia wanted nothing to do with him, how would he react? A ball of lead formed in his stomach, and he knew he'd get drunk. Very drunk.

He drove to the park and Olivia gave him directions to the recreation area. The place was hopping, and everyone they met stopped to congratulate Olivia on nabbing the killer. She always blushed, said, "I was just a gal doing her job." Then she'd point at her new toboggan, diverting attention from herself. "Toby Hendricks did the artwork. Isn't it gorgeous?"

Tucker found her modest streak endearing. But, he reflected, he found everything about her endearing. She left her hat on her head until they went down the slope. Then, every time they shoved off, she doffed it and held it on her lap.

Tucker sat on the sled, holding onto the rope, with Olivia in front of him. He was cold and uncomfortable. Rubber bands bit his wrists. Snow had gotten under his collar and into his shoes. His socks and neck were wet, and his cheeks and nose were numb. He couldn't feel his ears, and he wondered if they'd break off if he touched them. Olivia wiggled in his arms, and he wouldn't have traded places with any man on earth.

She turned to look at him. "I'm going to have to knit you a cap, Tucker. You look frozen. It's important to keep your head warm. One more trip, then we'll go for hot chocolate."

Tucker eyed the cup-shaped shack with the bright neon sign above it. They'd been down the steep hill half a dozen times, and the Cocoa Cabana looked more than a little inviting. He wondered what Olivia would add to her hot chocolate. He'd bet his car it wouldn't be marshmallows. Maybe peanuts.

He had to admit, the day was turning out to be fun. Tucker was grateful for that since he knew they'd be back often. Olivia was in her element.

"Any color preference for your hat? Do you want it to match your mittens?"

"I'll leave it up to your discretion. Since getting an eyeful of the toboggan, I decided you should be in charge of all color decisions."

"It is a doozie, isn't it?" She patted the top of the rainbow-embellished sled.

"That it is."

She turned her back to him, snuggled into his chest and said, "Let 'er rip!"

At the bottom of the hill, they followed a young couple into the café. Olivia sat at a table in a corner of the Cocoa Cabana, and licked her lips when he brought the hot chocolate. A froth of whipped cream rose high above the brims of the mugs.

She tugged a plastic bag from her pocket, and produced two licorice sticks. "Want one? I brought extra for you."

"No, thanks. I take my chocolate straight."

"Your call," she said before stirring her cocoa with one of the strips.

Tucker tried to shut his mind off as he sat in the warmth of the shack and chatted with people who stopped at their table. His mother's call haunted him, and he wondered what he should do. Would he regret it if he ignored her call? Would he, some day, wish he'd taken an afternoon to visit her? What nagged most was that he knew the answer to the biggest question. Would Olivia forgive her if she were in his place?

They decided to take one more trip down the slope. When they'd pulled the toboggan to the top, and settled on it, Tucker cleared his throat. "I'm going to my mother's place next week. Want to come with me?"

Olivia stiffened, then turned completely around, legs on each side of the sled, so she faced him. Eyes wide, she said, "You're going to see her? You've forgiven her?"

He shrugged. "It seems stupid to hang onto anger. Yeah, I want to see her. If I can, I want to forgive her. But I may need your help."

"You've got it." She threw her arms around him. "This is wonderful. It's like Christmas. You'll never regret it, Tucker. Letting go of bitterness is the best thing you can do for yourself. I love you for it."

"That's another thing I wanted to talk to you about."

She pulled back and dropped her arms from his neck. "Sorry. I won't say it if you don't want me to. But you can't make me stop loving you. I don't have any control over that."

"I don't want you to stop. I want you to love me forever because that's how long I'll love you."

"What?" she screeched.

"I love you, January Eighth. When do your parents get home?"

She drew her eyebrows together. "The end of the month. Why?"

"They should be here for your fourth, and final, wedding."

"What are you talking about?"

"I've decided not to be a monk. At the end of the month we'll both live by your rule and only sleep with someone we're married to."

Tears filled her eyes. "You're getting married? Do I know her?"

"I'm marrying you, if you say 'yes'. And not for one night. For the rest of our lives."

"Are you serious?"

"Never been more serious in my life."

"Whoopee!" In one swift movement she threw herself into his arms, knocking them both off the sled. It took off down the hill without them.

Tucker laughed and yelled, "Whoopee!" with her. They must be creating quite a scene, and he couldn't care less if people stared. As usual, she brought out a physical reaction in him. "I wish your parents were coming home sooner. This could get painful."

She looked at him. "You're in pain? What hurts?"

"Never mind. I'm sorry I don't have a ring for you. Maybe you can choose one. I have no idea what you'd want." Her fedora had landed next to him. He picked it up and held it out to her.

"Anything you pick out will be perfect. Go to Carat Top. It's a wonderful jewelry store. Ziggy Dermot, he owns the place, will appreciate the business. He's got bright red hair, you can't miss him."

"Did you help him name the store?"

"How did you guess?"

"A shot in the dark." Tucker wrapped his arms around her, feeling the peace of someone who's found where he belongs after a long search. "I'm not going to divorce you, Olivia."

He heard a sniffle, but when she spoke her tone was firm and strong.

"I'm not going to divorce you, either, Tucker."

About The Author

Cyndia Depre was born in Iowa, and has lived in Pennsylvania, Illinois and Minnesota.

She received a Bachelor of Science degree in Accounting, with a second major in Finance, from Northern Illinois University.

After running her own business for ten years, she closed the doors and began writing full-time.

She now lives in a suburb of the Twin Cities with her husband and their miniature schnauzer.

They keep an old, but much loved, boat at a marina on Lake Minnetonka, and use it as often as possible.

Cyndia is currently working on her third novel.

Visit her website at www.cyndiadepre.com.

LaVergne, TN USA
26 May 2010
184071LV00001B/2/P